Paper Boat

Discovering India
with a Master Storyteller

By Ken Kerkhoff

with True Life Stories by
S.M. Pejathaya

Andrew Benzie Books
Orinda, California

Published by Andrew Benzie Books
www.andrewbenziebooks.com

www.paperboatbook.com

Printed in the United States of America

First Edition: March 2015

10 9 8 7 6 5 4 3 2 1

ISBN 978-1-941713-11-2

Cover, book, and map design by Andrew Benzie

To my parents for all they taught me,
and the values they instilled in me

and

To the India-60 Peace Corps Volunteers and staff
who make this a better world,
in particular to Tom Carter, who gave me inspiration

and

To my children Matthew and Rachael

and especially

To my loving wife Dee,
for her patience, understanding and support

TABLE OF CONTENTS

INTRODUCTION

There are two enduring memories that stand out from the days of my travel and adventures in India. Above all, India is where I met Dee, the love of my life, my wife, my friend and constant companion for going-on five decades. The second is the friendships that evolved and the people with whom I worked in agricultural development, and especially with one man, S.M. Pejathaya (pronounced *pay-ja-thai-ya*). It is largely because of that man that this book was conceived.

The American Peace Corps program was established by Executive Order 10924, issued by President John F. Kennedy on March 1, 1961, and authorized by Congress on September 22, 1961. The program's purpose is to promote world peace and friendship through a corps of willing men and women who work with the peoples of interested countries in meeting their needs for trained manpower. Since 1961 over 215,000 Americans joined the Peace Corps and served in 139 countries. This true narrative chronicles how one group of Peace Corps volunteers (PCVs) in India learned to understand the lives, customs and religions of their host country citizens, and came to appreciate and love the people they worked with.

India States and Territories

DELHI

ANAND
(Amul Dairy)

CALCUTTA
(Kalkotha)

BOMBAY
(Mumbai)

BAY of
BENGAL

ARABIAN
SEA

GOA

HYDERABAD

MYSORE
STATE

MADRAS
(Chennai)

Mysore State
(Karnataka)

INDIAN
OCEAN

RAICHUR

SINDHANUR

BELLARY

UDUPI

MANGALORE

BANGALORE

PROLOGUE

Look at life as a journey on a ship. Calm seas can suddenly become rough and hazardous. The wind might blow a ship away from its destination unless the pilot knows how to manipulate the sails and tack the wind to an advantage. Many ships flounder in tide pools, or crash into rocks or icebergs. The friends who wait at the home port for their loved ones express great joy when their ship arrives safely. Just like the ship we are continuously presented with challenges through which we must learn to navigate.

One man, S.M. Pejathaya, compared his journey in life to a youthful pastime of sailing paper boats along a stream in his grandfather's compound. Is he a passenger on that paper boat, or does he have control over its ability to avoid all the obstacles by piloting his ship safely through them? Is he just a passenger or is he the captain of his own destiny?

My short period as a Peace Corps volunteer in rural India could have ended in a futile search for some nebulous dream. Thanks to Mr. Pejathaya my exposure to the people of India became a remarkable learning experience because he taught me how to understand India's culture and religion.

Pejathaya and I combined our stories in this book to let the reader experience the shock of being faced with an alien culture and then slowly progress into an understanding, and finally, a love for that culture and the people who live it.

In the narrative that follows we use many words and phrases that originate from the various Indian dialects. Although we try to explain as we go, do not hesitate to refer to the glossary at the end of the book to achieve a better understanding.

BAPTISM OF FIRE ANTS
AND SCORPIONS

There's a spider in the straw! No! It's a scorpion! Yikes! What the hell am I doing here? The horse flies are annoying, I fear those painful fire ants and the stifling cattle smells in the host farmer's barn are rank, but the insult of having to sit by myself with the bullocks and water buffalo stings the most. I don't understand these people or their language. I feel surrounded by a religion and a culture that I can't comprehend, and I crave American food.

My first village visit was the brainchild of the Peace Corps training staff, who sought to induce the trainees into a deeper understanding of the language and culture of rural India, known as 'village India.' Twenty-five of us were subjected to this experiment in volunteer survival, each to a different, remote village. Three of the trainees decided at the conclusion of this exercise that life in India was not their cup of *chai*.

I joined The Peace Corps in August 1968 to assuage an itch to see culture outside the United States. My parents were farmers in Minnesota, but encouraged all their seven children to study hard so they could attain a better living. Farming can be a tedious occupation, and my Dad had higher hopes for his children. Although I loved the farm life, I took his advice and went to college, where I studied accounting. The beckon of the farm, however, continued to whisper my roots.

Elementary school studies of distant places made a deep impression on me. Eskimos in Alaska, *Massai* warriors in Kenya, the Inca in Peru, *Kalinka* dancers in Russia and apple farmers in India's Kullu Valley virtually came to life in Sister Marian's fourth grade geography class. The mental travel from small town Minnesota to interesting, far away places was exhilarating. The desire to travel became more intense as I studied French in college and met students from other countries. My college associates kindled an interest in the American Peace Corps. Consequently, there I was, in Southern India, learning a language I had never heard of, and studying an unfamiliar culture. I may have bitten off more than I could chew.

Our training program began in August 1968 with 48 trainees. We came from New York, Minneapolis, Los Angeles and everywhere in between. After our first village visit, just two months into the program, we were 22 surviving trainees. Peace Corps referred to a trainee's departure as "de-selection." It happened voluntarily to those who decided they weren't cut out for the rigors of survival in a developing country, or those who had difficulty learning the language. For others, the Peace Corps psychiatrist (AKA "shrink") spotted real or imaginary character defects suggesting 'junior' was not "Peace Corps material." The current village visits, similar to my presence in this godforsaken place, had been the undoing of three of my compatriots.

Joseph, an Indian driver for Peace Corps Bangalore, crossed the Sindhanur *nullah* (a stream or river) around 9:00 A.M. that morning and dropped me off near a dusty lane leading to the small village of Udbal, about two miles from the *taluka* headquarters of Sindhanur. This was intended to be a spontaneous, one day visit. I had a forlorn feeling as the Jeep van pulled away, leaving me propped by the side of the road with nothing but my water canteen, a small bottle of iodine and my meager wits.

The sun was moving higher and the earth already warmed to induce perspiration with the slightest physical exertion. Up the dusty road I saw two high school-age village boys approach me as I walked toward the assemblage of mud-walled houses. The boys wore white, short-sleeved shirts, tailored khaki slacks and dusty sandals. Tailored, as I soon learned, was because there was no clothing store within a hundred miles, and adults wore either the simple white cloth called a *dhoti* or a *lungi* wrapped around their waists. School children, however, wore the shorts and shirts sewn by local tailors. I considered what they must have thought when they saw this gangly white man dressed in shoes and socks, a knit shirt and Levi's jeans walking down the lane to their village. My six foot-two inch frame had withered down to 165 pounds, and I must have looked totally bewildered by my surroundings. The two young men approached with stealthy caution and, in textbook English, asked me who I was. I gave my name and stated that I wanted to see the head person of their village.

Without hesitation they made an about face and escorted me into the village. There, they located Raju Gowda, the Chairman of the *Gram Panchayat*. My instructors had taught me that the *Panchayat* chairperson is equivalent to the elected head of the village council. The Peace Corps Associate Director had arranged my visit with this man, so Raju Gowda was expecting me. Not necessarily today, but he had a vague idea that some foreigner would descend into his domain and he was expected to host this stranger for one day.

We looked into each other's eyes with reserve and caution. Raju Gowda, an elderly man with sun-weathered features, had a thin, dark cigarette-like object in his hand and studied me with a wry smile before introducing me to the *Panchayat* Secretary. Both were sitting on an elevated stone and dirt platform under a large acacia tree. Like the Chairman, the *Panchayat* Secretary wore an immaculate white *dhoti*, which is a long cotton cloth wrapped around each leg and tucked at the waist. I couldn't help but feel amused to see them sitting on stones while wearing white, diaper-like *dhotis*.

The *Gram Sevak*, a government extension worker responsible for family planning and health programs in the village, soon joined us. He wore long pants and a button shirt. He also smoked the thin, brown cigarette, which I later learned is called a *beedie*.

These officials and several other farmers and village leaders were expected to attend a meeting in a nearby village. After 20 minutes of strained conversation in a mixture of village *Kannada* and British English they bowed their apologies and left me to my own devices. A number of remaining villagers gathered around me and began talking in the local dialect, *Kannada*. My ears were slow to pick up the unique sounds of the village's dialect, so I stuck with the limited vocabulary I had recently memorized. I asked to see the farmers' fields, but discussing agriculture with field workers, elderly women and school children was awkward. The farm owners had left for their meeting and the remaining villagers couldn't understand why I wanted to leave their shady, quiet village and go to the fields. They politely guided me to Raju Gowda's cattle shed and told me to rest while they prepared some tea and biscuits.

Conversing with only 100, or so, *Kannada* words in my vocabulary, was difficult. I could only ask to see their rice and wheat fields in two languages and neither seemed to convey my mission as an agricultural specialist interested in discussing local agriculture. The villagers preferred to talk about the art of tipping bullock carts. It seems that several years before my arrival to their village an American volunteer lived in this area. They referred to him as, "Big John." Apparently, Big John's forte' was demonstrating his brute strength by tipping over bullock carts, much to the enjoyment of some macho male villagers.

I believe the phrase the training staff taught us for introducing ourselves went something like, "*Namaskara. Naanu* Ken Kerkhoff, *amerikaada shaanti dalida swayam sevaka.*" Translated, it means something like, "Greetings! I am Ken Kerkhoff, an American Peace Corps volunteer worker." My *Kannada* was so bad that the only response I ever got was a stiff, textbook-like iteration of, "What time is it?"

Maybe my intonation was confusing, or possibly I mispronounced the words. The blank stares made me think that maybe I said something bad. It occurred to me that maybe the language training staff thought it would be humorous to teach me a line that translated to something like, "Greetings, I am a crazy American and now I'm going to take off all my clothes."

Throughout the first months of my stay in India, I was befuddled not only by having to communicate in a totally unfamiliar language and trying to understand local customs and rituals, but by having to contend with the difficulty of learning the bewildering number of gods and goddesses in the religious hierarchy. Add to that a caste system that I not only did not fit into, but had to navigate carefully to avoid offending my Indian hosts. Then, there was the unnerving experience of the unending curiosity of the village youth, who could be seen peering through the windows of my life at every move.

My undoing wasn't so much the discomfort of the host farmer's barn. After all, I grew up on a farm, and spent many hours every day feeding pigs, steers and chickens, milking cows, and cleaning up after all of them. Even the scorpion was just a bump in the road. No, my introduction to Indian food was the shock that nearly discouraged my dream of survival in India.

Sitting here in this *godown* (barn or warehouse) was the farmer's way of occupying me until he returned from his meeting. The host farmer attempted desperately to entertain me but was restricted by local cultural tradition, lack of knowledge about what makes an American happy, and the unavailability of a McDonald's Golden Arches. He asked his adult sons, who had studied the rudiments of the English language, to try to unwind the mystery. To some extent, I was able to communicate with the younger generation, but when the conversation stalled, the air was filled with empty space. Consequently, my village visit stalled only two hours into a planned eight-hour adventure.

Exasperated with my inability to communicate easily with the villagers, I said a polite goodbye and withdrew, heading for the main road whence I came. I crossed the shin deep stream through which the Peace Corps Jeep had carried me only two hours ago and trudged toward the larger town of Sindhanur. The cool *nullah* water felt good in the ninety degree heat. I was not yet aware that the water contained organisms that guaranteed amebic dysentery. Ignorance is bliss, so I enjoyed the moment. The town of Sindhanur was just a mile on the other side, and like a moth to a flame I shuffled in that direction. Wearing shoes and socks, however, is not recommended in a locale with numerous streams and no bridges. Taking them off was easy enough, but putting socks on wet, sand covered feet once I crossed the *nullah* was not.

Crossing that wide but shallow stream provided a visual kaleidoscope of color and living activity. Coming from the other side was a woman dressed in a green and orange *sari*. She carried a large straw basket on her head, a burlap handbag in one hand and her *chappals* (sandals) in the other. Her *sari* was wound between her legs and tucked at the waist to keep it out of the water. She walked behind a cart being pulled by a huge snow white bullock. The cart was decorated with colorful flowers and banners and looked smart enough to have been in the Rose Bowl parade. A man, whom I assumed was the woman's spouse, sat on the cart and drove the animal with sounds of, "Jtsk, jtsk!"

Also wading across the wide *nullah* were eight untethered, docile-looking water buffalo guided by a boy who appeared to be about 13 or 14 years old. The scene was like a National Geographic movie, moving in slow motion. On the far edge of the stream there were two women beating clothes against the few exposed rocks in the slow-moving water. Off to their left was another cart, this one harnessed to a water buffalo. A middle-aged man wearing a soiled white *lungi* scooped water from the stream with a tin kerosene can and emptied it into a 50 gallon drum on the two-wheel cart.

Warm air whisked above the broad water flow conveying new redolent smells to my senses. There was a natural freshness that reminded me of open space, foliage and cool water. For a moment my mind was transported to a simple walk on a flatland hiking trail. Gone for the moment was the memory of that disturbing odor of the large urban areas.

Leaving my host village and venturing out on my own was

not what the Peace Corps training staff wanted me to do. They encouraged the volunteers to immerse ourselves in discussions with farmers and other villagers using the local *Kannada* dialect. I had, however, a burning desire to discover the town of Sindhanur, which had one of the two tractor societies in Raichur District. Because of my farming background I had reason to believe that I would spend my two years as a volunteer in Sindhanur, if I could just survive the training program.

I heard the town before I saw it. Sindhanur was a dusty, dirty town, but it bustled with liveliness. Loud music blared from tea shop radios. Shouting children in ragged clothes manipulated sticks to guide large metal barrel hoops and car tires along the road, dodging in and out between the vehicles, bicycles and pedestrians. Bullocks pulled water barrels mounted on wheels, like the one I saw in the *nullah*. Whenever a water cart hit a rut some water splashed over the top, allowing splotches of mud to form on the roadway. Numerous brightly painted lorries (trucks) chugged through town, their diesel engines belching plumes of smoke and fumes from large, chrome-plated smoke stacks.

Men sauntered along the street wearing white *dhotis*, like the one worn by Raju Gowda. To a Westerner the *dhoti* appears cumbersome; however, I soon learned that the traditional *dhoti* is cool and comfortable. Later I saw an Indian playing tennis while wearing a *dhoti* and he was doing quite well. Other men wore white *lungies*, which are lightweight cotton cloths that simply hang straight down from the waist, like a sarong. Still others wore loose fitting cotton pants that looked like pajamas. Many of these various bottoms were topped with long white or pink shirts.

Numerous bicycles jingled around pedestrians, ringing their handlebar bells to warn slower beings of their approach. High-pitched motorcycle horns beeped a path through the crowd. Almost all these vehicles were loaded to the maximum. Several bicyclists had a second person sitting on the handlebars or sidesaddle on the crossbar. Some had large bunches of bananas or other produce draped over their crossbars.

A motorcycle putted by, loaded with what appeared to be a gigantic, rolled-up straw mat that was larger than both the motorcycle and the operator combined. The operator aimed his course by looking through the mat's weave to see an obstructed view of pedestrians and bullock carts in the general path of his wobbly advance. I gave him wide berth as I did not respect his navigation skills.

Lean, scruffy-looking dogs hung around the tea shops, hoping for a morsel of food dropped accidentally by a customer. The dogs were scrawny and shy. I saw a pair of mangy dogs locked in intercourse and running as one animal with eight legs toward an alleyway. No one seemed to be the owners of these dogs, and the dogs had no visible collars.

A group of young boys approached me from the opposite direction. They carried books attached to string or leather thongs flung over their shoulders. They wore sand-colored shorts and white, short-sleeved shirts. Three wore sandals and one sported shoes. The dust-covered shoes looked like they had never been shined. The boys greeted me with mischievous smiles and the text book question, "What time is it?" They were proud to be able to practice their schoolhouse lessons on a stranger with a wrist watch.

Another greeting question I heard more than once was, "English?" I wasn't sure if that was an invitation to speak English, or, if they were asking about my nationality?

I usually answered with my text book phrase, "*Nanu America da dalida svyam sevaka.*" That phrase always brought a questioning look, and these boys looked at each other with question marks on their faces. Either I said it wrong or they were surprised to hear me speak *Kannada*.

I was an obvious outsider, based on the clothes I wore and the sounds I made. My skin color, however, seemed to suggest that I might be British. After ninety years of British rule, many Indian people, seeing a white stranger, assumed that the stranger was English.

During their rule, the British *Raj* was oppressive, but also made major contributions to the development of India's infrastructure. The system of improved highways and the railroads were constructed between all the major cities during the period from 1858 to 1947, the year India won its independence from Great Britain. India created a postal system long before the British Raj, however, it was the British who led the way to an Indian department for a postal network that later included telegraphy and telephony, creating India's PT&T.

Great Britain's governance in the Indian subcontinent extended to almost all of modern day India. The British Raj supplanted the East India Company in 1858. The latter was a company of merchants, which was given monopoly privileges on all trade with the East Indies in 1600. The East India Company had private armies, and had the distinction of ruling an entire country.

As I sauntered down Sindhanur's main thoroughfare, some of my limited knowledge of India's history came back to me. This country has an extremely rich and colorful past. The very name of this town suggested a history reaching far back in time to the Great Ashoka and the Mughal Dynasty (from early 16th to mid-18th century). The Moguls were direct descendants of Genghis Khan. The names of cities, like the district headquarters of Raichur, and more distant Hyderabad, suggest of a Muslim influence. We also learned from our *Kannada* instructors that Bihar, India was the birthplace of Buddhism. Though Siddhartha Gautama was born in Lumina, Nepal, he attained "enlightenment" while meditating under a pupal tree in Bodh Gaya, India.

During in-country training we visited the ancient ruins of a place called Hampi, a historic landmark and religious center constructed by the *Vijayanagara Empire*, which ruled between 1336 and 1565. The city had been gutted by a Portuguese mercenary army and later laid siege to by the Deccan Muslim Confederacy. We trainees were amazed to learn of the level of sophistication the city of Hampi had achieved some four or five hundred years before we trod upon its soil. I was beginning to sense the powerful history that surrounded me.

At present, it was time to look for something to supplement the cup of tea and English biscuit the host farmer's family had provided me. So, I began to look for a place that served food. The primary road of Sindhanur was a pothole-marred tarmac highway that ran through the heart of town and continued northeast toward Raichur, 90 kilometers, and southwest toward Bellary, a distance of 89 kilometers. For a few short blocks in Sindhanur, the highway widened and accommodated provision stores, hotels and tea shops plus a wide range of impromptu roadside vendors. A small, circular spur served as the bus stop. In the direction of my southerly progress was the police station, an elementary school, a government hospital and public offices. Several small hotels prominently displayed advertisement signs along the route.

In time I would come to appreciate the casual vendors who crowded the street fringes. Today, they were a nuisance, shouting their greetings and pushing their goods at me. Soon, however, I would look forward to bargaining with them and tasting their juicy alphonso mangoes, the delicious jackfruit, kiwi and sapota. Today, I had no time for them. They only confused and frightened me. Doctor Johnson, the Peace Corps physician, had admonished, "peel it, boil it or don't eat it."

Along the left side of the road I spied an elevated shop with a hand-painted sign that portrayed a steaming plate of rice. I recognized the rice but not the other items on this weather worn sign. A happy looking Indian customer burped as he exited the shop, and, feeling that this was as good a place as any, I ventured up the single step and into air accented by a strong, spicy fragrance.

My spoken *Kannada* was poor, at best, but reading the hand-written *Kannada* menu was out of the question. A young man of about 20 years of age, approached wearing a dingy T-shirt and a *lungi*. The *lungi* was folded up above his knees and tucked into itself at the waist. The young man tested his dozen words of English on me then switched back to his familiar *Kannada* dialect to ask me what I would like to eat.

The only thing I recognized from the flood of *Kannada* he spewed out was the word "*koli.*" I was fairly sure *koli* meant chicken. He nodded in swift agreement as he took my order back to the chef, who straddled a steamy cauldron balanced over a wood fire in the darkened, smokey kitchen. I was in a non-vegetarian restaurant. That was fine with me, although the training staff had urged us to eat mainly vegetarian food. Most of our instructors were strict vegetarians, and, undoubtedly, many of the Indian farmers we were expected to work with were Hindu and, very likely, vegetarian.

The waiter brought my steaming food on a steel plate. I dipped the fingers of my right hand into the glowing sauce and instantly began my traumatic introduction to the spices of India. With the first bite of curry I realized that there was not enough water in my canteen to put out the fire. Never before had my lips experienced a burning sensation that a sip of water would not squelch. Before I swallowed the second mouth full, the sweat began pouring out of every pore in my body. Retronasal olfaction kicked-in and my nose started to run. My spectacles slid down my sweaty nose. To make matters inconvenient, I had to eat in the Indian fashion, with only my right hand. I also could not drink the glass of cool water the waiter placed on my table for fear of acquiring amoebic dysentery.

Our trainers drilled us on local customs and rules of etiquette. The most stern rules were, "Don't eat with your left hand! Don't touch anyone with your left hand! Don't show the bottoms of your feet to any living creature, and don't step on any books!"

The rule about the forbidden left hand relates to the method of personal hygiene observed locally. Flush toilets existed only in the major cities. Locally, people took their small water pots, called *tumbiges,* and headed for the open fields. The left hand was reserved for wiping.

With my right hand burning from the hot curry and my glasses steaming up and refusing to sit properly on my nose I somehow managed to get a trace of the hot spice in one eye. I could only see the food on my plate through one un-curried eye, but soon the river of salty sweat running off my forehead made the other eye nearly useless.

My clothes were sopping wet from perspiration, and the pain on my tongue and lips was excruciating. The dumbfounded waiter stood by helplessly, feeling a slightly amused concern for my agony. The only thing he could think of was to offer a small dish of plain, white curd. The yogurt cooled the fire enough so that I could pay the waiter and make a graceful exit. With burning lips and scorched fingers I scurried out of town, back across the Sindhanur *Nullah* and down the dusty bullock cart track to the village I had been assigned to without ever seeing Sindhanur's tractor society. When the Peace Corps Jeep came to pick me up several hours later I was making a concerted attempt to converse with the host farmer and his villagers.

This first village visit left me shaken and uncertain about my future as a volunteer. I realized how little I understood India's people and culture. A feeling of disillusion came over me. I considered that when a volunteer steps into the village he is under a spotlight from which there is no hiding. Whatever I know or don't know is exposed, like an actor on stage. How could I survive for two years?

That first solitary stroll through living, breathing India has been indelibly stamped in my memory. For the first time since joining the Peace Corps there was no one nearby to explain what I saw, heard, smelled and felt. I saw men with beards wearing saffron robes talking to themselves as they slowly inched their way through the market. Heads bent down and their long hair tied in tight braids looking like it had never been washed.

There were youths with inconceivable injuries lying on the ground, reaching up one mangled hand to ask for coins. I was approached by old men and women dressed in rags, some with no sight because their eyes had been lost in some horrific accident. They begged for food or coins.

On the same roads there were smartly dressed men, hurrying along with a briefcase in one hand and a banana in the other. The tough-looking lorry (large truck) drivers shouted at slow-moving pedestrians and the enervated farmers guided their bullock-drawn carts loaded with market goods toward the market place or their distant homes.

Back in the camp dormitory that night as I lay on my steel bunk under a mosquito net I seriously considered whether I could survive two years in India. My self confidence was shaken, and for the first time I doubted my future as a volunteer.

BACKGROUND

The trail of events that brought me to the point of sitting in a barn in a remote village in India began at a much younger age. Since elementary school days I had a desire to see the far away places described in my geography texts. I needed to see what was on the other side of the river or in the next state. I loved the anticipation of some imaginary change as my Dad drove across a state line during our family vacations. Travel and knowledge of geography and study of other cultures struck a resonate chord with my young mind. In the seventh and eighth grades I became interested in the Maryknoll Missions, and decided that I wanted to live and work as a missionary in Africa. Since I grew up on a farm near a small town in Minnesota, I saw the outside world as a marvelous adventure, a place to investigate.

I entered a Catholic seminary, hoping to one day travel to distant lands as a religious pioneer. However, after one year of conjugating Latin verbs and studying theology at Nazareth Hall Seminary near St, Paul, Minnesota, I decided to travel a different road. Later, in a midwestern university, the altruistic leanings of my undergraduate associates inspired a humanistic side of me that forsook the interviews with "Big-8" accounting firms in the Twin Cities in favor of returning to the dreams of travel to distant lands.

I joined a Peace Corps program for agricultural development in India. My volunteer group was called "India-60," because we were the sixtieth program designed to assist the government of India in it's efforts to promote development through volunteer programs and, in particular, to help implement India's "Green Revolution."

First used in 1968, the term "Green Revolution" referred to the spread of new agricultural technologies that were being developed and transferred to the developing world. The term was first used by former United States Agency for International Development (USAID) Director William Gaud. India adopted the term in a campaign that pushed for greater agricultural production and self reliance of village farmers.

My Peace Corps acceptance letter finally arrived in the summer of 1968. Federal investigators had interviewed my teachers, my college town landlord, my friends and my hometown banker and decided that I was an appropriate candidate to represent the United States as a volunteer. The Peace Corps assigned me to a men's program for agricultural development in India. The first two months of training was held in Hemet, California.

The training site was an abandoned itinerant worker camp on the outskirts of the retirement community of Hemet. Several miles from commercial stores and outside the companionship of local citizenry, we were destined to concentrate on learning the required elements associated with our prospective roles as Peace Corps volunteers. Surrounding our camp were alfalfa fields, crop land, orchards and irrigation canals. The closest sign of civilization was the "8-Ball" tavern about half a mile away; and even that was not entirely civilized.

Training consisted of three elements: agriculture, language, and Indian cultural studies. The agricultural element emphasized the development of raw land for irrigation but also included crop selection and cultivation, plant protection, composting and the use and development of mechanical agricultural tools. The majority of the 48 trainees had never previously worked on a farm.

The language spoken in our target area of Mysore State (changed to Karnataka in 1973), India, was *Kannada*. For language training everyone started from base zero. A few trainees had studied languages in high school or college, but most of us were neophytes in the area of foreign language, and

Kannada was very foreign to our ears. Only the then 40 million people of Mysore spoke *Kannada,* and to us it sounded like a contrived communication system. Native *Kannada* speakers from Mysore State grilled us six hours, six days a week on vocabulary, verb conjugation and sentence structure. On Sundays the trainees were encouraged to refrain from using English while in camp. We attended classes in the open air, and the instructors often injected language training into agriculture field exercises and during cafeteria meals.

The two dozen trainees who survived Hemet were happy to have ten days after training ended to see their families before reassembling at John F. Kennedy Airport in New York. I spent two days with my sister Mavis in Oakland, then caught a plane to Minneapolis, where I said goodbye to my parents and five other siblings.

We boarded a special charter jet in New York to begin our journey to the farm lands of Southern India. Mrs. Indira Gandhi, India's Prime Minister and head of the ruling Congress party, had been in the United States at the time and had chartered an Air India plane to take her back to New Delhi. She was in the U.S. to meet with the U.S. President, Lyndon Johnson and members of the U.S. Congress to discuss U.S. assistance to India and the current issues between India and Pakistan. Though her mission was not as successful as she had hoped, she agreed to accommodate several groups of new Peace Corps volunteers on her return to India.

When we noticed the tight security and the delays while boarding the plane, we became aware that the first class section accommodated a special person. Eventually, we realized that Mrs. Gandhi planned to travel with us. We were pleasantly surprised before take off when the door between the first class section and the main cabin opened and Mrs. Gandhi stepped into view. She was more diminutive than I had envisioned. She wore a magnificent blue sari laced with strands of silver. Her head was graced with traces of gray, but she proffered an angelic smile.

Several Peace Corps groups besides the India-60 trainees filled the main cabin, most of whom were destined for India. The loud talk and commotion quieted quickly as one of Mrs. Gandhi's staff asked for our attention. Mrs. Gandhi indulged the trainees with a short statement. She spoke in English, but her soft voice did not carry well in the packed fuselage. Those closest to the front of the cabin heard her thank the trainees for leaving their homes and loved ones to travel so far away to help her country's men and women. She referred to India's Green Revolution, and how important it was that India become self-sufficient in food production.

I didn't fully understand the significance of her presence, nor the importance of her address to us. Reflecting on that moment later I understood Mrs. Gandhi's concern for her people, and her desire to do everything in her power to help her country attain self-sufficiency in food production. She had come to America to plead for support in India's trouble with Pakistan, but had been given a chilly reception. Now, she was trying to present us with a warm welcome to her country. I felt inspired by her words. It was very appropriate that we received a warm welcome from the highest power in our new host country.

Our flight stopped in London, England; Frankfurt, Germany; and Beirut, Lebanon on an excursion that seemed to take days. When we stepped off the Air India jet in the New Delhi Airport the eyes of every trainee searched hopefully for signs of something familiar to sooth the trepidation that haunted our anxious minds. Our mouths were dry, our feet were swollen and a heavy feeling of exhaustion dulled our senses. A member of our India-60 group, Billy Danielson, had a painful earache, and several others complained of sensitive stomachs. Over 40 hours in airplanes and terminals, from our homes to New York, to the U.K., to Germany, to Lebanon and to India had disoriented the enthusiasm that was present at the start of our travel.

Until this day, most of us had extremely small understanding of India. What little knowledge we had before joining Peace

Corps was gleaned mostly from the writings of Americans and Europeans who had travelled the infamous hippie trail from Europe through Asia in the 1960's. *The Last Whole Earth Catalog* and *The Lonely Planet* guidebooks had been our best sources for information.

The sounds of strange languages in the New Delhi Airport assailed our ears as a dozen turbaned porters rushed toward us to offer assistance with our bags. We must have looked like innocent lambs as we stared in disbelief at the shouting and the commotion. Thankfully, our group leader shouted something, maybe in Hindi, a language our instructors had no time to teach us. The baggage clerks may have spoken *Punjabi* or *Urdu*, but certainly not the *Kannada* we studied for eight weeks. With looks of disappointment the porters reluctantly backed off when our leaders stepped in. Our limited *Kannada* vocabulary was useless here as even our Indian escorts were now speaking in other languages.

Looking back on that experience as a first time international traveler I acknowledge that I never would have made it on my own. Left to my own devices I probably would have crawled back into that Air India plane and refused to come out until it landed safely back in New York.

Making matters more bizarre was a disturbing odor that assailed our nostrils, further confounding our tired, foggy minds. Mixed in with the burned jet fuel, fumes from other diesel engines on the tarmac and the sweaty bodies moving like a slow whirlwind around us there was some unidentifiable, caustic and unpleasant odor, which we couldn't immediately identify. We would soon understand from whence it came.

The Peace Corps staff arranged for someone to pick up our luggage and load it onto a bus. They also arranged one day's stay in the Indian International Center. Like any good hotel it had air conditioning, flush toilets and European food. It was morning in New Delhi, but most of the trainees were exhausted and promptly passed out on their hotel beds. Little did we appreciate the luxury of that stop until several days later when we were introduced to our temporary living quarters on an agricultural training site twelve hundred miles to the south of New Delhi.

New Delhi, capital of the Republic of India, is located between her northern states of Uttar Pradesh and Haryana. The project location my fellow trainees and I were being trained for was on the Deccan Plateau in the southern state of Mysore, which was a long train ride south of Delhi. Tomorrow, we would make the journey to Hyderabad, and from there by bus to our training camp near a small village called Dhadesugur.

We had a day to explore New Delhi before embarking on the train to Hyderabad. We were told that Connaught Place was the most vibrant area of Delhi. Most of the volunteers chose, without hesitation, to investigate that claim. That is where I learned a cruel lesson on currency exchange while bargaining with merchants in the bazar. Feeling brave and adventuresome, several of us summoned a taxi and directed the driver by simply saying, "Connaught Circle".

Taxis and rickshaws buzzed busily up and down New Delhi's streets, zipping in and out of incredibly small spaces, challenging other drivers for a spot on the roadway. Buses roared down the main boulevards casting dust and diesel exhaust fumes on the hundreds of pedestrians whose excitement was seldom suspended. Shouts from street vendors parlayed our attention from one colorful display to the next.

My small hometown of Morgan, Minnesota never experienced sidewalk vendors or shoe shine boys. In Delhi, we were continually bombarded by the calls of merchants as we strolled the sidewalks of Connaught Place. Some food vendors displayed tempting fruits and delicious-looking prepared foods. We reminded each other of the words of Dr. Johnson, about eating food on the streets of India.

With that limitation on spending the few rupees of walk-around money, we focused on other local attractions. The circular markets of Connaught Place housed numerous fascinating craftworkers and artists. We rejected the calls of the merchants standing or sitting in their doorways and on the open ground but I was eventually coaxed by a street vendor into having my dusty shoes polished. He was a young man who appeared to be an honest looking soul. His loose fitting button shirt looked a little ragged and he was barefoot, but his earnest effort to get our business caught our attention. So, there he squatted near his little stool while he brushed the dirt off our shoes and applied a small gob of shoe polish.

He rambled on in an unfamiliar language as he worked, always flashing glances at the foot ware of passersby. When he finished with my shoes I asked him in my best *Kannada*, "*Ishtu corda-beku?*" Those words came reasonably close to the *Kannada* phrase for "how much do I owe you?" Even if he were able to understand and speak *Kannada*, the shoe shine boy would never admit it. He held out his hand in the universal gesture of 'give me money.' Suddenly aware that no one had prepared me for pricing the value of a shoe shine in Hindi, I reached into my pocket. My hand touched a ten rupee note, and while doing a speedy, but faulty, calculation in my head I handed it to the boy, who smiled appreciatively, waved a quick goodbye and disappeared.

The Indian rupee was worth about 14 cents in 1968. Therefore, the ten Rupee note I gave to the shoeshine boy was worth about $1.40 in U.S. dollars. Today, a dollar forty does not seem to be too much to pay for a shoe shine in the U.S. However, the true value of a shoeshine in 1968 in India was about 25 Paisa, or a quarter of a rupee. I had just overpaid that boy by a factor of forty.

That wasn't my biggest mistake. That came when I mentioned to Tom Carter, the Assistant Director for Peace Corps' Southern India Office, how much I paid to get my shoes shined. When he finally stopped laughing he told some of the staff and trainees. One by one the trainees, who also thought my error was humorous, speculated about how soon we would see the shoe shine boy driving around in his own luxury car.

Besides creating a little inflation in New Delhi's Connaught

Place, we also discovered what caused that noxious, ever present odor that seemed to permeate throughout the city. There were very few public restrooms, but many open sewers and public latrines. Many people had no hesitancy to relieve themselves by these open sewers or against the concrete walls that lined compounds. By the time volunteers left the country after their two plus years of service, that odor seemed to have disappeared. It wasn't gone; not only had we acculturated to it, we were not averse ourselves to "making a leg" as the local phrase goes, when the need arose.

However, we considered without a doubt that we could survive for a while in India. After all, the famous British singing group, The Beatles, had survived their recent stay while visiting the ashram of Maharishi Mahesh Yogi. So did Mia Farrow. Of course, these people were special guests of the esteemed founder of the technique called Transcendental Meditation, and were exclusively looked after. For sure they didn't have to worry about scorpions and snakes. Nevertheless, other Americans and Europeans before us had survived and so could we.

We also took some comfort in knowing that India, the largest democracy in the world, had a system of government that was not unfamiliar to us. Little did we realize, however, that there was turmoil at the upper levels of India's government. From our micro-perspective, food, drinkable water, heat and the monsoon rains were our main considerations, while in Delhi, Bombay, Calcutta and elsewhere there were serious battles for control of power over India.

National and international challenges raged, but remained distant from our view of life in the country villages. A constant religious war plagued parts of North India, and India's relations with Pakistan were persistently sensitive. During 1969 the Indian National Congress split into two factions; one led by Indira Gandhi, and another led by Morarji Desai. That year, Mrs. Gandhi nationalized fourteen banks, and India opened a facility to produce nuclear energy. Five years later India successfully detonated its first nuclear weapon.

THE MISSION

The mission of India-60 was to assist India's Mysore Department of Agriculture in Raichur District, to implement improved agricultural practices and promote proper use of irrigation methodology. The Green Revolution brought new challenges to rural Raichur District, where locally grown crops struggled to survive the limited annual rainfall on the rock hard 'black cotton' clay soil. Most villagers could barely eke out enough food to sustain life for their families, let alone produce crops for export.

Dr. Norman Ernest Borlaug was an American agronomist who is credited with the title of "the father of the Green Revolution." After his graduation from the University of Minnesota in 1942, Dr. Borlaug took up agricultural research in Mexico. His research resulted in new strains of semi-dwarf, high-yielding and disease-resistant wheat. Dr. Borlaug introduced these high-yielding varieties along with modern production techniques to Mexico, Pakistan and India. Wheat yields nearly doubled in India between 1965 and 1970, improving its food security.

Completion of the Tungabhadra Dam in 1953 in the Southern State of Mysore brought new hope for major development in the production of irrigated crops. Farmers jumped at the chance to grow rice, which is the staple in every villager's diet. Sugar cane had already been popular on land near rivers, where water was free and easily available. Now, sugar cane paddies multiplied quickly in the irrigation zone as canal water from the new Tungabhadra irrigation canal system became easily available to those fortunate to have lands reachable by canal water.

The Tungabhadra canal system was designed to make irrigation water available to as many Indian farmers as possible. Some 580,000 acres of land lay in the reaches of the canal system. However, as farmers harnessed the system for the heavy water demands of rice and sugarcane those farmers at the lower reaches of the canal system were left high, and dry.

To provide for a more equitable distribution of water the Mysore Department of Agriculture responded with a ban on using canal water for rice and cane, and instituted packages of practices for a wide range of what the government called "dry-cum-wet" crops. Crops such as maize, sorghum, wheat, sun flower, groundnut (peanut) and other crops could be grown with a limited amount of water.

Canal irrigation required some knowledge about leveling the land to make controlled application of water possible. Along with irrigation comes the challenges and responsibilities of water management to prevent overwatering, and proper drainage of the land. The absence of these two inevitably led to salinization and ultimate ruination of cultivatable soil. Our task was to assist the Raichur District Government in helping farmers level their farm land so it could be irrigated, select appropriate varieties of crops and teach them correct irrigation techniques to grow those crops. Along the way, we were to seek ways to innovate tools that would make their work easier.

I survived the village visits, the spicy hot curry and the total lack of privacy, and, just before Christmas 1968, I graduated to become a full fledged Peace Corps Volunteer. My *Kannada* language skills were somewhere around a two+ on the U.S. Federal Service scale of zero-to-four. My understanding of Indian culture was about a two, on a scale of one-to-ten. However, my enthusiasm was about 90 out of one hundred. In my mind, I was ready to save the world, but, until I met Pejathaya, I had no idea of how little I knew about India.

Training ended with a subdued celebration; enthusiasm mixed with anxiety. Happy to get out of camp, yet uncertain what the future would bring, Peace Corps staff delivered each of the 22 remaining India-60 volunteers to a village previously identified by Peace Corps and the local government officials to meet a "host farmer."

My assignment attached me to a cooperative tractor society in the town of Sindhanur, a growing community with a population of about 10,000. The town of Sindhanur is located in the administrative area called Sindhanur Taluka, which is an administrative division of a district, organized for the collection of revenue, somewhat similar to an administrative county in the U.S. There are a large number of villages and camps within the taluka, however, Sindhanur town is the Sindhanur Taluka headquarters.

I was instructed to apply my agricultural experience, along with newly acquired land-leveling training, to assist farmers in developing their land for irrigation of dry-cum-wet crops. I desperately wanted this particular assignment, as it meant working with tractors and machinery. It also meant living in a taluka headquarters, with all its modern trappings; such as a meat market, a movie theater, a government hospital, and the proximity of government offices.

The other 21 volunteers were each placed in one of the villages in Sindhanur Taluka or neighboring Manvi Taluka. Many were housed in dusty, mud brick rooms with cow dung slurry floors and walls, and roofs that leaked profusely in the rainy season. Some volunteers had no paved roads to their villages. A trip to the taluka headquarters for them often included a bus or bullock cart ride and a fair amount of walking. Most volunteers had no nearby shops from which to buy provisions, and they had to rely on their own wits and their Peace Corps-provided medical kits for medical attention.

Chuck Lenth, the volunteer stationed at the tractor society in Manvi, and I, in Sindhanur town, were two of only a few India-60 volunteers with measurable agricultural experience. Billy Danielson, a wheat farmer from Montana, was stationed in Balaganur. The rest of the group were distributed approximately equally around the towns of Manvi and Sindhanur, and were expected to use Manvi and Sindhanur as headquarters for their Peace Corps contacts. The furthest volunteer was about 20 miles from one of the two towns, no more than a half day journey by walk, bus, bicycle or bullock cart ride away.

My eventual accommodation was not immediately available so I spent the first several weeks staying in a government inspection bungalow with David Bowman, a volunteer from an earlier Peace Corps group (India-38), who had extended for a third year. Dave was able to introduce me to a number of the local leaders and government officials with whom I would eventually be working.

My home for over two years was to be an apartment in a partially completed concrete block building. The owner may have run out of construction funds when the first floor was completed. Rough concrete with protruding re-bar reflected his intention to eventually continue the structure skyward. There was no running water or heat in the unit, but I was at least thankful for a locking door and windows with bars to keep out most large animals and potential human intruders. The shared outside toilet facility was a dual unit, mud brick enclosure with no roof, an open sewer drain and a rickety door hinged with leather straps.

Bathing was done in an adjoining mud brick room, and the water was stored in a 50 gallon cement cistern. With no electricity or windows the bath room was always dark so we never knew what creatures swam in the cistern.

My two neighbors were Indian families. Mr. K. Rama Bhat, just next door, was a hefty man of 35 who worked as a supervisor for the Sindhanur Public Works Department. His wife and two young daughters lived with him, however, I seldom saw or spoke with any of the female family members. Mrs. Bhat was a good cook. The wonderful aromas that permeated the screened separator of our porches gave testimony. The girth of Mr. Bhat was further evidence, but the clincher was the delicious treats Mr. Bhat carried to my door on special occasions.

On the opposite side of the building lived Mr. Patel, MBBS (a general practice physician) and his family. Since their apartment entrance was on the far side of the building I only heard and almost never saw the good doctor and his family.

Saving the world doesn't come easy. Like many new volunteers, we struggled with attempts to become useful. New volunteers typically have all the positive energy in the world but they get frustrated when things don't go as planned. It takes from six months to a year to understand that just because the country is considered a "developing" nation doesn't mean that the indigenous people have no initiative, or progressive instincts. Once we understood a little about why things were done the way they were, we found it much easier to work with people rather than trying to force feed our American agricultural theories.

The Sindhanur Land Development Tractor Society is a cooperative association sponsored by the Mysore State Department of Cooperatives. It is a non-profit cooperative run by a local board of directors, who appoint a manager. The manager employs twenty to thirty tractor drivers and maintenance personnel to operate and keep the tractors and farm equipment in good working order. Village farmers rent the tractors for short terms at a nominal rate to help them develop and till their land.

Mr. Krishna Rao, the manager of the tractor society, was a recent college graduate. A proud young man, Mr. Rao came from a small and remote village called Talkahn, in nearby Lingsugur Taluka, just fifty miles from Sindhanur. Mr. Rao was the first of his siblings to make it to the university. He had a strong desire to show the board of directors of the tractor society that he could be successful in this his first assignment after graduation.

Mr. Rao seemed to wear a semi-permanent scowl on his face, probably because his youth, combined with the position of authority, made him super sensitive to failure avoidance. His apparently insecure disposition, and having an American so-called "expert" thrust into his domain made our relationship somewhat ambivalent. I later learned that he had nothing to do with deciding to host a volunteer, but was instructed by the Board of Directors to do so. Had he been asked he probably would have preferred to fly solo.

Mr. Rao was expected to make the tractor society bring in enough revenue to pay its expenses. That was the easy part. An incessant oversight by society board members as well as by a hierarchy of status-conscious farmers made his life unpleasant. I felt that he wanted to be left alone to run the tractor society, and that he hoped that I would not obstruct or criticize his efforts. I sometimes felt that he wanted the world to see him during public events as "in charge". I later learned that his apparent bad disposition was only the business face he put on when working with subordinates, board members, or government officials.

Mr. Subramaniam, an Indian from Madras State, was the tractor society's mechanic. Subramaniam had served in Burma with the Indian army as a heavy equipment operator and mechanic during the conflict with Japan. Subramaniam was probably in his early '50s and spoke fluent Tamil and Urdu, understandable English, and a little of the local *Kannada*. Approximately half of the tractor drivers were Moslem, and spoke Urdu. Others spoke *Kannada*, with some Hindi or English vocabulary. Subramaniam was the chief mechanic, and was able to communicate with all the personnel in some manner.

I took an immediate liking to Subramaniam, as he was the first person at the tractor society to introduce himself and show me around. His Indian Army experience working on diesel engines during the construction of the Burma Road made him comfortable around the thirty diesel engines in our tractor shop. Often, in the tea shops, I listened intently as he told many stories of his military exploits. He struck me as an honest, hardworking man.

I was surprised to learn that the German Volunteer Service had also assigned a German volunteer to the tractor society.

Peter Junker came with a sound background in diesel mechanics. He worked well with Subramaniam, and the two of them were not afraid to tackle any mechanical repair.

Peter Junker and Subramaniam working on a tractor

Though I tried early to spend most of my days at the tractor society, my responsibilities and interests eventually interfered with that plan. With the manager situated on site, a highly qualified diesel mechanic in the garage, and a German volunteer mechanic on staff, my responsibilities leaned toward training the tractor drivers. My assignment specified assisting the tractor drivers in working with land leveling experts to form contour border strips for land irrigation. This entailed showing the drivers how to follow the surveyor's markers to level land. I also tried to demonstrate safe operation of the tractors and equipment as well as simple maintenance and repair.

In Hemet, California, land development experts instructed us in surveying techniques. We learned how to measure the contour of farm land and, after staking-out a farmer's fields with markers at equal levels we used tractors with scraper blades to move soil into ten to twenty meter wide bands of land. These bands are called border strips, and follow the general contour of the farmer's field. With a slight drop in elevation of one meter per 100 meters and earthen bunds on both sides of the borders we could influence water to run like an even sheet from one end of the border strip to the other. At the Agricultural Training Facility in Dhadesugur, India, Mr. A. B. Bellary, Raichur District's Agricultural Development Officer, and his Indian staff continued this training, using actual farmers' fields.

This was my first exposure to land leveling and irrigation techniques. I enjoyed the spontaneity of the dry desert soil as it pushed up vigorous plants when I applied water. I learned the significance of water sharing, and the need for structuring one's timing to comply with the needs of other water users. I took great joy in learning how to control the flow of water to the crops by using syphon tubes. The resulting field layout was ideal for growing the government-prescribed dry-cum-wet crops using light irrigation. Border strips also allowed more use of mechanized equipment.

Many local farmers, however, had other ideas. They knew that they could make more money growing traditional crops. Since rice and sugar cane were grown for many generations they preferred to construct paddy fields and flood them with irrigation water. Local agricultural workers were not inclined to discourage the practice, so border strips were infrequently constructed. Our tractor drivers had more experience building paddy plots than I did, so, much of my land development training went for naught.

As a resident in the taluka headquarters, and as one of the few volunteers with an agricultural background, I had a responsibility for the volunteers whose villages were served by the commercial businesses and government offices of Sindhanur Taluka. Two blocks from where I lived sat the Indian Post and Telegraph Office. Messages to and from Peace Corps Bangalore often passed through my house. I was expected to assist the other volunteers with their work related to farming or machine operation. I didn't mind this, and at first I enjoyed working with the other volunteers and their many different projects. Later, however, I found it a challenge to dedicate sufficient time to the Tractor Society.

Much of my two-plus years as a Peace Corps Volunteer, therefore, was consumed with activities other than working at the tractor society. Each volunteer in Sindhanur Taluka had unique ideas for projects, and I enjoyed working with many of them in communicating their ideas and recommendations to the government authorities and Peace Corps Bangalore. We worked together on land development and irrigation projects, crop selection, plant protection, accessing agricultural inputs, and demonstrations of new implements and contemporary farming practices. The most challenging and interesting project I got involved in was spearheading a milk collection and distribution cooperative.

Most days would see one or more of the volunteers journey through Sindhanur while on a quest for agricultural inputs or information for their villages' farmers. I could not resist a request to help the volunteers make the connections to find solutions. I guess this is why I was christened by several of the other volunteers with the title, "Mr. Ken, Our Mother Hen."

A CHANGE IN VENUE

Around the same time the India-60 volunteers were seeing village India for the first time, life was also changing for a young Indian man named S.M. Pejathaya. Our paths had not yet crossed, but they would very soon.

Pejathaya grew up on India's West Coast, about 40 kilometers of dirt roads, ferry rides and trails from the city of Udupi. His birth place was in the Western Ghats, a narrow range of mountains that spans over 1600 kilometers along the western coast of India, close to the Arabian Sea. Pejathaya grew up not far from the sea, and his dream since childhood was to be part of the Indian Navy. As a student in elementary school, high school and college he belonged to the Auxiliary Cadet Corps and the National Cadet Corps (NCC). In his final year of college Pejathaya became the Junior Cadet Captain of his naval unit of NCC. In his mind, his future was set. He had developed a strong urge to sail the high seas as a naval officer, and wanted to join the Indian Navy after graduation. His dream seemed to be near at hand.

Family circumstances affected his plans when he graduated from college. Since his sister and brother-in-law had housed and supported him during his college education he felt an obligation to them. When they asked for his help to develop some forest land they owned he could not deny his assistance. Pejathaya felt he had no choice but to follow their wishes before he would join the Indian Navy. When the coastal farm was successfully growing rice and coconuts around 1968, Pejathaya was ready for his next adventure. However, things didn't work out quite the way he had planned. Here is his story.

GOODBYE TO SHIROOR
BY S.M. PEJATHAYA

By November 1968, I had harvested my six acres of rice crop. For Deepavali festival my small hut was filled up to the roof with freshly threshed 'paddy.' My sister and brother-in-law came over to the farm to celebrate the 'Dhaanya Lakshmi pooja', (Worshipping the granary).

Electric power had come to our remote farm due to the relentless efforts of my brother-in-law. He knew the top officials in the MSEB (Mysore State Electricity Board) and the State government had given top priority to provide power to the irrigation pump sets.

My man Friday, Cheempa Naika, had settled for good in the farm. I had fitted three electrical pump sets by the riverside and built strong sheds with granite stones to house them. I joined hands with the masons and the carpenters in transporting the building material on my power tiller trolley and together we built a two-bedroom cottage on the same knoll that housed my hut. The cottage was designed by my brother-in-law and my sister and it was very comfortable. The cottage stood next to the huge cattle shed. We had electrified all the buildings. After getting the electricity, our farm shone out with dazzling lights though it was surrounded by the thick jungle on three sides and the Swarna River on the fourth.

I taught Cheempa to operate the electric pumps. The pumps discharged water through 3 inch diameter pipes just outside our fence. In fact, from that level, water could flow down to all our coconut saplings and paddy fields by gravity through narrow channels dug for irrigation. Three laborers working at the water delivery points could irrigate the whole farm in one day. I encouraged a boy called Shastry, a Commerce graduate, to stay with me and taught him to look after the farm. I was certain that Cheempa, Shastry and our permanent laborers could look after the farm.

I thought that my mission was almost complete at Shiroor. I had done my duty of setting up a farm for my sister. I thought the time had come for me to say good-bye to Shiroor and seek my future elsewhere.

I applied to the Service Selection Board of the Indian Navy to appear for an interview for the NCC commission, as a career officer in the Indian Navy. Then, bad news arrived. I was informed by a letter that I had exceeded the age limit by six months for NCC entry. The same letter informed me that I could appear for an interview to take up a short service commission of five years with the Navy.

I was a bit disheartened. I had always dreamt of becoming a career officer with the Indian Navy and wanted to serve until my retirement. The India-Pakistani war had ended and I seriously thought of opting for the available short service commission entry.

At this juncture, I happened to meet Sri K. V. Biliraya, who headed the newly formed Agricultural Finance Division of the Syndicate Bank Limited, Manipal, during a progressive farmers' meeting of the Syndicate Bank's Agricultural Foundation. I had met Sri Biliraya earlier, during many farmers' symposiums. During the lunch break, I told him about my plans to join the Indian Navy under short service commission scheme.

He heard me patiently and did not comment. Within the next two days, I received a letter from Sri T. A. Pai, the managing director of the Syndicate Bank, stating that he wanted to offer me a job and I had to see him in this connection as early as possible.

Sri T.A. Pai was a well-wisher of our family and so was his brother-in-law, Sri K. K. Pai, who held the post of the General Manager of the Syndicate Bank. During my father's time, Udupi was a small temple town where everybody knew everybody. My father had loved, respected and always appreciated these two sharp young men who hailed from the highly industrious and popular business families of Udupi. The seniors of the Pai Family of Manipal were my father's friends. Sri T. A. Pai's elder brother Dr. T. M. A. Pai, the founder The Canara Industrial Banking Syndicate

Limited, which later came to be known as Syndicate Bank Limited with its head office at Manipal, was my father's contemporary and a friend. Furthermore, two of my elder brothers were already working for the Syndicate Bank.

I appeared before Sri T. A. Pai. He said, "Kesari Pejathaya, when shall you join our farm at Raichur district?" All the members of the Pai Family called me by my pet name. I had great respect for Sri T. A. Pai and when this question came from him, I felt I should reply in affirmative only. I said, "Sir, as soon as you would want me to be there."

"Please, go to Sri K. K. Pai to discuss further details," he said.

I went to the General Manager's office. Sri K. K. Pai asked me to take a seat in front of him. "Kesari. I am going to visit Raichur district day after tomorrow. Can you join me to have a look at the farm which is owned by the directors of our bank and their associates at Jawalgera? If you like the place we shall employ you and, your emoluments shall be at par with that of a bank manager. You shall get quarters and a cook. The accommodation is farm style. You shall be given actual traveling expenses when you have to travel on duty. You shall be solely in charge of the farm. This being a private farm you shall not be a part of the bank's staff. Being a proved farmer you shall easily follow the farming practices of the black soil, where we grow cotton, hybrid jowar (sorghum) and Mexican wheat at Jawalgera. Our farm is called the Tungabhadra Farms. You shall be answerable only to me and you have to correspond with me. You do not have to take orders from the Board of Directors. Sri T. A. Pai has just told me that you have accepted his offer without a question. We shall look after you and you shall look after our farm. You shall work hard as if it were your own farm and show us profits. We wish you all the best!"

For the first time, I went to Sindhanur, Raichur district with Sri K. K. Pai. It was evening when we reached the 'taluk' headquarters of Sindhanur. The local Syndicate Bank manager had arranged for our stay in the Circuit House (Travelers' Bungalow) at Sindhanur. That night all of us were invited to partake a sumptuous dinner at Dr. K. Anand Hegde's house. Dr. Hegde was a leading medical practitioner and a progressive farmer of Sindhanur. He had founded a cooperative society—the Tractor Society of Sindhanur, for which he was the honorary president. The society was hiring out tractors, their implements and spraying equipment to the farmers of the 'taluka' (taluk) at most reasonable rates. This was a great help to the farmers who had small acreage. Dr. Hegde owned a farm about a mile away from Sindhanur town.

We visited the farm at Jawalgera the next day. It was an expanse of plain land irrigated by the Tungabhadra dam's left bank channel. I could see miles and miles of open fields from our farmyard. We had all the machinery and labor required to run the agricultural operations. The dwelling houses were made of mud walls and the roofs were thatched with grass. There were a few thorny trees of the arid region, called 'Naganagowda Jaali' trees, along the field bunds. The trees had one inch long thorns and contained sparse leaves. They gave a very thin shade from the blazing sun. These trees of the arid region were very hardy and local people depended on the twigs of these trees for firewood. They used the hard wood to make implements. The soil of our farm was deep black, known as black cotton soil.

The staff and labor were very obedient. We had a wonderful pair of prize bullocks called Surya and Chandra. Sri K. K. Pai told me that these bullocks were the pride of the farm and they were not given the hard work of tilling or sowing the fields since we had tractors to do that work. They were treated as the farm's prestigious pets. They would be hitched to a beautifully crafted Bellary Cart (very expensive bullock cart custom made at the neighboring district headquarter city of Bellary) and had an exercise run of a few miles every day to keep them fit. I took a liking for the huge sinewy bullocks instantly. There were a few milch buffaloes and a watchdog called Lixo.

Sri K. K. Pai and Sri Baliga assured me that we had full support from the Agricultural Department and technical support from the U.S. Peace Corps Volunteers. He wanted me to take up the challenge of running the farm and prove my capacity as a good farmer.

That noon we had lunch at the farm cooked by my future cook Rajanna. The food was palatable and I thought his cooking was a margin better than that of my own. I really hoped to survive in the farm. As explained by my boss, the accommodation was rustic, yet functional.

Sri K. K. Pai asked me again as to whether I would accept the challenges and prove my capacity as a farm manager by growing the field crops like cotton, wheat, jowar, etc. at Jawalgera.

"Sir, I shall try my level best to grow the crops that I have not grown so far. I am sure that I would stay and survive in the farm surroundings. I have attended 14 training camps as a junior and senior NCC cadet in my high school and college life. I had stayed under canvas in the open with NCC and I may not resent having taken up a tough field job. I hope to work hard in the new environment to bring better profits to the farm. I am not hindered by the fact that there is no electricity or other urban amenities nearby as I have lived and proved myself as a farmer in the remote village of Shiroor," I said.

He asked me to report for the duty the next week.

MEETING PEJATHAYA

Before the sun could heat the streets of Sindhanur beyond a manageable comfort level, fellow PCV Merle Menegay and I set off for the office of the Assistant Director of Agriculture, Mr. Achyat Rao. Merle was an industrious India-60 volunteer, always on the lookout for an edge in helping his host village farmers grow more and better crops. Achyat Rao was a helpful and friendly agricultural officer who reported to the District Director of Agriculture in Raichur. He was always ready to assist the Peace Corps volunteers.

Government officials didn't seem to mind making their visitors wait to see them. They have busy schedules and loads of responsibility. I am sure they had massive amounts of paperwork. Luckily, the Assistant Director had two benches outside his office to sit while we waited for an audience. Within two minutes, another person arrived, and informed the office 'peon' that he also wished to see the Assistant Director. After being told to wait along with us, this young man took a seat at the opposite bench.

This man appeared to be close to our ages, maybe a few years younger. His appearance was not like either a local farmer or a government official, but he appeared to be Indian. His complexion was a clear, light brown, he stood about five foot-six, was slightly stout and he sported a gossamer handlebar mustache. He was dressed in denim jeans and denim jacket. He also wore a floppy hat and a pleasant smile. His spoken English and his clothes gave me the impression that he was well educated and not from the local area. Had he been a 'Gram Sevak' (village health and extension worker) I would have met him in one of the Agriculture Department meetings.

Before Merle or I could say anything, this man greeted us in a pleasant manner and introduced himself as the manager of the Syndicate Bank Farm in Jawalgera, about eight miles north of Sindhanur. His name was S. M. Pejathaya, pronounced "pay-ja-thai'-ya." We began a friendly, animated conversation about our respective missions.

Suddenly, the ADA's door opened and Mr. Achyat Rao came out to greet us with a robust smile. Asking us all to come into his office. He bade us to sit in his wicker visitors' chairs.

Our new friend looked somewhat confused and pointed to himself and said, "You mean me, too?"

"Yes, yes," said the officer, "come in and tell me what I can do for you."

The Assistant Director explained to the three of us that the agricultural demonstration plot inputs for *jowar* (sorghum) and cultivation instructions were being transported from the district headquarters in Raichur. They would arrive by the following week, "...at the latest." Then, he engaged us in small talk about life in India and our plans for the rest of our term. At one point, he turned to Pejathaya and asked, "What are you going to do when you go back to the States?"

After a brief pause, and with a surprised look, Pejathaya said, "Oh, no sir. I am from here. I am an Indian. I am one of you. I work for the Syndicate Bank's farm in Jawalgera, and I have no plans to visit the United States."

Pejathaya's denim jacket and jeans, his floppy hat and his precise British English apparently marked him as a visitor from the West, quite possibly Great Britain or America. Mr. Rao did not skip a beat, and welcomed Pejathaya to Sindhanur Taluka.

Pejathaya's easy laugh resonated in the veranda later as we strode from Mr. Rao's office. Merle and I were immediately attracted to this friendly guy, and accepted his invitation to join him for *chai* at the Ashok Bavan Hotel nearby. We consumed several cups of *chai* and several plates of *bhuja* (a spicy, exotic blend of crispy-crunchy multigrain noodles, peas, peanuts and *sultanas*) snacks as we talked for over an hour.

That was my first meeting with Pejathaya. I learned of his enduring devotion to farming, his background in turning jungle into valuable farm land, and his wonderful experiences growing up in the western coastal area of India. That day began a friendship that has endured over time and distance to this day.

We discovered that Pejathaya was a progressive farmer with many advanced agricultural ideas that he was interested in practicing. We also noted that he was exceptionally good at observing the world around him. He also wrote and narrated wonderful stories. I enjoyed listening to his many tales about his childhood, and about the people he met while clearing jungle in the coastal region of India.

Though a devote Brahmin, Pejathaya was considerate of other castes and religions. His religious beliefs never clouded his judgment of others, and he accepted every living creature just as it presented itself, on its distinct merits.

From that day forward, I relished my experiences in discovering the enormous richness of India, her people, religions and culture. I participated in many fascinating conversations with Pejathaya during my two-plus years stay in his country, and later, when we communicated over long-distances. His understanding of his countrymen and countrywomen, their religions, their struggles to survive and the history of this country served as a catharsis that shook me from my set Midwestern USA imprint and eventually gave me some insight into the wonders of India.

Pejathaya and I huddled frequently in *chai* shops, discussing Indian culture, agriculture, and his everlasting quest to build a 'perpetual motion machine.' As far as the latter goes, we both knew the required mechanics of such an imaginary machine well enough to know that there was little hope of anyone ever inventing a perpetual motion machine. Yet, the idea of energy efficiency was fascinating enough to keep our conversations flowing for hours.

The spicy hot curry, the numerous religious deities, the

colorful silk saris, the waiters in lungis, the farmers in *dhotris*, the smiling children and the cries of the vegetable vendors in the market-day commotion are but a few of the enchanting tastes, sights and sounds of exotic India. First time visitors miss much of India's enchantment because they only see the misery around the train stations and bus stops. In fact, each life is a treasure and a story in itself. The phrase, "slow down and smell the roses" applies, because there is beauty in the absorption of vibrant life beyond the bus stop that never ceases to excite.

Later, Pejathaya chronicled some of his tales in a manuscript called *The Voyage of a Paper Boat*. Pejathaya's writing shepherds the reader from his youthful memories, through his school years and into an agricultural journey into coastal jungle, canal irrigation on the Deccan Plateau, and finally, to the cultivation of coffee, pepper and *areca* nut in the highlands of Southern India. The following is the first chapter in his book.

VOYAGE OF A PAPER BOAT
BY S.M. PEJATHAYA

As a child, I used to sail paper boats in a small stream that flowed across my grandfather's courtyard in the rainy season. The 'stream' was the water that overflowed from a large well. The well had a small overflow sluice, and water would overflow in June, July and August. The overflow would stop at the end of the season and I would have to wait until it rained next year to play in the little stream again.

We lived in a valley covered with plains on either side. The laterite absorbed and released rainwater quickly. That was how our tiny stream would be formed. Along this small stream, two feet wide and hundred feet long, was my small world. There were rapids and shallows. There were deep whirlpools around the bends.

The whirlpools would try to sink some of my small paper boats, which I imagined to be large ships. The wild grass and weeds downstream were, to my imagination, the jungles of Africa, situated along the River Nile! There was a vast shallow with almost tranquil waters. This, I imagined, was the Pacific Ocean. There were stretches of water lined with rose and hibiscus bushes, in which the flowers were reflected. I imagined these to be beautiful ports like Rio de Janeiro.

I would make paper boats of all sizes, and follow these boats down the stream until they passed through an outlet in our compound wall. From there on, our little stream flowed further to join a bigger stream, which flowed down our village. In the water of our little stream, I could find small fish—the biggest of them, no longer than my little finger—and several water insects. These, to me, were the great fish and animals of the sea. The biggest of the fish, I would imagine, to be the great whales!

My ships sailed through these wonderful waters, all through the monsoon season. This was the most fascinating game of my childhood. I still miss the years I spent with my grandfather. Sitting in his huge reclining chair in the front room of the house, my grandfather would watch over me as I played along the stream. If I strayed close to the well, he would make a grunting noise, as if clearing his throat. This was a warning enough for an obedient boy like me to retreat from the vicinity of the well, which was indeed, very deep.

Sometimes, my boats would take in water and sink! Sometimes, due to the bad navigation of their respective captains—who were, of course, invisible—they would end up crashing into one another. There would be fair weather, as well as the storms. Sometimes, the heavy winds would moor them against the banks of the Great River. At times, they would go out of control and spin in the whirlpools, struggling to get out of the grip of the swirling waters. Sometimes, they would succeed in getting out of the whirlpools and continue their voyage. At times, they would not make it at all. Many of them, by virtue of their sturdy build, completed their journeys and went through the compound wall into oblivion. The sluice in the wall was their final destination.

Man's life has always been compared to the sailing of a boat. It is true that in life, one comes across many difficulties and problems. With a little help from fair winds and luck, some with good 'quality of build' may well succeed in the voyage of life. Others may finish their journeys with great difficulty. Some others may lose, despite possessing all the requirements – succumbing to their destiny. Some paper boats, in spite of their bad build and poor sailing quality, may still succeed – the fair winds of luck keep pushing them to their destination, without any mishap! But, all this depends on the fate of the individual boat.

Anyone who has sailed paper boats in his or her childhood, I am sure, will agree with me.

I always compare my life with the journey of the paper boats of my childhood. I have faced cruel storms and winds. I have faced rough waters, got stuck in the shallows, hit the rocks, corals or sandbars. I have 'taken in' water many times, but have been able to bail it out successfully. During the course of my voyage, I have been spun around like a top and tossed about like a paper boat during the great storms. I have been drawn into the vortex of the great whirlpools! Somehow, I have come out of them by sheer luck. At times, it has become evident to me that I have been guided and helped by the unseen hand of the Maker. Many a time, I have escaped from the total disaster waiting around the next bend. I have seen sunshine and fair weather too! I have been blessed with the bounties of life.

The voyage of my paper boat, up to this day, is very interesting. All along this voyage, I have felt the presence of that unseen hand—the hand that guides us through life.

In my writings I have tried to narrate my wonderful journey down the great river of life, in my own paper boat. There are the periods of sickness and the periods of good health, the days of poverty as well as that of relative wealth. There are people I have met, the places I have seen, and my experiences. There are the references to the animals, insects, plants and trees I have been familiar with.

I have tried my best to put down my experiences in writing, in my farmer's language. How far will I succeed in putting them across? That will have to be determined by my readers.

*   *   *

We each try to navigate our ship through the rough sea of life. Not everyone's journey is successful. Pejathaya had a way of simplifying the world around him and illuminating a positive interpretation to the actions of others. He has always known how to draw out the best in everyone near him.

Although he is definitely not Irish, when I think of Pejathaya I remember the old Irish proverb, that goes something like this:

> *Work like you don't need the money*
> *dance like no one is watching*
> *sing like no one is listening*
> *love like you've never been hurt*
> *and live every day as if it were your last*

Pejathaya wrote several books in his native *Kannada* language, and continues to write articles for several periodicals and agricultural newsletters. A book about his Great Dane, Raksha, is in its second printing, and a *Kannada* language book with a title like *"Paper Boat"* has also had multiple printings. A chapter from one of his books has been adopted into a college level textbook.

When the villagers celebrated holidays and festivals, like *Diwali, Dussehra* and *Holi*, it was Pejathaya who explained the significance of the celebration and taught us how to accept the rituals and join in the customs. During the festival of colors *(Holi)* for example, he warned us that adults and children alike love to spray pigment powders and colored water on others, without fear of retribution.

As much as we initially detested the thought of having bright colored pigments thrown on our hair and clothes, we learned to not only accept the spirit of the occasion, but to appreciate the people's joy and feeling of equality. In the end, we learned to accept the one day in the year when there is no division between rich and poor, or status in the caste system.

Pejathaya became the 'fair wind and luck' that guided our ship safely through troubling waters. Thanks to him, my Peace Corps associates and I were able to experience a much more meaningful and insightful India. His calm and intelligent manner helped us understand a deeper perception of the Indian people, their culture and their religions. He helped us accept the cultural ways of Indian life and to understand how the historical past shaped India's present. He gave us a new approach to the understanding of the many faces of Hindu gods and goddesses, and taught us respect for the way Indians practiced their religion.

An avatar of the Hindu deity Lord *Shiva* is a monkey whose features are depicted in numerous poses framed behind glass on the walls of Hindu homes and businesses. I asked Pejathaya why Hindus worshiped a monkey. He took a deep breath and valiantly began his attempt to explain the epic *Ramayana* and the relationship between numerous Hindu religious figures. His first attempt fell short of giving me full understanding, as the number of gods and goddesses and their interwoven stories was more than a Catholic can absorb in one day.

There is not only *Shiva*, but also *Vishnu, Lakshmi, Ganesha, Krishna, Rama* and many more. One has to read the *Ramayana* and the *Mahabharata*, two great epics of India's Hindu religion, in order to begin to understand the 'Who's Who' of the Hindu hierarchy. Pejathaya displayed amazing patience in helping me connect the dots.

One cool but windy October morning I sensed an escalating degree of excitement at the tractor society. The young drivers chatted excitedly as they showed more than the usual hustle around the repair facility. Mehboob, a rather pushy driver of about 22 years of age, was urging Subramaniam to please get his tractor running quickly. Other drivers manipulated grease rags in and out of engine parts, One driver had obtained a bucket of water and was caressingly removing road dust and field mud from his tractor. Another driver had festooned a garland of flowers across the front of his Escort Tractor, from headlight to headlight.

"What is going on?" I asked Subramaniam, who seemed to be taking Mehboob's prompting in good humor.

Subramaniam was dressed in clean, pressed pants, probably the best shirt in his wardrobe, and a smart neckerchief tied around his neck. He shrugged and said, "These boys want to show off their tractors in today's parade".

No one told me anything about a parade. Was this another festival to celebrate one of the Hindu deity? From the noise and excitement around me I gathered that this event had to be something important. I tried to ignore the drivers' antics as I helped Peter clean the fuel injectors for one of the International tractors. That accomplished, Peter and I strode across the street and down the road where the owner of a tea *ungadi* was preparing his usual breakfast of green chillies deep fried in dough.

As we stepped under the bamboo mat shelter of the tea shop we saw a gingerly stepping Pejathaya approaching from the opposite direction. His happy countenance suggested that the excitement of the day had inspired him to venture to Sindhanur. We greeted him with a hearty *"Namaskara,"* and offered to buy him tea and chilies.

"What is going on today?" Peter asked. "Why is everyone dressed in their best clothes, and why are they carrying strings of flowers?"

Pejathaya explained, "Ah! This day is special. It is called *Ayudha Puja*. The words mean '*Pooja* to weapons', and it is the workingman's favorite festival celebrated in Karnataka and Andhra Pradesh States. You see, it is a rejoicing victory day of *Pandavas* in *Mahabharata*. One version of the origin of this festival is that Arjuna, a great warrior, completed a 13 year exile and prepared to face the mighty *Kaurava* army alone in defending the King *Virat*. He prayed and performed *Pooja* to his weapons. The fierce battle which ensued ended in a great victory for him.

"The ancient stories suggest that after the victory in the 18 day war of *Kurukshetra* the warriors celebrated by honoring their weapons. That was the beginning of a ritual by the commoners who came to believe that a Pooja performed on this auspicious day would bring them luck and victory (prosperity). Thus, *Ayudha Puja* is the symbolic keeping of the weapons, tools and vehicles ship-shape and getting ready to face the war against evil. Farmers who depend on their implements for their livelihood perform the Pooja to equipment such as tractors, tillers and so on."

Sure enough, as the parade crept past us an hour later, we saw our tractor drivers proudly displaying every implement in our garage. The glistening machinery was festooned with garlands of colorful flowers. Puffs of pigment highlighted facial expressions on the machinery and some tractors had large pictures of Lord Krishna mounted on fenders.

This was the day the khaki-uniformed Sindhanur police

proudly displayed their polished rifles. The local tailors decorated their sewing machines and gave them the day off. Artisans worshipped the tools of their art, accountants took special care to brush the dust off their ledgers, writers honored their typewriters and the housewives scrubbed extra hard to get the charred stains off their cooking utensils before preparing special festive dishes for their families.

Decorated tractors ready for the Ayudha Puja Celebration

I felt a small sense of camaraderie as I witnessed the proud smiles on the faces of our tractor drivers. This was their day in the limelight as their families and friends witnessed their driving skills and the responsibility placed in them by the management of the tractor society.

Pejathaya noted that the Hindu *Ayudha Puja* festival is sometimes called *"Astra Puja"*, which means "worship of implements." The festival falls on a particularly auspicious day in September or October and is a part of the *Dasara* festival.

TIGER IN THE HOMESTEAD

Finding themselves in a strange environment, visitors to rural India often hold fears of the things they imagine but know little about. Americans living in rural India in the 1960s feared snakes, lack of edible food, scorpions and wild animals, somewhat in that order. It takes some time of living in the country before one establishes a level of semi-relaxed comfort.

Although a lofty respect for the poisonous snakes of India, like the krait, the cobra and the viper is healthy, most visitors will never see one of these poisonous serpents. The villagers accept the occasional death by snake somewhat in stride, as religion teaches one to accept life as it happens, i.e., their karma. In Hinduism and Buddhism, people believe in an informal destiny or fate; the sum of a person's actions in this and previous forms of existence is viewed as deciding their fate in future existences.

The plains of the Deccan Plateau, which includes much of Southern India, have snakes in abundance. If one keeps to the high ground, however, he could pass through life without a serious encounter with poisonous reptiles. There were very few other deadly creatures outside the animal preserves to threaten people. Scorpions and spiders were ever present, but not necessarily life-threatening.

The reaction of non-Indians on seeing a poisonous snake or insect is to try to eliminate it. They may erroneously feel that for every threat there is a "Rikki-Tikki-Tavi," Rudyard Kipling's legendary mongoose, that will defend them. The reaction of most Indians on encountering such a creature is to first avoid being bitten or stung, and second to preserve its life as a creature of God.

An incident occurred during my Peace Corps training that demonstrates the difference between two cultures. During a field trip to observe an improved variety of cotton Joe Emerson, one of the American instructors, parted the leaves of a healthy looking cotton plant to show us the development of the cotton bowls. An Indian instructor standing nearby grasped the American's hand and abruptly snatched it away from the plant. A krait snake lie along the main stem of the plant and was nearly invisible. One bite from the krait would have been deadly.

After recovering from the shock of the near catastrophe the volunteers attempted to attack the snake to kill it and prevent any future incidents. The Indian instructor was appalled and said, "No! No! Leave it alone! It has not caused any harm."

One day, while discussing snakes and other dangerous creatures, I asked Pejathaya to tell me where the infamous Indian tigers were. He said, "The Bengal Tigers were nearly hunted to extinction, mostly by foreigners. Previously," he said, "tigers existed in many states throughout India, especially in the jungles in Northeastern India, close to Nepal, and along the coastal areas".

He related stories of the famous English hunter, Jim Corbett, who hunted the man-eating tigers in Northeast India. Pejathaya became very interested in the subject, as he said that at one time there were many tigers and other large cats in undeveloped parts of India, but today they are primarily found in animal preserves. "In fact", he said, "there were tigers in the forests near Udupi, on the West coast of India, where I grew up."

That day, as we sipped tea at Sindhanur's Ashok Bhavan Hotel, Pejathaya said, "Let me tell you about my experience with tigers," and he began to relate the following story.

QUE SERA SERA[1]
BY S.M PEJATHAYA

One of my uncles, Subrahmanya Baglodi, was at home in my village of Kinnikambla, not far from Udupi to look after his aging parents and us children as well. He relieved my grandfather of his responsibility of caring for my fatherless family. He was very tall and brave.

I recall an incident. Probably I was a five-year old then. We brothers, and uncle Subrahmanya would often sleep in the spacious open courtyard in front of our grandfather's house, during the months of hot and humid summers.

It used to be cool outside the house, and we slipped into slumber gazing at the stars. The house inside usually was warm and stuffy. Electricity had not yet come to Kinnikambla and there were no fans. We used to light the kerosene lamps and study sitting near them.

One such night we slept in the open courtyard with our uncle. The next morning, when we woke up, we found ourselves inside the house! Our beds were spread neatly in the drawing room and we all woke up to find ourselves there, in utter astonishment. Later, we came to know that uncle

---

[1] Que Sera Sera in Spanish means 'what will be, will be.' It's a popular film song sung by actress Doris Day during 1956.

Subrahmanya had brought us all inside during the night, when we were fast asleep!

When we woke up in the morning, he was not to be seen around; he had already gone on his customary morning round to the fields. Our grandmother told us that we were brought inside during the night at about two o' clock, as two tigers were fighting in the paddy field next to our courtyard!

Probably they were fighting over a mate. Hearing the roars, Uncle Subrahmanya had brought us to the safety of the house at night. We did not have a gun in the house. Soon after putting us inside, he had gone alone, without even carrying a flashlight, to investigate. He had only a sickle in his hand for self-defense. He did not carry a flashlight, because the dueling pair of tigers might not have tolerated a man carrying a light in the middle of their battle! Chances were there that both of them would have attacked the intruder.

My uncle had watched the fight for nearly half-an-hour standing behind a hedge, until one of the tigers admitted defeat and vanished in the darkness of the night. The winner roared ferociously and proceeded in another direction, probably in pursuit of his mate.

The cows were in panic hearing the tigers' roar. My grandmother had been praying anxiously for the safe return of her son, while grandfather waited patiently in his armchair. My mother was totally confused as to what Uncle Subrahmanya was up to! Finally, he returned home to narrate the wonderful fight to us. He only wished he was with his film unit crew at the moment to capture it all!

The tigers were so common those days that we lost a few of our cattle to them every year. The dense forests were disappearing because of man's greed for timber and the prey of these carnivorous animals were thinning out in the forest. The big cats had to forage on farm animals to survive. We could hear the tigers and leopards roaring in the dusk, as they roamed hungrily near the villages in search of their prey. Occasionally, these hungry animals summoned their courage to enter the cattle sheds to drag away a helpless cow. The ordinary wooden doors of our cattle sheds were no match to their brutal strength. Every evening, my grandmother would place and fasten a specially made thorny fence outside the cattle shed's door to prevent these wild animals from breaking in.

Now I wonder where all these tigers and leopards have gone! The sad truth is that they are killed more by poisoning with pesticide than by the hunter's bullets. They stood no chance at all when their half-eaten kills were soaked with powerful pesticides meant for spraying on the crops. In a few years, these big cats totally vanished from the vicinity of our villages. Today, these majestic animals are on the verge of extinction. Children listen to me almost in disbelief when I narrate the true stories of my coming across tigers and leopards in my childhood. For, they have never seen these animals in the wild. They have seen these species only in circuses and zoos.

*   *   *

Pejathaya assured me that if I wanted to see an Indian tiger today I may have to go to the New Delhi Zoo.

I persisted. This man had my utmost attention, as I could not easily comprehend living so close to the wild as he apparently had in his youth. "What about farmers who had to be in their fields"? I asked. "Did they carry rifles to protect themselves from wild boar, buffalo and large predatory cats"?

"No," said Pejathaya, "most of the wild cats would shy away from heavy concentrations of population. There are, however, many stories about the man-eating tigers in the old days. Usually, these tigers attacked people only as an exception. For example, if a tiger was old or had been injured and was unable to chase and capture its normal prey it would look to human flesh as an easier substitute."

He related the stories he read in his youth from books such as *Man-eaters of Kumaon*, written by Jim Corbett, who chronicled his life as a hunter in India during the British times. Some of the tigers shot by Corbett had claimed the lives of hundreds of villagers before being brought down. Each man-eating tiger's taste for human flesh, according to Corbett, could be explained by some stress of circumstance beyond its control to adopt a diet alien to its nature.

"But as you may know," Pejathaya said, "we did have to contend with wild boar and buffalo that could attack humans if threatened, and there were other animals and snakes that one had to consider. Often, when one of our neighboring villagers was threatened in some way, we would join forces to try to overcome the threat. I did have the opportunity to know people who had been on hunts with British *shikaris* (hunting expeditions) during the days before Indian independence. Let me tell you about my friend Thaniya Naika."

Pejathaya began to tell a story from the early 1960s, when he was transforming his sister's dense coastal forestland into a coconut farm. There, in the Shiroor Forest, Pejathaya met a woodcutter named Thaniya Naika. Thaniya loved nature and had a high respect for all living things. He knew the Shiroor forest like the back of his hand, and had once been a guide to white hunters.

TIGER, TIGER…
BY S.M. PEJATHAYA

When I met Thaniya Naika for the first time, he was probably 55 years of age. He was strong and healthy. Though he had been a guide to many white 'sahibs' during their hunting expeditions, he never ate the 'shikar' meat, nor killed any animal or bird for the reasons of his own. He bought the fish or meat in the weekly 'shandy,' i.e. the weekly farmers' fair or farmers' market.

Having been born and brought up near the jungles, Thaniya Naika could guess time in the night by gazing at the stars. His hearing was very sharp. He could identify the animals in the forest by the small sounds they made and could locate them in the darkest night without using a flashlight.

Sometimes, this fearless Thaniya Naika would visit me around nine o' clock in the night as I was living alone in our farm. He would wolf whistle three times when he approached my cottage so that I would not mistake him for an animal of the forest and reach for my gun. On hearing the whistles I would shout, "Thaniya Naika, you can come!" He would sit near my 'paan' plate and accept my hospitality of some 'paan' and tobacco. He would return to his home after an hour. I always appreciated him for his daring act of walking alone during the dark nights without carrying light. Our farm sprawled along the northern bank of the deep river surrounded by the vast Shiroor Reserve Forest on all three sides. The thick forest stretched up to the Western Ghats many miles away.

Thaniya would reminisce about the great 'shikars' of the English 'sahibs' who were always big shots seeking a pastime in the jungles. Many of them were highly placed officers like the District Collectors, Military Officers and the Superintendents of Police. He narrated how he led them on "Search Light Night 'Shikars' and 'Haaka Shikars'."

The 'Haaka Shikar' was done by beating the bushes and creating great noise to scare the animals out from their hiding places and make them run towards strategic positions where the waiting gunmen could shoot at them. He would tell me of the great numbers of the Bengal tigers, the leopards and the wild boars that would be shot during those 'Haaka Shikars' of India's pre-independence days. He would narrate how the animals sometimes attacked and injured the 'shikar' beaters. He would tell of the instances when the tigers and big wild boars attacked the waiting hunters. The attacking animals were mostly the tigers and wild boars with bullet injuries, which had shed the fear of man due to their pain and rage. He mourned the death of his beloved nephew who died after being gored by an injured wild boar during one such 'Shikar.'

One day I asked Thaniya Naika if I could find tigers in our forest. I always dreamt of seeing tiger in its natural habitat. He told that one or two leopards might be there in our reserved forest but the Bengal tigers were totally wiped out long ago. They were too straightforward and daring animals to guess the cunning designs of man. He assured me that he would study the pug marks to locate a leopard within the deep forest.

Thaniya Naika was absent for the work the next day, but in the night he came to my cottage after giving his whistle signal. He told me that he had found the pug marks of a leopard by the side of a creek, which he called, "Copra Rock Creek." He had given this name to the creek since a big rock submerged in the creek looked like the dried half of coconut kernel without the shell. I had been there with him before. It was about three miles deep in the thickest part of the forest. Thaniya Naika asked me to wait patiently for about 10 days before we planned the trip.

"Why?"

"Ahead is the full moon in three days. The wild animals will be wary of man's movement in the forest under the moon light and hence, we should wait till the moon recedes." Thaniya Naika said, "I have certain conditions that you must follow, if you want to come with me to see the leopard."

The conditions were:

Henceforth, we would call that leopard as our 'Mamoo'[2] because he had vowed it to 'Pilichaundi' that we will respect the leopard like our maternal uncle and will not harm him. He had prayed to the spirit to show us the leopard and offered to perform a thanking ritual to Pilichaundi after we saw this leopard. He firmly believed that we would get to see leopards even in such difficult times, just because of Pilichaundi's grace.

Further, we have to be silent in the jungle. We have to mask our flashlight with dark cloth only to get a pencil of light to see under our feet while we walked in the forest. We shall not flash the masked flashlight horizontally because the beam might scare the leopard away. When we neared the spot, we shall switch off our flashlights and walk in the star light. We will walk barefoot to avoid noise. There will be no exchange of even whispers. We have to tap each other on the shoulders and use sign language (though, I did not have the practice).

I have to avoid using my Lifebuoy soap for my daily bath that day and I shall not use any talcum powder on that particular day, as our 'Mamoo' can smell fragrance of these items from a distance of about two furlongs. I have to keep 'Mamoo's' presence secret in our forest as the news may draw hunters. I can carry a gun for self-defense, but under no circumstance I shall be allowed to fire the same. I accepted all the conditions without a further question.

I was eager to see our 'Mamoo'. For me, each day seemed to have 240 hours during these ten long days. On the D-day, Thaniya Naika appeared near my cottage at 9 p.m.

I watched Thaniya Naika as he turned eastwards to pray to his holy spirit and he prostrated at the spot seeking the spiritual guidance.

I followed him with a gun and a masked flashlight in total silence. I walked in semi-darkness with great difficulty trying to make minimum sound. It seemed to be an endless walkathon, and Thaniya Naika was walking very sure-footed on his bare feet with great ease. Finally, we neared the Copra Rock Creek. There I was signaled to leave my canvas shoes and we walked on tiptoes.

We could hear only gurgle of the stream and see nothing. We walked about a furlong and sat behind a big anthill covered by a few thickets all

---

[2] Maternal uncle

round. After sometime, Thaniya Naika alerted me and pointed his nose to the other bank of the stream but I gestured him that I could not see a thing! He kept on tapping on my shoulder and pointing his nose in the same direction. Even when I requested in my poor sign language, Thaniya Naika refused to point his fingers in that direction. He gestured me to wait quietly and patiently. After straining my eyes in the starlit darkness, I sat blinking my eyes, but with certain despair. Two hours passed. Then some night bird started to call. The half moon began to rise amongst the high trees. A little later, I saw the reflection of the moon on the flowing water. I was very happy that I could see a little more in the moonlight. Then, suddenly, I heard a splash in the stream!

The leopard was splashing water in the shallow place, about 30 feet away. I was awed by his size! There he was! Though a little smaller than a 'pie dog', he was chubby! The baby fat was still on him. He was trying to catch fish in the shallow water of the stream with great concentration. He was hitting the shallow water with his paws. I thought, at times he succeeded in catching one. At times, he would wander to the side of the stream to chase some frog or a small creature.

I sat mesmerized by this baby leopard and watched him for quite a while. My fear of leopard vanished, for he looked like a pet cat playing with an insect. I wanted to go a bit nearer and have a closer look. I got up totally ignoring Thaniya Naika and walked forward. For a moment, the leopard saw me with astonishment. The next moment, he was alarmed! He bounded away into the shadows of the trees silently. I felt very bad for disturbing this cub while he was hunting his food. Yet, I was glad that I could see a leopard cub in its natural surroundings.

I was ashamed of myself. Tears rolled down my cheeks. I saw Thaniya Naika's face in the light of my unmasked flashlight. He too was in tears. We walked home talking softly about the beauty of the cub and our good fortune in observing it.

Suddenly, I asked why Thaniya Naika did not point his finger at the leopard. He asked me, "Sir! Would you point your finger at your maternal uncle? It is not the kind of respect you show to the most powerful and the respectable maternal uncle of yours, whether he is big or small! Sir, please remember, a tiger is a tiger and a leopard is a leopard. They are The Kings of our forests."

*　　　　*　　　　*

This story gave me a hint of the respect many Indians held for living things. For the first time I began to understand those holy men who wandered the countryside wearing masks over their mouths. They did not want to accidentally inhale an insect, causing its demise. They believed that they themselves were some other creature in a past life, and may come back as a different creature in the next life.

Later that day, as I walked in the dark, along the road from the village of a farmer whom I worked with, I realized that my fears were beginning to subside. Up ahead, I could hear a sound, but I knew instinctively that it was just a villager, walking in the opposite direction. People were friendly here, and there was very little violent crime. The man greeted me as we passed each other. He mumbled a greeting, "*Namaskaa ree.*" The ending on his greeting indicated to me that he used a very respectful form.

I replied, "Hi!" (the indubitable American greeting), and "*Namaskaara.*" The normal, polite greeting.

There was no light other than a glowing lantern from a solitary roadside hut, but he noticed from the way I walked, and from the sound of my return greeting that I was not a local. I could hear him turn around after we passed, to try to take a second look. I was beginning to feel comfortable in this environment, and my heart went out to this stranger, who had probably worked ten hours in the fields and hoped to see his wife and children before he ate his simple rice and 'roti' dinner.

LEARNING ENGLISH

There are at least 22 scheduled languages in India, plus countless local dialects. The country is truly an astounding mixture of languages, cultures and religions. Children quickly learn the rudiments of several languages, and, as they grow to adulthood they are able to communicate wherever they travel.

Although the national language is Hindi, the official language in the post-British era was still English. Most official documentation is written in English, or Hindi <u>and</u> English. In many of the states, official documents were also written in the local language script. Children learned their local dialect at home and in the schools, but in all but a few of the Indian states, they were also expected to learn Hindi and English. The various states were able to specify their official language. The state of Madras (later named Tamil Nadu) treated its local language, *Tamil*, as the primary medium and refused to recognize Hindi as the national language. During my travels in India, I visited Madras on only two occasions. The first time I was accompanied by a native Tamil speaker, who translated 90 percent of my communication.

The second trip to Madras State was after my Peace Corps service ended, and it was with another American, who, like me, spoke only American English, *Kannada*, and a few words of Hindi. We struggled to communicate through much of our journey in Madras State. However, every other place we traveled in India posed no language obstacle.

The state of Mysore borders on the states of Maharashtra, Andhra Pradesh, Tamil Nadu, Kerala and Goa. It borders the Arabian Sea on its western flank. Even though 60 per cent of the people of Karnataka speak *Kannada* in their homes, a visitor to the state can hear Marathi, Telugu, Tamil, Malayalam, Konkani, Hindi, Urdu and English in the market place.

My extremely limited knowledge of India, its history, its diversity and its fantastic people was expanded somewhat during Peace Corps training, but remained grossly lacking at the time I set up residence in Sindhanur. Total immersion in study presents fast results, but conversations with Pejathaya brought it all together. His ability to communicate freely in several languages made the learning process much easier. One day I asked Pejathaya, "Where did you learn to speak your refined English?"

"My learning of the English language began a long time ago, in my home village of Mijar, near the western coast of India, the place where I was born," said Pejathaya. "My grandfather, was a great scholar and astrologer. He lived nearby, in the village of Poomavara, and when my father passed away, grandfather took charge of my family."

Pejathaya speaks excellent English, with a hint of British accent spiced with his South Indian vocal inflection. He told me the story of how he learned to speak and write in English, and his story goes like this:

DESIRE TO LEARN ENGLISH
BY S.M. PEJATHAYA

I was eight-years old and studying in fourth standard in Kinnikambla Higher Elementary School. Because of my grandfather's tuitions at home, I was taken directly to the second standard. We were studying in Kannada medium. I was good at studies.

During that time, schools began English alphabet lessons in the fifth standard. The regular English classes started only by sixth standard. However, my grandfather had taught me English alphabet along with Kannada vernacular before I joined the school. He did not teach me further in English as he did not believe in overloading a child with too much information at a very young age. He told me that they would start English in my sixth class and until then I must concentrate on learning Kannada well.

I was happy at school and at home, I was trying to put together some alphabet to identify a few English words on my own. I had thought that I could manage in English language too and told so to my grandmother. She believed in me since she did not know English. She boasted with her friends that I had learned English at such a tender age.

However, my claims were put to test during the summer holidays when we went to Tirupati in Andhra Pradesh. My grandfather had decided to perform the 'thread ceremony' (initiation ritual)of my elder brother Balakrishna at Tirupati. 'Telugu' was the regional language in Andhra Pradesh.

During the two-day journey, we halted at Tumkur at night and reached Tirupati the next day evening. There were no comfortable lodgings at Tirupati in 1950s. There were several 'choultries'[3], which were constructed and donated to the temple by the devotees of Lord Venkateshwara. The sanctum of the Lord Venkateshwara stands on the hill called Tirumala. There was no accommodation on the hill for ordinary devotees like us. We found accommodation in one of the 'choultries' at 'Govindaraja Patana', now known as Tirupati.

The 'choultry' manager gave us utensils and a Primus kerosene stove on hire. Our apartment had running water and a small kitchenette. My Uncle Subrahmanya went to a nearby grocery shop to buy provisions while grandmother cooked 'Upma' and prepared coffee, which we wolfed down after the long travel.

Later in the day, she was busy cooking the evening meal with my mother's help while others were relaxing. Suddenly, grandmother asked me to go to the 'choultry' office and borrow a ladle from the manager. Assuring her that I would bring it in a minute, I ran to the office at the end of the corridor.

A portly person, the 'choultry' manager, was sitting there and I greeted him, folding my hands in a 'namasthe.' He asked me in Telugu, from which tenement I came from. I did not understand his question and I simply blinked at him. He understood my language barrier and repeated the question in English. Then I understood, and raised nine fingers to indicate that I was from tenement No. 9.

He continued to speak in English and asked me what I wanted. I just mimed that I wanted a ladle and pointed at the item on his shelf. All sorts of cooking vessels and accessories were kept neatly on the shelves. He handed me the item and asked me to sign for the same in his thick register after he made the necessary entries. I signed in Kannada.

He asked my name and in which class I studied. He continued to speak to me in English. I started to blush in frustration, as I could not converse in

---

[3] Free lodgings

English. I told him my name meekly and raised four fingers to answer his second question. He asked me to sit on a chair in front of him and went on questioning me about my school's name, parents name etc. I felt like a dumb person. I could not muster enough English words to answer the gentleman. I flushed and tried to reply in monosyllables. I felt as if I was sitting on an electric chair.

Finally, I managed to leave the place saying, "mmm... my grandmother wants this, Sir" and he nodded. I ran to my grandmother to deliver the ladle. My grandmother asked me how I could communicate with him. I replied, in a matter of fact way, that I had spoken to him in English!

She was very happy and proud of my language skill. She would narrate this incident to praise me in front of her friends at Kinnikambla later on. At the same time, I was trying my best to avoid any forthcoming confrontation with the 'choultry' manager. After the pilgrimage, I tried hard to improve my command over English, reading any printed English matter that I came across. I tried to learn new words. My tutor and great friend, my grandfather, passed away soon after this pilgrimage.

I had to turn to uncle Subrahmanya to help me with my English. He was a busy man. Yet, he would clear my doubts and tell me the meaning of the difficult words in the evenings. I tried to read and understand the articles in the monthly magazine, "Reader's Digest," which uncle Subrahmanya subscribed regularly.

Everyone at home listened to radio programs in Kannada. My uncle, elder brothers and sisters listened to the Hindi and English programs broadcast by our All India Radio. Hindi programs of Radio Ceylon were our favourite. As I grew up, I started listening to the cricket commentaries, which would be broadcast in English only. Later on, at night, I would listen to the Voice of America. The American pronunciation was a bit different from our Queen's English, but the Americans spoke more slowly and more informally. This Voice of America radio program appealed to me the most.

When we moved to Udupi, I joined the renowned Board High School. I was studying in Kannada medium and I was taught English for only one hour a day. Udupi was a small town, and I made friends with many elderly gentlemen who loved to speak in English with the school kids. I would join them during their evening walks and speak to them in English. These kind *elderly gentlemen spoke very fine English in British accent and corrected the mistakes in my speech. They suggested that I should buy a series of inexpensive classics. I started reading them. They would glance at the books during our walk and ask me questions on every chapter that I had read. I had to reply in English. This helped me a lot.*

When I reached my ninth class, which was then called the fourth form, our popular headmaster Mr. K. Vittappa took over the English lessons. He was a gold medallist in his English M.A. and he spoke the language like a veritable Englishman. Being a great disciplinarian, he laid emphasis on English grammar. He would always converse with us in English and encouraged us to speak to each other in English. He taught us very well. By the time I finished my SSLC, I was fluent in English. I had no trouble in switching over to a college where the medium of instruction was English.

MURALI THE ELEPHANT

The answers to my questions about India and her numerous and complicated religious hierarchy of god and goddess figures were only partially addressed by the cultural training element of our Peace Corps trainers. The Indians I worked with at the tractor society contributed to my education, but the variations in religion, language and culture among the staff made that experience somewhat confusing. The ease with which I could communicate with Pejathaya, however, smoothed and expedited the education process.

I enjoyed the many stories Pejathaya related to me about the days of his youth, as well as his experiences in his attempts to establish a career and his eventual fascination with agriculture. I delighted in his stories about the creatures he observed. These stories demonstrated his love of all living things. He had a deep respect for life, while his religion and family upbringing molded him into an appreciating observer.

He wrote a particularly interesting story about an elephant that played cricket. Growing up on a farm in Minnesota, I worked with a wide range of animals but I never saw an elephant in the flatland cornfields. The following is a story, in his own words, about the close association Pejathaya had with an elephant.

MURALI THE ELEPHANT
BY S.M. PEJATHAYA

Murali was a 14-month old calf when he came to Udupi in 1956. He was about five feet tall and had shiny small eyes. His body was full of rough juvenile hair, common in young elephants. His small trunk was always active and busy. He would keep on swinging it all the time. When he slept, he curled the trunk and kept its tip inside his mouth to avoid insects from entering his mouth.

The Forest Department of Mysore State gifted Murali to Admar 'Mutt' (temple). He was to become the temple elephant. Along with him came his 'mahout' (elephant keeper) Abdul, a young man of twenty.

The little elephant was the darling of the town. I was 12-years old and fascinated by this baby elephant. Every evening on my way back from school, I would visit Murali. My friends and I used to play cricket in the playground situated behind the 'Mutt'. The two friends, Murali and 'mahout' Abdul, were housed in a high-roofed elephant shed next to the ground.

Murali was not old enough to perform the temple duties. He was just learning his basic lessons in obedience. He would follow Abdul wherever he went. He would consume large amounts of selected green leaves, a small bundle of sugar cane provided by the 'Mutt', daily. At noon, he would be fed with about two kilograms of fine rice, 'ghee' and 'jaggery'. Abdul cooked the rice and jaggery together in a large vessel, added 'ghee' when it was still hot and made five to six big balls of this mixture. He would feed each ball of the sweet and fragrant rice to Murali's wide-opened mouth. The pachyderm swallowed them with great relish, squealing with excitement!

He would drink buckets of water, lifting each gulp with his trunk. He swished a trunk full of water into his mouth without spilling much. On week days, we would be at school during Murali's lunch time. However, we never missed to see him having his lunch during Sundays and other holidays.

Murali loved the company of kids. All the time he would be busy swinging his trunk, as if he were swatting flies around him. He would flap his big ears and he never stood quietly at a place. Even when he stood in one place, he would keep shifting his body weight from one pair of legs to the other. He did not like to be tied up. However, as part of his training, he had to be chained in one leg and tethered to a strong pillar.

When tied up, he would be restless. On seeing us, he would squeal intermittently so that he would be set free! Abdul would set him free and let him play with us. Gradually, he got used to his iron tether that fitted like a bracelet around his front left leg and the small iron chain with a bronze bell around his neck.

Whenever Murali moved, his shoulder muscles sagged and the bell rang. He was very intelligent. He knew how to keep the bell silent. He held it with his trunk! At times, when he was not chained up, he would roam within the 'Mutt's' spacious compound, he would use this trick to startle us! He would sneak up on us from behind and suddenly probe us with his ever wet trunk tip.

Usually the bell would be silent when he was asleep. We liked the way he slept. He would kneel down on all four legs and rest his body by leaning a bit to one side. He would leave his bulk mainly on the legs in one side and keep the other pair of legs ready, but at rest, so that they supported him whenever he decided to get up. Murali inherited this skill from his ancestors. Murali could wake up and stand on his legs at the slightest noise. Even his knowledge to keep trunk tip in the mouth to keep off insects came to him from his inherited instinct.

Murali had small, but sharp beady eyes. He could see small objects like toffees on the ground, and pick them up with his trunk easily. He could step backwards as easily as he could step forward! He was capable of walking in reverse direction for good distances at times with unbelievable maneuvering capability. His small eyes never failed to observe the minute details of the ground behind his back!

When we played cricket, Murali and Abdul would also join us. Murali loved to play cricket with us. He preferred fielding to batting. It was an impressive spectacle to see Murali run after the ball with his trunk outstretched to reach the ball. Though he was bulky, he could run faster than any one of us. At the same time, he would take longer time to stop because of his heavy weight. He would retrieve the ball expertly and swing it in our direction. Of course, his throw was not very accurate. Though he could not run and catch the ball in its flight, he could field well at 'long on' and 'square leg' positions! Probably, he was not much interested in lifting a dull-looking wooden bat with his wonderful trunk. Since Murali did not like batting and running from stump to stump, the 'mahout' would bat on behalf of Murali during every match! Abdul would take two turns in batting. He would seize this second opportunity without fail, especially, after losing his own wicket! We tolerated this, because Murali was a good fielder and Abdul was a fast scorer. Moreover, we needed Abdul's favors, as always!

Murali walked in front of our team when we went to face the other cricket teams in our local matches. Our jumbo teammate would always demoralize our opponent teams! If they did not allow Murali on the field in a match, we would declare that we were the winners, and we would return pompously! If they tried to talk of the rules and regulations, we would argue that Murali was more than any human player and any day he readily deserved his place. If ever they wanted to quarrel, our 'mahout' Abdul was a great hand at fist fights!

Abdul was older and stronger than any one of us, and he had a baby elephant to back him all the time. In every match, Murali would do his best in fielding and 'mahout' Abdul would bat twice. Abdul would always score well as he batted twice in each inning. Abdul was a good hitter and earned sixth and seventh places in the batting order. When he played as the seventh batsman, he would be representing his non-batting companion, Mr. Murali! Probably, our great 'Mahisha Mardhini' Cricket (MCC) team was the only team in the world to have a baby elephant as a cricket player!

During one such evening practice, Abdul sent the ball to a 'long on boundary.' The ball, unfortunately, reached a spot where the 'Mutt's' toilets were situated. The ball had bounced across the toilet building to stop over the septic tank area at its back.

Those days we did not have an underground drainage system. There used to be large but not so deep stone lined pits called septic tanks in every compound to absorb waste and water from the toilets. These pits would be covered with granite slabs or strong wooden planks on rafters and a thick layer of soil would cover their top. This pit happened to have wooden planks over wooden rafters and the top portion was covered by six inches of filled earth. Murali went across it to fetch the ball. The planks and the rafters buckled under his weight. We heard the snapping sound and Murali shrieking in fright as he went down! We rushed to find out. The most untoward had happened! Murali was in the pit, standing in about two feet of filth.

If ever the 'Swamiji' of Admar 'Mutt' came to know of the incident, he would be furious. We had to get the elephant out of the mess. Murali was in tears and crying helplessly as he could not clamber up the eight-foot deep pit!

Abdul tried to pacify him and shouted at us to bring pickaxes and spades to dig an inclined ramp into the pit so that Murali can walk out. We ran to the nearby houses to gather as many implements as we could and started the rescue operation at full throttle. In about half an hour, we could make a slow ramp for Murali. All the while Murali was coaxing us to hurry up! I can never forget the crying pleas of the baby elephant. Finally, Murali clambered out. Buckets of water were splashed on him to clear the mess to some extent. We were relieved to note that the baby elephant was not hurt. He was crying because of the horrible stench of the dirt that he was smudged with.

Abdul suggested that we take him to Maddela 'Saar.'[4] It flowed about a mile away from the spot. Abdul requested us to run home to bring several fragrant cakes of bath soaps quickly to the stream. We rushed back, collected every piece of soap available at home and appeared near the stream in minutes.

Murali was rinsed thoroughly in the fast flowing water of the stream at

---

[4] Dhobi's stream, in Tulu dialect

a deep point, and then brought back to the bank for cleaning with the soap. Cake after cake of different brands of soap were rubbed on him. Dozens of willing hands washed and lathered him. Murali was led to deep water again and brought back to be washed again with soap. The exercise continued for about one and a half hours! During this period, Murali would smell his body with his sensitive trunk, and would shriek in complaint. The stream frothed down as we washed the elephant again and again. We lathered and rinsed him until we exhausted all the cakes of soap we had procured.

Finally, Murali gave the squeaks of approval, nodded his big head and flapped his ears in delight and we brought him out of water. It was getting dark as we approached Admar 'Mutt.' The news of the disaster had reached the 'Swamiji' and we heard that he was upset! Fortunately, it was his evening 'pooja' time. 'Swamiji' was engrossed in the worship.

Instead of the 'Swamiji,' the mild manager of the 'Mutt' received us. Luckily, his son was the captain of our cricket team. He scolded us all including Abdul. However, the decent old man used 'not so bad' language on us. We apologized for the misdeed, pleaded pardon and promised that we would never include Murali in our MMC team henceforth. He, though deemed very kind, banned us from playing cricket on the 'Mutt' premises. We were glad that we were let off with mild rebuke. We ran home after feeling greatly relieved, though exhausted.

Later in the evening, after the 'Swamiji' got back from his 'pooja', 'Mahout' Abdul received a severe reprimand. The incident was soon forgotten. However, our hitherto invincible MMC team started tasting a series of defeats due to the absence of Murali and Abdul. Our pride too was hurt as we were vanquished in fist fights.

When Murali turned two, he was about six feet at the shoulder. He was as friendly with us as before. Abdul took him for long walks on Udupi streets to ensure that he got used to the traffic, the blaring sound of the vehicle horns and the milling crowds. He was trained in carrying a 'howdah' (palanquin, or covered litter) and to take a couple of people for a ride on his back, in an open ground on the outskirts of the town. Young Murali resented this exercise!

Whenever a 'howdah' was placed on his back, he would walk in reverse direction! He would never take a step forward! It was fun to watch him do this. At this time, Abdul had to teach him with a stick in his hand. The cane taught him obedience. Though not physically hurt, beatings certainly gave a blow to his pride. To escape the punishment, Murali began to obey Abdul's commands. He learned to carry a 'howdah' majestically and allowed two persons to ride on his back.

Many a times, Abdul gave my elder brother Balakrishna and me a ride home from school. Abdul would ask us to hide our footwear inside our umbrellas before climbing on the elephant so that no one should see us sitting on the elephant with footwear on! For, Murali was the holy elephant of the temple. He should not be climbed upon with footwear on! No one objected to our school bags, as books were considered very sacred. Of course, no one but us, God and Abdul knew about our footwear hidden inside our folded umbrellas! We would proudly ride home leaving our classmates back, to envy us!

Our mother liked the baby elephant very much. She would always be ready to receive Murali at our residence and offered him plantains, coconut kernel and plenty of 'jaggery.'

Abdul would get 'baksheesh' (a tip, or gift) of five rupees from my mother in addition to the hospitality of a large cup of tea and snacks, which he always accepted with relish. All were happy with this kind of arrangement.

In course of time, Murali learned how to carry a fully decorated temple 'howdah' and he would allow two people in addition, to ride on his back. He also learned how to walk backwards slowly fanning the chariot of the Lord Krishna with a silver-handled 'chamber.'[5] He learned all the etiquettes that were expected of a temple elephant. He had to stay almost the full day at the Krishna Temple. Eventually, his living quarters too shifted over to the bigger Krishna Temple's premises. I got to see him less and less till I had to leave Udupi eventually to earn my livelihood. I always remember him as a nice friend. The image of Murali with tears, stuck in a stinking pit, begging to be rescued, is etched on my memory.

---

[5] An Indian type of tousled fan with a silver handle

THE UNIQUE INDIAN

It is a major challenge to be air lifted into a totally alien culture, announce to the surprised villagers who curiously gather around that you have come to make their lives better, and then stake your claim to a worthwhile endeavor that accomplishes that goal. The villagers in your newly adopted home have no idea that their lives need any improvement. They are happy with the way they live. They eat, play, worship and work in the hot sun to raise their food. They have their families, their temple and their neighborhood transistor radio. What more is there?

A stranger sitting next to me on my flight from Minneapolis to Los Angeles asked me, "What is the purpose of your going to India as a Peace Corps Volunteer? What will you accomplish and who will benefit?"

Assuming, naively, that everyone knew that Peace Corps volunteers helped change the world and make it a better place for all humankind, I stumbled into the trap. He said, "You are only doing this for yourself. You couldn't possibly, in two years, change the way people have been doing things for centuries. Unless you are working with the CIA to gain information for the use of the U.S. government you will only be expending valuable U.S. resources to educate yourself. Or, maybe you want to avoid the military draft."

That hurt "like anything" as my Indian friends would say. Six months later it occurred to me that this stranger may have, in fact, been one of the earlier Peace Corps Volunteers, and actually had come to understand the reality of Peace Corps service. Nevertheless, at that moment, I placed that conversation in the far corner of my memory bank and continued on my quest to save the world.

Atticus Finch, in Harper Lee's book *To Kill a Mockingbird*, said that you should never judge someone until you walk a mile in his shoes. I came to India where over five hundred million people had established their personal views on the world long before I arrived there. The Indians I met tolerated my presence with great respect. A few of them were actually interested in what I might know that can help them improve their way of life. It would take me a year just to understand that the villagers will survive with or without me, and that the stranger on the airplane was somewhat correct.

Pejathaya was good at giving me small measures of reality to help me accumulate a better understanding of the Indian people I was dealing with. The subtle messages in his stories built a foundation that eventually guided me to an appreciation of the Indian people. One of my favorite stories was about a time in his youth when his family came to know of their neighbor who was a well digger. This man dug his own well inside his house.

THE FEAR FACTOR
BY S.M. PEJATHAYA

Fear is something that everyone experiences in life. It is part of each one's psyche. Even the bravest man has an iota of fear in him. It is because of fear that we assess the risks involved in every task. Many change their lifestyles because of some inherent fear. There are several kinds of fear. Many persons are known to have fear of darkness, fear of heights, fear of water, fear of lightning etc... The list never ends.

I narrate the consequences of a peculiar kind of fear, which nagged an old man who lived near my grandfather's village house. Thomara was about sixty-five and had a mysterious air about him. This reserved person had a very serious face and he never smiled. He had long silvery hair. He used to stare at people around him with his reddish eyes. Children of the village were afraid of him. His name was Thomara, and Lakshmi was his wife. The woman was as reserved as he was, but her looks were not as frightening. She followed her husband wherever he went. It was very strange that the couple never had any friends or foes in the village. They just stayed aloof.

Thomara eked out his livelihood by digging wells. He was an expert in his job and he had a few people working under him. He paid his men well but was not very friendly with any of them. The couple had no close relatives and no one had ever seen a guest in their house. They never invited anyone to their house. In fact, no one in the village had entered their house.

I always found Thomara busy throughout the year. During the dry months, he was engaged in digging wells, and during the rainy season, he would be cultivating his farmland high up in the hill. He had staked and established his claim over the land, which was later granted to him by the government. Such lands are called darkaast in the revenue jargon. All his crops were rain-fed. He grew paddy during the monsoon season. He had some horticultural crops like cashew, coconut and pineapple. Pineapple and cashew needed no water during the dry spells.

Thomara and his wife would irrigate the coconut trees during summer season by bringing water from their small house every evening. They would bring out water in shining round-shaped copper pitchers called kodapaana. These kodapaanas had a narrow neck around which a noose of rope would fit. With the help of these kodapaanas, every one in the village drew out water from their wells using coir ropes.

We wondered about this old man and woman bringing out enormous quantities of water from inside their house! The small kids of the village would stand at a safe distance and watch them bringing out kodapaana after kodapaana of water from the interior of their house every evening. As small children, we could never believe the existence a well inside their small house. Bore wells with electric pumps were unheard of during those days.

Thomara had built a small Mangalore-tiled house on the hill slope. He had miraculously found water on that hill. All the water he and his wife pulled out everyday was coming from a very narrow but very deep well dug by him inside his small house. It provided him with enough water for drinking and household purposes. Anyone who came to know about this fact wondered why the well was inside his house! The house had four rooms. Everyone in the village guessed that the narrow well was dug in the larger kitchen. People said that the man had dug that well alone and his wife had helped him to dump the excavated soil. He took no outsider's help in this task. The reason was his inherent fear! Thomara had the deep fear of 'kai maddu'[6].

Thomara was a hard worker. He dug deep wells. He worked in the dark confines of the deep wells that he always dug. He had an uncanny ability of water divining. He would mark the location of the well by himself

---

[6] Kai maddu means to put potent slow poison in food

and predict the depth at which he would strike water. Before commencing the work, he would inform the approximate depth of the well that he intended to dig and the estimated cost. His predictions would become true in most cases and majority of his wells gave out good yield. He went wrong in very rare cases; but, he readily owned up his mistakes. If he did not hit water at the estimated depth, he would dig down further, until he hit a good water source, at his own cost. He would complete the task at the predetermined cost. He never claimed or accepted the extra cost that he incurred in completing such a well. It was his professional pride! If he ever failed, he owned up the responsibility. And, he would never charge for that unyielding well. In such cases he would dig another well free of cost for the owner of the land. This proposition was most acceptable for the villagers too. Thomara always kept his promise despite reeling under poverty.

The village folks would joke at this well-known fact. They would say, "The water had to come! Otherwise, this stubborn fellow would keep on digging and he would come up on the other side of the globe!" At that age, when I had learned that the earth was round in my third standard geography, I really believed that this typical old man could keep on digging until his head appeared in the American Continent!

There were some very deep wells in and around our village as a testimony to the professional ethics of Thomara. They all yielded sufficient water. However, the women of such houses, cursed Thomara as they had to draw water from the depths of hell! They had to send down their water-pitchers down in these deepest of wells using very long coir (coconut fiber) ropes tied around the neck of their 'kodapaanas' and they had to pull them up with great difficulty, hand over hand.

During those days, electric or oil operated pumps were not known in the rural parts of India. By pulling these rough ropes frequently, the palms of the women would be full of blisters, which would turn into calluses. Drawing water was the most feared household chore in the Konkan Coast! (i. e. Western coast)

Most people along the coast of South Canara (Mangalore district) depended on well water only. The rivers drew saline water from the sea as they flowed almost at the sea level. The land near the sea was sandy and the rest of the elevated lands were lateritic moors. Because of the topography of the coastal land, a part of the rain water got absorbed by the earth and the rest flowed away to the Arabian Sea filling many ravines and rivers during the rainy season. Even today, the coastal population depends mainly on the well water since sweet water streams are very few in this region.

Now, let us investigate why Thomara dug a well right inside his house. Many years ago, Thomara had suffered from chronic stomach pain and the doctors at the district hospital could not cure him. Finally, he consulted an 'Ayurvedic' pundit in the neighbouring state of Kerala. The pundit diagnosed that Thomara's stomach pain was due to a witchcraft practice known as 'hand poisoning,' akin to slow poisoning. He was cured by the pundit after the administration of an emetic. The pundit, it seems had warned Thomara not to accept food or water from unreliable persons in future.

Thomara had no immediate relatives or close friends to put any such persons on his 'list of suspects'. Suffering unbearable stomach pain for about a year or two had compelled him to be extra cautious. Therefore, to play it safe, he and his wife just stopped taking food outside their home! They restrained themselves from attending any social or religious functions held in the village. Though this was only their personal dietary decision, it made the couple more unpopular in the village. They were looked down upon; as most people thought that this couple unnecessarily doubted everyone in the village. Thus the fear of 'slow poisoning' rendered them to the wrath of their fellowmen.

Rural people used to attribute any chronic ailment to this kind of poisoning during those days. They vouched that a few bad elements in the society had the habit of slow poisoning people out of pure jealousy. There need not be any reason to be a victim of this kind of practice. Social stigma nurtured by jealousy was deemed the motive. In most cases, people who indulged in such act never got any material benefit, but they just did it to keep the potency of their poisoning habit alive. It is believed that these poisons were used in very minute quantities. They were fed to unsuspecting guests who ate or drank in their houses.

It was told that such a perverted person, who dispensed this sort of slow poison, derived immense pleasure in seeing his victim's sufferings. And that someone who takes up this kind of poisoning habit, must have to poison at least one person in a year so as to keep his or her 'slow poisoning skills' active. The victim would suffer from some incurable pain that would make him weak and fatigued. They were known to suffer long periods of sickness and sometimes die a miserable death. The belief is that, no modern doctor, however much he is qualified, could cure such victims. Only the Ayurvedic pundits were said to diagnose and cure these victims. They would administer an herbal emetic to the patient. The patient would be told by the pundit to fast the previous day and to take the emetic the next morning in empty stomach. The patient would vomit a number of times. Finally, the emetic would bring out the poisonous material in its originally administered form. In other words, the original morsel of food or drink would come out in undigested form even after many years!

This is what I have heard. I have never verified the veracity of these facts. My grandfather told me that this phenomenon was a result of the fertile imagination, but saying so remains a taboo in the rural society.

Thomara, once cured, became very careful regarding his food intake. He stopped eating outside. He even stopped drinking water outside his house. Having built a house in the slopes of a barren hill, he did not have a well of his own. He had to get water from somebody's well downhill. Somehow, a notion got into Thomara's mind that even the wells could be poisoned!

He thought that he must have his own well for drinking water. The well should be within his house so that no one could poison it. He was obsessed with this idea. With the help of his wife Lakshmi, he started to dig one in his kitchen! Slowly, head loads of earth started coming out of Thomara's house. This extra earth was used to level up the space in front of his house. In the course of time, Thomara's house had a small courtyard. The well was of a minimum diameter, not more than three feet. It went ten fathoms deep and Thomara hit a good source of water. The well filled up as a testimony to Thomara's expertise in digging. The level of water had stood steady at around three fathoms! As the well was dug in the laterite moor, it kept its shape without the need of stone lining. The well had a circular parapet wall of about a foot in width. Two pillars were built on either side to support a metal cross bar, at the center of which hung a metal pulley. The specialty of the well was that it could be closed by a heavy wooden door and it could be locked too!

This lockable lid gave a feeling of extra safety against the fear of being poisoned for Thomara. The lock would be opened only when he or his wife used the well. The rest of the time it remained closed and locked with a *strong nine lever Aligarh lock. The only two keys of the lock hung in strong black strings around the necks of Thomara and Lakshmi. Thus, the phobia of being poisoned made Thomara to dig this wonderful well! There was no well of its kind in the neighbourhood. Many people heard about the wonderful well and they wanted to see it. However, the couple never allowed any one into their house.*

One summer, Thomara was deepening my grandfather's well. The rains were scanty the previous season and the well did not provide enough water for our household. Thomara worked two weeks with his team, and deepened our well. Thomara couple had no children and they had not adopted any child as they were always outdoors during the day.

Somehow, Thomara and Lakshmi befriended me as I watched them at work all through the day. The school was then closed for the summer vacations. They talked to me affectionately. I frequently asked Thomara and Lakshmi whether they would show me that wonderful well inside their house.

The day before they were about to finish the deepening work of our well, I put forth my request once again. I would not have been able talk to them about it if I had waited a day more! The next day they would work elsewhere. Both the old man and the woman looked at each other's face, and discussed the point in their tribal dialect. Then they nodded at each other in approval!

Finally, they said they would show me the secret well if my grandfather allowed me to accompany them to their house. They were quite sure that my grandfather would not allow me to go with them. Every one looked down on Thomara and his wife as they would not touch food or water in anyone's house in the village. They were branded as rude and headstrong couple. I told them that I would seek permission from my grandfather to visit their house the next day.

That evening, I went to my grandfather and told him that Thomara had hidden a well inside his small house on the hill, which could be locked like a vault, and he had promised to show it to me the next day. My grandfather told me that I would be the first person in the village to see that well, if Thomara ever showed it to me.

Next day, Thomara completed his work early by about two in the noon and was about to leave after taking his payment. I kept on pestering him to come along with me to see my grandfather again. I pleaded that he should ask for the permission from my grandfather and take me along with him to his house to show the well and return me safely to our house.

Hesitatingly, Thomara requested my grandfather, 'Sir, the child is pestering me to show the well which I dug inside my house years ago. I have not shown the well to anyone, but I have no heart to refuse this child. I shall take him home now, show the well and bring him back in an hour.'

To my astonishment, my grandfather gave his consent. I ran inside to dress up for my pilgrimage. I was elated that I would be seeing the eighth wonder of the world. I walked with the old couple for about half a mile up the hill to reach their house. I was given a stool to sit on. Thomara offered a tender coconut, which I readily accepted. The tender coconut water was very sweet. The old couple was very much pleased with my gesture. Just because this old couple never accepted the hospitality of the villagers, the villagers too had shunned their hospitality. Then they took me to their kitchen. There was the small well with a wooden lid and the lock!

Thomara opened the lock and the lid and let the pitcher down the well with a noose tied to its neck. About twenty feet below, I could hear the gurgling noise as the water filled the pitcher. Thomara pulled the rope up, took the pitcher outside the house and asked me to wash my face under a coconut tree. Crystal clear water flowed as he decanted the pitcher. It was as cool and fresh as spring water. I washed my face with it and at once I wanted to taste it. I drank a handful, it tasted cool and wonderful. I drank a few handfuls more before I washed my legs with it. Later, I came into their house to have freshly roasted and peeled cashew nuts with a small piece of solid 'jaggery' (course brown sugar). I enjoyed the snack that tasted very nice. Lakshmi asked if I liked the roasted cashew nuts and I replied that they were wonderful. Then, I told them that I would leave. Both of them followed me down to my grandfather's house. Thomara carried a large jackfruit while Lakshmi carried a small paper bag filled with freshly roasted cashew nuts.

As we neared our house, I ran ahead of them to narrate the wonder that I saw, to my grandfather. I told grandfather that I had a tender coconut and cashew nuts at Thomara's place. I told him that the water from his narrow well tasted cool and nice. The couple arrived behind me and thanked grandfather for sending me to their house saying that they felt *overjoyed to see me there. They told him how lonely and secluded they were all these years as no one visited them. They presented the jackfruit and cashew nuts to my grandmother as a mark of respect. My grandmother accepted them. She called the couple to the open veranda near the kitchen to serve them 'idlis'[7] with 'sambar'[8] and tasty mango pickle on plantain leaves. The couple hesitated to accept while my grandma told them that her grandson has accepted their hospitality without any hesitation and they must reciprocate by accepting food in our place. They did not hesitate further! They ate all that was served with relish and grandma brought second helpings. They were offered big tumblers of hot coffee, which they drank, enjoying each sip. When they were about to leave, they told my grandma that after a very long time they felt like social beings.*

After a period of over thirty years, they had accepted the hospitality of a neighbour because a child visited their house and accepted their humble hospitality. My grandma told them that they were always welcome.

After this incident, Thomara and Lakshmi were frequent visitors to our house. A new smile had appeared on their wrinkled faces. We kids visited their house to see the eighth wonder of the world many times after this incident.

My grandfather told us that the real eighth wonder was not that well at all. The real wonder was how this odd couple became social beings all over again! Thomara had become an outcaste because of his phobia about poisoning. This fear deep within his psyche had made him to dig a wonderful well inside his house.

Man takes to quixotic adventures to save himself from his phobias at unimaginable odds!

*   *   *

This story brings out the nature of life in the rural villages of India's Western Coast, but, more than that, it accents the curiosity and good nature of Pejathaya. His intense interest at an

---

[7] Steamed rice cakes

[8] A spicy vegetable curry

early age in seeing Thomara and Lakshmi's indoor well, coupled with his ease in dealing with others, saved an aging couple from a life of detachment and scorn from their neighbors.

A year after starting my work with the Sindhanur Tractor Society I finally started to understand that the Indian villagers around me were not to be stereotyped into a single conceptual Indian. It became clear that each person was an individual, with his or her own history and life dreams. I also realized that the only meaningful difference between a person living in India and a person living anywhere else in the world is just that, their location. It took all this time, and the pages from Pejathaya's diary to understand India's people better.

BLIND DIWAKER

India became an emerging economic power in the late 20th Century. The low price of labor in the cities like Bangalore, Mumbai, Calcutta and New Delhi encouraged international corporations to expand their industrial development in labor-intensive industry. Later, with the growth of computer technology, India became a world class competitor for software development and maintenance. Back in 1969, however, I had no idea about how resourceful and independent the people were becoming.

One story that Pejathaya related to me demonstrates some of the qualities of the people, including a high level of personal determination, love and perseverance. This story about one man and his wife took place in Pejathaya's coastal village, and plays out from his childhood school days through his adult life, when he heard the ultimate story of his 4th grade classmate, Diwaker.

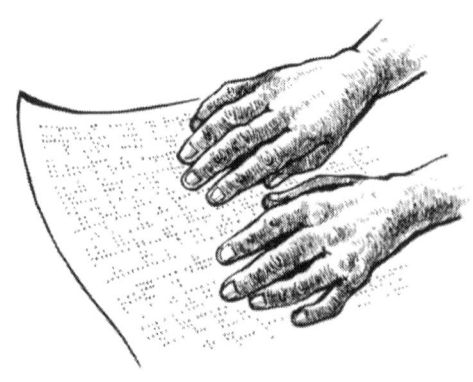

BLIND DIWAKAR
BY S.M. PEJATHAYA

Blind Diwakar* was a small boy who studied with me in the higher elementary school up to fifth standard at Kinnikambla. He was born blind. His parents were very poor small farmers. They owned one acre of rain fed paddy field and two acres of barren dry land. Diwakar's name is a misnomer. The word Diwakar implies Sun in Sanskrit. Unfortunately, he was blind from birth and could not see a ray of sun with his eyes!

He came to school with other children. The primary education was free as ours was a government school. Our kind headmaster had admitted him to the school and he tried his best to teach this blind boy. Fifty years ago, the blind children were refused admission in government school for normal children. Diwakar could hear the teacher and learn his lessons by heart, easily. He was a pleasant boy, very active and intelligent. He had a perpetual smile on his face. He had beautiful dark eyes that could see only darkness. He carried a stick to guide him as he walked on his own to school, though he seldom used it on his way. He was familiar with the road to school. He needed the stick only to know about the new obstacles that came on his way unexpectedly. Once inside the school, he left the stick in a corner. He could move about like any normal child as he had acquainted himself with the school premises.

The permanent loss of visual faculty was compensated by sensitizing his other capabilities! He could hear as well or better than any of us. He had a loud and clear voice. He could sing well. He always remembered what he

90

heard once. He could imitate the song of the birds, chattering of squirrels, monkeys and other animals. He could moo like a cow. He had a keen sense of smell. His skin was very sensitive to heat. He could feel the sun light by sensing the heat associated with the light rays. He could locate a window or a door by feeling the air currents that surged into a room, and he could sense the heat waves that came from the sun through doors and windows too! He could reckon the time of the day—morning, evening or night from the climate.

At school he could not read the blackboard. Still, he could write Kannada alphabet on a slate. His elder brother had taught him to practice writing by guiding his writing hand over and over neatly on his book or slate. He could write and count up to one thousand, and recite multiplication table up to twenty. He could even recite them in descending order too! Most of us could not do it. He knew all his lessons and poems. He could do the arithmetic sums by counting his fingers. He was admired by our teacher for his intelligence.

He passed every year until he reached his fifth standard. At the fifth standard, he was finding it difficult to learn Hindi and English alphabet. He found it impossible to understand Algebra, which made use of English alphabet along with the numerals. He could not see the questions on the blackboard or on the question paper. Inwardly, he felt he could not cope with the studies. This great handicap started killing all hopes of continuing education for the small boy.

It was in the year 1955 that a blind man from Madras (now, Chennai) came to give a benefit show of "Braille" in our school. The man collected two 'Annas' (twelve paise) from each of us to watch his show, in which he demonstrated as to how he could go about almost normally in the society in spite of being a blind person by learning Braille. Our Diwakar was most impressed with the man's capabilities.

Hearing that Diwakar was blind, he called him to the stage and showed him how he could read Braille by the feeling of touch. The blind person told him that Diwakar could write and do sums in Braille with the help of a Braille pencil.

Diwakar, for the first time in his life touched a Braille letter! He felt that a new door has opened for him. He enquired everything in detail about the Braille school in faraway Madras. He wanted to go to Madras to *continue his education in Braille and find himself a job after his studies. Later, he wanted to live like any normal citizen with the help of Braille education. He was glad he could achieve all this, despite his great handicap.*

He went home that evening with all hopes to tell his parents about the wonder of Braille script. He told them about the school for the blind, which taught Braille at Madras.

To his great disappointment, poor Diwakar was told that it would not be possible to realize his dreams. For, they were very poor to send him to Madras for his education. Moreover, he was too small a boy of ten to be sent to such a far-off place. There at Madras, the local language was Tamil, and no one could understand or speak that language in his house. No one at his home knew English or Tamil and communicating with the Braille school at Madras was their imminent problem. More grave were their financial problems and the family had to give up the idea altogether.

Diwakar could not keep up with his classmates in studies. He was compelled to give up schooling after his fifth standard, which he could pass with great difficulty. There was no way for him to continue his education. He stayed at home to help his poor parents in farming. He worked during the day as well as the nights, as he did not need any light during the nights. With his sensory feelings, he knew their farm inch by inch like the palm of his hand. He could roam in their small plot of land at all hours of the day and night. He could do almost any household chore or farm work as he was very intelligent and strong

Sometimes, I would remember my classmate Diwakar. Occasionally I would see him pass our school carrying a stick as he would go to the village's grocery store. I would talk to him on such occasions. He would always tell me that he wanted his beloved younger brother to study well. He dreamt of making him an officer. He wanted his younger brother to seize all the opportunities that he totally missed in life for being blind.

After my fifth standard, we moved to Udupi to continue our education, as my elder sisters and brothers were to be admitted to high school. As the years passed, the childhood memories remained green in my mind and I always wondered about poor Diwakar. I continued my studies and I was busy in establishing myself in life. All the while, the memory of Diwakar did not fade from my mind.

During the year 1997, I met a childhood friend from Kinnikambla at

Mangalore. I visited Mangalore to meet our coffee curers. There I chanced upon Sanjeeva, who studied with me at Kinnikambla School. We were very glad that we had met each other after nearly forty years! During our lunch we updated ourselves. Soon we were talking of our classmates. I enquired about Diwakar. I heard from him that our dear classmate Diwakar was not a blind person any more! Now, he had one transplanted eye, and he could see the world like a normal person!

Then he narrated this extraordinary story. Diwakar lived with his parents for a long time doing his farm work with great devotion. Because of his hard work, their farm prospered. His father died after a few years. Diwakar looked after his mother well. He managed to reap well from their land efficiently. Since Diwakar looked after the small farm, his elder brother felt that he could go out and earn and he sought work at Mangalore and settled there for good. Diwakar's mother and his youngest brother stayed with him. He took good care of his brother and took up the responsibility of educating the boy.

Diwakar, though blind was as active as any normal young man. Thoughtfully, he changed his cropping pattern. He planted coconut seedlings and grew pineapples as an inter-crop in the dry land. He found a good source of water in the well dug in the paddy field. He purchased a diesel pump and grew vegetables in one acre of paddy field. He could grow and sell vegetables to get a steady income throughout the year. The vegetable vendors came from Mangalore City to purchase the vegetables from his farm gate! His earnings improved. As the coconut trees grew taller, Diwakar stopped growing pineapples. He planted cashew in between the coconut trees.

In about ten years, his cashew trees grew up to give him a steady yield. Good market rates for coconuts and cashew nuts supported him. He improved his farm and rebuilt his house. He installed an electric pump set, and obtained power supply to the new house. The only irony was that he could not see those lights! His mother and younger brother were very happy.

When Diwakar was about twenty-five, he was considered to be an eligible bachelor, despite being visually challenged. He was very handsome to look at. Many alliances came for Diwakar from the poor parents who desperately wanted to marry their daughters to a good household. Diwakar refused such alliances, saying that he was a handicapped person. Any girl who would marry him because of the pressure of her poor parents might *certainly repent for having married a blind man in the later years. Diwakar's mother too agreed with her son's reasoning.*

A girl by name Netra lived next to Diwakar's farm. She hailed from a very poor but respected family. Though she had scored good marks in SSLC, her parents could not afford to send her to the college at Mangalore. She was fair and good looking, but she walked with a limp. Her legs were weakened by polio attack during her childhood. She had strong hands and worked hard. Her polio leg snuffed all her hopes in life! She was about twenty-two years old. She never hoped that she would get married, since she thought nobody would come forward to marry a cripple like her.

Netra had purchased a sewing machine, and she stitched clothes for women and children of the village. She began to earn enough for her livelihood by tailoring. She was a very kind and amicable girl.

Netra would visit Diwakar's mother often. When Diwakar's younger brother left for college education at Mangalore, she would come to his house every evening to read mail and newspaper to Diwakar. He would listen to the radio news everyday. But he had to depend on Netra for newspaper information. His mother was illiterate. Netra could read and write Kannada, Hindi and English, and could speak well in all the three languages too! She had taken a liking to Diwakar and his family.

Diwakar's mother became very ill and was confined to bed. Poor Diwakar had to cook the food too. He took up the responsibility though it proved to be a great burden on him. During the day, sometimes Netra would help Diwakar's aged mother to take bath. She would help in the household work, while Diwakar toiled in the fields.

After his younger brother left for his higher education, Diwakar found it impossible to pick the fallen coconuts and cashew apples in the dawn. He could not locate them. Diwakar was worried. Netra understood this point without anybody telling her. She would come every morning before sunrise and would pick all the fallen coconuts and cashew apples for Diwakar. She would deliver them to his house and go home. She would return a little later in the morning to look after the ailing old woman and help Diwakar in his cooking.

Diwakar was very happy in Netra's company since she made up for his handicap. She would do all the reading and writing work for him. Diwakar would never look down on this girl as a cripple, and she in turn, treated Diwakar with equal respect. They started liking each other.

One day, Diwakar proposed to Netra and the girl readily agreed! They were married in the village temple in a simple function to become husband and wife. Though Netra had passed her SSLC examination, she respected the dignity of labor. She worked hard in the farm from morning to evening, while most of the educated youngsters of our village preferred only white-collar jobs.

The word Netra means 'eye' in Sanskrit as well as in Kannada. The bride became the 'Netra' for Diwakar. He could see the world through her eyes! The couple was very happy.

The age-old longing for the study of Braille erupted from the dumped up heap of Diwakar's disappointment. He asked Netra to search for the address of the Braille school of Madras. He wanted to study Braille now. Netra told him that she would go to Mangalore next morning to find out about it. She went to a reputed eye specialist in Mangalore to seek his advice. The doctor told Netra that the science has progressed so much that eyes can be transplanted effectively during these days to make the blind see.

The eye should come from a donor. There was an Eye Bank in Mangalore that helped the blind, as many people donated their eyes to that Bank after death. She was told that her husband might have to wait in a long queue to get a suitable eye. Maybe, he would have to wait for years, after registering his name with the Eye Bank to get a suitable eye.

Immediately, Netra asked whether she could donate one of her eyes to her husband! The doctor said it was a good idea, but he had to evaluate the recipient first, and he should conduct the matching tests before he finalized on the transplantation.

Netra was very happy to hear this! She hurried back to Kinnikambla to tell her husband that she did not find out anything about the Braille at all! Diwakar seemed crestfallen. Then, she disclosed that the doctor in Mangalore had the technique of transplanting the eyes. She told Diwakar that she had taken an appointment with the doctor and she would take him there for evaluation, the very next day itself.

Diwakar was very much excited about the prospect. At the same time, he worried as to which donor would leave back his eye for him. It may be a long wait indeed. Next day, the couple went through the tests. The doctor declared that the transplantation could be attempted, as Netra's eye was found to be suitable. Netra would be wearing a glass eye to replace the donated one.

Hearing the news, poor Diwakar was worried again! He would not bear the fact that Netra would lose one eye to revive his sight. He refused the proposal totally! He declared that he would rather be happy if he learned Braille, and he would lead the life as a blind person.

Netra pleaded that she would not lose her visual faculty even if the operation failed. She would have a glass eye to make up for her looks. The doctor also persuaded Diwakar to accept the offer. Finally, he agreed for the operation.

The doctor was so much impressed with the mutual love of husband and wife that he waived off his surgeon's charges for the expensive operation. Furthermore, he promised to contact some of the charitable institutions as well as the Rotary and the Lions Clubs of Mangalore for financial help.

The famous eye surgeon's words carried a lot of weight in the social circles and the donor institutions agreed to pay for the entire operation and the domicile hospital expenses.

The rest was easy! Soon, after a successful transplantation, Diwakar saw the light for the first time in his life of 26 years! He could not recognize his wife until he heard her speak! He thanked the doctor and Netra for giving him a new lease on life. Soon after, Diwakar could come back to his farm to see his toil of several years. He saw his house, vegetable and coconut gardens in astonishment. Diwaker and Netra were the happiest couple who understood each other perfectly.

Thus, I heard the wonderful story of Diwakar. Self-reliance and sacrifice brought success to the couple in their lives.

Some day, I would like to take a copy of this article and go to meet the wonderful couple!

*The names of the persons and the name of the town they live in are changed to maintain the privacy of the true characters.

PEJATHAYA'S INTRODUCTION TO FARMING

The most exhilarating experience I had in India was watching the transformation of barren land into beautiful, productive crop land. The Peace Corps volunteers were witnesses to magical changes taking place on the Deccan Plateau. To some degree, the volunteers were contributors to the changes, although the Government of India and her Department of Agriculture were primarily instrumental in educating farmers in using improved crops, irrigation techniques, modern mechanization and plant protection methods.

That first bus trip across the planes of the Deccan Plateau exposed miles and miles of flat, dry black cotton soil. Sparse sticks of cotton rose 10 inches above the dry earth. The rusty-brown, withered leaves revealed one or two meager tufts of cotton on each spindly stalk. One picking per year was all the farmer could hope for, and if the monsoon rains failed that year his family made do with less income.

The black soil contained clay particles that absorbed moisture slowly, and released it slowly. Cotton could be planted with the first rains, and by the time the monsoons ended the cotton plants had burst through the ground. With luck, the clay soil would hold enough moisture to encourage the cotton balls to open before giving up the last drops of moisture to the hot sun.

Such was the way of subsistence farming in Raichur District before the arrival of the Tungabhadra Dam and canal irrigation system. My fellow volunteers and I had the great fortune to witness the miracle of transformation of a near wasteland into a veritable garden.

A farmer who could find sufficient resources and who could be encouraged to level his land for irrigation found wealth in the black cotton soil. We watched the smiles of excitement on the faces of enterprising farmers who watched the first planted seeds break ground. As the grass-like features of sorghum and maize plants pushed the earth aside and stood tall, we laughed with joy at the surprised look on the farmers' faces.

Some farmers tried sorghum. Some tried sunflower. Others wanted to grow vegetables, and soon learned that water had been the sole missing ingredient for bountiful harvests.

The grand slam came when the Department of Agriculture identified a plant that was well suited for the long, hot days, the black soil and a steady supply of water. Hybrid cotton changed the countryside from a struggling desert to a boomtown-like adventure. One kilogram of cotton seed would plant one acre. Farmers began lining up to buy the subsidized seed for this plant that grew like a tree. It produced a long staple cotton that had export quality, and farmers harvested their plants seven or eight times in one season.

Both Pejathaya and I considered ourselves somewhat experienced in agriculture. Our discussions usually involved applying our farming experiences to develop new ideas to enhance our agricultural endeavors in Raichur District. In the late 1960s, the possibilities for new agricultural techniques, implements, crops, irrigation and plant protection seemed limitless. We absorbed every issue of the *Farm Journal* from cover to cover. We attended every government-sponsored training session that was offered to us, and constantly talked with Indian and foreign experts on agriculture research.

My experience came from my parents and their 160 acre farm in Minnesota, where I lived from the age of three until I finished high school. The family farm was considered a "general" farm. We raised chickens for eggs, steers and hogs for the meat market and Guernsey dairy cows for their rich butterfat milk. We cultivated corn, oats, wheat and soybeans for market, and grew ample acreages of alfalfa for animal fodder.

My parents farmed an additional 200 acres of corn and soybeans on a share crop basis. Production from the two farms was sufficient to keep my six siblings and me in decent clothes and well fed, but we were not well-off. My chores began at an early age, carrying large buckets of grain and water to keep our egg-laying chickens well nourished. Later, I milked the cows, slopped the hogs, plowed the fields and cultivated those endless rows of corn and soybeans.

Most Minnesota crops are rain fed. My first experience with irrigation came in Hemet, California, where Cecil McCormac taught the Peace Corps trainees how to syphon water from a distributary canal into a field of corn. Pejathaya, on the other hand, started his farming experience by pumping water from a river to water his coconut saplings.

Pejathaya's personal goals did not originally include farming, but destiny changed his plans. His dream of sailing the high seas with the Indian Navy had to give way to reality. His dream was interrupted shortly after graduation. As mentioned in an earlier chapter, Pejathaya felt a great deal of gratitude for the support he received from his sister and brother-in-law. He offered to help them develop their forest land and to postpone his call to the sea.

I TOOK TO FARMING!
BY S.M. PEJATHAYA

In the summer of 1967, I was helping to clear my sister's agricultural land to develop it into a coconut farm. As the land was fallow and neglected for nearly two generations, it had become part of the adjoining Shiroor Reserve Forest. I cleared sixty acres of this agricultural land-turned-forest on the bank of Swarna River in Dakshina Kannada.

During May, I wanted to cultivate about five acres of land to grow 'paddy' (rice) and I had dug pits to plant coconut saplings in the rest of the area. The land had become a habitat for bison, deer and wild boar in the adjoining forest and I could not think of farming without a strong barricade. I fenced the entire plot with barbed wire and stone pillars

The farmland was in a remote place, almost amidst the jungle on the bank of the deep Swarna River and hence I had abundant source of water for irrigation. I had three diesel pump sets readily installed near the river. Nothing could be grown unless one stayed there to guard the crops. I built a small cottage with a kitchen. A veranda onto the side of the cottage housed our Japanese Mitsubishi power tiller.

I had to stay in the farmland for some time to prove that I could survive there alone. No human being from the nearby village of Shiroor, which was two miles away, would come and stay there. For, the villagers used to

100

cremate the dead[9] there as our land was left uncultivated for more than a hundred years and the owners of the land, my brother-in-law's family, stayed at far-off Udupi, never objected to this kind of trespass. Besides, it was a convenient place for cremations and final rites as the relatives of the departed could take bath in the nearby river. As per the Hindu customs, post-cremation rituals starting with collection of ashes have to be performed near a perennial source of water.

It was believed to be a haunted place. Right from the day one, the village folk discouraged us from farming this land, but my sister and brother-in-law were determined to develop this vast tract of land into a beautiful farm.

The forefathers of my brother-in-law made initial attempts to cultivate this land more than a century ago and they had failed, as it was a remote area with no proper roads. Even the bullock carts would not go there! The wild animals happily grazed on the crops as their makeshift fence of cactus planted in trenches posed no threat to them at all. Barbed wire fences were not known then. The nearest village was two miles away and no laborer would stay at the farmland. The monsoon floods in the river mercilessly washed away the standing crops. Tigers attacked cattle and there was the threat of malaria too. The farming attempts had therefore failed miserably, and the land was left fallow. In fact, I had no idea that I would go there and become a farmer. It was my destiny that led me there.

After my eldest brother started earning and purchased a house at Udupi, all of us shifted to Udupi for our high school and college education. When I was studying the pre-university course at Udupi, my brother shifted his business to the neighboring state of Tamil Nadu. My elder sister Dr. Shashikala and my brother-in-law Sri Vyasa Acharya offered to look after me. Sri Vyasa Acharya was a Commerce lecturer in a college at Udupi. The couple took me under their wings and helped me through the college. I am forever indebted to their kindness.

While studying at college, I dreamed of becoming an officer in the Indian Navy. I had joined the naval wing of the National Cadet Corps. I was ready to join the Indian Navy as an officer by the time I completed my graduation. I was looking forward to a bright future in the Indian Navy.

---

[9] Hindu death rituals included burning the deceased on a pyre, often constructed near a river

One of those days, we went on a picnic with my brother-in-law and his family to this neglected land. After visiting the place, my brother-in-law started dreaming of developing this land into a coconut farm. He told me that if I joined hands with him I could equally do well; I might even get better financial benefits than I would get in the Navy, if I succeeded in the farming. He told me that being a farmer is also as noble as being a soldier. He offered to pay me a stipend till we got the yields and later I could get a share in the profits as his managing partner. It seemed to be really an attractive proposition.

As an enthusiastic young man I craved for adventure. I never cared much about my own comforts or future during those days. I had no encumbrance and none but myself to take care of. I readily accepted the proposal. It gave me an opportunity to express my gratitude by helping my dearest sister and brother-in-law to some extent. They had paid for my college education. They had given me food, clothing and protection unconditionally. I inwardly wanted to establish that farm for my sister and get away later on to seek my future in the Indian Navy or elsewhere.

The riverbank opposite our land was the boundary of another village, Nirebailur. A scrubland extended up to the boundaries of a huge plantation of cashew nut trees planted by the government. There was a stretch of rough road linking the cashew plantation border to the Udupi-Karkala main road. The river marked the boundary of our Shiroor village.

If we laid a mud road to the cashew plantation from the opposite bank, we could reach the Udupi-Karkala main road, which passed through a small town called Hiriyadka. It was a tar road, three miles from the opposite bank of our river. This route, though longer by two miles than the walking trail, would enable transportation and hauling of materials to our farm easy. Otherwise we had to carry all our supplies on head loads from Hiriyadka, cross the river at a ferry point, a mile away from Shiroor. The total distance to the farm from Hiriyadka was six miles. Though it was eight miles via this road to reach Hiriyadka, it was worth the trouble as everything we needed for the farm could be unloaded on the opposite side of the river throughout the year. We purchased a canoe of about sixteen feet length for our use at the farm. We could reach the opposite bank easily now. A hired truck or jeep could come with some difficulty up to the opposite bank of the river. Our own boat could ferry the men and material to our farm. On our side of the river, I made a rough cart track up to Shiroor too!

From Shiroor, there was a mud road up to Manai, the ferrying point. This was our shortcut by walk to Hiriyadka. When the river was in spate, a boatman would ferry us in a dugout canoe. We used the public ferry canoe eight months a year at this Manai ferrying point and during the four dry months of summer, we could wade through the shallow river at this Manai ferry point. The river all along our boundary was very deep and we could not wade across. So, we were forced to buy our own canoe.

I whole heartedly agreed to start the farming project. The first step was to make motor-able roads on both sides of the river and at the same time I had to learn something about agriculture. I took a short-term training course at the Agricultural University of Bangalore in handling farm machinery and equipment. During the evening hours we were allowed to use the University library. We could meet the professors and visit their demonstration plots. This was a great opportunity for me, to learn methods of modern farming from the experts.

MY FARM ON THE SWARNA RIVER

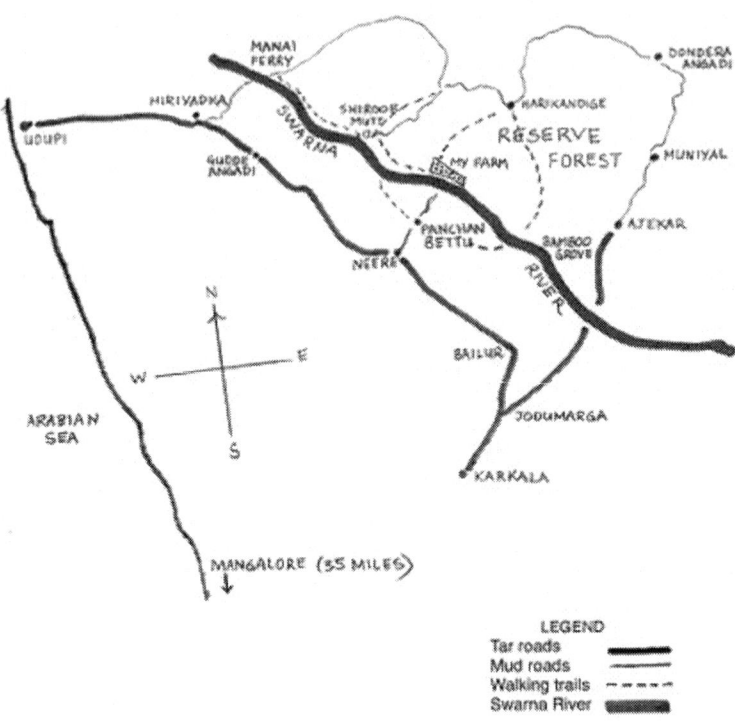

LEGEND

Tar roads	▬▬▬
Mud roads	────
Walking trails	─ ─ ─ ─
Swarna River	▰▰▰▰

Approximate distance between points of interest. Map is not to scale

* Udupi to Hiriyadka = 8 miles
* Hiriyadka to Manai Ferry to Shiroor Mutt to my farm = 6 miles
* Hiriyadka to Gudde Angadi to Neere to Panchan Bettu to my farm = 8 miles
* Hiriyadka to Ajekar to Dondera Angadi to Harikandige to Shiroor Mutt = 40 miles

I purchased a Mitsubishi power tiller at Bangalore and got it freighted to Mangalore. The Japanese instructors from Mitsubishi Company of Japan taught me to maintain their power tillers and other Japanese farm machinery. I purchased a custom-made trolley for the tiller at Mangalore and transported the tiller and the trolley up to Hiriyadka by truck. I brought them to our farm via Shiroor by driving through the mud road, as the river level was low at Manai during the summer. It was the first Mitsubishi power tiller in our village. Many farmers came to my farm to see the latest power tiller.

In the summer, I studied a lot of books on farming and agriculture, went to the large farms nearby, worked there for a few weeks and acquired some basic and experiential knowledge. I went to seek guidance from the farm experts of our district: At the same time, I worked with my senior at the college, Mr. Oscar Fernandes[10], who had already developed a farm in his father's neglected piece of land near Udupi.

After clearing the jungle and fencing the land, I built a small cottage with the help of a mason from Shiroor. I transported all the building materials in my tiller's trolley. I built a cowshed once I settled there since we needed a lot of organic manure for the farm. I had to maintain a big batch of local scrub cattle, the 'Malnad Gidda' breed. Being very hardy and available in the surrounding villages, they were well accustomed to the forest environment by birth. They grazed in the forest and returned in the evening on their own. Besides, they were available at affordable price. We had totally 42 heads of cattle, a few of them were cows, and the rest were oxen, young bulls and calves. They loved to sleep on the thickly spread bed of fresh green leaves in our cattle shed. This thick bed of green leaves when mixed with the dung and bovine urine would make excellent manure. This kind of traditional cowshed provided them the much-needed warmth and protection from the wild animals at night.

Every fortnight we would empty the well-trampled manure from the floor and transfer the same to our compost pits. We covered the pits with six inches of fresh soil to retain the moisture in the organic manure. We had to bring huge quantities of fresh green leaves from the forest and spread them in the floor of the cowshed everyday. I had detailed two men for this work.

I did not milk the cows in the morning. I would let all the calves drink their mother's milk so that they would grow up well and give me more and more manure. I could get a few pints of milk, though after being kicked at by the cows several times. I used to feel very sore about this evening ritual of milking where I got more kicks than milk! I remember one particular evening when I got only kicks and no milk at all!

The cows were not in a mood to give me milk for some reasons of their own. Maybe during that day, they had seen some carnivorous animals in the

---

[10] Oscar Fernandes later became India's Central Government Minister of Transport

vicinity of our farm or smelt one. They were very panicky and restless. The vicious kicks I received during the milking session nearly broke my ribs. The docile cows then appeared like ferocious wild animals to me. I felt like thrashing them in revenge.

But, I had a better plan. I hung a crude wooden nameplate with 'zoo' painted on it at the entrance door of my cowshed. I called them wild animals of our zoo! I swore at them until the pain subsided to tolerable levels. Later, I inferred from their strange behavior that a tiger might be prowling near our cattle shed and they could smell the tiger.

My insistent swearing and shouting loud while I received the kicks and putting up the nameplate must have probably scared the tiger to run back into the deep forest. Since then I stopped the milking session. I bought milk from Shiroor. My laborers brought milk daily. About one 'bele' or '12 kudte' of milk (equivalent to nearly two liters of milk today), cost me only 50 paise. Milk was that cheap at Shiroor since there was no buyer in that remote village and every house had livestock.

I would like to tell you about the first day of my cottage life. Initially I used to travel early in the morning from Udupi to reach the farm and leave by 5 pm to catch a bus back to Udupi. On the day my cottage was ready, none of the workers were willing to stay with me at night. They were afraid as our land was used as a crematorium or a cemetery.

It became necessary that I had to stay alone in my hut during that night and show up the next day very much alive, to prove that the spirits of the dead did not harm me! There was no other way. I had to stay and protect my crops from the wild animals. I was thrilled and very much excited about this feat of bravery."

FARMING IN THE JUNGLE

Pejathaya's stories revolve around his developing interest in agriculture and animal husbandry. He spent three years developing his sister's jungle farm, making it into a self-supporting enterprise. Before he moved on to farming on the dry-cum-wet land irrigated by the Tungabhadra Canal system Pejathaya dealt with wild animals that invaded his crops, an unpredictable river and muddy roads that hemmed-in his land. He befriended a litany of interesting neighbors who he learned to accept and assist, and he met with local creatures that befriended him and made his life full and exciting.

Large farms in the Midwest, U.S.A. resulted in families living a distance from each other. The expansive lands also required large machinery and long working hours. It was not common to hire laborers to help work the family farm. The isolation caused life to be less social than on the smaller farms of Southern India, where land owners needed to rely on the help and cooperation of their neighbors to operate a farm.

One rainy day in Sindhanur during the monsoon season, Pejathaya and I sipped *'chai'* in a small *'ungadi'* (a local tea shop) and traded stories about our respective farming experiences. I listened more than talked, since my stories seemed mundane when compared to his. He recalled the days when he had to stand guard at night to keep wild boars, buffalo and other animals from destroying his hard work.

Early in his first year he had to construct a high bamboo platform called a *machan*[11]. He would lie awake all night,

---

[11] A machan is a raised platform, often constructed on a frame of bamboo, used to watch over crops

prepared to scare off buffalo and wild boar. These and other creatures enjoyed more than one feast in his rice paddy before he took drastic measures. In contrast, the only wild "predators" I had to deal with were jack rabbits and pocket gophers. The most damage caused to Dad's corn crop was from our own dairy cows that occasionally broke through a fence to gorge on a nearly ripe corn crop.

Living near an Indian forest reserve, Pejathaya never knew what creature he would encounter during his nightly vigil on the *machan.*

WILD ANIMALS
BY S. M. PEJATHAYA

*My sister's farmland was fenced with five strands of strong barbed wire,
which were tied to eight-foot pillars of granite stone with galvanized binding
wire. The fence covered the three sides of the land while on the southern side
the deep Swarna River certainly made up for the fence.*

*During monsoon there were floods, and during summer, luckily, the river
was deep all along our property. Though the water receded, it flowed steadily
during summer. The wild animals would not swim across the river to graze
on our fenced property. We had formed a mud road along the periphery of
the fence, on all the three sides. We used this peripheral road for
transporting materials in our power tiller and trolley to the desired spot as
our land was about a furlong wide along the river. We passed the materials
over the barbed wire fence to the land from where we could use a
wheelbarrow.*

*As an alternative, we could use our double ender dugout canoe to
transport things on the southern side along the river. When we finished the
fencing we thought that we really had a wild animal-proof fence. But, soon I
found out that the wild boars sneaked through the barbed wire fence to
graze on our lush paddy crop. I had to build a 'machan'[12] and slept on it
with my transistor radio blaring until the radio stations closed their*

---

[12] A watch and ward platform. It is also called manchike in Kannada

transmission at late night.

I had to carry a gun to the machan to frighten the wild boars in case they came in during the wee hours. We had kept the main gate on the western side and it was the only entry to our property. My hut and the cattle shed were built just outside the main gate on a small knoll so that our farm animals would not wander into the agricultural land.

In the initial days of my farming, the workers from Shiroor village came in the mornings and left in the evenings. The workers did not want to stay there as our place was used for cremating the dead. The villagers stopped using the land as a crematorium once we began our cultivation. But the fear of the ghosts haunted them.

I had allayed their fear by proving that I could survive there alone. But the poor and ignorant folk assumed that I was not harmed, as I was a learned Brahmin. Moreover, I was a bachelor wearing the sacred thread across my torso and chanted Gayatri Mantra every day and hence, no evil spirit would harm me!

It was an uphill task to convince them that there were no evil spirits and the laborers could also lead a peaceful life if they stayed there. In the beginning of the monsoon season, I sowed my first crop of paddy. I had to double as the night watchman. Sundays were the weekly holidays for the farm workers. Since the wild animals never took a holiday, I myself had to be rostered for the night watch on Sundays.

I would be free on Sundays and festival holidays. I would row our double ender dugout canoe along the southern boundary of our farm. Sometimes I would go exploring into the Shiroor Reserve Forest. Unless provoked, no animal or reptile would harm a man. Yet, I would always carry an oversized pocketknife. Though I knew I might not need it, the weapon gave me a feeling of safety.

I happened to use the knife on only one occasion. When I was exploring the forest one morning in December, I found a clearing with a nice spread of golden yellow grass in the thick forest. The grass had grown knee-high and had put up ear heads of pale violet color. No animal had grazed on that clearing. The grass was swaying in the light breeze.

I felt like a kid on the beach. I started to drag my feet to create a sort of tail on the grass. It was fun to flatten the grass. I was wearing a pair of hockey shoes. I went round and round trampling the dew soaked golden *grass; I stopped suddenly as I stepped on something soft. Before I could realize, a snake coiled up on my right leg, up to my knees. I was wearing khaki shorts and stockings. I had trampled on the head portion of a krait! It had transverse silvery stripes on its shining black skin.*

Kraits are very venomous and the most dreaded reptile next to cobra. The victim would die a miserable death within a few hours of its bite. Even if proper antidote is given by a doctor, blood serums ooze through the lesions and recovery would be very slow as the wound gathers dead tissue around it and the patient would have to suffer a lot. As the wound grew ugly, it would be very difficult to cure krait bite. The part of the body with lesion would have to be amputated, or some times it would be deformed.

I had stepped on a fairly big sized krait and fortunately, its head was pinned to the ground by the sole of my right shoe. There was no use in trying to uncoil and throw the angry snake away. The very moment I moved the foot, it would be set free and it would bite me in rage. I stood still without moving my right foot for an eternal minute. I was deeply worried about my survival. The best way was to severe it's head with my oversized pocketknife. I had no other choice.

I grimaced as I severed the snake's head by running the sharp knife-edge along the inner edge of my right shoe. Its head got separated from its body. I had pinned its body with all my weight. Its severed head portion writhed under my shoe for a few seconds and went still. The snake's body tightened for about a minute and then it slowly went limp. Finally, I untangled the snake's body carefully without moving my right foot. I took extra care that its blood never touched my limbs. The cut-off segment writhed on the ground for a few seconds before lying cold.

As the snake's dead body and its blood were believed to be very venomous in the villages, as per the practice, I had to burn or bury the carcass of the snake along with the knife blade used to kill it. I did not have a spade or a matchbox to accomplish the task. I untied my shoes and laid it near the dead snake along with my knife.

I hurried to my cottage on bare feet to get a matchbox, a spade and a sharp sickle from my hut. I could locate the spot by finding my discarded shoes in the grass. I cut dry twigs, collected a big pile of dry firewood within minutes and burnt the snake with my beloved pocketknife and my good pair of hunter shoes. When the fire died I dug some soil and covered the ashes with thick layer of soil, so that no one would discover and pick up the remnant of my knife in that clearing and use them again.

*   *   *

The tea shop discussions with Pejathaya and Subramaniam, my tractor society mechanic coworker, were like school time for me. I'm not averse to hard work, but I loved to sit with these friends and listen to their stories. The refreshments were sweet coffee and *K-Tea*. The latter was made from Assam tea leaves and an assortment of spices boiled in milk. The coffee was also served with milk, as the idea of drinking black coffee had not reached Sindhanur. I believe the tradition of milk in tea and coffee came from the British, whereas most of the Americans I knew preferred black coffee.

I tried numerous times to order my coffee black, and was met with a disbelieving stare from the waiter and my Indian companions. In Bangalore, the restaurant operators called it *"decoction"* because they boiled the coffee beans. The result was a thick, hideously black sludge that would almost support the stirring spoon. That brew would guarantee no sleep for many hours. After attempts of ordering black coffee in Sindhanur I learned to drink the locally made milky coffee and *K-tea*.

Another interesting thing about tea shops in Sindhanur that always stirred conversation was the pictures on the wall. Every tea *ungadi* I visited in the *taluka* had framed pictures of important dignitaries displayed as if to show support for the persons represented. Not all the glass-enclosed images were of the same configuration, but usually included one or more of the following: Jawaharlal Nehru, Mahatma Gandhi, John Kennedy, a deity such as *Ganesha* (AKA *Ganapati*) or *Hanuman*, Indira Gandhi, and in a several instances, Jesus Christ and Pope Pius XII.

I was never very clear on the statement intended by the shop owner. Out of fear of upsetting someone's sensitivities, or getting into a political or religious discussion, I never asked.

THE SINDHANUR BUFFALO

The humble water buffalo is the traditional beast of burden for Raichur District rice cultivators. These docile animals stand only four and a half feet at the shoulder and their purpose in life is to work the *paddy* fields. This local breed, called *Hole Yemme*, or river buffalo, are much smaller than the breeds in the Northern parts of India, such as Gujarat or the Punjab. Those larger buffalo, called Surti and Murrah breeds, are the size of the American Hereford bulls. Although the stature of the local water buffalo was not intimidating, we needed to stay clear of horns that were sometimes awesome.

One year into my Peace Corps experience my dream of developing a dairy industry in Raichur District hinged on the milk-producing ability of this local breed. Not the least bit handsome in appearance, the Hole Yemme was known for producing high butterfat milk. I learned that the production quantity was small, but was rich in butterfat.

The milk *wallahs*[13] who traded in dairy products were known to extend the volume of their commodity by using water or other substances to dilute it. Hotels and middle class homemakers bought milk to produce the daily curd (yogurt) served with the family meals. They bought whatever the market provided because there was no government control, and no way for the individual to judge the content of the nutritious white fluid.

My vision was based on the understanding that milk was a

---

[13] A wallah is a person who does something. For example, a milk wallah sells milk

nutritious food and should be in everyone's diet. My interest was a carryover from growing up on a dairy farm. After doing a rather unsophisticated market survey, I plunged into the idea of making milk available to every Indian family.

My earliest solution was to suggest importing American cows and building a facility on the banks of the Sindhanur *nullah*. Tom Carter, India-60's Associate Director, suggested a more practical approach. He suggested that I study the experience of the famous Amul Dairy Cooperative in Gujarat, India, where the buffalo provided an abundance of quality milk. The Amul Dairy Cooperative provided collection, processing, sale and distribution for the rich buffalo milk. The Amul cooperative also provided veterinary assistance to the farmers, and financing to extend the herds.

With the Peace Corps' approval, John Kelly, the volunteer nearest to Sindhanur, and I took a train to Gujarat State and met the chief officer of Amul Dairy, Dr. Verghese Kurien. Dr. Kurien is internationally known for helping to create what became known as the most successful cooperative in Asia.

Two high level managers of Amul gave us a tour of the Amul facility, as well as several of the villages where milk was produced. They showed us the entire process of collecting, labeling, measuring, quality control testing, and transporting the milk to the processing facility. We met with farmers as they came to their village milk collection points and, through translators, asked questions about their experience with Amul, and the effect milk production played on their livelihood. Every farmer we questioned felt that the money raised through selling milk to Amul created more household income, even after paying-off the loans they incurred for feed, veterinary medicines and the purchase of animals.

There was a real sense of witnessing the magic combination of business, healthy food, agriculture and animal husbandry that resulted in a positive outcome for all the participants, even the Indian consumer, who now had a constant supply of milk, cheese and powdered baby formula. We left Amul Dairy energized with a wonderful feeling that we had witnessed a beautiful example of a successful cooperative.

After returning to Sindhanur, Dr. Kurien continued to fuel our interest and to provide answers to hundreds of questions. Through mail and a personal visit to Sindhanur by Amul officials, the people of Amul Dairy gave us support as we worked with local Raichur District farmers and Indian Government officials to create a cooperative organization in the likeness of Amul.

We had great difficulty selling the idea to local farmers and consumers. Both farmers and milk *wallah's* were content with the current situation. Farmers might dilute their milk before selling it to the *wallah's*. The *wallah's* might dilute it further before selling it to the customers. Hotels and households would have preferred to find milk in the local stores, however, there were no shops with refrigeration. Milk bought today had to be used today.

To complicate matters, we were scheduled to leave India when our Peace Corps contracts ended in eight months. Someone locally had to take the initiative to keep the idea alive. We met with groups of farmers to kindle an interest but found the local farmers reluctant to get involved. John and I talked to the Sindhanur hotel owners, who would be the major consumers. We spoke with any government official who would listen to us, and begged for their assistance.

Eventually, several *Andhra* farmers who lived in temporary encampments several miles from Sindhanur stepped forward and offered assistance to get the idea moving. Achyuta Ramaiah, a mild mannered *Andrah* farmer, saw some logic to having a cooperative do the collection, testing and marketing for his milk produce. When no one else volunteered he agreed to take on the presidency of the cooperative. Under President Achyuta Ramaiah the fledgling organization began to take shape.

The Cooperative Department of Raichur District finally approved the charter of the new cooperative (The *Sri Srinivasa*

Milk Producers Cooperative Society) in November 1970. Late one evening, ten *Andhra* farmers whose camp was four miles from Sindhanur raised their hands in a meeting in my crowded apartment. They agreed to meet us at 5:00 A.M. on the road next to their village and each would provide two or more liters of unadulterated buffalo milk.

The farmers who had emigrated from the neighboring state of Andhra Pradesh tended to be comparatively progressive. The family lands they left behind were becoming overcrowded, as most maturing young males wanted to till the land. However, as families divided the land repeatedly the farms became too small to provide a tenable family income. The arrival in *Karnataka* of irrigation waters from the Tungabhadra Dam created an opportunity for these *Andhra* farmers wherever land was available near the irrigation channels.

The immigrants brought their herds of animals with them, including a superior breed of buffalo. Each *Andhra* buffalo could produce twice as much milk as the local Sindhanur breeds. Like the milk from the local breed, the milk from these *Andhra* animals was very rich in butterfat. To be honest, one could have added a cup of water to a cup of buffalo milk and have a substance almost like the whole milk you buy today at your local grocery.

Soon after Achyuta Ramaiah agreed to a leadership role another *Andhra* farmer agreed to become the society's Secretary. Peace Corps Associate Director, Tom Carter, helped us greatly by agreeing to sponsor a trip for these two officers to the Amul Dairy in Gujarat. John Kelly and Billy Danielson, the India-60 volunteer from Balaganur, agreed to accompany these two gentlemen. Dr. Kurien and his Amul Dairy staff gave the two *Andhra* farmers the same personal attention that John and I had enjoyed three months earlier. The President and Secretary returned to Sindhanur with renewed vigor and a determination to get their fellow farmers to help them.

The inaugural milk collection day started early one morning in late November 1970. John and Billy hooked a two-wheeled trailer to a Mitsubishi power tiller that the India Department of Cooperatives lent to us, loaded a large milk can, a measuring ladle, and some small sample jars to create our milk collection vehicle. Waking at 4:00 A.M., to the irritating tweets from my trusty alarm clock, John and Billy cranked up the Mitsubishi, and, at a speed of 4 miles per hour, headed off towards the *Andhra* camp.

Billy, the chemistry major of our group, helped us set up a Gerber testing station and ran the first milk tests. The first day's collection was a mere ten liters of buffalo milk. From each milk deposit we took a small sample of milk. Billy measured ten milliliters of sulfuric acid into a graduated Gerber tube called a butyrometer. He then added 11 milliliters of the milk sample and one milliliter of isoamyl alcohol. He sealed and placed the tubes in a centrifuge and spun it for five minutes at 1100 RPM. After the spin cycle he could read directly off a scale on the butyrometer a precise measure of butterfat for each sample.

This butterfat factor was recorded in a log and matched against a graduated numeric scale that indicated a factor. The resulting factor was multiplied times the volume of milk contributed by each herdsman, resulting in the amount of currency to pay to each. The system was very objective, and mostly foolproof. Several farmers and milk wallah's challenged Billy's scientific processes, only to be embarrassed when they finally had to admit that they had adulterated their milk to increase the quantity. Once the word was out, no peccant suppliers ventured to deliver milk again. So went the Sri Srinivasa Milk Producers Cooperative Society.

The sulfuric acid used for this test had to be handled with extreme care. A careless spill can eat through most substances in seconds, and human skin is no obstacle. Billy took great care to keep curious watchers at a safe distance while he conducted his tests.

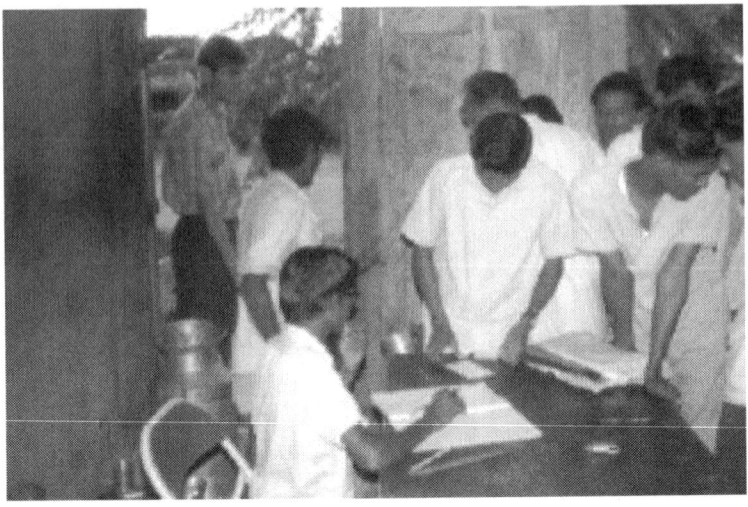

John Kelly with Achyuta Ramaiah supervising milk collection and testing

Eventually, the Sindhanur pharmacists could not supply enough sulfuric acid to maintain our growing requirements. They suggested a larger source in Bellary, about 89 Kilometers from Sindhanur. When our first supply of sulfuric acid ran dangerously low we didn't have time to wait for bus transportation to deliver more. Without prior planning, John and I hopped on my Jawa motorcycle and headed for Bellary. We hadn't considered how to transport the acid, but once we purchased it we had no choice but to hand carry it. I drove the motorcycle very carefully as John cradled the five gallon bottle of sulfuric acid behind me for the three hour ride back to Sindhanur. During the frequent rest stops I noticed that John was sweating profusely, even though it was a very cool evening. Apparently, he was envisioning what would happen if that container should burst in his lap.

The first tests the next morning shook us to the core. The milk samples burned up in a puff of noxious smoke the instant the sulfuric acid touched the milk. Billy leaned in a little closer to read the label on the bottle of acid and noted that John had just carried a highly concentrated bottle of acid on his lap over rough roads for three hours, on the back of a motorcycle.

Pejathaya saw the slow, painful process of getting government approval for a new cooperative. He encouraged us in our attempts to get the local farmers to organize themselves into a cohesive unit. He saw our struggling cooperative deal with collection and marketing issues and sympathized with our seemingly futile efforts to keep our milk transportation vehicle in workable repair. When the situation looked depressing, Pejathaya always showed up to offer words of encouragement and to add a positive perspective to bring us back to reality. He met his own challenges in getting milk from cattle that resulted in violent kicks and frustration, and eventually, terminated his desire for fresh milk. One day, as Billy and I stirred that day's excess milk collections to make '*doodh peda*', which is a tasty dessert made from milk, Pejathaya told us about a story he once wrote about buffalo of a different sort.

BISON
BY S.M. PEJATHAYA

On a summer day, I was walking in the jungle about half a mile away from my cottage. I knew a small clearing. It was about hundred yards by hundred yards, shaded by tall trees. One of them was a big 'jambul' tree (a tropical evergreen tree bearing a fruit like blackberry). The shadow of the trees covered the small meadow during the early morning.

I was whistling and walking happily in the forest. I had noticed a tall 'jambul' tree was about to give ripe fruits. I wanted to check on it. The violet fruits, though tiny in size, would be delicious during the height of summer. I entered this small hidden clearing with tall grass and some high thickets. I suddenly bumped on a herd of bison that were relaxing in the morning sun. I stopped as soon as I saw them. The bison too were surprised to see me. Probably, they too thought that a human being may not come there whistling all the way like a bird.

We were staring at each other face to face. The huge leader was resting his body on the ground with his head held high. He watched me with a hint of surprise. It was a magnificent sight. Their skins and shapely horns were shining in the bright morning light. I could smell the bovine scent emanating from their bodies.

My whistling had stopped without my knowledge. I would be dead if they decided to attack me! I only hoped that I did not alarm them. I wanted to retreat as quietly as I could. Before the bison could react, I reared without making a sound, took shelter behind the nearest thicket, and retreated a few more steps. I felt that there was no chance of them chasing me, but, I heard them getting up and stepping towards me as if to investigate. Might be they wanted to get a closer look again! At the same moment I turned and ran towards my farm as fast as I could zigzagging through the thickets and tall trees.

I think I had beaten the Flying Sikh Milkha Singh's (a former Indian track and field *sprinter) record that day! Fear was the catalyst for my speed record. Never in my life had I run that fast nor did I any day later. I had great respect for these creatures after the incident; I loved their majestic looks and gait.*

The Indian bison are called 'Gaur' in North India. They are wild buffaloes. Their size is double that of domesticated ones. They have white socks on all the four feet and mostly the males have a large white spot on their forehead. They have symmetrically bent shiny horns. They are shy. They seldom attack human beings unless frightened, provoked or wounded. The grown up ones are about six feet at the shoulders and weigh about a ton; as they walk on solid dry ground, they leave a deep impression of their hooves. They personify speed and strength. During 'Haaka Shikars' when they flee in panic, they break the thin trees and saplings that stand in the way. Any one can make out the way they had run. They leave a track and their panic run would appear like locomotive engines let loose in the forest!

During the normal course, they walk quietly across the jungle and prefer to graze on the grassy clearings within the forest or grassy plains in the surrounding. They drink water from rivers and rivulets. They live in groups and follow a leader. Next to the elephant, they are the biggest and the strongest animals of our forest. Elephants were not found in our part of the forest.

Our fence was ready when the monsoon rains approached. We planted coconut saplings brought from Sullia. We had six acres of paddy field near my cottage. I ploughed in a good lot of green manure into the soil by using the power tiller and flooded the paddy fields. I had raised a paddy nursery in a small plot. In mid-June we planted the fields in time. By July, we de-weeded the paddy fields and applied the fertilizers. By August end, the paddy fields were lush green and started to flower. The scent of the paddy crop filled the air.

One night I heard our pie dog[14] barking. He had come to our farm as a malnourished puppy and befriended me. He lived on morsels of food I gave him. He was the only one who appreciated my cooking. Sometimes, it was very difficult for me to eat what I cooked. But, the nameless puppy ate all that was served to him without complaint. In addition, he devoured all the leftover that I threw out the next morning. He had survived my cooking and put on weight too!

He hid behind my power tiller in the veranda and was whimpering. I was too confident of our fence and I was very sleepy as any youth of my age would be. I didn't get up to investigate. Next morning, I could spot the big hoof marks of a few bison, right outside the fencing of our paddy field. They had stood there for some time and retreated into the forest in the night. I was very proud of our fence and I thought they would never come through our fence.

Next day, the dog was barking and whimpering again. After sometime, it started barking into the darkness endlessly. I relied more on the barbed wire fence. Assuming myself as a 'securely fenced farmer,' I slipped into deep sleep. Next morning, I looked out of the window; I could see that half an acre of my paddy crop near the fence had disappeared totally. The remaining portion of the big field, which measured about an acre, was badly trampled upon.

I hurried to inspect the fence. Four or five granite poles were bent towards the ground. The strands of twisted barbed wire were untwisted as they were pulled to expand and the imbedded nails had fallen on the ground. It looked as though a bulldozer had attacked my fence.

There were a number of hoof prints to indicate that a herd of bison had entered our field. Their systematic grazing had left about an inch of green paddy stub on the field. I was at my wit's end. I went to consult the forest officials at Hiriyadka. He was a stout and tall officer with broad shoulders and gruff voice. He looked like a bison himself. He told me that no one can shoot at a bison. I was at liberty to scare them away with a gunshot fired in air. He advised me to build a 'machan,' lie down there and stay awake armed with some firecrackers. He advised me to carry old kerosene tin and

---

[14] A pie dog is an ownerless half-wild mongrel dog common around Indian villages

122

a small stick to beat it. During those days, we used to get eighteen liters of kerosene in a sealed galvanized tin. He asked me to beat the tin throughout the night and sing! The kerosene tin would produce a scary hollow sound and when combined with my singing, which was even scarier, the commotion would convince the bison that a man is hollering and beating the drum to scare them away.

In case the beating of the tin and my loud singing failed to scare them away, he asked me to burst a volley of crackers or use a "licensed weapon only" to fire a few shots into the air. Shooting at a bison or any wild animal is an offense attracting imprisonment for years, he warned me, as it was his duty to do so. He of course said the benevolent Forest Department was turning deaf ears to the complaints regarding shooting of wild boars, as they were the biggest menace for the cultivated crops.

Browbeaten, I did not know what to do! Time was running out and I had to be in the farm by evening to protect my crops. I hurried to Udupi to see Ammanna Master, a retired high school teacher. He was a big game hunter and a wildlife expert of great repute. Ammanna Master told me that I and my dear brother-in-law were the virtual wrongdoers! For, we had left the land fallow for nearly a century and now it has become a part and parcel of the forest. And now, we are claiming it back all of a sudden from the animals of the wild!

However, he told me that shooting the bison is certainly not the solution to the problem. They would strike again as soon as they forget the death of a fellow member; and most animals do forget such facts very fast. Now, we had to convince the herd that the place is 'our dwelling area' and we had to put a scare in them, so that they shall be afraid to enter our territory.

The modern fence shockers or electrical fences were unheard of during those years. I was yet to obtain power supply to run the pumps in the farm. Electrifying the barbed wire fence using the domestic or irrigation power was strictly forbidden as per law as it was lethal to animals as well as human beings. He asked me not to think of this option even in future. Ammanna Master too agreed that the best way was to keep watch all through the night beating a kerosene tin for the time being.

However, he suggested I try one thing, if I dared. He asked me to procure a good muzzle-loading gun. First, put a powerful charge as this is for the bison. Then, top it with coir pith, On top of this charge, put an *ounce of well dried green gram seeds instead of the lead pellets, ram some more coir pith to secure the load and finally, mount a percussion cap (fulminate cap) on the gun's nipple and wait until the leader of the bison herd gets within thirty yards. Then, fire at the leader, aiming the gun away from its eyes and ears. This is very important, because the bison shall lose sight if the projectiles like whole green gram seeds hit the eyes. If aimed at the ears, it may lose its hearing; the chance is that the projectiles shall create great irritability and loss of balance to the animal in that case. As the result, the bison may become mad with rage, and it may launch a ferocious attack on any human being or domestic animal in the vicinity. This would create a dangerous situation in the forest. But a nice lashing given to the rump of the leader would scare the bison leader to lead his herd away from the vicinity of our agricultural land. He did not forget to warn me that the injured bison may attack in retaliation.*

However, he assured me that he would attend a 'Haaka Shikar' if arranged in our forest. He would try to drive the bison away from our part of the forest. This may save our crop of the season for sometime.

Thus reassured, I purchased a good lot of crackers at Udupi. The shopkeeper was quite pleased with my off-season purchase. By that time the last bus to Karkal had already left. I took out my bicycle from my sister's car garage and started pedaling the long distance of 14 miles to the farm. Had I gone by bus I had to walk the last four miles from the bus stop to the farm. Though I had missed the bus that day, I could ride and cover the last four miles distance faster.

I reached the riverbank as the sun was setting. I loaded my bicycle on the double ender canoe and paddled across the river. The workers who were waiting to go home left immediately after I arrived. They were scared of the bison herd too.

There I was. All alone in the tranquility of the farm! I cooked some dal and rice for dinner. I had not fabricated a machan, I had decided against it. The new machan would warn the bison of a man's presence.

I would sleep on the bund of the big paddy field with two blankets, one as to cover myself and another to spread beneath. A big kerosene tin contained all the crackers that I had purchased that evening and I could beat the tin with a stick to produce a loud and hollow sound in case of an emergency. I had my stock of crackers and a matchbox ready with me. I did not have a muzzle-loading gun.

I did not dare to light a fire that day. The fire could have kept me warm that night; but animals would certainly get scared of the fire and may not turn up at all. I decided to wait for them in my hiding place amidst the paddy crop, which had grown to about three feet height. I decided to lie down on the bund of the field that was ransacked by the bison the previous night. The 'pie' dog stayed with me until it started to get colder as evening progressed into night. He straight away made it to my hut to sleep under the shelter of the lean to roof of the veranda. Fortunately, that day it did not rain. I was afraid to switch on my portable transistor radio. I thought the sound of the radio would warn the animals. I had to lie, wait silently and scare the animals by lighting the high-sounding crackers.

I managed to stay awake up to my bedtime of about 9 p.m. Lying on my back; I was gazing at the bright stars shining in the moonless sky. The night sounds of the forest reached me with more clarity and greater intensity. The insects in the paddy field chirped and I could hear the plonking sound of the frogs as they jumped into stagnant water of the field. A nightjar cried. The jackals gave long hoots in the depth of the jungle.

The fence was purposefully not repaired during that day and the path was open to the bison. First, I wanted them to come into the fields, and then, I would light my stock of crackers and drive them away. As they ran, I would shout at them saying, "This is my field, and I have grown this paddy with great difficulty. You have no right to devour my crop!" I earnestly hoped that they would listen to me.

It was about 11 pm and the half-moon rose in the east. The fresh dew started falling. I covered my blanket over me and kept looking out at the direction of the flattened fence from time to time. Everything was quiet except for the night sounds of the forest to which I was very much used to.

I removed the plastic bag of crackers and the matchbox from the big tin and kept them closer to my body to keep them warm. This would make them easier to light in the humid surroundings. Due to the day's exercise and evening's long bicycle ride, I was very tired. My eyes were burning and I thought that I would give them a couple of minutes rest. I shut my eyes with a determination to open them in two minutes.

Without my knowledge I had slipped into deep slumber. I woke up to the barking of the 'pie' dog well after midnight. He was barking from a distance! I opened my eyes with a jerk. The half-moon has risen. I brought my neck up to peep over the paddy crop. I looked at the break in our fence across the paddy field in the moon light. I could see some movement near the fence.

The breeze was blowing towards me. I could smell the bovine scent. This is the same kind of smell you find in a buffalo shed. Slowly my eyes adjusted to the dark. Near the fence the majestic looking leader was standing and looking in my direction. He seemed to be little hesitant to proceed further.

I wished I had a muzzleloader loaded with a projectile of green gram seeds to give him a lashing. The herd was about fifty yards away. I could have crawled the distance of another twenty yards on the bund of the paddy field easily to accomplish the daring act. Alas! I did not have a gun.

As I was contemplating as to what to do next, the leader took a step forward to approach the field. I thought that this was the right time to scare him. I took out a string of 'electric crackers' called thus, because these crackers give out a flash of lightning like flash of electric blue light as they burst with a sharp and loud bang. I lit them with a matchstick under the blanket, and threw them along the paddy field's bund. If they fell into the paddy field they would soak in standing water. Fortunately this did not happen. The series of explosions rocked the tranquility of the forest. The startled bison herd grunted and galloped away! In their confusion they just ran into the forest blindly felling small trees. They ran like a group of locomotive engines and the ground reverberated to the beat of their hooves. I could hear the saplings break deep within the thick forest as they ran in fright for quite some distance. From their flight, I could easily guess that they would not come back again in near future.

Satisfied that I have done my bit, I retired to my hut and fell fast asleep. Next day I repaired my fence. A few strands of barbed wire had to be replaced. The operation of bursting crackers found some success. The bison never bothered me again that season.

The rabbits lived in peace in our farm. I had the trouble from monkeys and langurs. The monkeys were the residents of our forest and langurs (Black Monkeys) were the occasional visitors. Monkeys went into hiding when the aggressive langurs came to our forest. The larger and stronger langurs attacked monkeys at sight and drove them away. When the langurs left our forest the monkeys re-established their dwelling rights.

The village God of Shiroor village was 'Hanuman'[15] and no one would harm a monkey in our village. When the monkeys created havoc, the farmers tried to scare them away by firing their muskets in air. Nobody would hurt them and none wanted to hurt them. The monkeys were aware of the villagers' weakness.

Next to bison and wild boars, the monkeys proved to be the next great menace. Finally I had to try 'Ammanna Master's medicine' for monkeys too! I fired green gram seeds at the leader's back from a distance. Of course, I put a smaller charge into a muzzle-loading gun. The nice lashing of the grains worked, right after the first try. The intelligent monkey leader stayed away from my farm as long as I was there in person. If I ever came out of the farm to go to Udupi, the monkeys would come to attack our crops. Monkeys are keen observers and they were weary of my presence. The same trick worked on the group of langurs too. The deer and the sambar never dared to cross our barbed wire fence."

∗   ∗   ∗

Pejathaya's buffalo were, obviously, not the milking kind. We may never know the quantity or quality of milk from his forest buffalo, as no brave soul is willing to secure a sample. Even at his Tungabhadra Farm, he left the milking to others. He was interested in being a supplier for our milk cooperative, but our small co-op was not ready to expand in his farm's direction.

March 1971 brought my Peace Corps contract extension to an end. Thankfully, the Peace Corps asked Tony Ganey, the India-60 volunteer stationed at Turvihal, to move to Sindhanur to continue to support the *Sri Srinivasa* Milk Producers Cooperative Society. Tony had extended for a full year and still had most of that year remaining. Milk collections increased dramatically under Tony's supervision. The government assisted the co-op by obtaining a used Land Rover to collect and deliver milk. Before Tony left India at the end of 1971 the society was

---

[15] The monkey-shaped disciple of Lord Rama

attempting to distribute milk as far away as Raichur and Bellary.

Thanks to the Sindhanur buffalo, milk may have been slightly more available, at least for a short time.

SHIKAR

Farming in the jungle gave Pejathaya ample opportunity to see the resplendent beauty of India's coastal region's natural wildlife. The wild creatures were awesome to encounter, even though some could be persistently pesky, and some downright dangerous. The large, wild forrest buffalo were generally peaceful grazers until disturbed by humans. Then, they could be very dangerous to a human on foot. The big cats were shy, and generally left man to his own pathways. Wild boar could be insufferable when they ravaged rice paddy and other crops.

Pejathaya relates his experience with wild boar.

WILD BOARS
BY S.M. PEJATHAYA

Greater menace came from the wild pigs. They dug up under the barbed wire and entered the fields. They loved to eat the delicious ear heads of paddy. The ear head portion of the paddy grain filled with milky liquid soon after the flowers pollinated. This damage was devastating.

A person by name Cheempa had volunteered bravely to keep watch over these wretched pigs. Keeping watch meant beating the kerosene drum and shouting all night. This job, he did gleefully every night. May be this old man was suffering from insomnia. He would collect double his day's wages for his services. He worked in the day shift too.

About a month back he had come to graze our scrub cattle during the day in the forest. He knew the clearings in which the grass grew well amidst the forest and he knew where the streams flowed to provide drinking water for our cattle.

After working for about a month on day wages, he volunteered to stay in the farm. Thus, he became the first resident laborer of our farm. He was a widower and liked the light work of cattle grazing. He stayed in the room adjacent to our cattle shed. The 'pie' dog liked him more and more as the days went by. It took shelter in his bed during the nights.

One day, many of the villagers of Shiroor came to my farm and requested me to organize a 'Haaka Shikar.' Bison and wild pigs were having a greater share of their crops in Shiroor, two miles to the west of my farm. They had gone to the forest officials to seek un-official permission to conduct a 'Haaka' to drive the bison and pigs away from our parts of the forest. They very well knew that it was easy to drive away the bison from our part of the forest, but the stubborn pigs would not migrate easily. A few of them have to be killed in the hunt. The forest department would not take official notice of killing of these menacing pigs. The villagers requested me to invite Ammanna Master.

Ammanna Master was no stranger to the forests of Shiroor. He would come with his friends to participate in semi-official hunts like this. The village folk knew that whenever Ammanna Master came for a hunt, he never returned without bagging a wild boar. A good-sized wild boar meant the villagers would get sufficient quantity of meat to every household.

As per the accepted rules of the 'Shikar,' each participating person would get his rightful share in the meat. The shooter shall get one hindquarter known as loin meat. The other hindquarter shall go to the organizer of the hunt. Here the villagers found an advantage. If I were the organizer, I being a vegetarian, my share would be distributed equally amongst the hunting team. The dogs that participate in the hunt shall get a share of the shikar meat too! As always, the shikar meat would be a welcome delicacy for the simple villagers. The daytime 'Haaka Shikar' was a well-organized sport in the villages of South 'Canara.'

I requested Ammanna Master to preside over as the chief 'shikari' of our hunt. He came with a few friends by a jeep up to the opposite bank of our farm. All of them were carrying licensed guns. The 'haaka' party of villagers assembled and I, as the organizer, had to offer 'tambool' to the participants. The 'tambool' consisted of a basket of 'betel' leaves, slaked lime, high quality Tellicherry chewing tobacco and 'areca' nuts were to be offered by me at the beginning of the hunt and at the end of the event. This was considered to be a great honor to the participants.

Ammanna Master put the gunmen at strategic points before the beat of each segment of the forest began. The 'haaka' begins with shouting and beating of drums and kerosene tins. Big stones would be hurled into deep thickets to scare the animals. Ammanna Master had warned every gunman not to shoot at the bison or any harmless animal like rabbit, sambar and deer. I was provided with a hefty muzzle loader in which I had to load the "special lashing load" for the bison. I had put one extra thimble full of gunpowder more over the usually allowed four, upon which I had rammed in *about one-and-a-half ounces of very dry green gram grains.*

Ammanna Master took his position at the best vantage point. I was asked to stand near him with my muzzleloader. He had instructed me to be all eyes and ears as the 'shikar' began. My mission was to watch for the bison leader, wait until he passed my hiding position. I had to release my green gram charged shot on his posterior so that he would receive a good lashing on his rump. In case the leader got angry and turned to attack me, Ammanna Master would come to my rescue. I was confident that Ammanna Master would protect me under any such circumstances.

The first to move out of the forest were nimble-footed deer and sambar. We would let them pass, without firing. Next would come the turn of the bison. They would come running in panic behind their leader. I had to do my job carefully.

When any promise came from Ammanna Master, it sure was a man's promise. He would protect me at any cost risking his own life. So, I did not have to worry about the safety of myself as I stood there in my shown position.

Ammanna Master stood by a great big anthill. I stood by his right side on the level ground behind a thicket. From the distance, we could hear shouting and beating as the 'haaka' beaters entered the jungle. It was by about 11 am.

There was a sound of dry leaves as a couple of sambar appeared before us and passed us from our right, followed by a small herd of deer. Ammanna Master, in his khaki dress, stood like a statue slowly chewing his paan. Then, we heard the drumming of the bison hooves and staccato sounds of the breaking saplings. He pointed his finger in the direction of sound and gestured me to get ready. I stood patiently readily poised. Within seconds the great big leader followed by the herd of seven came to my view. They were galloping in our direction. I could guess that the herd would appear in front of us and pass us at about twenty yards to the right like the sambar and the deer.

The herd appeared in front of us and took the same route as expected. That was to our right. The leader glared at us and veered to his left. As the leader exposed his flanks, I lifted the gun, aimed and followed the leader for a second and I emptied my muzzle loader at his rump, hoping that he would not turn back to attack me. He did receive a nice good lashing on his butt from my special charge.

The herd of bison accelerated their speed further after my gun fired and we heard the faster drumming of hooves and continuous sound of saplings being broken. We heard the distant splash as the group jumped into the river to swim across to the other side to enter another on the opposite bank. The 'haakadars' were spellbound for a few seconds as they heard the musket fire and the startled commotion of the fleeting bison. Soon after, the men resumed the 'haaka' with more enthusiasm.

The much-dreaded bison had gone across the river and it was the time to drive the pigs to the waiting gunners. Ammanna Master patted me on the shoulder and whispered, "Well done!" He ran back to resume his stand on the anthill, as his sharp ears had already picked up the approaching sound of the wild boars. I ran and stood behind him to give him a clear firing field. Within half a minute, a big herd of wild pigs, may be more than twenty in number, came rushing towards their escape route on to our right. For a split second Ammanna Master looked at the herd without moving. He was gazing at the herd to select his targets. As they were about to pass us, his gun went to his shoulder in a flash. There were two reports as the twin barrels went off one after another. The big herd vanished into the jungle. The herd had scattered a bit and assembled again as it hurried away.

Two large tusker boars had fallen one behind the other a few yards apart. They had fallen down the trail about ten yards to the right behind our hiding position. They were both motionless. The first one's head had been pierced by a rifle action special cartridge ball near the right ear. The second one had its snout almost blown off by the buckshot fired from the gun's left-hand choke barrel.

I had witnessed the finest gunmanship of Ammanna Master that day.

Unperturbed, he reloaded the gun and was ready for further game. He seemed oblivious to what he had just bagged. The 'haaka' was over within a few minutes as the 'haakaadaars' approached us. No one was interested in continuing the hunt as the bison were driven across the river and two big boars had fallen.

Our famous shikar meat dispenser, Badiya Poojary, appeared ready to distribute the meat according to the unwritten rules and regulations of the 'haaka'. As Badiya Poojary approached the carcasses, I retired to my hut.

I did not want to witness the butchering. My share of meat would go back to the common pool.

Later, that day I heard that each person got a sizable share of meat. Each dog that had participated in the hunt got its rightful share too! Cheempa collected our 'pie' dog's share and took it to his quarters to cook it with his own share. Both looked contented after the meal that night. He must have left the bones to his companion, the 'pie' dog. After this 'shikar,' we could harvest our first crop of paddy without any wild boar menace that year.

*   *   *

Wild boar could be very dangerous. They were powerful creatures, and sported nasty tusks that could disembowel another animal or a man with one sweep of its muscular neck. Because of their unpopular and feared status, the local leaders and police occasionally permitted hunting the wild boars. An organized hunt was called a '*shikar,*' a word taken from the Urdu or Persian language, meaning hunting as a sport.

Pejathaya tells a story about a '*shikari*' who nearly lost his life hunting for the boar.

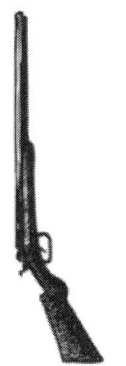

SHIKARI SHEENA SHETTY
BY S. M. PEJATHAYA

Shikari Sheena Shetty was not a professional hunter. His love for hunting had earned him that sobriquet in Shiroor. He was a small hotelier in suburban Bombay (now, Mumbai).

In the 1920s, like most of the youths from South Canara district, he went to Bombay to seek his fortune. He worked in various hotels to earn his living and studied in the evening schools. By 1945, he had earned enough money to start a small restaurant (referred to as hotel henceforth) in Bombay. The business thrived and he led a comfortable life. By 1950s, his sons grew up and ran his hotel very well. During the sixties, Sheena Shetty returned to his native village to see his widowed elder sister, the only surviving member of his family. She was leading a miserable life of a landless laborer with her two young sons. Like any 'Bunt' (a community) gentleman, Sheena Shetty gladly assumed the role of the guardian for the poor little boys. The Bunt community in South Canara followed matriarchal family system in which maternal uncles took charge of the nephews and nieces.

Being rich by then, Sheena Shetty purchased some land and entrusted its responsibilities to his nephews. Being a farmer by birth, Sheena Shetty loved this piece of land very much and took interest in its development. He raised an excellent coconut garden and lush fields of paddy, as he had enough money to invest from his hotel earnings. In the course of years, he did not

135

have to work very hard as his sons looked after his hotel well in Bombay, and his nephews looked after the coconut garden and the paddy fields at Shiroor.

Sheena Shetty was not a trigger-happy hunter. He loved to roam the forests around Shiroor carrying his excellent Webley & Scott 12 Gauge Double Barrel Shotgun. He always dressed himself in khaki shorts and a black 'banyan.' This helped him to camouflage in the forest. He was a good shooter but hated killing unnecessarily. He never killed any bird or animal which was not harmful to man and his agriculture. More than hunting, he enjoyed roaming and watching the flora and fauna of the jungles. He would volunteer to join the 'Haaka Shikars' held commonly to check the wild boar menace to the paddy fields. There were a few leopards, which occasionally preyed upon the cattle of the village. These were sought in the daytime 'shikars.'

The 'Patel' or 'Sarpanch'[16] of the village used to invite eminent persons like the District Collector or the Superintendent of Police as honored guests for the shikars. These hunts were organized with the cooperation of the government officials since hunting was part of measures to protect crops and village cattle.

Sometimes, the bison ransacked the paddy fields of the village. The villagers on such occasions gathered together to arrange a 'haaka,' only to shoo away the bison from the nearby forest. Nobody killed monkeys and bison in Shiroor as the village God was 'Hanuman', and the bison were considered akin to the 'holy cow'.

Sometimes, during the shikars the animals would be wounded and they could not be traced before the sun set. On such occasions the brave persons of the village would follow the blood spoor, trace and finish off the wounded animals with the help of their dogs. If the wounded animal was a tiger or a wild boar it would attack the shooter in a fit of rage. A little delay in firing the gun or a small miscalculation as to the position of the wounded animals in the thick bush would prove fatal to the shooters. There were many instances of the hunters getting fatally wounded during such adventures, and everyone feared the loss of human lives.

Sheena Shetty was always eager to finish off the wounded animals. He

---

[16] Village head man

had an upper hand in this sort of shooting, as he had a superior type of breach loading imported double barreled weapon, which an ordinary person in the village could not afford. Most of the villagers carried their old and rusty muzzle loading weapons to this sort of risky 'shikars.' If they ever had to take a second shot, they had to stop to reload the gun by putting a measured quantity of gunpowder first into the barrel of the gun and ram in some fine dry coir pith to hold that charge down securely. Then, select the correct sized lead pellets required for bringing down the game and put them on top of the rammed-in "charge," and make secure again with another twist of the coir pith. Finally, they had to put the 'percussion cap' on the nipple that lies beneath the hammer of the gun. It would take at least five minutes to reload their primitive weapons. The size of the lead pellet was to be determined carefully beforehand.

A shotgun 'shikari' had to carry a number of different cartridges loaded with different sized lead pellets. 'Cylindrical balls' or the 'spherical balls' were used to bring down the big game. The set of six small balls, called 'buckshot' was used to bring down medium sized game like deer and wild boar. Three different sizes of small pellets were used for small game and birds. The 'muzzle loaders' had no option of changing their pre-loaded charge or the size of pellets at will. With a double-barreled breech-loading gun, a hunter had the choice of loading the required type of cartridge recommended for the hunting game within a matter of few seconds and it could carry one big game cartridge in one barrel and a small game cartridge in the other. The hunter had the option of loading a set of the big or small game cartridges in both the barrels of his gun according to the need of the moment. Furthermore, after the first shot, he had the second shot ready in the other barrel. Two shots in succession could bring down almost any animal. With the help of his superior weapon Sheena Shetty was the best 'shikari' in Shiroor. His dogs were good in following the blood trail.

It was a Sunday in the middle of September; a 'haaka' was organized by the 'Patel'. A police inspector was invited as the honored guest. The 'Patel' had assembled the gunmen and the 'haakadars' in the village pasture next to the forest at 9 a.m. The inspector was welcomed, and through his hands the 'paan' tray ('tamboola') was passed on to the participants. The tray usually consists of fresh 'paan' leaves, betel nuts, which are finely scraped and cut into quarter segments, and strong smelling

Malabar chewing tobacco. Every one had to accept the 'paan' from the VIP. It was an honor. Those who were used to chewing tobacco could take a twist of tobacco too. The dogs would be waiting with the 'haakadars' who appear with drums and big kerosene tins for the beating of the forest.

It was cloudy. The haakadars could not raise much noise due to the drizzle and dogs were not in a good mood. Still, the beating on the different parts of the surrounding forest went on. Towards the noon, a herd of bison was alarmed and they bolted towards the river in panic. They ran to another forest across the river as usual and no one bothered to shoot at them. They splashed into the Swarna River and crossed over to another smaller forest across the river. The dogs barked in frenzy, and many a participant climbed the nearest thick tree to save himself from the stampede of the desperate bison.

Finally, the rain stopped by about 4 p.m. The warm evening rays of the sun shone over the green forests. The next beat was in the thickest bit of forest called "Malla Kadu" (Big Forest). When the beaters were almost half way through the forest, a herd of wild pigs emerged out of the forest to appear where the 'shikaris' with their guns lay in wait at the designated vantage points. The chief guest fired two shots from his double-barreled gun one after another. One of the bullets hit the biggest wild boar, which was in the lead. The bullet seemed to glance past its neck and the boar bolted to the thickets across the vantage point into a smaller scrub jungle next to the big forest. There was a small but visible trail of blood.

Unfortunately, it started to rain continuously again; and the beat was to be stopped. It was getting dark and the inspector sadly returned to his car parked on the main road across the river two miles away.

He left after requesting the villagers to trace the wounded animal next morning and finish it off. Otherwise, the wounded animal, which had entered the thickets near the village pasture, was sure to attack the villagers who passed by the next day.

Every one went home shivering in cold and very hungry, cursing the rain that played spoilsport and the dogs were amongst the most disappointed.

Next morning, Sheena Shetty appeared near the hiding place of the wounded animal with his dogs. His friend, Kariya, accompanied him with his long barreled muzzle loading gun, duly loaded with six smaller sized spherical balls of lead (i.e., buckshots) meant for the boar. The buckshots would be scattered within a small periphery when the gun fired. Loading this type of buckshots was the usual practice of wild boar hunters.

The dogs picked up the wounded animal's scent and led the two men to an almost impregnable bush of 'lantana.' The dogs stopped dead on their trail and refused to move forward into the bush. They were pointing nervously to the center of thick thorny bush. It was an impregnable bush of 'lantana' that spread about twenty feet across and about thirty feet long inside the scrub jungle.

Now, Sheena Shetty asked Kariya to go across to the other side of the bush and throw stones to the bush from the other side and asked him to holler as loudly as he could to scare the wounded wild boar out. Sheena Shetty stood readily poised to shoot the wounded animal, once it exited from the bush.

Kariya holding his own gun in his left hand, started to throw big stones into the thicket with his right. Nothing happened for sometime! The dogs kept pointing to the thicket with an angry growl. Kariya found a big piece of wood near him. He kept his gun down and flung this big piece of wood into the thicket by lifting it high.

What happened next was too difficult to comprehend! The wounded wild boar, instead of exiting from the other side, turned towards unarmed Kariya headlong. Kariya gave a cry of alarm and his legs froze in fear. Within a second the wild boar was on him trying to gore him with its tusks.

The wild boar attacked him head long. Fortunately, the animal's head entered between his legs and caught its head within the folds of Kariya's 'lungi.'[17] There was a great sound of grunting and snarling of the confused wild boar combined with the desperate shouts for life from Kariya.

Sheena Shetty came round the bush running to find Kariya and the wild boar wrestling with each other on the ground. The boar's head was entangled in Kariya's lungi and its head could not be seen properly!

To scare the boar from Kariya, Sheena Shetty fired a shot in the air. The report of the gun gave a shock to the enraged boar. It backed out. The lungi that covered its eyes got untangled. Then, the startled boar tried to attack the man who had fired the gun. Within a fraction of a second, before Sheena Shetty could point the gun to shoot it with the other barrel of his

---

[17] Colored loin cloth akin to sarong

gun, the boar had pounced on him. Sheena Shetty went down with boar to the ground.

In the mean time, Kariya who was almost unscathed, got up and grabbed his own gun. At this point blank range he thought that he could not miss the beast, and he fired.

There was the big roar of the gun as the boar gave a loud grunt. Its grunt was followed by a cry from Sheena Shetty. The boar had received the full blast of five pellets in its flanks, but one pellet had managed to enter the lower abdomen of Sheena Shetty. The wild boar collapsed to one side as Sheena Shetty sat clutching his bleeding lower abdomen.

He moved away from the carcass and called loud to Kariya who had gone into a trance in bewilderment. Kariya had almost thought that he had shot his friend Sheena Shetty along with the wounded wild boar!

Clutching at his bleeding wound Sheena Shetty told Kariya in a cool and collected voice not to worry. Taking off his black banyan he requested Kariya to tear the same into thin long strips. With these pieces, he pressed the bleeding wound and asked Kariya to tie up a bandage around his belly to staunch the excessive bleeding.

Hearing the gunshots the villagers rushed to the spot. The nearest hospital was six miles away and a makeshift stretcher of a blanket and two bamboo poles was fabricated in a hurry.

In the meantime, Sheena Shetty was carried to a nearby house, where he asked for a piece of white paper and a pen. He wrote with great difficulty that his own gun had gone off by accident and he had wounded himself. He declared that no one else was responsible for the injury. He signed the paper in ink and endorsed the document by affixing his thumb impression in his own blood. This document, he gave to the village 'Patel' who had appeared there on hearing the gunshots.

The village Patel accompanied Sheena Shetty who was being carried in the makeshift stretcher to Hiriyadka. Fortunately, the only Government Hospital doctor was in the Primary Health Center. He asked the 'Patel' to summon the police sub-inspector to register a case of gun wound before the treatment began.

Fortunately, the Patel found the sub-inspector and submitted Sheena Shetty's statement. There was no delay in the treatment of the wound. The doctor said, luckily, the wound was not very deep and he excised the bullet easily. Within four days Sheena Shetty could walk home.

It would have taken many hearings in the court of law to prove the innocence of Kariya, though the hunting of the wounded wild boar was not illegal as it posed a threat to the villagers' life. Sheena Shetty had already submitted the statement to the police and hence, there was no court case.

This incidence never deterred Sheena Shetty, who roamed the forests with his gun till he died a natural death recently. Soon after this incident Kariya sold his gun and surrendered his gun license. He never participated in another 'shikar.'

BAMBOO RAFTING

The standard eight foot Douglas-fir two-by-four is the American common denominator in residential construction. The first thing we do when starting a project is to load up on those eight foot boards that constitute framing for most of our homes. One of the differences between India and the U.S. that we noticed when first arriving in New Delhi was the ever-present use of bamboo for some of those traditional projects.

I gazed in wonder at the eight-story building along Mahatma Gandhi Marg in Delhi. I was interested not because the building was tall, but because the scaffolding that ran up the entire height of the eight floors was made of bamboo. A combination of straight and crooked lengths of bamboo of differing thickness were strung together with what looked like grass ropes. The scaffolding was interesting by itself, but I was speechless as I watched workers climb bamboo ladders with pans of concrete or mortar on their heads, and worm their way to the top floor, risking certain serious injury or death if they misstepped or the bamboo gave way.

The secret to the success of this bamboo scaffolding, I later realized, was that the people who walked on it many meters off the ground were the same workers who constructed it. The worker was not about to trust his or her life to a structure assembled by a stranger.

Once I moved to the rural villages of Raichur District, I saw that bamboo was the ever-present medium for home building, *machan* structures (*elevated field watch platforms*), walking bridges, and just about anything that needed strong bracing. Properties of bamboo, which is technically a grass, include a resistance to decay and insect penetration. It is more flexible than steel, and it gains strength under compression. Bamboo is one of the fastest growing plants on earth, and when harvested at the correct time, can maintain considerable strength for several years.

There were no eight-story buildings in Sindhanur at that time, however, there were plenty of construction projects that used bamboo for bracing, form building, scaffolding and more. Before I finally completed my work and left India, my wife and I lived for three months in a bamboo-framed grass hut.

Our bamboo house was on the outskirts of the agriculture training camp in Dhadesugur, situated on the banks of the Tungabhadra River. It had walls and a roof of woven *apu* (pronounced, aa-poo) grass mats attached to a bamboo structure, and a cow dung slurry floor. The house was so light that we were startled awake at daybreak one fine morning when a gigantic bullock used the corner of our house as a rubbing post. The entire house moved up and down with the animal's incessant scratching.

Pejathaya used bamboo for many projects when he developed his sister's land along the Western Coast of India. He told me an interesting story about finding bamboo for his projects. Here is his true story in his own words.

BAMBOO RAFTING
BY S.M. PEJATHAYA

Daadoo was my foreman at Shiroor farm. The 50-year-old was immensely fit for his age. He had dark brown skin, shining white teeth and sliver-streaked long hair tied into a knot at the back of his neck.

He knew all aspects of farm work. He wielded his large machete-like sickle with great dexterity. With his loud and clear voice he could command our laborers and extract work from them efficiently. He never used harsh words on anyone. Daadoo was also adventurous and ready to try a hand at seemingly impossible tasks.

Bamboo is necessary for many tasks. We did not have bamboo in the forest near our farm. I had planted some suckers along the boundaries, but they would take years to come up. The bamboo poles would cost us dearly if we purchased them at a bamboo dealer's yard at Hiriyadka. After buying, we had to haul the bamboo poles by cart or truck to the opposite bank of the river. We had to tie them up into a big bundle with strong ropes and drag them to our side of the river. This exercise would cost us a lot of money and time.

For the naturally available bamboo, we had to go nearly eight miles up the river to a bamboo forest that stretched up for miles and miles, along the Swarna River. It was quite an adventure to go to that place by rowing a boat up the river during the rainy season. We could bring bamboo down to our farm by making a bamboo raft and guiding it carefully down the flooding river. It was quite a dangerous mission too, as the river flowed rapidly over many submerged rocks. The river water, when at flood levels, would be very muddy and no one could see those submerged rocks. During the dry months the river level would go down so low and bringing a bamboo raft down the river was not possible. Nobody in recent years had ventured into this.

On a sunny day in July, there was respite from rain. Paddy transplantation was over and we had very little work to do in the farm. We had employed only a handful of workers to look after the daily maintenance of the farm.

Daadoo suggested that we could paddle up the river to collect bamboo and bring them down the river by making a nice bamboo raft! The bamboo raft would float down the river as the river was flowing in the optimum level.

He said that when he was a boy he went on such adventure with his father and the spirit of adventure was waning out in the present generation. "These days the villagers found it more convenient to buy bamboo from Hiriyadka", he added.

The word 'adventure' roused my curiosity. I asked about the risks involved. He said there were not many risks except staying in the bamboo forest for three to four days. We had to cook our food, fend for ourselves from snakes and animals of the forest. Finally, we would fabricate a strong bamboo raft and bring it down the river without crashing it on the rocks.

And, the requirements are:
- *a good dugout canoe which would carry five people*
- *ration and implements*
- *a team of five strong men to paddle up the river against flooding waters*
- *and willingness to camp and survive in the jungle for four to five days*
- *a pair of long-handled extra oars to steer the bamboo raft*
- *a gun and ammunition for self-defense*

I considered the list and nodded in approval. Our dugout canoe was good enough. There were three more strong men willing to join the expedition.

The ration consisted of lots of tea powder, 'jaggery,' matchboxes, five liters of kerosene oil, rice, wheat flour, grocery, vessels, mugs, plates, and vegetables like onions, carrots, potato, sweet potatoes and white sugar. The sweet potatoes would double up as snacks when roasted or they could be cooked like any vegetable.

We carried a few aluminum pots for cooking and enameled mugs. We carried roasted peanuts, pickles and good supply of dry 'rice rotis' called as 'Kappal Rotis' (dry rice cakes used by the ancient Indian sailors) that would stand for a week. These 'Kappal Rotis' were the favorite food of ancient seafaring people in the Konkan coast. These dry 'rotis' would stand the humid conditions of the sea for weeks. The extra oars were not a problem.

Daadoo had a licensed muzzleloader gun. I asked him to buy enough ammo. The gun was only for self-protection from wild animals. Hunting and cutting of timber were not allowed in the reserve forests of South Canara, but farmers were allowed to collect dry leaves, dried up twigs, green fodder and bamboo for self-use during those days.

I had to send Daadoo for provisions etc. to Hiriyadka. I packed a plastic bag with two extra pairs of clothing, a blanket, a rug, a flashlight, a pocketknife and my farm's first aid kit.

I could not carry any sophisticated food like biscuits (cookies), dry fruits or chocolates as my fellow adventurers did not give them any food value! They would laugh at such food and call them kid stuff. For them, even the bread that we found in the only bakery at Hiriyadka was a 'diet food' meant only for the patients suffering from fever! I didn't want to become their laughing stock and hence didn't pack any such stuff.

We decided to start early on the next day. The next morning the five-member team started up the river. Surprisingly, there was no personal luggage with my teammates! They had an extra loincloth tied over their heads, as turban. They had put on two shirts one over the other and each carried a coarse hand-woven blanket. All of them together would share the contents of a small waterproof plastic bag that contained a few packets of 'beedis' (local small cigars), matchboxes, small bundles of 'betel leaves,' areca nuts, slaked lime and some chewing tobacco.

The boat was full with ration and implements comprising a crowbar, a pickaxe, a spade, an axe and six heavy scythes especially designed to cut bamboo. *All items were covered with tarpaulin to protect them from rain.*

As we rowed up the river, I was disappointed, as I didn't find any rope on board. When asked, Daadoo said, we didn't need any, as we would get nice creepers in the forest. They are stronger than any rope and would never slip when tied even in wet condition.

I sat at the tiller end of the boat and used a steering oar to guide the dugout canoe up the river while the four of my companions rowed tirelessly against the current. I had learned to steer a boat from my Indian Navy's boating and sailing instructors during my NCC Naval Wing days in the college. I could expertly avoid the obstacles as we rowed up the river.

The upward journey was slow, as we had to paddle against the flow in the fast flowing river. We took nearly eight hours to go up to the bamboo grove. The thick forest suddenly ended to make room to an immense bamboo forest. We paddled until we found a rivulet joining the river.

We paddled up into the rivulet to cover about two hundred yards into the forest, where we found a big rock that stood up in the forest. Daadoo ran ahead asking us to stay in the boat. He returned with a broad smile on his face. He told us that he found a suitable place for us to camp. The nearly fifty-foot tall rock had a projected top to the West and it would provide us shelter from the rain. Under this great natural canopy Daadoo had found a fairly flat surface, which was relatively dry and convenient for us to camp.

We tied the boat in the sand-bottomed shallow pool. First, Daadoo went into the bamboo clumps to find poles of bamboo that would support a 'pendal.' Daadoo and his team dug holes in the ground and erected the bamboo poles to support as pillars. They tied the top end of the bamboo pillars with bamboo rafters securely with the readily available creepers. The creepers that grew along the side of the river were indeed very strong. After fashioning a framework, we spread our tarpaulin on the frame. This was to be our home for the next few days!

We lit a kerosene stove to make some black tea sweetened with sugar. We had to make do with black tea because there was a severe shortage of milk powder in the market those days. After tea, we scattered to collect dry twigs and firewood in the scrub jungle that grew along the river. We collected enough of dry twigs, driftwood as well as firewood to suffice for four days. It was not an uphill task, as it had not rained at all for the last two days.

By evening, we cooked our food over wood fire and sat by the warmth of the fire. As we ate our dinner, it started to rain! The rain did not bother us much, though the tarpaulin danced over our heads as the heavy winds blew. However, we were cozy under the canopy of the canvas and the rock ledge above. By morning, the rain had stopped. After breakfast of 'Kappal Roti' and dry chutney, we went out to gather the creepers, which grew along the river. By about ten, we gathered enough and had another round of black tea before heading to the bamboo clumps again.

I was not at all proficient in wielding a heavy scythe, and I was yet to learn the skill of cutting bamboo at the nodes. As I attacked a bamboo clump, most of the time, I was missing the nodes! This splintered the bamboo and they became more difficult to cut. Due to my poor skill, the bamboo that I selected and cut would not come out of the clump easily, even if I pulled with all my strength. During this effort the heavy thorns of bamboo hurt my body. I could cut one bamboo while others could cut a dozen. My teammates seemed to cut them as easily as they would cut the sugarcane stems. They could select and cut a bamboo; extract them out of a clump easily without any entanglement problem. They would slash the leafy branches, cut the tip portion to get straight poles of uniform length and they would stack them neatly in a pile with ease! They looked very comfortable doing this job.

I was bleeding at several places as the thorns showed no mercy on me. It became evident to me that even if I toiled for a full day I could not do what they could do in just half an hour.

Daadoo came to my rescue and flashed his teeth, "Anna! Please take the muzzle loading gun and keep watch as we cut the bamboo. It is an important job to stand on guard." The word 'Anna' is the polite form for 'brother.'

I knew inwardly that it was unnecessary because we had slept the previous night there without anyone keeping watch. Daadoo assigned me the watch and ward duty to save me from the ordeal. I had to accept the idea gratefully. Otherwise, I would have looked like a pincushion within hours! I started my gallant duty of sitting on a small stone and watching them at work. They worked nonstop until lunchtime. We had some rice, lentils and vegetable cooked with spices. They took half an hour's rest after lunch and resumed the work until dark. We had 'khichdi'[18] for dinner. We slept well as Daadoo did not insist on my guard duty during the night.

Next morning, it started to rain more heavily, but our team of four bamboo cutters worked nonstop in the pouring rain itself. My next day's duty was just to mind the fire under the teapot and the cooking pot. From time to time, one of the four would come to warm himself and look after the pot in which our lunch was being cooked. All the four of them had excellent idea about camp cooking. I had no experience whatsoever in cooking over a wood fire, nor had I cooked for anyone else but myself until then. With me, cooking food was only a survival trick. The food cooked by me always tasted awful and very bland. Had I tried my cooking skills in the bamboo forest, my faithful companions would have deserted me then and there! I stayed clear of the cooking pot and enjoyed the camp meals happily! All the four of them seemed to be good cooks. The food was very tasty but they used a little more of red chilies which forced me to drink more water during my meals. Otherwise, in the cold jungle atmosphere, the food seemed just right spicy.

The rain continued to lash incessantly for the next two days. Our work of cutting bamboo too continued without break. They folded 'Kambli'[19] along the breadth once and once more along length to make a 'Koppe' or rain cover. They would seal the top with a steel wire. They wore the sealed end on their head. The 'Kambli' covered them and kept them warm on all three sides allowing them to work with both hands free. The blankets resisted the rain to some extent and kept their heads and backs relatively warm and dry. Their hands and legs were soaking in the rain. Somehow they felt that they were protected by this blanket. Every evening they warmed their blankets near the campfire to dry them. After they dried, they rolled the same blankets around them to sleep soundly until morning.

Each member, while feeling too wet and cold, came into the tarpaulin-covered camp to sit by the fire to partake a hot cup of black tea. Then, he would eat 'paan' with a twist of tobacco and supervise the cooking pot before walking into the pouring rain to resume bamboo cutting. As a mark of

---

[18] Rice and lentils boiled with sautéed vegetables

[19] Rough hewn woolen blanket

respect they never smoked in front of me, but our stock of 'beedis' and matches depleted fast, as these people toiled in pouring rain. The work progressed despite heavy rain.

The water in the river rose to high flood level. Daadoo was very happy at this! For, he said the process of drifting the raft down the river would be easy, as we would face less and less hindrance from the submerged rocks.

On the third day my team finished cutting the bamboo poles. Next morning Daadoo started building the raft and others helped him. He first made a layer of bamboo of forty-foot length and twenty-foot wide and tied them together with close knots, using strong creepers. He slid the frame into the shallow water of the inlet. He made fast eight tiers of such bamboo layers on the frame and secured them tightly to make an oblong raft. He built a center platform of one foot height in the middle of the raft leaving six feet border space on all sides. He built a railing around this one-foot high platform with strong bamboo poles. He told us that this railing served as back support for the 'guiding pole' pushers. They needed a back support as they pushed at the rocks, fallen trees, sand bars or the banks of the river itself. As they pushed their guiding poles, the whole raft should move in the opposite direction. When they pushed with the support at their backs the heavy raft would respond to their push. This needed great strength and our companions looked quite capable.

At the stern, he made two bamboo davits for the steering oars. These davits helped to hold our steering oars in place and we can use them as tillers by keeping at the required angle.

Daadoo selected four strong forty-foot bamboo poles to serve as guiding poles and scraped them nicely at every node to make them smooth, so that they did not hurt the hands of the handlers.

Three persons would handle three handling poles, while the fourth pole was carried on board as a spare. In case one of the handlers was thrown overboard, chances were we would lose his pole in the river water. At such an emergency, the fourth one would come for use.

Daadoo would take one of the steering oars while he entrusted the other one to me. He knew that I could handle the steering oar as I had steered the canoe up the river. Daadoo told me that he would handle most of the steering work with his oar and I was to immerse and man the second steering oar only when the raft needed extra steering power. Only during *such emergencies I had to insert my extra steering oar to the davit and dip the blade into the water to follow the same angle as that of Daadoo. This would enforce a steady steering power.*

That night we sat around the fire and took instructions from Daadoo about the next morning's rafting. None but Daadoo had any experience in this adventure. Yet our captain Daadoo assured us that it was going to be great fun. At the same time, he cautioned that we would be seeing death face to face in swirling muddy waters too!

He asked us not to panic under any circumstance. Even if one gets thrown overboard, one should not panic. He asked us to swim and just to keep our body afloat that's all! The others would save him by extending a guiding pole.

All that night, I dreamt repeatedly of being thrown into muddy waters and had a very fitful sleep. Next morning we decamped.

Daadoo took meticulous care to leave the place as clean as we had found it. We dismantled our temporary home of three nights, we extinguished our campfire, buried all the cinders and ashes making a deep pit. Daadoo told us that we had no authority, whatsoever, to spoil the beauty of such a wonderful camping ground. I appreciated his aesthetic sense. His love for nature was inherent.

Our raft was ready to take off down the river. Daadoo tied our dugout canoe with a short rope to trail behind the raft. He broke a coconut at the front portion of the raft, lit incense sticks and we all prayed for a safe journey down the river.

We loaded all our implements and belongings into the center platform portion of the raft, which was covered by the railing on all sides. We draped the tarpaulin over all our belongings and secured it. With a silent prayer, we set ourselves afloat!

It was fun floating down the river, at good speed, until we came to a portion where the water frothed upon hidden rocks! Daadoo guided the raft expertly over this hurdle but we were sweating with the fear of hitting the submerged rocks. Next, we were to approach the place where the river took a small bend. He asked the three men handling the guiding poles to stand at the ready position, one in the front portion and the other two on flanks. He asked us not to panic. They were supposed to use the poles only if our raft carried over to the bank or an un-submerged stone. Daadoo asked me to insert my steering oar into the bamboo davit and be ready. He asked me to hold on to the course that he was steering by keeping the same angle with my steering oar. I held at the steering oar as tightly as I could, next moment we were in the whirlpool! I braced myself to hold on to the tiller oar with all my strength. As we passed over the whirlpool, we saw that the raft was being sucked into the water with great force! The water level came up by about six inches by the great suction of the whirlpool. I could feel the great force of suction and the feeling was more pronounced in my stomach! I felt as if the innards of my abdomen were being pulled towards the strange depths as the lumbering raft slowed down to almost a standstill! The raft started to rotate in an anti-clockwise direction. Daadoo's dark brown face turned pale with fear. A few turns in the whirlpool would make our low buoyancy raft sink to the whirlpool's depths! The other three onboard were praying loudly! I was looking at Daadoo's tiller oar, as I had to keep the same angle. Daadoo yanked the tiller, the prow of the raft turned in the opposite direction to stop the spin, and I too simultaneously simulated this maneuver. The spinning obviously stopped. Our raft seemed to halt at the spot as it struggled to stay afloat!

Then, like a shot from a catapult, our raft was flung out of the whirlpool as it lumbered down towards the left bank of the river being pushed by the mysterious current of the swirling whirlpool with great speed! Within seconds, we were nearing the left bank to crash on the rocks! All the three men extended their poles towards the rock bank and as soon as the poles made contact; they pushed hard with all their strength. The raft responded slowly as we headed down the river. At the same time one of the pushers had lost his balance and he was thrown into the river!

Daadoo shouted to me to steer the raft, and he pulled up his steering oar in a flash. Before the man passed the aft side of the raft, he ran to the side of the raft. He extended the long handle of the steering oar to the man overboard. The man by instinct caught the handle, and climbed effortlessly upon the raft. Everyone was grinning happily!

The raft came down the rest of the way in good speed along the current without much trouble. All along, Daadoo and I handled the tiller oars. The pushers had to use the poles once in a while only. After what we had gone through at the whirlpool bend, the rest of the rafting seemed like a picnic!

Finally, we arrived at the farm and we tied the raft to the trunk of a big tree after beaching it properly. We untied the canoe from the raft and tied it in its usual place. We had enough and more of bamboo poles to suffice us for the next two years! I asked each of the crew to take home as much bamboo poles as they wanted.

The rafting down the river in a bamboo raft was a great experience. Our escape from the whirlpool was really miraculous!

If you ask me, "Would you repeat the adventure again?"

"No!"

Because, I gather that Daadoo has retired long back from my sister's farm. Though he is still alive today, he may not have that great strength now to make it again with me.

Without Daadoo at helm of a skillfully fabricated bamboo raft, I would not think of rafting down the tricky waters of the flooding Swarna River again."

KNOWN DELINQUENT (KD)

Jangling bells and rhythmic *tabla* drums disturbed my thoughts as I sat in my room, bent over an old issue of *The Farm Journal*. My concentration vanished as I sensed a commotion not far from my apartment. Pushing myself upright I stepped outside my door and looked past the mud wall that surrounded the clay tennis court below my building.

Dust stirred in the warm evening air. Through the weak light clouded with dust I could make out a makeshift tent and the heads of many people milling about. At that moment, my neighbor, Mr. Bhat, also emerged from his front door.

"Mr. Bhat, good evening. What is going on over there?" I asked.

"Hello, Mr. Ken," he replied. "They are having a *Bharatnatyam*," he said. He explained that it is common for a troupe of dancers, often from the southern state of Tamil Nadu, to move from town to town performing traditional dances. He added that the *Bharatnatyam* dance was considered the dance of fire. It is the mystic manifestation of the metaphysical element of fire in the human body.

"You should go over, and enjoy the dance. They do not charge admission, but the dancers often like to ask for a donation during or after the performance. You will enjoy seeing the beautiful women and their colorful costumes," he said.

I told him that I was surprised to learn that women danced in public, as I had been told that it is considered improper for women to be seen this way. He commented that the *Bharatnatyam* dance is based on religious beliefs. It comes from the ancient temple dances and is popular throughout India. Not all *Bharatnatyam* dancers are women. As in many of the Indian plays, men sometimes play convincing roles as women.

Mr. Bhat invited me to go down to the open area just beyond the tennis court walls and join him for a couple of minutes to watch and listen. I followed his lead as he moved into the crowd and stood at a point where we could clearly see the stage. Local Sindhanur townspeople left their shops to stand near the stage floor. Uplifted faces beamed smiles of satisfaction as they inhaled the fascination of the performing artists.

A *tabla* beat out a loud, steady rhythm and an unseen hand shook an instrument similar to a tambourine. Dancers in spectacular costume energetically performed various poses and danced across the stage highlighting their specially made and very colorful costumes.

The dancers wore white leggings ornately hemmed with silver and gold thread. Their blue skirts displayed intricate, colorful patterns. The ankles of the barefoot performers were hemmed with small bells that jingled with the rhythm of their movements and the beat of the *tabla*. Their hands and feet bore red designs in *henna*[20], matching the color of the kumkum on their foreheads.

As the dancers completed their second dance, Mr. Bhat and I deposited respectful donations for the performers and found our way back through the crowd. As we walked across the back area of the tennis court I asked Mr. Bhat, "Were the dancers men or women?"

"Oh," he said, "these dancers were definitely women. But," he added after a moment of consideration, "sometimes it is very difficult to tell. Usually, in *Bharatnatyam*, the dancers are women. It is in the cultural plays where the women characters are normally played by men."

"What kind of man would spend his career posing as a woman." I asked him. It seemed to me that it was a very unusual thing for a man to do. "Are these male performers homosexuals?"

---

[20] Henna refers to the intricate tattooing from the dye made from the henna plant

Mr. Bhat wasn't sure what I meant, but indicated that these male actors devoted their lives to the art, and they saw their art form as very normal. They do not carry a stigma if they are good performers, and can, indeed, become famous. He admitted that he believed that once a man became a female impersonator he usually had difficulty moving into other careers.

Several days later I related this experience to Pejathaya. He agreed with everything Mr. Bhat had told me the evening of the *Bharatnatyam*. He added that these dances were not as common on the Western Coast where he came from, but he was familiar with both the *Bharatnatyam* dances and the cultural plays. He also said that, in cultural plays, it is considered proper for the women character to be portrayed by males.

This exchange ignited additional conversation about the comparison of our two cultures. A man's identity is unique, and follows him everywhere. Whatever action we take today will identify who we are forever, for better or for worse.

This prompted Pejathaya to tell me a story about an unusual man who worked with him while he developed his sister's coconut and rice farm. This man was just and kind, but a series of actions in his youth became a stigma that haunted him throughout the rest of his life. Circumstance prevailed, and an unfortunate juncture in his road determined whether this man would be destined to be a hero or a goat, dependent on timing.

It is indeed sad that a man can carry a stigma for his entire life because of one mistake made in the heat of the moment. Was it an act of patriotic valor, or was it a criminal act? The answer depended on the government in power at the time. Even so, one mistake does not always mean that the man is a bad person.

K. D. THIMMA
BY S.M. PEJATHAYA

K. D. Thimma is no more. But his memories are green in my mind. He lived in Shiroor. He was about sixty years old when I first met him. But, he was the strongest and the best built man in the village. He was dark, but his skin had a healthy glow. He looked like a Greek statue chiseled in black granite stone. He was a giant of a man and stood more than six feet tall. He was a good worker and very straightforward man. He was the stalwart of our village. I use all these adjectives, because, he was like a powerhouse of physical strength. He was my close acquaintance and I am proud to say that he worked for me. The villagers feared him because of his sheer size and reputation. He was short-tempered and never tolerated any nonsense.

K.D. stood for 'Known Delinquent.' It always stood with his name to remind others of the dark side of his unfortunate personal history. He was an ex-convict as per the police records. He went to Hiriyadka Police Station five miles away every week to put his thumb impression in the police register to confirm his presence in the village. The police demanded that he should do this as per the standing orders of the District Magistrate of South Canara passed during the pre-independence days.

In his youth, Thimma was very aggressive. He had frequently got into fights with the fellow villagers. As the result he was remanded by the Hiriyadka Police many times. Thimma was never known to tell a lie, *thieve, or commit adultery. He feared none. This fearlessness became a real setback for Thimma.*

During the freedom movement, Thimma, a boy then, had joined the extremist group of the Congress party. He had taken part in uprooting telegraph poles and attacking the machinery of the British Government with the other extremists of the Udupi 'taluk'. Subsequently, he was caught and interrogated. He confessed to his deeds but didn't divulge the names of his friends, supporters or associates. He was punished and jailed several times for his confessed crimes against the British Government.

Unfortunately, Thimma was not treated like a political prisoner, but was branded K.D. by the British judicial authorities because of his previous records at the police station. With this label, he was treated like an outcast in the village and he was held responsible for any untoward incident in and around Shiroor. He would be dragged first into the police custody for interrogation. Nobody in the village supported him or arranged his bail, though everybody knew that he was not guilty. This made him even more angry and morose. When the police used the third degree methods on him, young Thimma would retaliate, only to receive more of beatings and punishments; he had lost all his teeth due to the merciless blows. It was sad to look at such a healthy figure without teeth.

When our country became independent, no one recognized Thimma as a freedom fighter as his name was included in the K.D. list. Being a Known Delinquent, he had no social standing.

Had he been a little craftier to give a political color to his unintentional crimes against the British Government and to his small term imprisonments, he could have thrived by posing himself as a freedom fighter and become a local politician. Unfortunately, Thimma was not cut to project himself as such a person; he had neither the craftiness nor the aptitude to become a small time politician. He never looked forward to any sort of reward for his endeavors during the country's freedom struggle. This proved to be a very unfortunate trait that marred his post-independence career

He farmed one acre of land as a tenant farmer. Since the income was not adequate, he had to work as a farm laborer. He lived with his wife in a small thatched hut. They had no children.

He did not allow his wife to work in other people's fields. He looked after her well. Thimma's wife was a good-natured woman and the villagers respected her. His ways had become rough and tough over the course of time as he was always treated like an outcast and a criminal. He never cared for the elders or the 'so-called bigwigs' of his village. Though the villagers knew very well that he was not a thief, no one hired him permanently. Everyone hired Thimma for tasks, which needed great strength like moving timber and heavy stones or loading grains to convoys of bullock carts.

When he worked, he worked very hard and turned out the work of four normal persons. Yet he would accept only one man's pay as per his own policy. At times, he would be paid a little extra by way of tips.

Thimma was always very soft to the children and he respected women. The elders in our area told tales of when the great floods came in 1946, Thimma had swum daring the floodwaters and rescued many a family.

When children asked him for fruits, he would climb tallest trees of mango and jack fruits which no one else in the village would dare to climb. I always felt that Thimma never deserved to be treated with such unfortunate disdain in his own village. However, the K.D. tag projected him as a bad man and made him suffer the ignominy of the past. Just because of the fact that he had to go to the police station every week, he was always called and branded K. D. Thimma.

Thimma stayed aloof due to the humiliation. He and his wife never attended the village festivals or any other social functions like marriage ceremonies etc. Nor did they attend the temple feasts.

He never carried vengeance on anyone and the villagers individually harbored no ill feelings towards him. But, when the mischief mongers provoked him, he would simply bundle them up and throw them into some puddle, or lift them, shake their wits out of them until they pleaded for his mercy.

While developing the coconut farm for my sister I had to depend on the laborers from Shiroor. First task was to construct a road to Shiroor. During the first week of the road works, we found a big boulder right in the middle of the path. Six of us struggled hard to move a big boulder. We tried hard using the biggest crowbars as the levers to move this big stone for nearly an hour, but in vain. As we were struggling, we heard a woman's voice from behind, "What are you trying to do there? Why are you playing with those crowbars? It takes only one man and one crowbar to move that big boulder."

We turned back in astonishment. She was K.D. Thimma's wife, my helpers told me. I had not seen the couple until then though I had heard a lot of K. D. Thimma's stories. I was annoyed, but did not display my anger: "Please, call that strong man who could move this stone, if he is nearby."

She told us to relax in the shade for a few minutes and she went off to call her husband. We waited under the shade of a tree. Soon, she returned with a giant- sized person.

He greeted me by folding his hands in namaste and I reciprocated. He gazed at the boulder and took hold of one of our biggest crowbars. He judged the weight of the stone and pierced ground deep under the stone with one stroke of the crowbar. Under the crowbar, he placed a small stone to lever the crowbar and he yanked the crowbar with his great strength. The stone rolled by a foot! Within two minutes, the stone was rolled away from our path.

I applauded and thanked Thimma for his great feat of strength. He did not even smile. He gestured namaste with his folded hands and left without a word. His wife followed him.

I was impressed. I really needed such a powerful man to help me in my farm. I sent word to Thimma through my foreman Daadoo and offered him permanent job as a laborer in our farm.

Thimma agreed to come and appeared for work in time the very next morning. Thus, Thimma joined the workforce of our farm. He worked tirelessly and turned out more than two men's work easily. I told him in the evening that I would hire him for a higher wage to compensate his work. But, he refused the higher wages politely saying that he is as good as any other laborer, and the God has given him a bigger body and little more strength for which he cannot seek more wages.

He told me that he would be very happy if I hired him as a permanent laborer henceforth. That was all he wanted. I appreciated his simplicity. After Thimma joined our team, our work progressed well. He worked with great zeal and encouraged others also to work hard.

He was very punctual, obedient and disciplined. He was a man of few words. Thimma, in course of time, became a bit more friendly with me and started to converse with me. Whenever I asked him about his past tussle

161

with the law, he would dismiss it saying that was all over and it was no use talking about all that was past.

The years went by and I drifted away from Shiroor. Whenever I went to Udupi, I would always enquire about K. D. Thimma with my brother-in-law and sister.

Of late, I heard that he died of cardiac arrest in his sleep. He had attended the farm work until the previous day!

Today, I remember our stalwart Thimma as the gentle giant of our farm. I only wish that he didn't have that prefix – K.D to his name.

ORGANIC FARMING,
AND LUNCH WITH A PRIEST

A visitor to one of India's major cities might get an impression of just one side of India's culture and lifestyle. That perception may be totally different from what that person would experience in a rural village. That is not to say that the traditions of religion, culture and lifestyle do not exist in the city. It only means that the big city shows first its hustle and bustle before the visitor meets the inhabitants.

Modern airports and transport vehicles bring the foreign visitor through a succession of experiences that transition from the sights and sounds of the airport to related stimuli in the destination. Speeding cars and rickshaws dash around pedestrians and bicyclists to flood the newcomer with a new range of fears, anxieties and excitement. The glitter of neon, the steel and glass high rises, and the store displays leave one's thoughts far from the humanistic side of India.

Step into the rural Indian village, however, and hear the silence. Feel the creaking wheels of the bullock cart. See the barefoot children running carefree across the dusty dirt floor of the village central plaza, which is anchored by the giant neem tree. Here you can observe the reverence for life in its simplest form.

When you meet the villagers you begin to understand their simplicity, and their tendency to be very hospitable as they welcome you into their homes. There is a protocol to follow, but you may not know it until you observe. For example, it is expected that your introduction be made through the village leader. Usually, the *Panchayat* Chairman will be an elder male, and he will ask who you are and where you come from. You are expected to accept his invitation to join him in drinking a cup of tea or water.

The Chairman will likely introduce you to other prominent villagers, some may be the more progressive farmers or merchants. You will soon learn to avoid direct eye contact with the women of the village, and to refrain from commenting about any woman or post-pubescent girl, as that is considered improper. The villagers allow a certain amount of latitude for first time visitors, as long as they are respectful.

You may see a member of a religious sect in long saffron robes or you may see a Brahmin priest wearing a white *dhoti* and no shirt. There are many religious sects in India, and most villagers treat all of them with appropriate respect. Most visitors never see the differences between the religious orders, and even fewer grasp the significance of the various religious beliefs. Pejathaya tells a wonderful story of a Brahmin priest who lived not far from his coastal coconut farm.

UPADHYAYA
BY S.M. PEJATHAYA

Upadhyaya was his surname. Nobody called him by his first name. He lived in a place called Pundit House. He was an orthodox 'Brahmin' of eighty plus when I first met him. He followed the Hindu way of life and certainly believed in what he followed. His lifestyle was similar to that of his ancestors. He was a 'Sanskrit' scholar. He was taught by his father who ran a 'Gurukula' (a residential school of ancient tradition) in their big house. They were landed people and they cultivated acres of paddy, areca nut, coconuts and cashew. During his ancestral times, a good number of boys studied Sanskrit and the Vedas there and hence the surname — 'Upadhyaya' (teacher).

I met him during the end of 1967 when he had come to visit my farm at Shiroor. It was an honor for me. Probably, it was in June, the tall and straight old man with a white cloth covered umbrella hailed me as I was engrossed in puddling—final round of irrigated plowing and leveling a muddy paddy field with our power tiller.

When I saw the white cloth covered umbrella, I guessed some 'Brahmin' scholar had come to see our farm. Carrying a black umbrella was supposed to be inauspicious for a learned Brahmin. Probably, it was akin to carrying a black flag!

I stopped to cut off the engine, and sloshed towards him in the muddy field. I climbed over the bund of the field and exclaimed "Namaste" as I neared him.

The fair, lean and tall elderly gentleman, with glittering gold studs on both the ears, was wearing a snow-white dhoti and a green filigree embroidered Kashmiri shawl. He wore no shirt. Reciprocating my greeting, he introduced himself as 'Pundit House Upadhyaya.'

At once, I uttered my 'Gotra and Pravara' with my name and touched his feet in respect. This was the custom with my family to greet the wise and educated Brahmin elders. Sri Upadhyaya blessed me: "Ayushman Bhava" (May you be blessed with long and healthy life!).

I invited him into my humble two-roomed house. He wanted me to show my power tiller machine first, and explain its various parts, which I gladly did in a few minutes. He watched the demonstration of my machine in the field with a great interest. He asked a few questions, got his doubts cleared and said, "Shall we go to your house?"

Looking at the tall sinewy man, I remembered my late grandfather's generation. He displayed the same manners and cultured qualities befitting a landlord. At the entrance of my cottage, I offered him water to wash his hands and feet, before I did. He accepted the water and washed his feet, hands and face thoroughly. He did not accept the towel that I proffered, but used his own. I offered him the only chair that I had in the house and requested him to sit. He gestured me to sit on my cot and then only he took his seat.

He sat straight in the chair, and in his loud and clear voice he asked many questions about the power tiller, its price, fuel consumption, efficiency and its maintenance.

He questioned me about the use of chemical fertilizers and pesticides so common with the new generation of farmers. I told him the fact that I used chemical fertilizers, pesticides and the fungicides. He said he was an organic farmer and never used fertilizers or pesticides. Then, he asked, from where I had brought my seedlings of coconuts. He had already noticed that they were of a different variety. I said, most of the seedlings were from a farm at Sullia, and they are called locally, 'Pachche Kundri'. He spent nearly an hour with me discussing many aspects of farming. He was well informed in chemical farming too. When he was about to leave, he cordially invited me to his place, about four miles away at the western end of Shiroor if I walked on a trail along the river.

After I finished transplanting all our paddy fields that season, I determined to visit the 'Pundit' House. I thought of wearing a white 'dhoti' *around my waist. I was not used to wearing 'dhoti,' if I ever wore one, I could not wear my ankle boot. Wearing a 'dhoti' over an ankle boot was not an imaginable combination. Without the pair of ankle boots, I would not dare to walk in the slippery forest path filled with mud, stones and thorns, by the river. Even if I did wear a 'dhoti,' it was raining that day; the color of my white dhoti would certainly change upon reaching Pundit House. The orthodox Brahmins always would offer a 'dhoti' and a towel to their guests before they are sent to wash their face, hands and feet, as a custom. Still, I decided to carry my own 'dhoti,' a towel and shawl in a small shoulder bag to suit the orthodox surroundings of the Pundit House.*

Upadhyaya was a very gracious host. He introduced me to his wife, who prepared traditional food to honor my visit. After partaking of lunch and a relaxed talk, he suggested we go round his farm.

I liked the lush green of his paddy fields and the robust plantation of coconut and areca. I asked how he developed such a fine organic farm. He told me that it was the result of years of hard work and planning. He narrated his personal history and went on to describe how he became an organic farmer.

"In the beginning of the nineteenth century, farmers concentrated only on production of rice in South Canara. A few people had taken to the serious farming of coconuts and areca nut. I joined this league of farmers with forethought. The transport facility had improved and the commodities started to move inside the country, and there was a greater scope for the export of our agricultural commodities. I developed the first systematically placed and properly irrigated plantations of coconut and 'areca' nut. I tried to grow some pepper as a side crop. I took interest in beekeeping too. I looked after the dairy animals well, though there was not much demand for milk in this forest area. Once a week we could send out accumulated stock of butter or 'ghee' to Udupi market. The excess of coconuts were turned into 'copra' by drying coconut kernels under the sun. Someone had started an oil mill at the nearby town of Karkala, and they could purchase all our 'copra.' Small quantities of 'copra' could be squeezed locally with the help of the mangle operated by bullocks, and coconut 'poonac' (residue after extracting the oil) was an excellent cattle feed. I planted many types of fruit trees, as I loved horticulture. These fruits are being used up by my household and my neighbors. As you see we have no market nearby and we grow all our

vegetables and fruits. In the border of our property, I planted large tree varieties like mango, 'jambul,' jack, wild jack, teak, soap nut, 'kapok,' 'tamarind' and 'champak.'

"In the adjacent scrub jungle that belongs to us, I planted 'Karmar' saplings. Karmar is a variety of fast growing fuel firewood that can be used immediately after harvesting. These woodcuttings need not be dried before use. They have a high content of volatile oils and they can be used immediately after cutting. This firewood can be profitably harvested once in every eight years. I kept on planting a plot of 'karmar' every year until we had eight plots. As you see now, I have no shortage of fuel firewood. I always keep enough for the household use, and sell the rest every summer. These days, even the Malnad farmers are facing firewood shortage. The forest department restricts cutting trees for firewood. Thank God for this forethought or else the "Brahmin Lady" of the Pundit House would have turned me into a firewood 'poacher'!

"Our property lies in a valley and it is surrounded by forestland. We can collect fallen dry leaves for manure. Our permanent laborers, who stay in the small cottages that I have built along the boundaries of our property, can collect the fallen twigs for their daily use. The stream that flows all along the deepest part of our valley is a perennial one. In the summer it would slim down to a small trickle. So, I dug up five big tanks on its path to hold great quantities of water. Each tank is hundred feet by fifty feet and all are about ten feet deep. During the rainy season all of them overflow. During drought they act as reservoirs. I have terraced the plantation plots on either side of the main stream, so that all the rainwater does not run down the slope. The rainwater slowly settles to sink into the ground to improve the efficiency of the stream. These tanks collect silt every year during the rains. The surface erosion of the soil in our valley though minimal, forms this silt. We take out this silt every summer to put it around our plantation of coconut and areca as it forms a rich supplement to the manure. In the beginning we could grow only one crop of paddy in the ten acres of paddy fields, as there was not enough water available for irrigation from our stream. As the years passed by, my methods worked and now, we can grow three crops of paddy in all of our land. However, I do not like to take three crops of paddy without rotating the crops. I usually take a crop of pulses like, green gram, black gram or beans. I always grow an acre of

sugarcane. Sugarcane has got so many clients from the adjoining forest—wild boar, porcupine and bison. I keep a watchman armed with a drum to scare them away at night.

"I took the full responsibility of managing the farm leaving my father free to pursue his 'Purohit's' profession and teaching. I worked from morning to evening very hard, with a dream to develop this place into a modern farm. Slowly, our yields improved and the dairy animals and oxen became healthy. I visited the big farms and the government research farms in the neighborhood to gather more information. In my early years of agriculture, my best crops and best dairy animals in our taluk brought me a few prizes.

"I liked to rear buffaloes. I had a good herd of buffaloes and cows. I had a good batch of healthy heifers and young buffaloes coming up.

"As per the norms of the community, plowing the field was prohibited as it involved beating the oxen or buffaloes to follow the furrow after furrow. Beating an animal, that too, a 'holy cow,' was treated as an act of violence. Now, you plough your fields with a machine, and nobody can object to you!"

Sri Upadhyaya went inside his room, came out with a well-maintained Webley and Scott DBBL gun and showed it to me. He told me that he had paid only one hundred rupees for the weapon. It was a lot of money then. The gun had given him a sense of security. He had scared away wild animals that came down to spoil his crops, though he had never killed any animal with it.

He took me round his farm, showing and explaining each plot. It was the most wonderful and well-planned organic farm I had ever seen. There was no mechanical pump anywhere. The water flowed by gravity. There were compost pits in every block. Enough number of dairy animals supplied the required manure as he followed composting methods. He only grew the local strains of paddy, as they were resistant to most pests and diseases. The farm was self-sufficient, and needed neither diesel power nor electricity for its maintenance. He never used the artificial fertilizers or pesticides. By his fifty years of hard work and meticulous planning, he had realized the 'ideal farm' of his dreams.

I developed a great respect for this orthodox farmer and religious man.

We returned to the house and I was offered a nice cup of coffee in a silver *tumbler with snacks.*

A team of six children returned from the school with their shrieks and ringing laughter as they reached their home. The house became alive with the sound of children, as they went to wash and all of them changed from their school dress. They suddenly became silent as they watched me sitting with their grandfather. He introduced me to them and they said 'Namaste' to me and marched into the kitchen for their refreshment.

When I entered my farm later that evening, it was almost dark. I tried imagining as to what would go on at dusk in Pundit Upadhyaya's House. Probably, the children would be singing the 'bhajans' (devotional songs) as the women prepared the evening meal. The young Upadhyaya's would be discussing the summary of the day's work, at the same time, planning the next day's work schedule while the patriarch would be busy writing the day's accounts. Almost a perfect picture of the activities that went on in my grandfather's house in my childhood!

I was suddenly aware that this is our culture! We grew up and absorbed it without our being aware of it. Everything went according to an unwritten timetable.

I remember my college teacher Mr. Robert Peres quoting, "Civilization is what we have and Culture is what we are!"

After the visit to Pundit Upadhyaya House, I came to a conclusion: Hard Work, planning and perseverance are the essence of a successful farmer. The love for the environment and self-contentment in life should be the basic principles of a farmer's life. I realized that it takes a lifetime to become a successful farmer. I can never forget the wise old Sri Upadhyaya in my lifetime, for he had all the best qualities of a good farmer.

*   *   *

Pejathaya's story conveys the reverence most Indian people hold for the elderly, the priestly class and the *pundits*. Indians hold elderly scholars in high esteem. By touching the feet of this man Pejathaya was showing his respect for the personal scholarly attainment and he was invoking the ancient traditions of his own family.

I observed many high statured persons being honored by my

Indian associates in this traditional way. Not all of the priestly class lived off charity. Many were farmers, who got their hands dirty in their fields. Others were teachers or businessmen. Although some made their existence solely off the generosity of their followers.

There were also the religious sects whose followers wore simple saffron cloth. Some of these refused to kill any living thing and would cover their mouths with cloth to prevent accidentally ingesting an insect and thereby causing its demise. They placed their feet carefully to avoid stepping on crawling insects or living plants.

I watched foreign visitors react to some of the fanatically religious men and women, and treat them with disdain, or even laugh at them. Through his stories, Pejathaya was helping me to understand that the Indian *Hare Krishna mantra* was not just a Western fad but a pure outlook on life. The *Hare Krishna* movement began in India in the 15th century. The *Hare Krishna* movement in the U.S. may have become a misguided cover for detachment from society, much to the chagrin of observers in the Indian community.

My education moved ever so slowly forward, like a trickle that debouches into a lake of understanding.

The night bus to Bangalore was my primary, if not sole, means of making the two hundred fifty mile journey to the South India headquarters of the Peace Corps. Bangalore still is the major commercial center for the state of Karnataka. In 1968 it was also a haven or refuge, where American volunteers could go to reacquaint themselves with a strong hint of Western culture.

During the 1960s Bangalore still reflected vestiges of past British colonialism. Many Indians in Bangalore spoke English. Cold beer was served in places named "The Old Bull and Bush," "The Green Door," and "The Three Aces." Movie theaters occasionally showed a selection of English language movies, some of which were relatively current releases. In addition, one could order a cheeseburger with a side order of fries at Haroon's Regent Guest House. Street names, like "Brigade Road," and "Nelson Way" added a flavor of British military installations placed in colonial times to protect the Commonwealth. The Peace Corps office was located on Alfred Street.

A potential passenger on the one express bus that traveled from Sindhanur to Bangalore had to either be very lucky, very early, or rich enough to pay a stand-in to wait in line to procure a seat. There were no facilities for making reservations, and we soon learned that the two dozen, or so, seats were usually garnered by businessmen and wealthier clientele. The bus was called the 'luxury bus' because, admittedly, the seats were quite comfortable, the bus was air conditioned and the service was express. There was no standing room, as the journey took nine or ten hours, leaving Sindhanur around eight or nine p.m. (sharp?) and arriving central Bangalore around six a.m., just in time for breakfast.

On my second trip on the luxury express night bus to Bangalore, I was fortunate to claim an available seat without waiting in line. I had worked a nine hour day in the hot sun, and was quite exhausted. My Associate Director for Peace Corps' Southern India Office asked me to attend a meeting with Agricultural Department officials in Bangalore the next day. He did not tell me what was expected, "Just be there!" I was relieved to have found a seat.

Darkness set in before the bus was but twenty kilometers out of Sindhanur. I laid my head against the side window, using my towel as a shock absorber, and stretched out to my full length to get some sleep. Apparently, my feet touched a parcel or bag that the person in the seat in front of me had placed under his seat.

The formally clad Indian man in front of me rose in his seat and turned to say something to me. I didn't catch what he said as I had dozed-off. Then, in my fidgety slumber, I must have kicked his parcel a second time.

This time, the gentleman turned in fury and shouted at me in English to please not kick his bag. My natural response would be to offer an apology, but there was something about this man's attitude that angered me. Before I could stop myself, I said in a loud voice, "Please don't put your damn bag in a place where feet are supposed to be."

I was immediately appalled at my audacity, and regretted my behavior. I also noticed that the people sitting in my vicinity went quiet. They stared at me with looks of horror, as though I had committed some grave crime. I was beginning to understand that the person in front of me was not just a wealthy executive, but a religious person of high renown. I don't know who was more embarrassed for our respective outbursts, the priest or me.

In a flash, I realized that I had committed a serious faux pas, and that I had just displayed the 'ugly American' side of me. I had also shown great disrespect for a highly respected, high caste person and the people around me would take this moment as proof that these white foreigners bore no sensitivity or care for their fellow Indian citizens. Their cumulative attitude seemed to sum up my behavior as less than savory, and categorize me with their former enemy, the "bloody" British. In my imagination I saw myself with a sign around my neck written in Hindi script that said, "Ugly American."

My only salvation would be to apologize profusely, and make my best efforts to regain some amount of reconciliation with this gentleman. In an attempt to salvage the moment I leaned forward and said to the man in English, "Sir, I apologize for shouting at you. May I suggest that you place your bag in the overhead storage area so that I don't accidentally kick it?"

That was not the right thing to say either, though the facial expressions on the people sitting near me seemed to soften. They looked at me sympathetically. The offended passenger, however, responded with a gruff, "Humph!" and continued to leave his bag under his seat. This was a bad start to a long bus ride.

Although I tried to fight off the thought, my mind tore me away from this place and plunked me down in my Uncle

Herbert's farm house kitchen, where I looked up at a plaque he always displayed prominently on the wall. It was a picture of a horse from the rear. Around the outer edge of the plaque were the words, "Why is der more 'orses asses den 'orses?" It was that thought that helped keep my mouth in check for the remainder of the trip.

ADJUSTING TO LIFE ON
THE DECCAN PLATEAU

The small village of Jawalgera was just eight miles from my home in Sindhanur. The Syndicate Bank's Tungabhadra Farm was an additional two miles from Jawalgera. As Pejathaya was adjusting to his new position as farm manager in his farm near Jawalgera, the Peace Corps India-60 contingent in Sindhanur Taluka was adjusting to its own role in agricultural development.

The adventure was probably as daunting for Pejathaya as it was for us volunteers. He left the cool, moist area of his youth to travel to the hot, dry Deccan Plateau, very much unlike the coastal hills in many ways. His advantage was that the language was the same as in his first home, and he already had a good idea about farming, irrigation and agricultural markets.

Pejathaya kept meticulous notes when he arrived in Raichur District, and later included his reminiscing as part of a book. I found his descriptions of the area, the people, the structures he lived in and the type of agriculture he was to master more thorough and compelling than my own descriptions. Because we were both new to Sindhanur Taluka we experienced similar surprises.

He compares the thatched hut that was to be his office to the temporary homes of the farmers who immigrated to Raichur District from the neighboring state of Andhra Pradesh. These immigrants came to buy land and to take advantage of the canal waters from the Tungabhadra irrigation network. That style of thatched hut later became very familiar to me when a similar hut became my honeymoon home.

The local Karnataka farmers, whose ancestors lived in this area for centuries, built more permanent structures. They used stones and adobe bricks for their thick walls, and the mud and grass roofs were supported with long timbers. The thick walls with few, and smaller, windows made the local structures seem stuffy and dingy.

The Andhra structures were light and airy, with more windows, but were not expected to last for more the 15 or 20 years without major remodeling.

Here are Pejathaya's thoughts on what he saw when first coming to Tungabhadra Farm.

FARM AT JAWALGERA
BY S.M. PEJATHAYA

My office was nothing but a thatched hut measuring twenty-five feet by ten feet. The mud walls were regularly plastered with thin film of cow dung and the floor was of 'Cuddapah' stone (limestone, from Andhra Pradesh) slabs. The roof was thatched with 'Apoo grass' which grew in abundance along the water channels. The doors were made of bamboo frame imbedded with bamboo mat. The windows had bamboo strips laid crisscross on bamboo frames with the diamond-shaped bamboo grills. Our windows sported eco-friendly screens of jute sacking. These could be rolled up and tethered with jute twine. These primitive screens would be let down during the wind blown dust waves.

Our farm buildings were just like any other progressive farmer's buildings of new settlers in Raichur district. All the farm buildings in the neighborhood were built in the same fashion to suit the arid climate of the plains. The construction materials were available locally. These buildings kept us cool in the very hot summers and dry and cozy during short winter season. There were no instances of theft or housebreaking in our area as people were very honest. If ever someone dared to thieve, it would have been the end of such person as no one tolerated theft. A thief if ever caught red-

handed had to succumb to merciless beatings of short-tempered 'Lambani'[21] workers. I never had to worry about thieves or burglars. We seldom locked our doors or our personal belongings even though we had few valuables in the farm. The office records and the petty cash were kept in a steel cupboard to give us an extra feeling of enhanced safety though it was never needed. The office furniture consisted of a few steel folding chairs and tables.

As a farm manager I was happy in my bachelor quarters, which in fact was another thatched hut next to our office shed across a farmyard. It had a 'Jaali' wood frame camp cot with coir (fiber from coconut husk) netting over which my cotton bed was spread. I had a bamboo dresser shelf, which held my only tin trunk in the lower shelf. The metal trunk contained my life's belongings. On top of this shelf there stood a small 6"X 8" size mirror that I used for shaving. The middle shelf contained a few books. Next to my bed was a cane teapoy, which held a hurricane lantern, the newspapers, magazines and a small three-band transistor radio, which gave me the information of the outside world.

We had no power in the farm. There was power supply to Jawalgera village but even the post office did not have telephone or telegraph. To avail such novel facility we had to go to the taluk headquarter of Sindhanur. We had to buy our petrol and diesel at Sindhanur. The petrol cost 62 paise while diesel was 38 paise a liter (about $0.09 and $0.06 in 1968 equivalent). Much needed sugar and kerosene were available at the ration shop in Jawalgera.

Next to my quarters was my kitchen shed with many aluminum vessels and a few stainless steel utensils, a few cups, saucers and eating plates made of porcelain. We had few drinking glasses and an earthen pitcher for drinking water. The water remained very cool in the earthen pot. We had a kerosene stove and an open chulah[22] on which my cook Rajanna cooked my jowar rotis, dal, rice and vegetables.

Next to the kitchen was an "open-to-sky" bathroom and "camp toilet". In the bathroom there was a big metal oil drum with its top carefully cut

---

[21] A nomadic clan akin to the Gypsies

[22] A fire place where the small tinders and dried up branches of Jaali wood were made to burn with a little quantity of jowar straw

away. This drum was filled with water; a bucket and a mug were kept near it. The floor was covered with a big granite stone slab at a sloping angle. I always took cold-water baths. The water flow from the bathroom was led by a small channel into the adjacent field. The camp toilet consisted of a ten feet deep pit of about four feet diameter. Upon this circular pit, a bamboo frame with a central window was mounted. Fresh lose earth was collected in a heap by the side of the pit. We poured lose earth into the pit after each use of the toilet with a small spade kept for the purpose. These military type camp toilets really proved to be very hygienic and stench-free.

All the sheds faced north so that they did not face the scorching sun during the morning and evening times. There were four more sheds behind my office. They were the store or godown, a large tractor shed, a spacious dormitory like staff quarters with a staff kitchen similar to mine, and large cattle shed. My living quarters and kitchen were in front of my office, across the spacious courtyard. This space was lined with periwinkle and other hardy flowering plants. Our labor camp was far away quite out of our earshot.

The summers were very hot and the temperatures would exceed 44 degree centigrade (111 degrees F) at times. During the height of summer we would start fieldwork at five in the morning and finish by one in the afternoon. The scorching sun became unbearable after one in the afternoon when the mercury level soared. All of us took rest in the shade of our dwellings.

The only source of water flowed in a small sub-channel, which ran east to west along one side of open courtyard that housed all our sheds. The group of these sheds was called a camp. Though the official name of our camp was Tungabhadra Farms Camp, the local people referred to it as The Syndicate Camp. The camp derived this appellation, as the owners of the farm were former directors of a large banking institution, The Syndicate Bank Limited. After the nationalization of banks in India, the name of this pioneer banking concern was eventually reduced to Syndicate Bank.

The entire water requirement of our farm was met by an outlet coming from the main channel No. 54 of the Left Bank of Tungabhadra dam. The dam was about sixty miles away. The channel would be closed for about forty days every summer for repairs and maintenance work. During this dry period, we had to store water in the ground level storage tanks near our establishment to survive the scarcity every year. The closure would be soon after the harvesting of summer crops. We had no source of water nearby due to depleted water table. Raichur district was a place with scanty rainfall.

We had about 150 permanent laborers living on our farm. They were mostly from a tribe called 'Lambani.' The labor camp was put far away from our office and living quarters since our 'Lambani' laborers sang as a group all through the day and sometimes all through the night. They sang in high-pitched tones in their native dialect, which seemed to be an admixture of all Indian languages. Theirs is a spoken dialect with no script of its own. The laborers would sing, as their moods would guide them, day in and day out. They sang like free birds. It was the way of their life and they would be deeply offended if someone asked them stop singing.

Even during the time, they were working in our fields, they would sing in their gypsy language non-stop and we had to tolerate their collective singing. Only during the rare intervals of their singing, we could communicate with them and instruct them regarding the work at hand. These 'Lambani' people lived with the nature and they were very hardy and honest people. They would sing all night during the full moon days and the new moon days. Singing their folk songs was their cultural activity and main source of entertainment too.

During holidays and festival days, they would sing louder and sometimes dance forming a wide circle or would gyrate forming a few smaller circles. On festival occasions and Sundays, they would have a drink, sing, dance round, and round for hours.

The Lambani labor folk lived in their camp by constructing individual huts for each family. Their cone-shaped huts that looked like American Indian teepees were covered with jowar straw, supported by 'Jaali' wood or bamboo supports. Each family cooked and lived happily in the confines of their small tent. They occupied about one acre of land while we occupied about two acres of land for our dwelling purpose.

The 'apoo grass' thatching on our hut roofs had to be changed once in every two years. The shallow rooted apoo grass grew in abundance on the banks of our water channels, in fact, this kind of grass held the earth on our channel banks intact. When harvesting the grass each summer, we could get new thatching material for our roof.

I had a vast area of farmland to manage and we grew cotton and wheat as main crops. At the same time, we were experimenting with many new crops in a few experimental plots. We wanted to test the feasibility of new crops and their adaptability to the climatic conditions of the Deccan plateau.

We were under the prescribed 'Light Irrigation Area' and we were allowed to grow any crop other than paddy and sugar cane. Paddy and sugar cane crops need heavy irrigation. These two crops were allowed in 'heavy irrigation' area only.

Our soil was 'deep black cotton soil' with ample clay content. The land was flat and we could see for miles and miles. The nearest village was two miles away and Sindhanur town was 12 miles from our farm. Life was very challenging for me as I lived in a very remote and interior place in the plains of Deccan."

*   *   *

The India-60 volunteers were learning about spicy Indian food, crowded buses, leaky roofs, and "Indian Standard Time." Unlike Pejathaya's new experiences, we had to decipher an entirely different culture as well as a new language. A Peace Corps volunteer's typical day contrasted greatly with Pejathaya's experience. A villager's days began at sunrise and ended when darkness made it difficult to see. The daylight in between was measured in very flexible terms.

Most villagers did not own a watch. When a volunteer agreed to meet a farmer in his field we were likely to set a precise time, say, 9:00 a.m. To farmer Patel, this was a general agreement, not enforceable with precise clockwork. At 9:00 a.m., it is quite possible that farmer Patel was not in his field where you patiently awaited him. He may be waiting for you near his house, or he may be sitting with his friends in a local tea *ungadi*, enjoying a traditional dough-soaked and deep-fried chili pepper. Whoever heard of such a scheduled meeting as 9:00 a.m.; in the fields, yet?

When the sun began to heat up the great outdoors, around 10:00 a.m., you surrender and head for farmer Patel's house, feeling humiliated and moderately angry. You confront farmer

Patel in a civil manner, assuming that a consequential circumstance delayed his progress to the field. However, Mr. Patel, who has no instrument to tell time, understands that there was never a precise time for the meeting and, for him, there are certain formalities he expected to employ before actually going to the field, like offering you, his guest, a cup of tea. Oh yeah! You should have known that!

Indian Standard Time

It only took one, maybe two such occurrences before the volunteer fully understood the real meaning for the word "*narle*." That word, *narle*, in *Kannada*, (according to our Indian *Kannada* instructors) means "tomorrow," which is an exceedingly clear concept to most Americans. The Indian village farmer, however, used that term to indicate a non-specific time in the future, usually a future day, but not necessarily the very next day. Hence, the sunburn PCVs acquired in the early days while waiting in fields.

Directions

In addition to "Indian Standard Time" there were other idiosyncrasies that we had to learn. Receiving directions to an unfamiliar place, for example, was always a challenge to interpret. When I asked, "Where is the village called Sirruguppa," for example, the local villager gave a barely discernible wave of his head, or his arm, in a general direction and stated, "Just this side." Of course, there were no street signs in the villages or mile markers on most roads, so the direction-giver could be very general. Sirruguppa could be fifty feet or fifty miles "just this side."

Crop Thinning

Another interesting phenomenon I found with farmers was their reluctance to thin their crops. The printed 'Package of Practices' for a particular crop may advise the farmer to sow seeds every four centimeters, and after germination to thin the plants to every eight centimeters. I would carefully notch a stick to exactly four centimeter intervals, and another to eight centimeter intervals. The farmer had no problem understanding the planting space but was excessively reluctant to pull out every other germinated plant. It was against his entire being to see a plant survive the birthing process, only to be cast away. One farmer I worked with finally agreed to remove some plants, but I noticed that he did it very carefully. I suspect that after I left he put them back in the ground.

Bus Etiquette

Bus transportation could also be a disconcerting adventure. My first exposure riding the local bus from Sindhanur to Turvihal was an exercise in cultural shock. The country bus was designed to accommodate 48 people, but, at the mid-point of our 11 mile journey, there were about ninety people on the bus, including the ten or fifteen brave souls who rode on the roof with the baggage.

As was normal in those days, the bus was late in arriving, late to depart and at full capacity, or so I thought. Men, children and women, some with goats and baskets of chickens or handbags full of produce, pushed and shoved to get in the door. Each stop was a frenetic scene of human confusion, as people getting off the bus were smothered by people getting on.

That day I travelled with Peter Junker, the German volunteer assigned to work with the tractor society. We planned to diagnose and, hopefully, repair several tractors near Tony Ganey's village of Turvihal. I carried my metal tool box which weighed about twenty-five pounds. My first instinct was to stand back and let the women and small children board first. Peter said, "Go! Go! if you don't push to get on you'll be left behind."

I felt a little foolish elbowing a 90 pound woman aside, but she did not hesitate to push right back. In fact, due to my temerity, she captured a spot ahead of me, and heralded her victory with a haughty, "Hah!"

The hot, dusty ride was made even less comfortable by being compressed into a small space with little air circulation, not to mention no air conditioning. We were being pushed against other hot, sweaty bodies. The men tried to talk over the din of the village women's discordant, high-pitched voices and the braying and clucking of the traveling animals. Every time the bus lurched unexpectedly all conversation paused, as bodies were forced into each other in rhythm with the violent swaying of the bus.

The excursion to Turvihal that day was successful. In all, Peter and I saw four tractors that were out of commission. Two of them only needed minor adjustments, and one was beyond our help. The foreign distributors of farm tractors were quick to sell tractors to the Indian farmers, but less than spontaneous when it came to providing spare parts. Later, with Tony's help, we wrote to the dealers to argue the plight village farmers suffered in keeping their tractors in working order. Response from the dealers was sluggish.

The fourth tractor was not on our original agenda. An Andhra farmer approached us as we waited for the bus to return to Sindhanur. He said that his International tractor was new but was not running well; could we come to look at it? He said it was smoking, and using too much oil and petrol.

The farmer gave us a ride on his bullock cart to his camp, and treated us to tea and English biscuits while he sent a runner to the field to instruct the driver to retrieve the ailing tractor. We saw the tractor coming from half a mile away, as it belched smoke into the blistering hot air. Before the tractor came to a stop, Peter had a pretty good idea of what the problem was. A quick look at the oil dip stick proved that the farmer, in his innocent attempt to make sure there was enough oil in the crankcase, had overfilled the crankcase.

The farmer readily admitted that he was eager to protect this major investment, and was putting almost as much oil in the crankcase as petrol in the fuel tank. He was much relieved to learn the meaning of the markings on the oil dip stick. Peter and

I sat on the wide flat fenders of his tractor as the farmer drove us back to the bus stop where he had found us. We caught the last bus back to Sindhanur, just as the sun hung low over the thorn bushes and tumble weeds. We were too tired to be upset with the pushing and shoving as we meekly stood in the crowded bus isle for the ride home.

As the bus neared town and motored on the road that passed by the Sindhanur Tractor Society we noticed that at least twenty of our tractors were parked in and around the tractor shed. Normally, the only time a driver would return his tractor mid week was for repair, or a change in assignment. Peter observed that there must be a new movie playing at the Sindhanur cinema theatre. According to his past observations, the drivers always seemed to find some minor thing that needed repair late in the day whenever there was some interesting activity in town.

We were very relieved to crawl down off that bus when it finally came to a stop in the center of Sindhanur. We were covered from hair to feet in sweat that had turned a layer of dust into mud. Right after this bus excursion I put in my request to Peace Corps Bangalore for a motorcycle.

Riding Bicycles

None of the volunteers had the good fortune to have been issued personal motorized transportation. Each volunteer was issued a bicycle. Our bicycles were the rugged, single speed type, with coaster brakes, and bells on the handlebars. Those loud sounding ringers on the handlebars were the most important attachments to the bicycle. Weaving one's way through traffic was impossible without warning the mass of pedestrians of one's approach.

The universal pecking order in road protocol became clear early on. Large lorries and buses ruled. They had the loudest horns, the smelliest exhausts and the noisiest engines. Everybody got out of the way for them. Next came big cars, little cars, jeeps, rickshaws, motor cycles and motor scooters, bullock carts, bicycles, pedestrians with large bundles on their heads and finally the walking public. All of the above, of course, came to a near dead stop when bullocks, sheep, goats or water buffalo crossed the road.

My worst experience on a bicycle came just a few months after I settled into the Sindhanur routine. I had the habit of strapping my heavy tool box onto the rack on the back of my bicycle. I kept my tools close at hand for emergency field repairs. The weight in the back made the bicycle unstable, but I learned to control the wobble.

Pedestrians tend to zig-zag down the crowded streets of Sindhanur, so I continued ringing my handlebar bell to caution them. Ahead, I saw a little girl of about three or four walking with an older girl of about eleven. The older girl was carrying a baby. They walked along with the surge of pedestrians moving in the same direction that I travelled. I sounded my bell at them even though they were off to the right side. I had almost overtaken them when the three year old suddenly bolted to her left to cross the street. I swerved my bike to avoid her, but she collided with the tool box strapped to the back of my bike.

The girl's head struck the tool box with a resonating bang and rattle of metal wrenches and sockets. The impact spun her around once and she landed flat on her back, screaming. I quickly got off my bicycle and went to help. Within seconds, about twenty people gathered around the little girl. Some of them were looking at me for an explanation. The looks were not entirely accusatory, but they unnerved me just the same. There wasn't much I could do to help the young girl. She would have a nasty bump on the side of her head, but there was no blood. She would be fine after her headache dissipated.

Tractors

Before I could be of much assistance or spend any time lamenting over the incident, word came to me from one of the tractor drivers that several of our tractors were hopelessly stuck in a farmer's field and the manager had urgently requested my assistance. It was already 3:30 in the afternoon on a very hot day, but I couldn't leave our tractors, the drivers and the manager stranded. I grabbed my water canteen, threw my sleeping bag on the back of my bike and headed toward the village of Kolpur.

Eleven miles from Sindhanur I found three of our society tractors stuck in mud up to their engine rails. Mr. Rao, the manager, was there with his Jeep, and seven of our tractor drivers were idling off to the side. The drivers were covered from head to toe in mud, and twenty or thirty farmers, villagers, children and dignitaries stood by discussing the situation. The elderly gentlemen were probably cracking jokes about bullocks versus tractors.

We applied some physics and plenty of muscle power, and finally we managed to get two of the tractors and one power tiller out of the mud before dark. One of the farmers from Kolpur invited me to his village for tea. That was an offer that I couldn't refuse, having not eaten since morning. We crossed a small irrigation channel on the way to Kolpur. While attempting to lift my bicycle over the muddy water, I lost my footing. My foot sank a good ten inches into the soft mud, and a group of young villagers thought it was very funny. They jeered as I struggled to locate my sandal deep in the muck.

The farmer helped me wash off the mud, but the sandal was marginally serviceable in its present condition. After a short stop for tea I needed to start the journey back toward Sindhanur. Unfortunately, while walking my bicycle in the dark, I stepped on a thorn bush. One thorn went deep into my unprotected foot. I realized that I was not going to make it back to Sindhanur that night, so I decided to journey cross-country to Basawapur, John Kelly's village, about three miles away.

I cautiously pushed my wounded two-wheeler along the dirt path as I watched for thorns, rocks and snakes. My bare feet would be no match for those natural obstacles. I reached the outskirts of John's village just as the last vestiges of twilight faded into total darkness. Three barefoot children led me to John's humble lodgings. There, I was informed that 'John Sahib was away and would not return that day.'

However, someone located John's cook, Mrs. Barnabas, and summoned her to the *'Sahib's'* house. She was most helpful, as she cleaned the mud off my feet. She then used a tweezer from John's Peace Corps-issued medical kit and, with the light of a kerosene lantern, removed the thorn. Walking on that broken thorn had forced it three-quarters of an inch into my foot. What a relief! Now, I only had to worry about the infection that was sure to follow.

That day ended with a warm meal prepared by Mrs. Barnabas, and a sleepless night under the stars. Seeing John's mud brick, one room accommodation made me appreciate my apartment in Sindhanur more. On the other hand, sleeping under the stars in a quiet remote village is a wonderful experience.

Pejathaya admits that his initiation to life in Raichur District was different, although still very challenging. He left behind his comfortable bungalow in the coconut farm and was now living in an airy, thatched structure on the flat farm land. The black cotton soil tortured his body as the wind whipped it through the thin walls. The only trees to shade his house and office were the thorny acacia bushes.

The wire that brought electric lights and energy to his coastal farm had not yet reached his Jawalgera hut, and there was no nearby river to supply free gravity fed water to his crops. There was, however, a relatively new system of canals and channels that brought the universal solvent to the vicinity of his farm. He just had to learn how to channel that water so it could nourish his farm crops.

The Caste System

Social stratification in India defined communities into thousands of hereditary groups commonly thought of as an ancient fact of Hindu life. Outside the four major groups in the caste system were the untouchables. The Peace Corps volunteers struggled to cope with the caste system, whereas

Pejathaya had experienced this system since his youth. The volunteers found it difficult to treat one person so dissimilar to another. One of the India-60 volunteers in Manvi Taluka found it unpalatable to deal with the peoples' treatment of the low caste Hindus and *Harijans* (untouchables).

Mike Quaid, who came from Brooklyn, New York, and had studied law, worked with several hard working *Harijan* villagers who strove to improve the lives of their families. *Harijan*, which means 'children of god' in Hindustani, was below the Hindu caste system, and those people were considered untouchable.

The story is told of Mike's trip to a Sirwar tea *ungadi* (stall) with a *Harijan* friend one day shortly after Mike's coming to live in that village. The *ungadi* owner refused admittance to the *Harijan*, but allowed Mike to enter. The *Harijan* sat on the dirt floor outside the shop, and was served tea in a dirty cup. Mike asked to be served his tea in a similar cup while he sat with his friend on the dirt outside the tea '*ungadi*.'

This, of course, created a significant stir among the villagers. Mike, however, never wavered in his attempts to stress equality among all people. One man, trying to break a long-standing cultural tradition throughout a country of five hundred million people can make a few people aware of a situation but he cannot change a nation. Some people loved Mike for his gesture, others hated his interference.

LIFE ON TUNGABHADRA FARM

A little over eight miles from Sindhanur, Pejathaya was experiencing his own challenges. As the 'new kid on the block,' Pejathaya had a lot of catching up to do. Most of the crops he was expected to nurture in his Raichur District farm did not grow in his Shiroor area. He had to learn the package of practices for *jowar* (sorghum), wheat, maize, cotton and sunflower, plus he was expected to experiment with other varieties. He had to analyze his labor requirement, assess the needs of his limited staff and fill positions to assure that the farm work was carried-out efficiently and timely.

Several months after we met, Pejathaya told me about his first experiences with the people who came to work for him and the interesting people in the area. His story about his tractor driver, Mehboob, follows.

MEHBOOB—THE HELPER
BY S.M.PEJATHAYA

Mehboob told me that he was seventeen years old when I questioned him. He had come seeking the job of a "tractor driver's helper" at our Farm. He told me that he hailed from a very poor family.

Mehboob was a short boy with lots of energy and enthusiasm. He almost begged me to employ him as a tractor driver's helper and told me that he would be eighteen soon and get a driver's license. However, he looked not a day older than fifteen to me by his looks. He was less than five feet tall. I told him that he was too small to go on our tractor and I asked him to leave. However, he would not budge. I told him again that he was too young for the job and asked him to come next year and try again.

Mehboob kept on insisting for my permission to clean our tractor. He wanted to display his competency in the cleaning job, and told me that he would gladly leave, if he failed to impress me. I asked him to go ahead.

After about two hours, Mehboob asked me to come and see his work. I went there to see an impeccably cleaned tractor. It had no trace of mud or dust on it! Then he asked me to have a look at the farm's jeep, and my motorcycle; they too were well cleaned and shining!

I feigned that I was very angry and asked him in a raised voice as to why he cleaned the jeep and the motorcycle without my permission! Mehboob replied that if he were ever given the job of a helper in our farm, he would work hard and take care of all the vehicles and the farm machinery, in addition to his duties. He assured me that in short future he would get driver's license and drive all the vehicles.

I asked him whether he could drive a tractor.

"Yes Sir."

"Jeep?"

"Yes, Sir."

"Motorcycle?"

"Yes Sir"

"Caterpillar bulldozer?"

The answer was positive, to my surprise! Then, I handed over the keys of the tractor and asked him to give me a driving demonstration.

Mehboob accepted the keys in his outstretched cupped palms and said, "Thanks Sahib." The very next moment, he folded his hands in a polite namaste and said, "Sir, I can drive the tractor and all the other vehicles which you would want me to drive, provided you teach me how to drive them!"

I was neatly bowled by Mehboob's wit. I liked the gentle humor, positive attitude and enthusiasm. At once, I employed him as our tractor driver's helper boy.

On that day, Mehboob started his career in our farm at 'rupees' eighty a month. He was shown his quarters next to that of our driver Raj. He set up his kitchen in his quarters borrowing a few utensils from the other staff.

After a few months, I learned that every month Mehboob sent a major portion of his salary to his poor parents in his native village by money order. He told that his parents were very poor and he was the eldest of six siblings. Mehboob worked with great dedication. He won the confidence of our stubborn tractor driver—Raj. Occasionally our long-faced Driver Raj would smile at his assistant. After about six months, I could observe that Driver Raj was teaching steering controls to his disciple.

Mehboob worked so hard and I raised his monthly salary to 'rupees' one hundred and fifty. Then came the summer of 1969 and the 'Holi' (Festival of colors[23]). In our farm, we did not play with colors to celebrate 'Holi.' In fact, my bosses had banned the use of colors in the farm. The previous

---

[23] Holi is an ancient Hindi festival that usually involves people throwing colors on one another

'Holi' festivities had turned out to be very unruly and violent in the farm. Our laborers had found a little too much to drink on that day. In their festival mood they used too much of harsh colors like cloth dyes which they hurled in little too much quantities on our field supervisors and staff! There was a fight between the staff and laborers. My predecessor had to call the police to quell the never-ending fistfight and quarrel. Even after the festival, the harsh colors would not wash off for weeks from their skins and hair. The coloring materials had caused fearsome irritation in the eyes and grave skin problems. The farm, in turn, had to pay a huge medical bill.

After the unpleasant incident, playing with colors was banned on the premises. Thereafter, no one splashed colors during 'Holi' in the farm. The festival became only namesake after the ban. The day after the 'Holi,' I found to my utter surprise that all the animals in the farm were smeared with bright colors. Not an inch on their bodies showed their original color! Dog Lixo was painted red. Buffaloes were smeared in yellow and black to look like Bengal tigers. The farm staff and laborers were displaying multi-colored feathers. Cook Rajanna's cat was painted in green. I gave out a sigh of relief when I went to check on our bullocks. Fortunately, our snow-white bullocks were not touched with paint. I asked my supervisors to find out as to who was involved in the mischief. The inquiry went on and finally it was proved the act of our helper Mehboob!

I was very upset about Mehboob's mischievousness. I had to hold an inquiry and take necessary action. I feared that I might have to sack the poor boy! I chided Mehboob for his thoughtless act. Duly after begging for my mercy, Mehboob tried to put forth his defense by himself. As per the boy's logic, the ban on 'Holi' coloring was issued only for the staff and the laborers; naturally, the animals were exempted and he had tried his hand at coloring them by purchasing five rupees worth of cloth dyes at a shop in Jawalgera. As a result, we had a bright fluorescent green cat, a scarlet colored dog, many multi-colored fouls and tiger-like buffaloes.

I asked Driver Raj and my field supervisors to reprimand and convince Mehboob that he had violated the rules and regulations of our farm. He must therefore tender a written apology assuring that there would not be any 'Holi' coloring for animals in the years to come.

A violent Driver, Raj scolded Mehboob for half an hour. Finally, a tearful Mehboob signed a written apology and begged for my mercy. After a *word of warning, I excused Mehboob that day.*

Two years passed and our helper Mehboob grew up to become a tall and strong young man. One day Mehboob came to my office to ask for a loan of five hundred 'rupees' to get his heavy vehicle-driving license. I told him that I could not help him as my bosses never permitted me to give loans to the staff.

He started to shed tears and stood there silently. I told him that there was no use in crying, as he should have planned on saving some money for this purpose. Mehboob meekly said that he sent one hundred 'rupees' every month to his parents and he barely managed to eat properly and get by with the balance of fifty 'rupees'. Finally, he told me the hard truth – his parents and siblings would starve if he did not send that hundred rupees.

I had no way to raise his salary as I had already given the increment that I could within my powers. At the same time, I wanted to help this boy. After thinking for a while, I asked him to eat in my kitchen for the next one year to save this much money he needed for his heavy vehicle driver's license. Moreover, I told him that he certainly should wait for one more year, because he does not look like an eighteen-year-old boy, and no officer would grant him a driving license. He gratefully accepted my advice, and started to eat in my kitchen to save that amount of 'rupees' five hundred.

Mehboob got his driving license the next year. He was given a tractor to operate independently. He worked as a tractor driver honestly. His salary promptly raised to 'rupees' two hundred and fifty. Mehboob thanked me for my kindness and said he did not know how to repay my gesture. I told him that he could do this easily, by passing on the gesture to some needy person in future.

Mehboob worked faithfully for the farm. Soon after, during April 1971, I had to leave the farm to work on another project. Subsequently, my bosses decided to sell our farm to a gentleman by name Katasuri Surya Rao, a leading businessman of Sindhanur. Soon after, I completed the land registrations, handed over the farm, lock stock and barrel with all our staff and labor to Sri Surya Rao and bid adieu to Jawalgera. After the farm was sold, I lost track of Mehboob.

Nearly ten years after my stint at the Tungabhadra Farms, I happened to go to Raichur district with my family. I met Dr. Anand Hegde and his wife Janaki akka at Sindhanur. Then, I visited our old farm. Many of the farm labor and staff had left in the course of ten years. There were many new faces. Even then, I was glad to meet those few, who were my staff and labor. Sri Surya Rao welcomed my family and me and treated us to a nice feast. He took me for a trip of the farm in his jeep. He had improved the farm well. The saplings of the fruit trees that I had planted on the bunds of the fields were bearing fruits then. I was glad to see the fruit bearing trees of pomegranate, guava, lime and sweet lime, which were a rarity at Raichur district.

We proceeded to Raichur City and stayed in a very comfortable hotel. We stayed at Raichur for only a night. My two daughters were school going kids. Early next morning, we proceeded on our pilgrimage to Sri Raghavendra Swamy 'mutt' at Mantralayam, about one hour's drive from Raichur.

As I was driving out of the town in my Fiat car, a trailer-truck of the Electricity Department, laden with heavy concrete poles was following my car in a mad haste. The truck was hooting its loud horn and flashing its headlights behind my car. I slowed down to give way for this 'honking and flashing monster'.

As soon as the truck overtook my car, it swerved to a grinding halt in front of my car. The trailer truck driver was signaling me to stop behind his vehicle. I pulled behind the trailer and wondered as to why I am being forced to a stop like that!

A giant of a man, more than six feet two inches tall jumped down from the driver's seat, and came towards me grinning. He saluted me and said, "Salaam 'Saab'! Haven't you recognized me?" I looked at him from head to toe, but could not recognize the young man and I sincerely told him so. Then he said ,"Why Sir? I am your tractor driver, Mehboob."

Suddenly I recognized him! The mischievous glint in his eyes had not faded at all after all these years! He politely saluted my wife and shook hands with my children. I asked him about his life after I left the farm at Jawalgera. It seems he worked there for a few months for the new owner. Ambitious Mehboob did not want to work as a tractor driver all his life. After leaving Sri Surya Rao's service, he went to Bellary City. There, he spent all his hard earned savings to take lessons to drive the "Super Heavy Vehicles," and succeeded in getting a license to drive them. During the course of time, he found a good job with the Karnataka Electricity Board to drive their super heavy-duty vehicles. He told me that he liked his present job and was happy. He told me he was a married man now and had three children. He invited me to his house at least for a cup of tea in the evening. I had to decline that humble invitation as I was leaving the town. He offered to bring some sweets for my daughters from a nearby shop. I denied the offer politely.

I asked Mehboob to tell me the truth as to how old he really was when he came to our farm seeking a job. He replied very shyly "Sir, I was about fourteen then. I was ambitious and very anxious to get that job. Therefore, I added three years to my age. Now, I request you to forgive me for telling a lie."

As I correctly guessed, he must have been over sixteen when he got his drivers' license! I appreciated Mehboob's sincerity. I can never forget his positive approach to life.

NEIGHBORS

Pejathaya was getting to know his farm, his workers and his neighbors several months before our paths crossed in the office of the Assistant Director of Agriculture. Our respective work sites were located about ten miles apart, and we were both heavily involved in learning our new jobs and environments. While I tried to make an impact at the tractor society, he was trying to understand how to grow dry-cum-wet crops.

He later wrote about his experiences of settling in at Tungabhadra Farms. I did not know all of these stories until much later. His neighbors included some very rich land owners as well as some farmers who could barely make a living off their small parcels of land. Many farmers did not own their land but cultivated it at the will of wealthy land owners. Others owned very small plots, some considerably less than an acre.

Not far from Pejathaya's Tungabhadra Farms was a large farm the local people called the "Russian Farm." This farm was one of India's Central State Farms. It was a research farm owned and managed by the government of India's Ministry of Agriculture. It consisted of several thousand acres divided into large demonstration plots. Its purpose was to research the potential success of various crops in that area as well as the use of large scale machinery and advanced irrigation and land reclamation methods. The government hoped to eventually assist the Agricultural Department by identifying crops that were ideal for the black cotton soil and Raichur climate. During my stay in India, I visited the 'Russian Farm' several times to observe the progress of their research.

Interestingly, there were no Russian people permanently living in the farm camp. Most of the machinery, however, was provided by the Russian government as Russian foreign aid. The farm had large combine harvesters, giant ridgers and ditch makers, 60 horsepower Belarus tractors with hydraulic steering systems, Czechoslovakian Zetor tractors, Russian bulldozers and earth movers, levelers, road graders, large seed drills and planters, fertilizer applicators and huge tractor mounted sprayers. The farm employed Russian-made diesel-powered sprinklers that could irrigate an acre in just one hour.

The farm experimented in both irrigated crops such as hybrid sorghum, maize, cotton, hybrid cotton, Mexican dwarf wheat and sunflower as well as rain fed crops, such as white sorghum, local cotton, and safflower. For the irrigated crops the farm drew water from the canal system and sprinkled it rather than using gravity irrigation. The 'Russian Farm' became a frequent destination later, when I researched soybean growing.

Pejathaya, in the warm evenings after the farm work was finished, wrote about his experiences and the people he encountered. Some of his other neighbors proved to be interesting subjects. What follows are some of the stories about farming in Raichur District, especially about the people who farmed nearby. Janekal Mallappa, for example, may have been one of India's pioneers in the move toward organic farming.

JANEKAL MALLAPPA THE ORGANIC FARMER
BY S. M. PEJATHAYA

Janekal Mallappa was my neighbor at Jawalgera. He was about sixty when I first saw him; but he definitely looked younger as he had no sign of grey hair. He had an athletic body and sharp wit. He was a medium sized man. He owned five 'koorigis' of land. In local dialect, one 'koorigi' is four acres. He cultivated his twenty acres situated next to our farm.

Though he had channel water for light irrigation, he never used the water to irrigate his crops. He liked to do his dry farming and was happy with whatever yield he got from his traditional rain-fed farming. He used to grow 'Bili Jola', (white sorghum) the local staple food variety of sorghum. He inter-lined the sorghum with safflower ('kardi' oil seed) and 'Hutchellu.' 'Hutchellu' is a variety of oil (sesame) seed which every villager uses in the preparation of 'chutney' powder, which goes well with their staple diet of 'jowar roti.' He took only a single crop per year. He had a few buffaloes whose milk he sold to get a small additional income. He was a friendly person and a contented man.

He had a strange logic. He never wanted to make use of irrigation. He would say that the irrigated crops attract pest and diseases and he would have to use chemical sprays. Finally, he would get a marginally lower yielding crop. This smaller crop may just compensate the extra expenses incurred for buying and spraying the pesticides and the fungicides. He would declare that he would never like to do this 'modern circus' of chemical farming. He definitely did not want to spray poisonous chemicals on his sacred daily food. He asserted that never in his life he would do such an act.

201

He, his family or his livestock would never eat any product that was sprayed with poisons. Mallappa certainly believed in what he said.

Whenever free, Mallappa would come down to my farm and spend some time with me. Over a cup of tea, he would talk of old times. Before independence, the Raichur district was under the rule of the 'Nizam' of Hyderabad. Mallappa had grown up in the time of 'Nizam' rule. Since generations, Mallappa's family had been faithful to the 'Nizam.' Mallappa's family was a family of patriots. His ancestors had served in the 'Nizam's' army. Just as India got its independence, the 'Nizam' did not want to join the Indian Union or The Republic of India. The faithful followers of 'Nizam' supported him. There was 'Razakar Movement' in which the faithful subjects of 'Nizam' opposed the new republic. These 'Razakars' offered resistance to the rule of newly formed Republic India. Mallappa was one of such active 'Razakars' in his younger days!

Mallappa never knew why he became a 'Razakar.' The quality of being faithful to the king was in his blood. His father and his forefathers were faithful subjects of the 'Nizam' of Hyderabad. Being uneducated, he never knew much about the Indian freedom struggle nor the newly acquired independence. When the 'Nizam' wanted to oppose the Union Government of India, young Janekal Mallappa joined the rebel movement as a volunteer. The brigade consisted of Afghan mercenaries fighting against the Indian Government. The 'Pathan' mercenaries accepted this "diminutive 'Razakar' and used him as a scout and a spy during the skirmishes. Young Janekal Mallappa would roam freely near government offices and police stations to collect information for the 'Nizam's' forces.

However, very soon, the city of Hyderabad was surrounded by the forces of the Indian Republic, and eventually the 'Nizam' surrendered to join the Union of India. Janekal Mallappa narrowly escaped punishment, as he was not directly involved in fighting. He returned to his village to continue farming and led a peaceful life. He did not like the politics of the post-independence. He would tell me that people were happy under the 'Nizam'; and then, there was only one 'Nizam' to respect and salute! After getting Independence, he had to salute so many people – right from small time politicians to a good number of government officials.

He had scant regard for all the development works planned and taken up by the government. He did not believe in the prosperity brought about by the Tungabhadra Irrigation Project and neither in the use of chemical fertilizers, fungicides and pesticides.

He continued to farm in the same manner as his father and forefathers did. There were few changes in his life style. He firmly believed that irrigation would increase the salt concentration in the alkaline black cotton soil and he always warned me that one day or the other, the irrigated lands in Raichur district would turn saline and be rendered useless by this unwise irrigation. I would say the government had also foreseen this aspect, and had made it mandatory to grow only lightly irrigated crops under irrigation and we were growing cotton, wheat, sorghum and maize as our main crops.

To certain extent, Janekal Mallappa was right! A few farmers, who used the irrigation water excessively to grow forbidden crops like rice and sugarcane year after year, had already suffered problems due to high concentration of salts in their soils. Such lands became useless as the salt deposits formed a hard pan and salt logged their lands. The reclamation process was indeed very expensive and time consuming.

Due to the extensive irrigation in Raichur district, the humidity in the air increased and consequently the annual rainfall did increase. More frequent rains improved the yield of rain-fed crops. The farmers who stuck to the traditional dry farming like Janekal Mallappa were happier compared to their forefathers.

The well-adopted traditional strains of "Bili Jola" (white sorghum) yielded well. These traditional crops never required any pesticide, as these old strains were resistant to most of the pests and diseases. Whereas, we people, the so-called modern farmers used a lot of chemical fertilizers, pesticides and fungicides to protect our high yielding crops. Since we irrigated our crops, we worked throughout the year. Though we rotated our crops, we did not give enough rest to the soil. This of course resulted in lesser yields at times.

Giving soil some rest period refers to a few months natural exposure of soil without irrigation. During these exposures, the soil would dry up and very deep cracks would develop in the deep black soils to give enough aeration. This natural process certainly would help the salts to leach down the accumulated salt deposit.

When irrigated constantly, the topsoil cements up, forming a clayey seal and leads to formation of a much-feared salt pan in the upper crust of the soil due to evaporation of irrigation water. Heavy investment and labor are required to reclaim such soils.

Running bigger establishments like the Tungabhadra Farm called for more investment. We had to grow high-yielding irrigated crops so that we would be able to maintain our establishment costs. The humid conditions of the fields attracted and encouraged pests and diseases. We had to spray more of poisonous materials on our crops. This really formed a vicious cycle. We had to grow more to make up our higher cultivation costs. Once we began as chemical farmers, we had to continue in the same style.

People like Janekal Mallappa led a life of ease without many tensions. Their needs were limited, and an average but steady yield from their handful acres of land kept them happy and contented.

After the harvest Janekal Mallappa could relax. He would look after his cattle and attend to his dairy animals. He would attend the nearby 'jathraas' and look forward to celebrate the festivals; he would sing the folk ballads in the evenings and sometimes see the dramas and an occasional movie at Sindhanur. He would budget on the sale proceeds of his farm produce and live a simple but contented life until the rains came next year and his next sowing season started. On the other hand, we struggled with our farm machinery and chemicals to grow two or more crops per year to get enough profits to repay the bank loans and keep our permanent labor paid every week. We had to run our show and this rigmarole went on without a break. We led a restless life.

Recently, I hear a lot about organic farming and sustainable agriculture. I think I had seen a 'real example' in Janekal Mallappa right in the sixties."

*   *   *

Another of Pejathaya's neighbors was a woman named Adivamma, who lived in the nearby town of Jawalgera. Adivamma farmed forty acres of land adjacent to Tungabhadra Farms.

ADIVAMMA
BY S. M. PEJATHAYA

A lady called Adivamma was my neighbor and owned about forty acres of land. She too farmed in traditional organic method like Mallappa, my other neighbor. Adivamma is a Kannada name. 'Adavi' means forest and 'amma' means mother Goddess. The name Adivamma suggests the name of Parvathi, consort of Lord Shiva. She was over eighty years old, but strong for her age. Though she had weathered and wrinkled skin, she looked very distinguished and she wore lots of gold on her old self. She always wore a heavy chain to which a good number of gold sovereigns were attached. This is called 'Kaasina Sara'—a status symbol of the rich ladies. She was well to do and traveled the distance of two miles from her house in the village of Jawalgera to her fields by her 'covered bullock cart' locally known as "savaari gaadi" to which she would hitch young trotting bullocks.

The old lady had visited our farm with Mallappa, a couple of times. On one occasion I invited Adivamma and Mallappa to join me for lunch. The old lady agreed to dine with me provided I made it a point to eat in her house at my earliest. I agreed for the sake of decency, but never made it.

During the year 1966, several years before I arrived on the scene, the old lady sold twenty acres of her land to our farm. She had received the price of the land in full by cash and signed a voucher. On the day our farmlands were to be registered, Adivamma could not attend the registration, as she was indisposed. Subsequently, the previous manager of our farm had forgotten to register her twenty acres of land to our name.

Though we were in possession of that land and farmed it, the title vested with Adivamma. This fact came to my notice as I verified the land records in the taluk (county) office. I went to see Adivamma in her field and told her that she had to come to the sub-registrar's office at Sindhanur to register her land in our favor. I reminded her that she could not come for the registration three years ago, as she was indisposed. Without her co-operation, the land registration was not possible. In addition, her non-cooperation would imply that we had to seek legal recourse, which could go on for years together in the court.

Furthermore, we had no formal agreement of sale executed on the day we paid her, and she had taken the full land value in advance. During the three years, the land value had jumped up by three times. We had leveled her land for irrigation purposes. We had a flourishing hybrid cotton crop on it. We were the first to develop the land for light irrigation in our village and many people had followed suit. This had increased the value of land in our area. As per the land records office, she was the rightful owner of the land and I had no way to stop her from harvesting the crop on it.

While we paid the land revenue every year, the receipts were issued in Adivamma's name by the revenue authorities, as she was the rightful owner according to their records. When I brought this discrepancy in the land records to the notice of my bosses, they suggested that I should set it right immediately, at any cost. They did not mind paying an extra sum of money to Adivamma, in case she demanded the present market price.

That noon, as I explained our problem in detail to Adivamma, she suddenly got agitated! She told me straight away that she shall not co-operate to set right the records! She told that it was my predecessor's fault and he had not bothered to get the sale deed registered on a subsequent day. She added that the managers of our farm were always haughty young men who knew no civilities! As I knew, my predecessor was a nice gentleman. He had left our farm, as he was engaged to get married, and his fiancée refused to set up home in our remote farm after marriage. My predecessor was upset and he had requested our bosses to transfer him to a city. Being the directors of a huge commercial bank my bosses had obliged him by transferring him to an urban branch of a city. Eventually they had employed me, a bachelor, without any encumbrance to look after their farm in the year 1968.

The previous manager was courteous to Adivamma whenever she visited our farm. Yet, he did not bother to visit her house in turn to accept her hospitality, not even once. Eventually, when he was transferred, he had left abruptly, without even telling good-bye to her. These facts had turned the old lady very cross. When I took over the management, I too made it a point to invite my neighbors to my quarters and host them tea or lunch. Every time Adivamma visited our farm, she had invited me to her house at Jawalgera, and each time, I had promised that I would visit her at the earliest. Unfortunately, I had not kept my promise.

Adivamma spoke to me: "Look Sahib, You have visited my farm today on your business matter. Yet, you have not been my guest. You have not paid a visit to my house even once. If you can talk business, I too can react in the same manner. If you want to meet your good neighbor Adivamma, you have to go and meet her in her own house. Will you come tomorrow noon to my house by about eleven?"

I told her that it shall be my pleasure, and returned to my farm. All that day, I worried as to what I should do if the old lady did not extend her co-operation in registration of the land. Next day, I went to Adivamma's house in Jawalgera.

It was the second house off the main street on to the right. The solid house reflected the local architecture as it was built with locally available materials. The house had granite boulder foundation, thick mud walls and huge granite slabs for ceiling over which a thick layer of black soil mud coating was laid to insulate the stones from the heat of the sun and to protect from rains. The walls were plastered with nice clay, and they were freshly whitewashed. The doors and windows were made of rough-hewn strong wood. The doors were small, about five feet in height. One had to bow and enter the house.

Leaving my footwear outside, I entered the house. The windows were small to prevent the hot drafts of the Deccan wind entering the house, but they were laid in such an angle to keep the house dimly lit. The windows provided good cross ventilation. The house remained cool and comfortably dark.

It took a couple of minutes for my eyes to adjust to the light in the interior of the house. The house had a couple of divans in the drawing room.

There were a couple of stools. The walls were decorated with the ethnic designs drawn with red earth. The wall had many niches, to keep the 'til oil' lamps at night. There were a few more niches for keeping the odds and ends like betel nut and paan platter etc. There was a big photo of Lord Shiva on the wall. The photo was decorated with fresh flowers. The house had neatly polished mud floor, which felt very cool to my bare feet. Adivamma told me that she lived alone with a servant woman for company. She told me that she owned one more bigger house next-door, where she housed her cattle and a few of her workers with their families. She did not wish to speak about her own family and she said that she was left all alone in this world to live her miserable life.

I imagined that some sort of calamity had befallen her family years back. It might have been the bubonic plague or smallpox. In the olden days many people died an early death due to these kinds of ravaging diseases, as there were no known preventive measures. She welcomed me by saying, "Sahib, you are welcome." She suddenly became silent, may be engrossed in some thoughts. Her eyes looked distant and focused far away.

She asked, "Sahib, do you mind, if I addressed you, the way I would address a grandson?" I replied her that I would be honored at that. Then, she offered me a clean towel and said, "Son, don't sit in the drawing room like a guest. Please wash your face, hands and legs at the backyard of the house. Come back here and say a silent prayer to 'Shiva,' and join me in the kitchen as I would cook a few 'rotis' for you." I obeyed Adivamma as I would obey my grandmother and after saying a silent prayer in front of the big photo, I entered the kitchen to squat on the floor, on a piece of hand woven grass mat.

She offered me a big glass of cool water from a huge earthen pot, which stood in the corner. The water glass was made of brass and it shone like gold. She laid a large bronze platter in front of me. It too shone like a plate of gold and I could see the reflection of her cooking fire on it. The cooking fire illuminated the immaculately clean kitchen. There were different vessels made of brass, bronze and copper. There were some earthenware pots too.

She opened a round-shaped brass box and took out a cold but crisp 'Bajra Roti' (millet roti) and laid it on my plate. She served a large dollop of freshly churned butter and two kinds of dry chutney powders, one made of groundnuts and the other of "Hutchellu" (sesame, 'til' or 'gingili'). She reached for the porcelain jars in the kitchen shelf and served me fragrant mango pickles and "tamarind 'thokku' (a kind of tamarind chutney).

When I ate the dry and crisp 'roti,' she patted dough to bake thin and soft hot 'rotis' of 'Bili Jola' (white sorghum) and served them with fresh salad and a curry made of fried brinjals and another curry of sprouted cowpeas. There was a pudding made of fresh plantains. Food was very tasty and I ate eight soft rotis. She was about to serve more rotis while I said, "Adivamma, I am already full. I have already eaten eight rotis!"

These words offended her! She angrily declared that I shall not utter such words during a meal! "Never count your rotis and eat. That is done by people whose days are numbered! You have just passed your teenage and you should never do that!" Saying so, she took a pile of rotis that lay near the cooking fire and dumped all of them to my plate!

Good God! There were so many of them, and I was forbidden from counting them! On the day I took up farming as a profession, I had vowed that I shall never waste food on my plate. Food is sacred and every man toils to earn his food. We, the farmers, work so hard in the field to grow our food and it is a disgrace to waste food on one's plate. The food that we waste on the plate could be fed to someone else. I did not want to waste food on my plate. Therefore, I sat there wondering as to how to finish it all. Moreover, I had not been half through Adivamma's menu! I requested Adivamma for another plate to pile all those extra rotis and told her that I would carry them to my farm and finish them off at dinnertime that night. She smiled and agreed for the proposition. Then she continued to serve. She served a maize kernel dish called 'Kattambali' with crisp fried stuffed chilies. Then she served 'Holige' and 'Payasa.' Further, I was forced to eat some rice with 'Rasam,' 'Sambar' and curds (plain yogurt)". I ate so much that I found it very hard to get up from my mat and wash my hands.

After the huge meal, I carried myself to the divan in the drawing room to sit there. Adivamma appeared there with a plate of neatly sliced apples, along side she laid a plate of 'paan' and 'areca' nuts. She asked me to relax while she ate her lunch.

I told Adivamma that I would eat a piece of fruit and I had no habit of chewing 'paan' with 'betel' nut. After a hurried lunch, Adivamma came and sat in the opposite divan and kept the plate containing 'betel' nuts and 'paan' by her side. She chewed her 'paan' with some tobacco in a leisurely mood and conversed with me. She asked about my native place, my mother, my schooling, my brothers and sisters. She enquired about the rain pattern in our South Canara district and the crops that we grew there. Finally, she told me that she was happy that I visited her and she had the honor of reciprocating my hospitality. I replied her that the food that I could offer in my humble bachelor quarters was a frugal fair cooked by my 'Lambani' (gypsy) cook, and it cannot be called a meal at all compared to the lavish one she had served me. I thanked her for the meal and admitted that I had not eaten such a grand lunch of Deccan food in my life.

As I was ready to leave, she declared that she was ready to accompany me to the sub-registrar's office the next day morning to register her twenty acres of land in the name of our farm. She went inside to pack those extra rotis with some more in a big brass Tiffin carrier along with all those dishes that were served for lunch. She asked me to eat them all at my dinnertime and return the utensil the next day. That night my cook did not have to prepare dinner. Together, both of us could not finish what Adivamma had packed for us!

Next day, Adivamma proclaimed in front of the sub-registrar that she had received the rightful value of the land three years back and given possession of the land on the same day to us. It was her fault that she could not register the land because of her poor health condition. The land rights were transferred to us without any problem, as Adivamma did not raise any objection.

I cursed myself and strongly regretted my foolishness to suspect an honest grandmotherly lady like her. All she wanted from me was a human gesture, a cordial visit to her house, as expected of any friendly neighbor. My visit to her place and accepting that wonderful lunch, resolved the issue. When I dropped Adivamma at her home that evening after the registration work, I apologized to her for my adamant behavior of not visiting her house earlier. She said. "Son, forget all that. I am like a grandmother to you. Now, promise me that you shall come to my house often and have food in my kitchen. Now, have a cup of tea before you leave."

After this incident, Adivamma's bullock cart would come jingling to our farm more often. As soon as she alighted from her chauffeured bullock cart hitched with trotting bullocks, she would call out, "Son, how are you?" she would shout at my cook with all her 'maternal authority,' to make some *strong tea for her. Sometimes, she would join me for lunch. My cook always shivered at her arrival as Adivamma would walk into 'his domain,' and take him to task for his untidiness and poor cooking skills. Each time she visited my place, I had to go over to her house in the village, as a rule. Every time, I had to have a huge lunch, I had to fill my stomach to full capacity or else Adivamma would chide me. This great friendship continued until I left Jawalgera. She fed me like a mother and she was never tired of serving food for me. Even today, I remember Adivamma's lavish hospitality and all those mouth-watering dishes.*

*   *   *

Pejathaya's office was frequented by local villagers who hoped to get employment on the Tungabhadra Farms. One persistent lad was Lakpathi, who became Pejathaya's office boy. Here is his story.

LAKPATHI
BY S. M. PEJATHAYA

Lakpathi was my office boy and was about fourteen years old. He had never been to school as his parents were migrant laborers. He belonged to the Lambani (gypsy) tribe. His parents pleaded with me to give him a job as an adolescent field laborer. I employed him as my office boy, as it meant light work and he had a chance to refine himself for better prospects in future. He loved his job and kept my office premises spick and span.

Lakpathi would appear at 7 a.m. to water the rows of periwinkles in the courtyard space between my office and quarters. He nourished them with great care. No cattle would touch these hardy flower plants. He would maintain boiled and cooled drinking water in the earthen pot with a tap in my office. Everyday, he would bring in my 11 a.m. tea to the office from my kitchen. He would be present with cups of tea whenever visitors came. He would go on a bicycle to Jawalgera Post Office every afternoon and bring in our mail and the newspaper on every postal working day. The newspaper would come by post and I would get the same next day. There would be no newspaper on Sundays, as the Post Office remained closed.

We used to grow mainly cotton, hybrid sorghum, maize and Mexican dwarf wheat in addition to local 'Jowar' (local sorghum). Lakpathi was an intelligent boy though he had no education. In the evenings he would listen to my radio. He would look at the pictures in the newspapers. He would ask many questions about the affairs of the world. If ever he saw a movie in the tent cinema in Sindhanur, he would learn the film songs by heart at the first viewing itself and he would repeat some of the dialogues too!

I tried to teach him alphabet but failed miserably. Lakpathi had no aptitude to learn. He had no patience to learn the alphabet. He could pronounce the words correctly before he learned how to write them. He did not feel like going through the lengthy procedure of learning to write the same words that he could pronounce. I think he thought that he was wasting his valuable time! However, I could not understand the logic behind his thinking.

One morning a relative of our field supervisor, Sri Veerabhadra Gowda, came to visit him. Gowda was supervising work in our cotton fields, which were about a mile away. I found Lakpathi busy cleaning the premises. I asked him to dispatch one of the laborers from the nearby wheat field with a bicycle to summon Veerabhadra Gowda and request him to come to the office on the bicycle to meet his relative. I told Lakpathi to brew some tea for our visitor.

Lakpathi disappeared with the bicycle and returned in few minutes. I asked him as to whom he dispatched. He said he had sent one of our permanent workers, Manappa.

After serving tea to the guest, Lakpathi resumed his work of rigorous cleaning. The relative of Gowda was getting impatient as the few minutes of waiting turned into an hour and a half. I too was astounded about this delay. I went to check in the direction in which our supervisor was to come. I could see Veerabhadra Gowda struggling to push a bicycle about a furlong away! I thought the bicycle had a puncture and I sent Lakpathi running to fetch the bicycle. Young Lakpathi ran like a squirrel and reached Gowda within a minute. He took hold of the bicycle and started riding it towards our office to my great astonishment. I asked Lakhpathi what was wrong.

He said nothing was wrong at all! The truth was that our Manappa as well as supervisor Gowda did not know how to ride a bicycle and that is why they took such a long time to come with it! I felt like eating my hat for relying on most obedient fellow like Lakpathi. It turned out to be my absolute mistake.

I had to tell Lakpathi that he should send someone who knew to ride a *bicycle to call Gowda. In addition, I had to ascertain whether Gowda knew how to ride a bicycle.*

To the word, my orders were executed.

What really happened was Manappa, who did not know how to ride a bicycle carried it all the way to Gowda and instructed him to bring the bicycle to my office as per my orders! Gowda accepted the bicycle and pushed it all the way back. I never knew that Veerabhadra Gowda could not ride a bicycle! A sweating and panting Gowda conversed with his relative and sent him off. Lakpathi and Manappa went about their work as if nothing had happened! I was the only one to be frustrated by this strange incident.

The local coffee powder in our village shop of Jawalgera was very bad and stale because only a few people drank coffee in that village. I picked up a jar of instant coffee at Raichur, our district headquarters, when I went there on official work. I sent it through Lakpathi to our cook Gangappa. I forgot to tell him that it was soluble instant coffee and it needed no filtering.

Next morning, when I asked for a cup of coffee, Lakpathi ran to the kitchen. After sometime he appeared with the cup of coffee with a crestfallen face. He begged me not to drink that coffee. I ignored his remark and I started to drink my coffee with great relish, but found Lakpathi shedding tears in the corner.

I asked Lakpathi as to why he was crying. Lakpathi replied me very sadly that I was going to die soon and he would miss me very much. I was astonished at this sudden prediction and asked him to inform me of the impending cause of my death. He replied with great awe "Sir, the coffee that you brought the yesterday is poison! Because when its decoction was filtered, no used up powder remained on the strainer. Gangappa thought that this coffee powder was abnormal and it might be poisonous to drink such coffee. Sir! I too saw it dissolve in hot water completely!"

His mind had inferred that I would die by drinking of this abnormal coffee, which might be poisonous as the cook told! I called Gangappa to my office and explained both of them as to how the soluble coffee is manufactured. I told them that the coffee decoction is prepared in a large factory and sprayed into a hot chamber to get granules of instant coffee. The used up powder called 'coffee grounds' is readily disposed at the factory level. Thousands of people drink this kind of instant coffee everyday and it is as good as freshly brewed coffee. Finally both of them refused to be convinced of this fact. Lakpathi insisted that he would throw away the weird coffee. Finally, I asked him to do so. Lakhpathi was happy that I may not die soon!

The time came when I had to leave the farm. A doctor friend of mine at a place called Manvi wanted a boy for his clinic. He offered a better salary, food and shelter. I recommended Lakpathi to him. He had seen Lakpathi in our farm and liked him. The doctor promised to send Lakpathi to night school too. I felt happy as the doors for better future were opening for Lakpathi.

After some persuasion from my side, Lakpathi and his parents agreed to the prospects of the new job. One fine day I took Lakpathi in my jeep to Manvi. He readily agreed to work for the doctor. When I started back to the farm, Lakpathi bid a sad farewell to me.

Ten days passed and I received a telegram from my doctor friend to come immediately to fetch back Lakpathi to the farm. I started the same evening to Manvi to find a totally disheveled Lakpathi. He had lost some weight and looked very sick. His eyes were bloodshot. He looked like someone who had not slept for many days. The doctor told me that the boy worked very well and he liked his work very much. Yet, Lakpathi could not use the bathroom or the toilets and insisted going to the channel for his ablutions, as he was not used to the confines of four walls. The doctor agreed and sent him out for his bath and toilet purposes.

However, the main problem was that Lakpathi could not sleep inside the house. He could never sleep a wink but he did not bring the problem to my doctor friend's notice. Lakpathi had no one to talk to in the new surroundings. He wanted to sing his 'Lambani' songs loud but was afraid to do so. As he could not sing, he had problems of pent up emotions. He lost his appetite in about two days and finally refused to eat saying that he was not hungry.

Yet, he was very obedient and hard working as ever, but he was miserable in his new place. Though he was put to the night school, he had never picked up anything there and behaved like an alien in the night classes. He never seemed to adapt to the new environment of Manvi. I talked to Lakpathi and came to know of his problems. I explained the plight of the poor boy to the doctor. The doctor quoted me the famous lines "How can a bird that is born for joy sit in a cage and sing?" He asked me to set the singing bird in its natural habitat!

Once Lakpathi came to the farm, he slept for a full day in their hut. From the next day he ate and slept well. He became normal on the third day. Thus, Lakpathi returned to the farm to follow his fate like the others of his clan. There was no way I could help him.

∗   ∗   ∗

Pejathaya's workers were an interesting lot. Most of these youth came from poor beginnings. They struggled to find even the simplest jobs, and, once employed, they often used their earnings to support their parents and siblings. The more aggressive youth, like Mehboob, pushed hard to get any job, then looked for every advantage to promote to higher paying jobs.

We found that no matter how lowly paid a worker might be he would often send a significant portion of his earnings to his family. Sometimes the money sent home helped provide education for a sibling. The joint family adhered all its members together, as one. Each individual helped the 'family' reach a higher level of existence, just as Pejathaya's family had supported him through his college education. In exchange, the individual, like Pejathaya, did his part to help the family in return.

Another neighbor of Pejathaya, was a vestige of the Nizam feudal system. Pejathaya tells the story of meeting the Elder Raja.

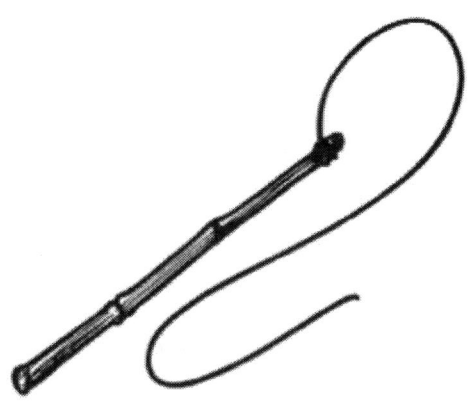

THE ELDER RAJA
BY S. M. PEJATHAYA

The Elder Raja, who lived in a castle-like manor near our farm, was a feudal landlord in his younger days. In the true sense, he was a 'Jahagirdar' (landlord). It seems that in the good old days of the 'Nizam' rule he owned nearly four thousand acres of land, which, he distributed amongst his innumerable tenant farmers. It appeared that he farmed about a thousand acres on his own even in those times.

The size of his manor was astounding. It had vast high wall surrounding it. In addition to the manor, the fort-like high walled compound contained cattle sheds, stables, armory, barns, godowns and even a building called the dungeon. People said he even had an execution chamber that was used by his ancestors. The dark dungeon block that still stood to exhibit tiny cubicles certainly asserted his feudal lineage. His ancestors were supposed to punish and jail the wrongdoers, criminals and the enemy captives.

His house was a fortified manor. The main door was to be approached by a maze of winding paths through high walls built of granite stones. The huge main door opened into an inner courtyard. It was a fact that his house had an underground treasury room. The fort-like compound contained two sweet water wells. The rest of the wells in at least ten-mile surroundings yielded only hard water. The ancestors had chosen the 'oasis' to build their fort-like house to dominate the surrounding villages. Before the advent of

Tungabhadra canal waters, his villagers and those of the surrounding villages took drinking water from these wells only. The despots of the manor could refuse water to any person or household as they pleased. Such person had to migrate away from the area. In other words, water was denied to any household that did not obey the despot.

Water was a rare and precious commodity before the irrigation channels came to the area during the middle of the twentieth century. The elder Raja had the village's two sweet water wells within the compound of his manor. The people of the village had to depend on Elder Raja for drinking water.

The Elder Raja had spent his younger days like a despot ruler though he was a 'Jahagirdar' under the 'Nizam' of Hyderabad. In other words, he was almost an absolute ruler of his village 'jahagir.' He had a small army of agricultural workers who were housed inside the fortified walls of the manor. He would go over to Hyderabad each year to pay his fixed yearly tribute to the Nizam. He, in turn, was authorized by the Nizam to collect revenue at his own discretion from the tenant farmers and the small farmers surrounding his manor. He would issue them revenue receipts under the seal and signature of his own. His 'Munshi,' (chief of accounts) maintained the revenue records of his 'jahagir.' A predetermined sum was paid to the 'Nizam' every year and the rest of the collected amount went to the coffers of the 'Jahagirdar.' However, the 'jahagirs' were abolished after India gained independence and the 'Nizam' State surrendered and joined the Union of India. The Elder Raja became only a big landlord. Then came the Land Ceiling Act and Land Reforms Acts of Karnataka. These Acts were enforced by the Government of Mysore, later to be called as the Government of Karnataka. This reduced the size of his holdings to limited number of acres. The eligible adult members of his family could hold maximum of about seventy acres of dry land allowed by the present government.

The Elder Raja showed a number of adult cousins and uncles, who could own lands to this maximum limit fixed by the government. They could get the 'khatas' (land holding rights) of the best lands available near his manor. The 'Jahagirdar' family was quite big. Even after the government curbs, the Elder Raja, being the eldest in the family, farmed and managed all the lands belonging to the members of his family. Instead of being the 'Raja' of the village, he became the 'Raja' in his manor. Very much like the olden days, he was respected and revered in the confines of his manor.

The tenant farmers, who farmed for him, became "independent farmers" in pursuance of the above said legislations. The dam water flowed and irrigated the land of the rich as well as the poor. There was no shortage of drinking water in the area. The dependence for drinking water on his private wells gradually ceased as people used the channel water.

The Elder Raja suddenly realized the loss of his power over the people of the village. He started to stay aloof from all the social activities of the village and confined himself to his manor. He became a very reserved person. He would ride out of the manor in full gallop every morning by about eleven to supervise his farming activities. He would not slow down his horse in the narrow village road nor did he ever stop to speak to anyone. He would use his riding crop without any hesitation if someone happened to obstruct his way unawares or unknowingly.

The younger brother of Raja was called 'Chikka Dhani' (junior boss) and he was very popular with the villagers. He was about fifteen years younger to the Elder Raja. He had grown up like any other aristocratic young man of modern India. Elder Raja loved him dearly and looked after him like his own son. 'Chikka Dhani' was well educated as he studied at Hyderabad. Being brought up in the modern ways, the younger brother kept good political contacts. Naturally, all the liaison work of the family and the record maintenance of the farmlands were taken over by the younger brother, while the elder one looked after the administration, financial matters and farming activities. Elder Raja was a good farmer and believed in orthodox organic farming.

I knew 'Chikka Dhani' very well, as he would drive a jeep like one of us, while his elder brother always preferred to ride his big stallion and loved to carry a riding crop in his hand. He seldom spoke to the villagers nor looked our way as he rode past our farm on the way to his lands. I heard from his younger brother that the Elder Raja was a very short-tempered and reserved person. He was feared in the neighborhood, as he was known to wield his riding crop mercilessly on anyone who offended him. People confirmed that the Elder Raja still lived in his old style of a despot. I never had an opportunity to talk to him, as I had no business with him. However, a day came when I was to confront this man all of a sudden!

It was a January morning. My laborers reported a big heard of cattle happily grazing in my Mexican dwarf wheat fields. I saw nearly thirty heads of cattle, neatly finishing off my good crop of wheat! I was upset and enquired my laborers as to whom the cattle belonged. They said that all of them belonged to Elder Raja and the cattle strayed into our land from Elder Raja's grassland next to our field. The man in charge of the cattle was not to be seen around.

As a custom, any stray cattle that came to graze on our farm crops would be tied in our cattle shed until the owner came to ask for their release. In this particular case my laborers were afraid to tie them up as the cattle belonged to Elder Raja.

I told the laborers that our farm rules cannot be bent for a VIP's stray cattle and I personally saw that the cattle were corralled in our huge cattle shed. I ordered our workers to provide grass and water to the animals so that they may not starve.

By evening, I heard the drumming of hooves near my office. I looked out to find the Elder Raja approaching our office. I came out to receive him. He stared at me with fire in his eyes. I said, "Namaste," and asked him come into my office, which he did after a moment of hesitation.

He entered my office carrying his riding crop. I offered him a chair and asked our office boy Lakpathi to bring a glass of water for our guest. I also asked him to order for some tea with cook Gangappa. The elder Raja was still staring at me and I pretended not to notice his wrath. Then, he spoke to me in a well-controlled voice. He said, "I want to speak to you."

I coolly replied, "Not until we have a cup of tea, because you are my honored guest". After we had our cups of tea, I offered him 'supari' (fragrant 'betel nut granules) though I do not chew supari. I offered him my brand of State Express cigarettes. As if to observe the niceties, he reluctantly took a piece of 'supari' and lit a cigarette.

Then, the Elder Raja spoke, "Manager Sahib, you look like a sensible young man from a good family, and I have been observing you as I pass by your farm. You are a hard worker too. Who gave the idea to corral my cattle? This may not be good for your health. Now, I want you to release them immediately."

I replied him with equal respect, "Raja Sahib, you are most welcome to our farm. You have set your foot on our premises for the first time, and I am honored. As per your request the cattle shall be released immediately, but I want to know the reason as to why they were grazing unattended on our wheat."

He replied, "I was told by my cowherd that one of our cattle accidentally put it's snout onto your wheat crop, and your people scared him away by beating him up, and you ordered your men to corral all my cattle. Is this true?"

I told him that the second part of his statement was very true while the first part was not. I told him about the damage done to my wheat crop that morning by his herd of cows and I had personally verified that there was no cowherd in attendance. Therefore, I had to do the inevitable. I told him that he might not have been aware of the fact. He got up from the chair and went out to call one of the laborers. A group of laborers had just arrived; they had followed him on foot. They were carrying staves, sharp sickles and axes. The fellow came trembling inside the office to fall prostrate at Elder Raja's feet begging for mercy as he admitted to the fact that he was away from the heard that morning. He begged for mercy repeatedly.

The Elder Raja handed over his riding crop to me and asked me to beat the liar until my arms got tired. I refused to take the riding crop, saying that it was not my concern. Next moment, I heard the wailing of the poor laborer as the furious Elder Raja wielded a rain of blows on the poor man, as he pitched and rolled on the floor begging him that he will never commit the same mistake again.

I could not bear the sight and I requested the Elder Raja to stop. He stopped beating the wretched man. He declared that the villain needed some more beatings but he stopped at my request. He came back to his chair and sat down as if nothing happened. He began in an embarrassed tone, "I am sorry for listening and believing this lowly man and coming down all the way from my manor to fight it out with you. But for your smiling hospitality, I would have impatiently lifted the riding crop on you too without caring for consequences in my fit of anger! I know the fact that you work for the most respected persons with lots of money and influence. Now I know that I would have committed a great mistake. Please excuse this impatient old man used to the old ways".

I told him that I could see that the mistake was not his and I was trying to forget the unpleasant incident already. He replied that it was very noble of me and tried to relax. He requested me for another cup of tea. Within a minute, Gangappa, who was watching the drama from behind the window screen, reappeared with two cups of tea.

I was really impressed by the Elder Raja's sincerity and the straightforward way in which he apologized. He never beat around the bush; he was straight. I could tell from his embarrassment that he has never used the word 'sorry,' much less, beseech apology!

It was a magnanimous act on his part. I appreciated Elder Raja and my respect for him doubled a hundred times more. After our tea, he stood up to take leave.

In a gesture to make amends, he invited me for dinner in his manor the following Sunday. This was a very rare honor indeed! Everyone around, who knew Elder Raja, congratulated me for having been invited for dinner at his residence. He is known to be a very reserved person and he had never invited anyone home.

The next Sunday, I drove my jeep through the narrow winding pathway that led to the courtyard of his manor. I could see a number of big granite boulders poised on top of the high walls. Probably, they were laid there in the past to take care of any unwanted visitor from entering the manor. The house too was built like a fort with thick walls of granite stone. The heavy wooden doors and windows were reinforced with thick strips of steel and had metal knobs on them. I was personally received by the Elder Raja. He ushered me into his private drawing room.

We sat on one of the thick mattresses spread on a huge antique carpet. Cool water that smelt of cardamom was served in tall silver glasses. The Elder Raja inquired about my native place, our family's farmlands and about my family members. After a few minutes I was invited to the dining room. The dinner was served on silver platters in the spacious dining hall. We squatted on the carpet and the plates were kept on four inch-high rosewood pedestals with intricate carvings. It was a lavish vegetarian dinner loaded with 'ghee' and sweets. There were 'jowar' and 'bajra' 'rotis' and wheat 'chapatis' in addition to flavored rice. I lost count of the side dishes. It was a dinner to remember. After dinner, tea was served in Hyderabadi fashion and 'betel' nut and 'paan' were offered. I thanked the Elder Raja for his hospitality. He told me that it was a pleasure for him too as he had no local guest to his table for many years. I thanked him and said good-bye.

After this incident, the Elder Raja started to lift his right hand in *greeting as he rode past me in our farm. I used to feel elated while exchanging such greetings. I was the one and only person in our village to be recognized by the Elder Raja. It was a matter of great pride for me to receive a wave in recognition from the Elder Raja.*

Our friendship grew with time. Occasionally, if I were to be found near our office, he would drop in for a friendly chat with me and have a cup of tea. Nervously, for decencies sake, I would invite him to have dinner with me in our farm, but he would politely refuse the invitation, saying that he was not a youngster like me to survive the cooking of a great cook like Gangappa!"

A VILLAGE CALLED MUKKUNDA

While Pejathaya entertained his neighbors and studied the local agriculture of Sindhanur *Taluka*, the India-60 volunteers were assimilating their roles as agriculture extension workers. The hours we spent in technical instruction during Peace Corps training in Hemet, California and Dhadesugur, India focused primarily on developing land for irrigation and assisting Indian farmers in cultivating dry-cum-wet crops. In truth, some of our group never constructed a contour border strip during their two years in India. I believe several volunteers in Manvi 'Taluka,' including Mike Quaid and Richard Wines did, however, get involved in making border strips.

Many of the volunteers actively worked as intermediaries between their more progressive village farmers and the India Department of Agriculture to demonstrate the growing of irrigated crops. Although most of the volunteers did not have agriculture backgrounds, they embraced their new roles with vigor and dedication.

George Franco, an India-60 volunteer, was from New York State and the Washington, D.C. area. He earned a degree in sociology from Boston College. His interests lay in studying foreign languages, writing and philosophy. The closest he came to seeing a farm before venturing to India was during his part-time work as a bricklayer. By his own admission, mowing lawn was his closest contact with living plants. Those of us who observed him during training had a difficult time envisioning him getting into the farmer mentality. Although he soaked up the *Kannada* language training with ease, George found agriculture an interesting diversion from his previous experiences. He enjoyed the change of pace but was somewhat befuddled with this new subject. He listened attentively during the long sessions on plant selection, crop protection and methods of irrigation with Mr. Cecil McCormac our technical instructor.

Once training ended, Peace Corps placed George in Huda, a secluded village about 15 miles from Sindhanur. Unfortunately, the deputed host farmer gave the impression that hosting an American was somewhat of a status achievement. As the "big man" in the village he was more interested in pursuits other than farming. George received very little cooperation from the villagers, and he found his endeavors to be ineffectual. In frustration, he sought the attention of anyone who wanted to hear his message. Farmers from the nearby village of Mukkunda, on the other hand, were very disappointed that they were not selected to host a volunteer. They lobbied George to move to their village, and promised him a good house to live in and their best cooperation.

That is how George eventually settled in a village that turned him into an extension worker dynamo. His new home away from home was the village of Mukkunda. This village was about as isolated as a village gets. Five days each week, when the road was deemed passable and a bus was in operating condition, a driver would attempt to leave Sindhanur to make the 22 kilometer trip to the outskirts of Mukkunda. That was on the good days.

The bus creaked to a halt at a wide spot in the road to let off its passengers so they could walk the last two kilometers to the village. I traveled this route with George several times, and noted that when the bus arrived it would be met by several bullock carts and a handful of family members and household servants. They were there to help carry the goods purchased in Sindhanur to the village. The last two kilometers were a miserably dusty walk in dry season, and featured ankle-deep mud during the monsoons.

A visitor to Mukkunda immediately felt something special

about this village. For one thing, the people seemed to be cheerful, and very cordial to each other and to outsiders. Even though I was a stranger, the first time I visited Mukkunda it felt as though the villagers were welcoming me home. There was pattern and organization to the lush fields surrounding the path, and once inside the village you could see an order to the streets and a pleasant appearance to the buildings. On closer inspection I could see why.

Each rectangular structure was built of precision, hand-cut stones. The stone fitting was so well done that you couldn't slip a credit card between the stones. The structures had perfectly square corners and straight, vertical walls. Most of them had been built more than one hundred years before I strolled the pathways of this ancient village. Mukkunda was famous for its ancient temples. These included the *Murari Ranga*, *Eshwara* and *Baajeshwara* temples, which were built during the rule of the *Sindha* dynasty, an ancient civilization.

The best part about Mukkunda, however, was the attitude of its 2000 plus inhabitants. George's host farmer was Mudiya Gowda, but George also worked closely with several other progressive farmers, including one Sri Chandrappa. These two farmers had insatiable appetites for information. They wanted to know everything we knew, and more.

We were perfectly surprised when George gained a significant amount of agriculture knowledge once he started working with his more progressive farmers. During the few short months George lived in Mukkunda he accomplished a lot. At first, George would come to my Sindhanur house in a panic, "Ken! Help me! What is the best spacing for hybrid jowar? What pesticide should they use for cotton stem borer? How much does a tractor cost?"

He had a list of questions about crop selection, plant protection, mechanized equipment and he always wanted the information immediately so he could hasten back to Mukkunda with the answers. Later, Mudiya Gowda and Chandrappa would come to Sindhanur with George. They wanted to get answers 'from the horse's mouth.' They would look through my *Farm Journals*, and ask questions about the machines they saw in the pictures. Their English was limited, but they were so hungry for information that they learned English from George and the other volunteers in a shorter time than it took us to learn *Kannada*.

True, Mudiya Gowda and Chandrappa had insatiable appetites for agriculture knowledge, but they were also good leaders, and immensely sensitive and cordial to others. They easily espied people they could learn from, as well as people whose ideas they needed to disregard. I heard their names dropped by high-ranking government officials, who aimed their cutting-edge research in the direction of progressive people, like these two gentlemen.

Mudiya Gowda and Chandrappa were the kind of people who make others shine. Their enthusiasm drove George to be a first rate Peace Corps volunteer. Their questions opened new avenues for the rest of us by making us ask questions we had not considered. When I had difficulty getting the local farmers interested in a milk collection and distribution plan it was Mudiya Gowda who said, "Why don't you approach the Andhra farmers. They have healthy animals and seem to listen to new ideas."

People like these two gentlemen have pure, unadulterated intentions to be the best they can be and to help the people around them. The world needs more people like them.

THE MANDHANUR BUFFALO

Pejathaya was also beginning to make his mark and expand his horizons. He eventually met all the volunteers who stopped by my house, and he was able to get involved in many of our projects. He listened to our ideas and contributed his own. He almost seemed like one of the volunteers.

We would find time after work to converse, sometimes for hours. The volunteers realized that Pejathaya was experiencing the same adjustments to the local climate, culture and type of agriculture as they were. To our tremendous advantage, he was like a brother, who could explain the things that would have made the transition to life in India difficult for us. He clarified the understanding of the confusing religious deities. He explained the behavior of the caste system, and he shared his ideas on the Indian culture.

During the monsoon rains of 1969, several of the volunteers were stranded in Sindhanur when bad roads prevented their buses from transporting them to their villages. Tony was there because his house in Turvihal leaked so badly that all his belongings were wet and there was no place to sleep. He was an utter mess when he dragged himself into Sindhanur and presented himself at my door. His eyes were bloodshot from lack of sleep. He hadn't eaten a decent meal in two days because he could not find a dry match to start a fire in his soaked kitchen. He also had a disturbing cough.

Thankfully, my roof was holding up. The outdoor toilet did not have a roof but we could, to a certain degree, time our visits between the rain showers. The humidity, however, was beginning to make our paper files swell with moisture, and my typewriter showed signs of rust.

We fought over the most recent issue of Monroe's *Time* magazine, and then sat around the gloomy rooms trying to amuse ourselves with 'war stories' as darkness began to set in. Conversation led from stories of our trifling successes to dreams of what we wanted to accomplish with the last year of our PCV contracts. Tony and Monroe spoke of sharing ideas between us volunteers, the Department of Agriculture officials, Peace Corps Bangalore and our village farmers. Someone came up with the idea of writing a cooperative newsletter that could be circulated to interested people.

In the flickering candlelight, one of the group came up with the idea of getting the PCVs from both Manvi and Sindhanur *Talukas* to contribute articles about their work. It was further suggested that we could include articles and notices from the government officials as well as from Peace Corps Bangalore.

By this time it was too dark to clearly see their faces so I wasn't sure if they were serious or not. Who would have the time to write articles? Moreover, who would have the time to compile articles, edit and type them, and then reproduce and distribute the final product? Who would pay for the paper and the mailing costs?

Despite my concerns, or maybe because of them, Monroe and Tony decided to take this up with the 'powers that be." Swifter than a hungry snail, the 'powers that be' signed off on the proposal and Peace Corps agreed to buy the print stock, mimeograph the edited product and mail it to all the interested parties. All we needed to begin the newsletter idea was a name for the paper and some articles.

The name came from our surroundings. Sindhanur and Manvi are two adjoining *talukas* in Raichur District. The volunteers were evenly divided between the two *talukas*. The most interesting creature that lives in Raichur District is the water buffalo, or "*hole' Yemme*," (river buffalo) as dubbed by the local farmers. I considered them the ugliest beasts of burden you will ever see. Even the East African wildebeest looks handsome in comparison. But these guys are very docile. Their true value is their ability to work in the water-filled rice paddies. They have rough curved horns and leathery thick, black hides. They might be slow, but these animals are ugly. They have a mind of their own, if, indeed, they have a mind at all.

Tony Ganey disagreed. He never thought of the buffalo as ugly or mindless. He said, "Perhaps stubborn, definitely tireless, and when set in motion he could not be deterred—thus the common observation 'brake inspector.'" He explained, referring to vehicles encountering buffalo on the high roads, "If you came upon animals walking along the roadway only the buffalo would not vary his pathway. Cattle, goats and sheep would split in all directions and create numerous hazards to anything else a foot, but not the buffalo—sure and steady, moving forward without varying from his set direction."

It was this image in Tony's mind that helped him find a voice for the India-60 journal. He said, "We want our 'Buffalo'—its words—to prompt the Buffalos of Raichur to wade thru the water rather than wallow in the mud."

The newsletter was called the *Mandhanur Buffalo*. The front page of each issue was adorned with a cartoon sketch of a water buffalo, sometimes with a fly buzzing around its head. We asked Pejathaya for his advice. We did not want to violate any religious or cultural sensitivities.

In the beginning, the volunteers expended great quantities of pent up enthusiasm and ideas to contribute articles with prolific regularity. After several issues, however, Tony, our Charminar-smoking Editor-in-Chief and Monroe, our Assistant Editor, had to shake us down for articles to fill the pages. This is where our Indian partners, like Pejathaya, stepped in to add ideas and articles. Pejathaya became an avid reader of the *Mandhanur Buffalo*, and created articles to supplement its pages.

Pejathaya wrote serious articles and letters to the editor about agriculture in Raichur District. The quality and sincerity of his articles revealed a unique writing deftness. He had a latent talent for expressing himself in a charming and entertaining manner.

He started sharing some of his ideas through his writing. Several years later I read his best works. The following example is a story he wrote about the bullocks on his Tungabhadra Farm not far from Sindhanur.

THE HOLY BULLOCKS OF OUR FARM
BY S. M. PEJATHAYA

Surya and Chandra (the Sun and the Moon) were the holy bullocks of our farm. They were king-sized sinewy bullocks of milky white color. These were called our holy bullocks since they were maintained more for grandeur than for work. My boss, Sri K. K. Pai, loved these bullocks very much. He had specifically instructed me not to work them in the field, but to see that they get their daily exercise.

To exercise the bullocks, we would yoke them to their magnificent 'Bellary 'Gaadi,' made to order upon the instructions of my boss at a famous cart-making concern of Bellary. They pulled at this cart with great zest during their exercise runs every day except Tuesdays. Tuesdays were full holidays for our bullocks as it was a custom in the villages not to work the beasts of burden at least for one day a week.

Lingayya was deputed to look after these bullocks. He was a devout 'Lingayat.' All Hindus worship the cow and 'Linguists' worship bullocks as they call them as the reincarnation of 'Nandi'—the bull of Lord 'Shiva.' Lingayya spent most of his time in the bullock shed. He would sleep in their shed during the nights as he stayed alone in the farm. He would feed and massage them with great care. He would clean and oil their cart every day. Lingayya was unmarried and used to say that the bullocks were his family.

We grew a native strain of sorghum called 'Bili Jola' in about two acres of land exclusively for the sake of our bullocks. My boss's instructions were to see that we use the tractor to till and sow these two acres of land too so that his beloved bullocks are not strained. Lingayya would harvest two large bundles of green sorghum plants and feed the bullocks every day.

Lingayya would feed and water the bullocks first in the morning. Then he would put 'kumkum' 'Tilak' on their forehead and say his prayers folding his hands in front of them. Being an ardent 'Lingayat,' this daily ritual gave him immense pleasure. The bullocks too loved this man dearly. They resented anyone else touching them. Whenever my boss came to visit the farm about once in six months, he would first go to the bullock shed to lay his eyes on his favorite bullocks and then only step into my office.

In the cool of the evening, Sri K. K. Pai would ask Lingayya to hitch the bullocks to the cart and he would go for a jolly ride. We all enjoyed this sight. A jet-set Managing Director of a commercial bank in full suit, enjoying his evening ride on a bullock cart! A fully suited figure of a man riding on a bullock cart was quite an unusual sight in the villages of Raichur. The villagers watched the scene with great astonishment.

On their daily exercise runs, the bullocks would keep a steady trot for about an hour. Yet, they would never show any sign of exhaustion. I would attend Jawalgera, Pothnal and Thimmapur 'jaathras' (local fairs) with pride riding on our bullock carts. These 'jaathras' were huge assemblies of farmers where each one exhibited his prized bullock pair. I would wear my blue blazer, flannel trouser and striped tie. I would sport a bright turban over my head. The turban would be neatly tied up by taking the expert help from my field supervisor Veerabhadra Gowda. I would be invited to these 'jaathras' and I, like any other local landlord, always made it a point to attend such 'jaathras' in the traditional style of the early nineteenth century.

These trips were mainly to showcase our prized bullocks and our custom-built Bellary cart with intricate designs. I would stand in the cart while Lingayya would drive our Rolls Royce of a cart into the crowded 'jaathra' street. The farmers' crowd appreciated this gesture every year and the organizers of the jaathras always insisted that I must attend the 'jaathra' in the same style every year. It was, of course, a matter of pride for me to exhibit Surya and Chandra.

During one of the exercise runs, our bullock Surya suddenly got tired and started to froth. He was wheezing as he had difficulty in breathing.

When the cart returned from the ride, Lingayya was frightened to death, as our boss would be very angry. I too was worried about Surya. My boss would certainly take us to task for our negligence, as to how we could ignore such a serious symptom of ill heath in Surya. I immediately sent the jeep to Sindhanur to fetch the veterinary doctor.

We all collectively reported to the vet that the bullock was fine until the previous day and we never noticed any problem with him. The vet gave a thorough medical check-up to Surya. He declared that Surya exhibited excellent signs of good health, except for the fact that he got tired easily that day and he inferred that it might be due to some allergy. The allergy might have been caused by some kind of grass it had as fodder the previous day. To pacify me, the wise vet gave some injection to the bullock and prescribed two days' complete rest.

Next day, my boss was informed of Surya's sickness in my daily work report. I received a long letter giving me 'special instructions' to arrange for the best treatment for Surya and to report his condition in my daily work reports without fail. He had asked me to take extra care of Surya.

The vet visited the farm every day for several days but the symptoms with Surya continued to persist. Finally, the vet gave his verdict that Surya had a sort of breathing problem like wheezing, which he could not cure at once with his medicines.

I informed the same to my boss in my report. I got a reply asking me to try the 'Ayurvedic' or native treatment for Surya at the earliest. I consulted Janekal Mallappa of Jawalgera who was an elderly friend and neighbor of mine. Mallappa used to give native treatment for the local cattle and he cured most of them. He spent nearly half a day with Surya and finally said that the disease was of a serious nature and he had no cure for such ailment. He declared that the bullock can only be cured by the native medicine of the Hakim[24] of Pothanaal village.

Next morning I was at Pothanaal to meet Hakim Saheb. Janekal Mallappa was with me to show me the way to his place. Mallappa introduced me to the old Hakim. The Hakim reciprocated my 'Namaskara' with 'Walaikum assalaam' (meaning, may peace be with you also). He looked like a very pious man. He was very tall and stood

---

[24] Muslim physician

very straight. He wore loose fitting 'Pathan suit' of ash color and a green turban. Hakim Saheb had a long flowing beard dyed red with henna. The aged Hakim seemed to be a well-to-do farmer and had a large house. He offered us tea, and then patiently heard the problem with our prize bullock. After thinking for some time, he told me, "A membrane inside the belly of the bullock has become brittle." For which the treatment was very simple. A pellet of native medicine was to be forced through the bullock's gullet first and a live monitor lizard was to be released inside the belly of the bullock! He told me that the treatment shall be performed free of charge on a full moon day. He coolly asked me to procure a young monitor lizard of about one foot length and come to him. Then he would get the herbal medicines ready by the next full moon.

I started to sweat at the idea of this treatment! I pleaded that our Surya is a strict vegetarian and he would not swallow a live monitor lizard. The old man adamantly told me that I had to follow his instructions, if I desired the cure. I wanted to buy time. In the meanwhile, I immediately decided to consult the veterinary doctor of Sindhanur who had studied in a University Veterinary College before agreeing to such weird treatment. I told the Hakim that we shall try to procure a monitor lizard of one-foot length and then see him again in the next few days.

The wize Hakim, who was as old as my grandfather, could sense that I was fidgeting. He straightaway told me that I can never catch a monitor lizard by myself nor buy it from any known source that easily. He told us that he had his tribal supplier of the lizards, who always obliged his indents without fail. He wanted me to give him an advance of two hundred rupees and book one for our use immediately, so that he can appear with the lizard at my farm on the next full moon day to treat Surya. He told me that he would never charge for the medicine part of his treatment.

The next full moon day was twenty days away and there was sufficient time for him to procure the monitor lizard. I paid two hundred rupees advance on the advice of Janekal Mallappa. However, I thought I had twenty days to decide on the matter. I could always refuse the treatment if my boss objected. I went to the vet at Sindhanur next day and reported the line of treatment of the native doctor. The learned vet told me that he did not know of any hardening membrane in a bullock's stomach that would cause wheezing problems. The vet told me that the Hakim had cured a number of bullocks in our neighborhood of similar wheezing problems. He assured me that the Hakim was very reliable and advised me to let him have a try.

Despite the clinical advice, I was afraid to give my consent for the treatment. If something untoward happened to Surya, my boss would be offended and I would certainly lose my job. Yet, everybody in the farm asked me to give a try for this treatment. At last I wrote a letter to my boss seeking permission to follow the native treatment. In the letter I mentioned that the Hakim wanted to use a live monitor lizard along with some native medicine. Surprisingly, the approval for the treatment came by way of a neatly typed letter duly signed by my boss. This relieved most of my tensions, until the day the Hakim arrived at the farm for the treatment, with Janekal Mallappa.

The Hakim opened his small brass sheet trunk and took out a number of herbs and roots. To these he added some strange smelling powders from various bottles he carried in his trunk. He asked for a food grinding stone and about a quarter liter of fresh milk, which we readily supplied. He ground all the ingredients to a juicy paste. Then, he slowly rolled the paste into a tennis ball sized pellet. It smelt very acrid and must have been very pungent too. Then, he showed me a cylindrical shaped earthen pipe-like container with two small breathing holes. He told me that inside that container he had brought the live monitor lizard.

Suddenly, my stomach started to churn and I was sweating all over the body. The very thought of releasing a live monitor lizard into the stomach of our bullock appalled me. My throat went dry and without my knowledge, I was praying for the mercy of all the Gods to save our Surya from any calamity. The things happened in a quick frenzy. The Hakim asked Lingayya and Janekal Mallappa to hold the bullock's snout high. Within a fraction of a second the aged Hakim thrust the ball of medicine into Surya's gullet. Surya resisted, but he had to swallow that pellet as his nose was tightly closed by the Hakim. Surya agitated and reared in his stall. He could not back up anymore as he was tied. Resisting the awful taste, he brought his snout down in a quick movement to bring out the pellet. At the same time, the Hakim had held the cylindrical container and opened the small lid right under his open mouth! Simultaneously he was tapping the container, to frighten away the poor monitor lizard.

In a flash, I saw the monitor lizard clambering into the cavernous mouth and the downwardly extended neck portion of Surya. Probably, the monitor lizard thought that he was being released into a hollow tunnel that lay before him! Surya once again brought his neck up trying to cough-out whatever thing that crawled in through his gullet. The monitor lizard was faster than the gentle bullock. The lizard had already entered the alimentary canal of the bullock. It took a couple of minutes to calm down Surya. He looked normal again to my great relief.

The old Hakim said that the treatment was successful and he was in a hurry, as he had to attend some family function in his village. I did not want to let him go for another half an hour! I invited him and Janekal Mallappa for a cup of tea in my office.

I quietly excused myself and got into the kitchen to tell our cook Gangappa to serve cookies and tea as slowly as he could so that the old Hakim would be retained for at least for some thirty minutes! So, Gangappa took his sweet good time to bring empty glasses first. Then, he appeared with a jug of water. Next, the empty plates were laid on table. After few minutes the cookies were served. Followed by my few angry calls (feigned, of course!) cook Gangappa appeared with very hot mugs of tea. He did not bring tea in cups and saucers. Our intelligent cook had the mugs sterilized in boiling water for more than ten minutes, so that the tea remained scalding hot for the next few minutes. Immediately after serving tea Gangappa cleared away water glasses, to prevent Hakim from using one of them to cool down the tea, by tossing the scalding liquid from the mug to glass. Poor old Hakim took more than ten minutes to finish his tea in the forty plus noon temperature of Raichur district.

Thus, more than half-an-hour went by before Hakim was ready to leave. We inspected Surya once again. He seemed to be doing fine. Hakim promised me that the bullock would be cured of his ailment in a couple of days. He advised two days' complete rest for Surya. I thanked Hakim Saheb and bid farewell to him as he got into our jeep. I instructed our Driver Raj to drop the old Hakim to his destination.

Two days went by. On the third day, we hitched the cart to Surya and Chandra. As usual, they eagerly pulled the cart in a steady trot. Two bullocks returned after covering the customary two miles. To our great amazement and joy, Surya was doing well. No froth in the mouth and no wheezing! I was thrilled. I jumped into the jeep to rush to Sindhanur to give an express telegram to our boss relaying the success of the treatment. Next day, I received a long congratulatory telegram from my boss requesting me to visit the Hakim with fruits, betel leaves, a couple of coconuts, and a woolen embroidery shawl and thank him on his behalf. I was too willing to execute the orders of my boss with great relief. I drove up to Sindhanur town to buy the most expensive embroidered green shawl for the Hakim. Without my knowledge, I was singing to myself happily, as I drove up to Pothanaal village!

The old Hakim was immensely pleased with our gesture. He thanked my benevolent boss, Sri K. K. Pai and me for the honor. I was a very happy boy that day. I certainly would have lost my job for good had something happened to Surya.

The days went by, and one day, we were to sell the farm to one Sri K. Surya Rao of Sindhanur, as my bosses decided to wind up the farm. I was to be married during that summer of 1971. My boss told me that he wanted to put me on another project. He came over to the farm for negotiations. It took almost no time as the deal was struck through a media. Once the price was agreed upon, my boss agreed to sell the farm lock stock and the barrel, except the pair of bullocks.

When it came to Surya and Chandra, my boss told Sri Surya Rao sternly that he would never sell his beloved bullocks for all the silver and gold in this world, and intended to take them to Manipal, his hometown. Sri Rao on the other hand insisted that he should kindly sell them to him at any fancy price. He tried to convince my boss that these bullocks were accustomed to hot climate of Raichur district and their main feed was sorghum and sorghum straw, which would be unavailable in the coastal town of Manipal.

This statement did not cause much worry for my boss as he had already contemplated the prospect of importing the sorghum and sorghum straw from Raichur district for his pet bullocks.

Sri Rao put up a new tact! He begged my boss not to sell the bullocks for money at all! But, to give them as a present with his blessings! He revealed to my boss that he had made up his mind to buy our farm, only after he had the fascination to own and look after the prize bullocks. He promised my boss that he would never work them in the field and he would worship the holy bullocks. He promised to take over Lingayya under his employment. My boss told Sri Rao that he would think over about the matter and let him know his decision the next day, and sent him off.

Then, my boss called me aside to ask my opinion as to whether our bullocks may adopt to the coastal climate of Manipal. And, what to do in case our bullock Surya developed the wheezing problem there again. I was not sure about the answer. He asked me to verify with the old Hakim of Pothanaal village.

I went to the village to seek the expert advice of the Hakim. Hakim Saheb told me that the coastal weather may cause the breathing problem to relapse again. I requested the Hakim Saheb to come along with me to explain the matter to my boss as this was a very delicate issue. Old Hakim readily agreed to come with me. He met my boss and my boss thanked him profusely for curing his bullock, Surya. He discussed the issue of taking the bullocks to his hometown. During the discussions, my boss went even to the extent of air-conditioning the bullock shed for his pet Surya and Chandra.

Hakim Saheb kept on saying that the arrangement may not work at all. He feared the disease could relapse in the humid coastal climate and it would be difficult to get him out of it in case the problem relapsed.

Finally, our boss bid farewell to the old Hakim and retired for the night in a grim mood. Next morning, Sri Surya Rao arrived to request for Surya and Chandra again. My boss Sri K. K. Pai asked Lingayya to bring the bullocks in front of the office. He took the lead ropes of both the bullocks in his hand, summoned Sri Surya Rao and handed over the ropes to him and said, "With our compliments I am handing over Surya and Chandra to you. Please look after them well." Next, he climbed into his big car and asked the chauffeur, Mr. Jathanna to drive on to Sindhanur. He never looked back.

*   *   *

Although Pejathaya's story was very descriptive of an owner's love for his magnificent bullocks, the article didn't get past the desk of the editor of the Mandhanur Buffalo. "Too long," Tony said, "and not of immediate interest to the local farmer. It is a good story, however. Maybe you should write a book."

Eventually, Pejathaya did write a book. Select chapters of it are included here.

During India-60's final year in India, a total of eight issues of the *Mandhanur Buffalo* were printed and circulated. It should be considered a success. For the first time, a line of communication was available that linked the volunteers not only to each other but also to the different governmental and commercial offices and to the English speaking public. It was a vehicle that assisted the Raichur District residents in gaining a better understanding of the Peace Corps, and what the volunteers were attempting to accomplish in India.

Finally, the Mandhanur Buffalo served as a valuable tool to announce in a semi-formal manner the newest findings of the greater agricultural community. The newsletter contained information on the proper utilization of chemical pesticides, the hazards of over irrigation, locations and prices to acquire agricultural inputs such as seeds, fertilizers and pesticides, and, occasionally, a cartoon or a joke.

GETTING INVOLVED

India-60 volunteers in Sindhanur *Taluk*; John, Merle, Tony, George, Billy, Tom, and Monroe presented themselves at my doorstep less and less frequently after the first eight or nine months. Each of the volunteers became more involved with their assignments. They began to identify needs in their villages that required their attention.

For example, John noticed that there was almost no visible medical facility available for the poor people in his village. He saw young and old suffer from local treatments that caused more pain and distress than the original injury or disease. He could not stand to see another human being suffer. John dedicated much of his time to assist the ailing villagers.

Tom discovered that the Andhra farmers in his host camp had the capacity to grow more crops than the local market could handle. He also saw a need for reliable supplies of crop spraying equipment, chemicals and fertilizers. There were some industrious villagers who made it their business to attend to those needs but they were not organized sufficiently to operate in a sustained manner. Tom helped organize an agricultural marketing cooperative.

Tony listened to frustrated farmers who had access to power equipment such as tractors and power tillers, but struggled with keeping the machinery maintained and operational. There were diesel engine water pumps, several power tillers and a number of 35-horsepower tractors. These machines provided very important assistance to the farmers when they worked. When the machines failed, parts were almost impossible to find. Even if the parts were available there was no mechanic with tools to repair the machines. Tony contacted machine manufacturers and distributers to help find parts and service.

Billy, who graduated from the University of Montana with a BS in chemistry, had visions of applying his academic achievements to practical endeavors. His creativity came of use not only through promoting safety in use of pesticides, but in more imaginative undertakings such as repairing power sprayers and researching potential production of alcohol from local plants. Billy also stepped in to lend his expertise later in our program when we needed to learn how to test local buffalo milk for butterfat content.

Billy, who grew up on a 4000 acre Montana wheat farm and operated large machinery, was very interested in the "Russian Farm". He heard about the large combine harvesters and massive tractors on the Central State Farm and he yearned for the chance to clamber up on one. When he finally visited that experimental farm the Chief Information Officer, Mr. Khetarpal, refused to let Billy climb aboard. We speculated whether that refusal was related to the status of U.S–Soviet Union relations or was just standard farm protocol.

Billy, Richard (in Manvi Taluka) and John observed the struggle farmers had with insects that destroyed large portions of their crops. When they noticed that the row spacing of some crops accommodated the wheels of the standard bullock cart they devised a cart mounted boom sprayer that could cover several acres in a few hours. It was an unwieldy contraption that looked like something from a Star Wars movie set, but it was effective.

Monroe saw that his farmers wanted to use backpack sprayers to fight the infestation of pests on their crops but were deterred by lack of safe insecticides and parts for their Aspee Bolo hand pump sprayers. He organized a weekly appearance at the Sindhanur weekly market where several of the volunteers would gather on the steps of the Syndicate Bank to repair sprayers and sell plant protection equipment and sprayer parts. This informal market-day booth became a popular way to disperse agricultural brochures and literature of safe plant protection.

Monroe also received a small grant from CARE, and set up a sprayer rental office in his village of Alabanur. Pest Control Rentals of Alabanur (PCRS) bought five hand operated Aspee Bolo sprayers and several hand operated dusters. The PCRS also sold pesticides, safety equipment, fertilizers and seeds from its rented office. This facility eventually served not only Alabanur but also ten surrounding villages.

Merle was determined to make the desert bloom. With relentless energy he sought out every available crop demonstration plot to find plants that could grow in his Salagunda farmers' black cotton soil. A frequent visitor in the government offices and at the regional research stations, Merle became well known as an industrious agriculture pioneer.

The India-60 volunteers from Manvi *Taluka* were also becoming independent as they developed strong relationships with their more progressive farmers and delved into special projects. Chuck Length was developing a good rapport with the manager and drivers from the Manvi Tractor Society, and was having success in developing land for irrigation and agricultural production.

Willy James was deeply concerned by the poor nutrition he observed in Chagbhavi Village, and throughout parts of Manvi *Taluka*. He wanted to introduce healthy foods into the diet of villagers. He pushed for high protein crops, such as soybeans, to improve nutrition. He advocated household vegetable gardens to get quality foods on their tables, and traveled widely to find seeds and advice to get his ideas started.

Willie, David Mamulski and Richard Wines came through Sindhanur occasionally and related their successes with their agriculture work. Michael Quaid directed his energy to not only help the average Sirwar farmer improve his agricultural production, but discovered a special spot in his heart for the often overlooked poorest people. His work with low caste villagers was legendary. All of these men had learned their spoken *Kannada* well and were loved by their villagers. Richard and some other volunteers also learned the *Kannada* script and were able to communicate in writing at a respectable level.

The volunteers were becoming very comfortable with the various avenues for getting help from government authorities, regional research centers and from other developmental organizations, such as USAID and private agricultural product manufacturers and distributors. The consultants at the local agricultural research facilities introduced themselves during our earlier training and had volunteered their help. The Department of Cooperatives helped with existing or potential cooperative societies. There were numerous research institutes to assist in questions on growing crops, developing land, irrigation and drainage and land reclamation issues. Private agricultural companies began promoting their products by contacting PCVs directly.

India-60 volunteers were fortunate to have excellent cooperation with government officials. The Assistant Director of Agriculture (ADA) in Sindhanur Taluk, Achyat Rao, was eager to assist the volunteers in their work, and became a friend and a great resource.

Mr. A.B. Bellary, served as the The Assistant Director of Development and was very helpful to the volunteers. He had earlier served as a technical instructor for India-60 during our three months of training. Mr. Bellary was one of our main contacts during our entire two years. He also spearheaded the search for the ideal crop to grow in Raichur District's black cotton soil. The Deputy Director of Agriculture in Raichur was J.R. Bhaktul, who was incredibly helpful to the volunteers and a great supporter of the Peace Corps. Casting a benevolent eye over the entire enterprise was the District Collector, Mr. Jayakumar Anagaol.

This was the most productive time during our two years of service. We had learned enough of the language and customs to be able to communicate, and we had a plethora of resources to help us attain our goals.

THE NOT-SO-GREAT INQUISITION

Several months after the India-60 volunteers were placed in their respective host sites, we were invited to the district headquarters in Raichur for meetings with officials from the Department of Agriculture. We were informed that other Peace Corps groups would also be attending these April 1969 meetings.

Most of us were at first comforted to learn that there were other Americans not far away. It gave one a modicum of solace to learn that others had suffered the same circumstances and survived. It was also an opportunity to get news of home, swap war stories and maybe listen to some American music, as well as get some survival tips. The volunteers in Raichur were part of a *Village Level Food Production* unit.

The meetings with Agriculture Department officials went well. We met the District Agriculture Department leaders as well as our Indian counterparts and reviewed the goals and progress of our joint mission as agricultural extension workers. Between meetings some of the Raichur PCVs directed us to local eating establishments that were popular with volunteers. Most of the volunteers decided to spend the night in Raichur, because buses to Sindhanur were not easily available late in the day. Also, the Raichur volunteers invited us to a party at the home of one of the local volunteers.

Late that evening several of us went to the house of the volunteer hosting the get-together. We were not convinced that we were up for a party, as it had been a long day and all the volunteers were tired. The sun had descended below the horizon and darkness was falling fast as we approached the PCV's house. We could hear loud music, but there were very few lights emanating from the house. We got a distinctive whiff of something strange as we stepped in the door. It was too dark to see much, but when our eyes became more accustomed to the dark we could discern about two dozen human figures. One of them pointed to a stool and, over the loud sounds of rock 'n' roll said, "Have a seat."

As I moved toward the seat Merle pulled my sleeve and said, "I'm going!"

"Let's stay a minute and meet some people," said I. "We can leave soon."

Merle was having none of it. He understood better than did I that the smell we met with on entry was likely *ganja*. *Ganja* is the Sanskrit term for cannabis. *Ganja*, or any form of mind-altering drug, was strictly forbidden. Its use was against the law in India, and the American Peace Corps threatened to expel from the country any PCV suspected of possessing, selling or using any outlawed substance. No amount of cajoling could get Merle to change his mind. The front door opened again and he was gone.

It was too dark to recognize anyone, and I could hear no familiar voices over the loud music. So, I just sat there and tried to get into the swing of the gathering. Something was being passed around the room and my instincts told me it was not something people wanted to advertise. Soon it was handed to me. It looked like a pipe and it smelled like something I had not experienced, however, I instinctively knew it had to be some form of marijuana.

It was a situation I had never confronted. Through my college and young adult years I never once tried marijuana, even though I once saw plants growing along the roadside, where my Dad pointed them out. It was just not something I ever felt the need for or had the time or inclination to try. That night, at what could be a crossroads of my life, I hesitated to lift the bong to my lips. I passed it along to the closest person to me without tasting the sweet smoke of its burning leaf. I decided this house was not a place I wanted to be, and I left.

Several weeks passed back in Sindhanur with no further

mention of this event. Then, one afternoon, a volunteer who lived near Raichur came through Sindhanur to catch the overnight bus to Bangalore. He wasn't sure why, but he had received a telegram from Peace Corps Bangalore instructing him to meet with the Associate Director, immediately.

I didn't think much of this until two days later when another volunteer was called to Bangalore. Then, I became curious and started to ask questions. The next thing I knew, one of the Raichur volunteers stopped by my house to say goodbye. He was given a one-way ticket back to his home in the U.S.

George Franco, the volunteer in Mukkunda, was called to Bangalore next. A day later, he was driven back to Sindhanur *Taluka* in a Peace Corps van, and given two hours to pack up his personal belongings and say goodbye to his host farmer and village friends. The villagers loaded George and his personal belongings onto a bullock cart and walked alongside the cart for the two kilometers to where the Peace Corps driver was waiting for him.

George was in tears when he stopped by my house to plead with me to please help his farmers. He asked me to spend at least a week with Chandrappa when his new tractor arrived, and to make sure the new hybrid cotton seeds made it to the village. He also asked me to not tell Chandrappa or Mudiya Gowda that he was being kicked out of the country for violating the banned substance rule.

It wasn't more than a week later when a telegram arrived for me. "You are requested to meet me in my office in Bangalore, immediately."

I gulped. This sounds like a shakedown. Does this mean someone suggested to the Associate Peace Corps Director that I smoked pot? What is going on?

Two days later Tony and I caught the overnight bus to Bangalore. I presented myself in the office of Tom Carter, the Associate Peace Corps Director, the first thing the next morning. The bus ride is a nine hour trip, leaving Sindhanur around 9:00 p.m. five days a week and arriving in Bangalore around 6:00 a.m. the next day. There was not much opportunity to sleep during the trip. After traveling all night I was a bit shaken with the prospect of defending my honor in the Peace Corps Office.

It was immediately evident that the last two weeks was taking more of a toll on Tom than on anyone else. He did not like to be put in a position of judging volunteers, and felt very ill at ease in sending home those who admitted wrong doing. He was obviously losing sleep over this inquisition and his red eyes were the evidence.

Tom politely asked me to come into his office and have a seat. He came to the point quickly. "Were you at the party in Raichur after the meeting with the Department of Agriculture on April 2, 1969?

"Yes, I was."

"Someone said that they saw you there and that you smoked pot. Did you?"

"Yes, I was there. No. I did not smoke pot. I held the pipe in my hand but I did not partake. I left the house immediately after I sensed what was going on."

"Can you tell me who else was in that house that night?"

"It was too dark to make out anybody specific." I went on to say that I may have recognized a couple of faces but I cannot say for a fact that I saw them smoke *Ganja*."

He looked me in the eye, and studied my face, as if to read my hidden thoughts. Rather than pressing the issue further he instinctively knew that even if I had recognized other volunteers using the *ganja* I was not likely to reveal their identity. He shrugged his shoulders and said, "Ken, I can't tell you how glad I am that you were not involved. Now, go back to Sindhanur and get back to work."

I picked up my travel bag and trudged out the door. I bought a breakfast of fried eggs, steak, toast, jam and cold milk at the Regency Guest House, ran a few errands and caught the next bus back to Sindhanur, feeling relief for being vindicated. I also felt regret that not only had I not done anything to discourage my friends from tasting the *ganja* but I already had lost several of my fellow volunteers to this incident.

As a result of the Raichur incident we eventually lost seven volunteers from India-60, and a number of others from the Raichur PCV group. The swift hand of Peace Corps India made everybody sit up straight. The effects of the 'great inquisition,' as we called it, on the remaining volunteers was not overwhelming, as we all had our work to do and immersed ourselves in it. The exception to that was the departure of George. This guy had impressed us with his sudden interest in helping his host village excel. All the Mukkunda villagers, but especially Chandrappa and Mudiya Gowda, had adopted George as one of theirs. They believed in him and trusted that he was there to help make life better for the villagers.

The volunteers were impressed by Chandrappa and Mudiya Gowda and their insatiable interest in learning everything there was to know about agriculture. We were at a stage of introducing new varieties of crops and improved methods of growing them. India had breakthroughs in scientific advances in animal husbandry and farm mechanization, and these two farmers were absorbing information like sponges. They had tapped every bit of George's knowledge on these things and wanted more.

During the 3 short months in Makkunda, George had imported and provided one of his farmers with enough vegetable seeds from the United States to plant an acre of experimental garden. He showed them how to cultivate hybrid corn bred to produce fodder, and he somehow acquired a silage chopper. He showed them how to store the silage in a pit for future livestock feed. He also managed to acquire a new set of books and desks for the local elementary school.

As George prepared to step back into the PC Jeep for the ride to the Bangalore Airport, he asked me in earnest to help his farmers. He handed me a list of things he was still working on for them. One was to advise them on planting the newly introduced variety of hybrid cotton. Another was helping

Chandrappa purchase a tractor.

The day after George left for Bangalore, both Chandrappa and Mudiya Gowda came to my house. They did not understand what had happened. They asked, "Why did George leave?" They asked in *Kannada* if something they said or did had caused George to leave. Was George unhappy with his living arrangement? Why did he leave so quickly, without telling us more? We thought we were working well with him, and we need him in the village. Will Peace Corps place another volunteer in Mukkunda?

Indian men don't cry. Yet, I saw tears in Chandrappa's eyes as he pleaded for an explanation. Both men sat on the metal folding chairs in my dusty room and hung their heads. They stayed for nearly an hour, looking sad and out of sorts until one of the India-60 volunteers walked in the door. George had specifically asked me to not tell his villagers that he was kicked out of the Peace Corps and India. He wanted to preserve a modicum of respect he hoped they had for him.

All I could tell Chandrappa and Mudiya Gowda was that George had been very happy living in Mukkunda, and that he had the highest respect for them and the other Mukkunda people. I told them that George asked me to let them know that he was sorry he could not stay his full two years but had to leave abruptly. I also told them that George had asked me to assist them with the projects that he had been working on. I promised that I would make myself available, here or in Mukkunda, to work together with them. Without actually lying to them, I let them believe that George had to leave because of urgent family matters back in the States.

I didn't hear from George until many years later. When I returned to the States in 1971, locating my friends was far from my mind, with finding employment and supporting my family a higher priority. Later, when I did consider touching base with George, I hesitated, thinking that maybe he would not feel comfortable hearing from those he left behind. It was 2013 before I finally contacted George, who was by that time a successful neonatal doctor.

I spoke with George recently and he said, "I am extremely grateful for the chance to have gone through the Peace Corps experience. I only wish I could have accomplished more."

George also said, "Modiya Gowda and Chandrappa are two of the finest individuals I ever met."

Mukkunda's progressive farmers eventually overcame their loss of a very special friend, and Chandrappa and Mudiya Gowda prospered when the new hybrid cotton was introduced in Raichur District.

Hybrid cotton became the main cash crop in Raichur District. Mr. A.B. Bellary, ADA, had found his magical crop. Farmers waited in line to buy the seed. The more progressive farmers became very excited about this long staple cotton that yielded several times more than local varieties. It was a high quality cotton fibre that could be exported in bulk or in woven cotton fabric. Both Chandrappa and Mudiya Gowda became well known throughout the district as progressive growers of hybrid cotton, and before my service contract ended they both owned tractors.

So much for the inquisition. The "weeding out," as J.R. Bhaktul called it, resulted in thirteen painful departures and hurt some sensitive feelings, but nobody lost their lives over it. A few were better for it as they concentrated more intently on the work at hand.

MIDNIGHT MASS

That first full year in India was an education of a lifetime. We had experienced a dramatic adjustment from our comfortable lives in the U.S. to survive in a very alien (to us) culture, speaking a language essentially unknown to most Americans. The experience of hot sun, dusty roads, spicy food, lack of privacy and unrelenting rains of two annual monsoon periods made us appreciate life in a new way.

We now had friends in India. We accepted much of the culture, understood some of the religious activities, and no longer cringed at the segregation in the caste system. We were beginning to feel confident about getting around the countryside on buses and bicycles and surviving without all those crutches we felt so necessary one year ago.

John Kelly and I decided to celebrate Christmas 1969 by attending midnight mass at the small Catholic church in Jawalgera. We had become good friends with Father Archie, the parish priest, who I met on one of the many trips through Jawalgera to see Pejathaya. Father Archie also managed a 100 acre farm near Jawalgera, where he employed local parishioners to grow food and crops to support the members of his parish. Father Archie made a special effort to invite John to Sunday Mass, and attending midnight mass was customary in John's family in Vallejo, California. John invited me to join him.

As agreed, John left his village of Basawapur early in the evening. He caught rides on a bus, a bullock cart and a government Jeep to get to Jawalgera before midnight. I rode my bicycle the eight miles from Sindhanur. A flashlight strapped to the handlebars helped warn me of potholes in the thinly paved road. The only other obstacles were silent pedestrians, bullock carts, meandering buffaloes and various small animals that skittered across the road.

Father Archie was happy to see the small congregation that braved the night to celebrate the anniversary of the birth of Christ. It was an exhilarating feeling to join the local villagers in song in the small, candlelit church. We sang familiar carols and joined in the laughter at Father's lighthearted sermon. Father Archie made a special point of greeting us after the Mass, and wishing us a merry Christmas and a happy New Year.

If dark could get darker than black it sure seemed to do so in the early hours of Christmas Day. There were no buses or Jeeps headed toward Basawapur at this hour. Without wheels of his own, John decided to brave the handlebars of my bicycle for the eight mile journey to Sindhanur, in the dark.

John had withered down to just over 140 pounds, but he was still a formidable obstacle to my vision as I peddled my wobbly bicycle down the darkened highway. There was very little car or lorry traffic, but when a vehicle did approach we made sure to get far off the road to avoid even the slightest chance of a collision. Luckily, there were no significant hills to climb or we never would have made it back to Sindhanur with two people on that simple, single-speed bicycle.

After a tiring ride we made it to Sindhanur around 2:30 a.m., on Christmas Day. From somewhere, John produced one of his "Care" packages from California. He must have stashed it in some obscure hiding place in my apartment, for, as we arrived in Sindhanur, exhausted, hungry and thirsty, John held forth with an assortment of specialty foods, including a canned roast beef.

This was the only time and place in India to eat roast beef. The bullocks and cows are sacred animals in this part of India, and when they die it is only due to old age. There is even a sanctuary for old, retired cows and beasts of burden, where they spend their declining years. Moreover, the Hindu castes would cringe at the very thought of consuming any meat, especially beef. So, in the still of night while my Hindu neighbors slept we enjoyed our Christmas feast.

John carefully opened the tin and we consumed the entire can of evidence. It was not like eating a home-cooked roast right out of the oven, but it had delightful traces of home-cooked aroma and flavor. By daylight, not even the wrapper was anywhere near my residence. We washed down the roast with warm Kingfisher beer, and topped off the delicious meal with the two Hostess Twinkie's that had lined John's "Care" package.

A surprisingly large number of Sindhanur townspeople stopped by during the day to wish the Americans a happy Christmas. We were touched by the gesture of their warm greetings, since most of the visitors were Hindu or Moslem, and do not normally celebrate this Christian holiday. Their sincerity brought tears to our eyes.

WINDING DOWN

It was not long after the new year when Pejathaya's employer invited him to attend an urgent meeting in Udupi, the headquarters of Syndicate Bank. When he returned to Jawalgera several days later he announced that he was engaged to be married. His future spouse, Sarojamma, was heiress to a portion of her deceased father's coffee estate.

Pejathaya was determined to work one more year at Tungabhadra Farm to complete his assignment as farm manager before getting married. Incidentally, one year later the Syndicate Bank owners announced that the Tungabhadra Farm was being sold. One of the owners of the Syndicate Bank invited Pejathaya to accept another position with the bank.

All the PCVs were happy for Pejathaya's good fortune, but sad to see him leave Raichur District. Pejathaya remained friends with the volunteers and continued to correspond with us and to share his writings. Some years later he wrote the following story about his departure from Raichur District.

ADIEU TO JAWALGERA
BY S. M. PEJATHAYA

During the month of February 1970, I received a telegram from Sri K. K. Pai asking me to meet him in person at Manipal at the earliest. I caught a night bus to Bangalore on the same night and from Bangalore, I boarded the first day bus to Udupi. I reached Udupi by about six p.m. and called Sri K. K. Pai's office for an appointment as soon as I reached my sister's house.

Mr. Pai seemed to be in a jovial mood over the phone that evening. He said, 'Kesari! Well, you have arrived. Can you see me in my residence tomorrow morning by 8.30 a.m.? You shall have breakfast at my residence. Good night!'

"Yes Sir! Good night." I replied.

I stayed at my sister's house and kept on wondering as to the purpose of summoning me so urgently. Having breakfast with my boss was not unusual for me. He would often invite me for breakfast with him whenever he wanted to discuss the farm matters. His son, Dr. Arvind Pai, was my senior in the high school and he was a NCC cadet too. Dr. Arvind's younger sister Geetha was my junior in the college and she is married to my high school classmate Dr. Prabhakar Kamath and they have settled in the USA.

Mrs. K. K. Pai is the younger sister of Sri T. A. Pai, the managing director of the Syndicate Bank Ltd. She was a very kind lady and loved me like a son. She would always feed me to the brim whenever I went to their home. Sri K. K. Pai and family were our family friends for two generations and I had no hesitation at all to enter the Pai residence situated at Kunjibettu Extension of Udupi. Their house was right opposite our MGM College.

Next morning, at 8.30 sharp I was at Sri K. K. Pai's residence. Mrs. Pai called me into the kitchen table and offered me a cup of coffee and told me that her husband would join me in a minute or two. She enquired about my mother's health and the rest of the family as usual.

Sri K. K. Pai came over to the kitchen table and we had a sumptuous breakfast of dosa, uppittu and freshly cut fruits with lots of coffee. Sri Pai would not talk of any business during breakfasts. He would always see to it that his guests ate heartily. We came over to sit in their drawing room. Sri Pai shot his first question, "Kesari, how old are you?"

"I am 24, Sir."

"Why haven't you thought of getting married?"

"I have to prove my capacity in my job and I have to be financially sound enough to start a family," I replied.

"That is a good answer," Sri Pai said. "I have called you here as I am a well-wisher of your family. Now, I am requesting you to go over to Mangalore tomorrow with your eldest brother and sister-in-law to see our deceased planter friend Sri Raghupathi Hebbar's daughter. Please meet me day after tomorrow to discuss some matters of the farm. You can catch the night bus to return to the farm."

Next day, I went over to Mangalore and saw Saroja at her sister's place and came back to Udupi. I assumed that she would not consent to marry me. I had a beard and I was wearing blue jeans and a T-shirt during a time nobody preferred such a garb. Next day, my mother was informed over telephone that the girl had consented to marry me.

I told my mother straightaway that I shall not marry immediately. I am agreeable if the girl is prepared to wait for one year. I told her that I needed this one-year period to prove myself in my job. To my surprise the girl as well as her mother consented to my request instantly. I returned to Jawalgera after meeting Sri K. K. Pai in his office.

When I entered his office the elderly person and my well-wisher Shri K. K. Pai congratulated me for having consented for the proposal. He gave me some instructions regarding the cropping pattern at the farm for that year *and sent me off the same evening.*

As promised, I got married on ninth of May 1971. By May end my boss had decided to sell the farm to Sri K. Surya Rao at an attractive price. At the same time, Sri K. K. Pai offered me a good position in the Syndicate Bank. In the meantime, without my knowledge, he had held a meeting with the auditor and the members of Late Raghupathi Hebbar's family and formed his own opinions regarding my future. However, I was not aware of this fact.

Soon after my marriage I was asked to help with the registration of the lands in Sri Surya Rao's name. After handing over the farm I appeared before Sri K. K. Pai and told him that I was ready for the next job with the bank. He asked me to take a seat in front of him and put a simple question, "Kesari, what shall you do after retirement?"

I sincerely replied him, "Sir! If I ever lived up to my retirement age, I may buy five acres of land somewhere and settle down to lead a peaceful life."

"Why don't you assume that you have already retired right now? You have more than ten times that area of land right now and the land is rightfully inherited by Saroja as per the will of her father. Her late father wanted our Syndicate Bank to be the trustee and executor for all his self-earned estates. We could not take up the responsibility due to the imminent nationalization of the Bank. Now, I ask you to go over to Kalasa and take over the management of Saroja's estate. If you do not like the environment you can always come back and work in the bank. You need not tender your resignation. We shall just loan your services to the registered firm, M/s Raghupathi Hebbaar's Estates (Regd.) with its registered office at Shimoga. One year ago Sri T. A. Pai and I had discussed and decided on your future and the future of our departed friend Raghupathi Hebbar's daughter.

"We had seen profits in our Jawalgera farm only after you took over the management. However, Raghupathi Hebbar's daughter may not survive in the climate of Raichur district, which records more than 42 degrees Celsius during the summer months. She has been brought up in the cool climate of coffee country. I wish you to go over and help Saroja and sisters to look after the four estates. In case you do not like the place at all, you can come back and our doors shall be open for you."

At this, I rebelled that I shall not work for my wife and be a slave. Sri K. K. Pai asked me to relax and he coolly explained: "Since Saroja has no brothers, one day or the other you shall have to take up the responsibility of at least Sulimane Estate which she has inherited from her father. Whatever belongs to her is yours and whatever belongs to you is hers. There is no demarcation between husband and wife's property. Moreover, the coffee rates have fallen to the lowest after the demise of your father-in-law and the estates are facing a financial crisis. I have promised your sisters-in-law and mother-in-law that our bank shall finance the group of estates. If you take up the field operations I am sure all the daughters of Raghupathi Hebbar shall prosper. You may say that you do not have experience in coffee cultivation and I agree. Being a professional farmer you can learn the tricks in a couple of years. As I have seen, you are good at the judicious use of chemical fertilizers and of the modern sprinkler irrigation systems. Please give it a try. I am sure that you can handle the situation and help others too. Do not say no. It is a challenge for you. If you succeed you shall be the happiest man on earth. My blessings are with you. Please go to Sulimane Estate and be in touch."

I felt that I must not argue on the judgment of my boss who loved me like a son. I said, "Yes, sir!" And, I turned towards the coffee hills and I never had to look back.

*   *   *

After Pejathaya returned to Raichur District to complete his work and hand over the farm, he and I were each heavily involved with our respective assignments; he with perfecting the cultivation and harvesting the lands under his charge and, later, handing over the reins of Tungabhadra Farm to the new owners. I was deeply involved in the milk collection and distribution project as well as the tractor society work. Pejathaya would occasionally stop by my apartment to chat, and we would sometimes sit in a nearby tea *ungadi* to enjoy a cup of K-tea and some good conversation. These infrequent visits were welcome but rare.

The year of 1970 was very busy for both of us. Eventually,

Pejathaya felt that he had accomplished his work at Tungabhadra Farm, and was ready to move on to his marriage and his new life as a coffee farmer in Chikkamagluru District. We didn't meet again until several months after Pejathaya left Jawalgera and I took a temporary assignment training new volunteers in our earlier Peace Corps training camp at the Dhadesugur Agricultural Training Center.

My Peace Corps extension period ended in March of 1971. The Peace Corps gave me a thorough debriefing, a complete physical exam, and an airplane ticket to Minneapolis. Returning PCVs were allowed to route their air travel to the States by any route they wished and to take as long as they wanted. I joined a friend who had researched soybean cultivation in Raichur and Dharwar Districts with me. We agreed to spend as much time as possible in the mountains of Northern India, and then pick our way back to the U.S. through the Far East.

My traveling companion and I saw much of India, then moved on to Nepal, Burma (now named Myanmar),Thailand, and Japan before returning to her home in Hawaii, and eventually my home in Minnesota. En route to the latter, we had barely touched down in California when I received the invitation from Peace Corps to return to India.

The Peace Corps preferred to have at least one seasoned volunteer work in their training programs. They felt that a retired volunteer bridged a gap between the stark reality of what trainees experienced in-country and their U.S. experience.

India-60 returning volunteer, John Kelly, was invited to serve that role, but he canceled just before the program started. John had applied to the University of San Francisco and wanted to finish his education. Also, his father had contracted pneumonia and John needed to be there to care for him. Mr. Byron Haderlie, an agriculture specialist from Idaho, was working with the Peace Corps to help recruit staff for the training mission. I briefly met with Byron in Sacramento, California. He had me sign a contract and gave me a plane ticket that took me from San Francisco to Minneapolis to Bangalore. After a brief stop to see family and friends, I returned to India.

Two groups of Peace Corps trainees arrived in India three months apart to be trained in agriculture, language skills and local culture over the next seven months. I worked for Peace Corps as an agriculture instructor for the first group's training, and as Technical Coordinator for the second training session.

Pejathaya was married to the late Raghupathi Hebbar's youngest daughter, Sarojamma, in Udupi on May 9, 1971. Soon thereafter he completed his move to Sulimane Estate in the coffee-growing hills of Karnataka. One afternoon, during my second training program, Pejathaya presented himself at the Agriculture Training Center in Dhadesugur. His new bride accompanied him. I was happy to see him again. However, he seemed to have changed. He now was a married man, and had serious responsibilities.

He was the owner and manager of a coffee estate. He had to demonstrate to the people who helped him achieve this position that he was worthy of it. He had to maintain the appearance of the status to which he had now been installed. He did not seem to be the carefree, fun-loving guy I had come to know.

He was no longer sporting his blue jeans and T shirt, and didn't have that happy-go-lucky smile on his face. He wore the clothes of a wealthy land owner, with a long string of beads hanging from his neck. He was now a serious man of status. He now had a spouse to support and was responsible for managing a coffee estate. It was great to see him again but our meeting was abbreviated because of my training program and his need to continue his journey, so I could not spend much time with him.

Although our days together in Raichur District were history, we communicated by aerogramme and snail mail for many years until Pejathaya acquired his first computer. Then we began communicating regularly by e-mail. My wife and I visited Pejathaya and Saroja at their coffee estate in Chikkamagaluru District in 1971 before returning to the States. In 1999 Pejathaya brought his wife and two daughters to our home in California for a two week visit.

Pejathaya often reminisces about his mingles with the India-60 volunteers. He found the experience as interesting and stimulating as did the volunteers. Shortly after leaving Raichur District, he wrote the following in his journal.

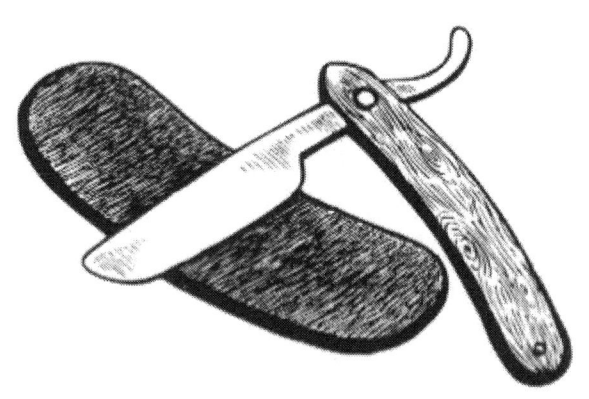

LIFE IN ANOTHER PLANET
BY S.M. PEJATHAYA

We believe that friendship is something that is expected to last for a lifetime. In many cases it is not so. Sometimes, I sit back and remember my best friends. I remember some of my schoolmates of whom I thought I would never lose contact during my lifetime. Now, I have lost track of them all!

Now I can count a couple of college mates who are still in touch with me. They are as busy as I am, and except for the occasional swapping of greeting cards, there is nothing much to say of our "constant contact" now.

On the other hand, I have several American friends who have been in regular contact over many years. They were almost as old as I was, when we first met during 1969. We were all in our early twenties. They worked as the American Peace Corps Volunteers at Sindhanur Taluk of Raichur district in Karnataka.

They belonged to a batch called Peace Corps Volunteers India – 60 (PCV). I was working as the manager of Tungabhadra Farms at Jawalgera, which was a very backward village eight miles away from the taluk headquarter of Sindhanur. Ken was working with the Sindhanur Tractor Society and John was working in the remote village of Basavapur. The American boys were hard workers, and they were really concerned about the environment and the welfare of the people around them.

They tried to improve the quality of life of the agriculturists around them. Often, Ken and John very much resented the poverty that plagued the villagers of India. The poverty had put a full stop to many planned developments. People in the rural areas were always busy in their struggle to earn a decent living. Many of the village farmers could not think of investing anything extra for their planned development. Poverty was a curse to most of the villagers.

Ken had more friends from the U.S. Peace Corps working in the other areas of Raichur district. The associate directors of the 1968 U.S. Peace Corps project in our State coordinated with our Karnataka and Central governments. These directors lived at Bangalore and had their own Chrysler jeeps as they had to travel extensively.

The volunteers around Sindhanur and Manvi worked in close association with the agriculture department and they were provided with bicycles to move around. They dressed like local boys, ate Indian food and spoke broken Kannada with some difficulty. Yet, they could communicate with our villagers with relative ease. They were first trained in California, USA, and later at the Farmer's Training Center in Dhadesugur of Raichur District. They had learned little of Kannada during their brief training period in California and picked up a little more when they trained at Dhadesugur Farmer's Training Center. They were put there for a few weeks to orient themselves to the Indian climate, environment and food. There, they had to study the ways of life of Raichur district villagers. Later they were installed as "Peace Corps Volunteers" in their pre-designated villages, where they tried to live and befriend the local population.

These volunteers visited the farmers in their work area and introduced them to the improved methods in agriculture. Their aim was to increase the productivity so that the farmers could earn more and the quality of life of the villagers improved in course of time. These boys joined their neighbors in the fields, to work with them side by side as volunteers.

The time thus spent together in the field was really "quality time" as both the parties could understand each other's culture. Ken was a good mechanic and he worked hard at the Tractor Society. He put in some eight to ten hours of work everyday on an average. He often worked late into nights. He lived in a rented house at Sindhanur. His house was a concrete structure with electricity supply but had no running water.

The other guys, who lived in the villages, roughed it out in thatched houses or the houses that had mud walls and large stone slabs for the ceiling. Many of them had to live in the villages where there was no electricity, or toilets. They had to learn to go to the Tungabhadra canal for their bath and had to get used to the kerosene lamps. They adapted to the local food of 'jowar' 'rotis' (sorghum bread), lentils, leafy vegetable called 'pundi palle soppu' and little rice. Basically, all of them were young and adaptable. They were honest and friendly with the people around them.

Living in the remote villages of Raichur district was like "Living in another Planet" for most of the Peace Corps Volunteers. They could not find even bread and jam in their villages, let alone, chips and soft drinks. The food they could find in the village teashops or the small restaurants of Sindhanur were strange and too spicy. Many of the preparations contained a lot of very hot chillies, 'tamarind' and other spices. I used to see them all very red and flushed with tears as they ate occasionally at Ashok Bhavan, our best restaurant of Sindhanur town. All the food items available at Ashok Bhavan were strongly spiced and they had to down them all with sweet tea or a local soda or a cool drink. The cool drinks were "something special" as Ashok Bhavan was the only restaurant in Sindhanur that boasted of a refrigerator. What a luxury it was! To sip a cool drink after cycling miles and miles on the unpaved canal bank roads in the black cotton soils of Raichur district in the summer temperature of 42 degree-plus Celsius!

These volunteers always had to move around on their rickety bicycles as no buses plied to their remote villages. If they came to the main road after riding a good distance of a mile or two, they would find one of the very few buses that plied the roads to Sindhanur. The village folk traveled in these buses, which were packed to triple their specified capacity. A good lot of village men and even women chose to ride on the top of the buses. Thirty to forty persons would ride on the roof of the buses, as they would find no room for themselves to stand inside the jam-packed vehicles. Hence, most of the volunteers preferred the luxury of those long rides on their bicycles to avoid harrowing bus travel.

Each volunteer was allowed to keep a kitchen assistant who would cook something at home for his survival. Ken got his washing water from Sindhanur 'Nullah'[25], a stream that flowed near the town. It came through

---

[25] Stream

in huge metal tanks mounted on a bullock cart. The left bank irrigation channel of the Tungabhadra dam flowed about a mile away from the town. The water was cool and sweet. This was the source of drinking water for all.

The toilets were primitive — as they were of 'service type' in the town of Sindhanur. The Town Municipality's health department serviced these toilets. There was no underground sewerage system at Sindhanur. Wastewater flowed in open drains that lined the roads of the town creating a sanctuary for pigs and mosquitoes.

The folks like us who lived outside the municipal limit dug camp toilets for our use. Our washing wastewater flowed into fields or kitchen gardens. There were no mosquitoes in the farm as no water stagnated in the vicinity. We, who lived away from the stinks of the town, certainly considered ourselves lucky!

In many villages of our 'taluk,' folks used to take bath in the 'nullah' or the water channels and used the open grounds for toilet purposes. They washed their oxen and buffaloes in the 'nullahs' too! Many a times we could find hordes of water buffaloes wading into the channels of Tungabhadra dam to wallow in summer heat. The water turned turbid by these lowly buffaloes. On such days, we always made it a point to boil our drinking water well.

For the PCV volunteers who had seen only cow's milk in the United States, the very thought of consuming buffalo milk was a nauseating affair for them during their first weeks! They were pacified when they realized that they were consuming the buffalo milk since the day they arrived at Raichur district. In fact, they were consuming curd, buttermilk, coffee and tea prepared with buffalo milk right from the day one! Finally, the volunteers had to accept and relish buffalo milk as good milk. Like everybody, they too learned to consume buffalo's milk, as cow's milk was a rarity. It was not preferred by local folks because of its lower fat content and poor taste.

For Continental or American cuisine, one had to visit the distant cities of Bangalore or Hyderabad. To reach these cities one had to travel long distance by night buses and the journey time always exceeded twelve hours. This kind of food they could find once or twice a year during their holidays.

All the Peace Corps Volunteers were advised by the health department to drink boiled and cooled water. If they ever tried to cook something akin to their home food, they had to burn their fingers in cooking over open stove called 'chulah' in India. The concept of an oven is unknown in rural India. They had to suffer through the spicy cooking of their kitchen assistants, who naturally believed that the food without the strong spices is no food at all. They would always wait for a letter or an occasional piece of pie or chocolate from home! Mail used to take about a month to arrive. The daily English language newspaper would arrive at the village only on the next day by post!

The entertainment was by way of radio only with lots of static disturbances. In the evenings there would be the short wave station of The Voice of America program or the English program of Radio Ceylon. Sometimes antiquated English movies were shown in cities like Raichur and Bellary as morning shows only. The BBC and All India Radio gave news in English and there would be an occasional English program by All India Radio. The lone cinema hall of Sindhanur showed only Kannada and Telugu movies. They screened Hindi movies occasionally.

The word TV was unheard of. We heard that there was a TV station at Delhi. I had witnessed a live TV show only once, at one of New Delhi's Science Exhibitions in 1967. Ken played tennis regularly as he was staying next to the Sports Club at Sindhanur. The other PCV boys came to Sindhanur and stayed with Ken on Saturday evenings and Sundays. During these weekend trips they had to buy their grocery etc. for the oncoming week.

They would get a haircut at Modern Hair Cutting Saloon situated by the main road. It was housed in a large wooden box. The shop was much smaller than a cargo container. Yet, it was the macho place! The wooden walls of the saloon displayed semi nude posters torn out from some girlie magazines along with a 'Hair Cutting Style Chart'. The barber made his customer to sit on a high throne. He would wring and bend the neck of his customers to a convenient angle as he gave a haircut. Sometimes, he inflicted small cuts and wounds. Before one could complain, he would dab a big slab of potash alum on the wound. We had to bear it all!

Usually, no one complained, as there was no use in complaining! If ever you needed a haircut, you had to suffer through the barber's blunt pair of scissors, antiquated shearing equipment and that horrible shaving razor, which he would hone on a piece of hung leather strip or a slate honing stone. Fortunately, we had not heard of AIDS in India during those years. At the touch of the alum, the blood flow would stop. As there was no other *barber in town with his own hairdressing hall, we were forced to patronize him only. We had nicknamed him—THE BARBARIAN!*

His primitive competitors practiced their trade by the street side. Their customers had to sit on a low stool in the scorching sun. Every fashionable man of Sindhanur town who sat in the only throne offered by Modern Hair Cutting Saloon seemed to accept all these cuts and nicks from the famous barber's razor blade as part of the game! Nevertheless, the famous barber's hand-operated shears instead of snipping the hair pinched and pulled the hairs mercilessly, along with the surrounding skin. Sometimes, they drew a steady flow of blood. Occasionally, our ears would be nipped here and there by his scissors.

After the hair cut, our external brain surgeon, I mean the barber, would give us a nice head massage. During the course of which, without warning, he would wring our neck once to the left and once to the right. It came as a shock to me when he tried this wringing trick on me. I could hear the ligaments protesting each time with a noise. However, after this wringing, I felt good.

I did not dare to face this special treatment once more in my lifetime again! Before sitting on the throne, I would request him, "No massage, please!" I was really afraid that he would wring my neck and break it once and for all!

Every time before I sat for the haircut, I would request him not to wring my neck. He would laugh; but oblige! No one seemed to complain about this wringing of the neck or those minor cuts and nips; and nobody was 'cruel enough' to comment on the expertise of the one and only 'decent barber' of Sindhanur. Whenever we touched the cities like Raichur or Bellary, we rushed to some decent barbershop to downsize our overgrown manes!"

THE CHRISTMAS PARTY

The India-60 PCV's completed their two year contracts in late 1970. It was time for many of them to finish up their projects, say goodbye to their hosts and head to Bangalore to collect their homebound airplane tickets. For those of us who extended our stays to complete various projects it was a sad parting.

After two years in India the volunteers had fostered a bond of friendship. We shared the rigors of a Spartan training camp, learned a new language, and shared our fortunes and misfortunes over two exciting years. We traveled many miles on poor roads and cattle paths, riding our bicycles to visit farmers and their fields. Together we laughed at our sad condition as one by one we experienced the effects of unboiled water or ultra spicy food.

Two years can slip by amazingly fast even though the first months had seemed agonizingly slow. Now, we had outgrown our temerity and had become tenacious problem solvers. In a way, we had succeeded in making a mark. Now, it seemed to be coming to an abrupt end. I felt a deep sadness as the volunteers passed through Sindhanur on their way south to Bangalore.

On a much brighter perspective, I was beginning to feel comfortable with my life in Sindhanur. I was making an impact with the tractor society, the milk cooperative was marginally successful and I had become friends with several progressive farmers and a number of townspeople. Some were farmers with whom I worked directly, or they were the more progressive farmers working with other volunteers who frequented my house to learn from the cumulative experiments and research of the volunteers and to simply share news. And then there were the staff members of the tractor society, the cooperative milk society farmers, my tennis-playing friends and other Sindhanur residents.

Subramaniam often invited me to enjoy festive meals with his family. Some of the hotel owners and managers became good friends after I released my cook and began eating meals at their establishments. (The word "hotel" has a broader meaning in parts of India, where a place that prepares food is called a hotel, rather than a restaurant).

After the exodus of most of the India-60 PCV group I was feeling a bit down, but was in the spirit to celebrate the Christmas season anyway. I decided to host a holiday feast. Having limited knowledge of Indian cooking, I placed a huge order for festive food at a friend's hotel. I then extended invitations to all my Indian acquaintances for a "Holiday" party.

The hotel staff prepared mounds of delicious food, most of it non-vegetarian. The fact that I ordered chicken biryani and mutton dishes suggests that after two years I still was not tuned in to the seriousness of the wide range of religious and social principles of the people of Sindhanur. My Moslem friends had no problem with the chicken and mutton dishes, but some of my Hindu friends only shared a bottled drink, because eating food cooked in a place that prepared meat was a violation of their religious beliefs.

In spite of my poor planning, many people came to the celebration. There was a very pleasant and festive mood. Even though Christmas is not a holiday on most peoples' calendars in Sindhanur, a very small percentage of the population being Christian, people like Subramaniam and Pejathaya came because they were friends and wanted to share their wishes of goodwill. After several hours of eating, drinking, singing and celebrating, the participants began to bid their final best wishes and disperse to their respective homes. Even as friends said their goodbyes I still did not realize the social blunder I had committed.

About the time some people started to leave the party, Pejathaya mentioned that he might have missed the last bus to

Jawalgera. I said, "No problem; I will carry you to your house on my motorcycle." He agreed, and after I bid farewell to the last of the party goers and paid the food preparers and servers, we set off to my house to get my Indian-built Czechoslovakian Java motorcycle.

By the time we reached Pejathaya's bamboo and river-reed manager's quarters it was near midnight. He had Lakpathi, his office boy, prepare tea for us. A cup of chai would refresh me for the journey back to Sindhanur. The chai was good, and conversation easy, as we covered subjects in agriculture, education, politics, foreign travel and our respective childhood adventures. The hours flew by and we talked into the wee hours of the morning.

When the conversation turned to religion, I bluntly asked Pejathaya if he was Hindu. I always assumed that he was, but we had never discussed our personal religious beliefs before. He always seemed, somehow, different than most Hindu people I knew. I nearly fell off my bamboo stool when he told me that he was raised as a Brahmin. I suddenly realized the grave mistake I had made in serving food prepared in a non-vegetarian establishment, and I began to apologize profusely. High caste Hindus are strict vegetarians and follow strict rules.

It is a serious affront to a high caste Hindu to serve meat or even food cooked in vessels that previously cooked meat. I suddenly realized that I should have made separate arrangements for each of the various religious groups in the gathering. However, Pejathaya's response also made me realize his true nature, and I will never forget the manner in which he proved his friendship.

Pejathaya said, "No, no, no. There is no need to apologize. I went to your party because you were celebrating a very special feast in your own culture and I was pleased that you considered me a friend and invited me. I respect everyone's choices, and I was happy to be able to celebrate with you. I can look beyond my religious beliefs for a chance to honor a close friend."

It was at this point that I knew what a special person this

man is. He would do anything for a friend. To this day, Pejathaya has never betrayed his religious beliefs, and I have learned to be more sympathetic to the beliefs of others.

That day I vowed to overcome my blind blundering over peoples' cultural and religious beliefs and practices. There could not have been a better awakening for me to change my assumption that my culture and religion are the only important ones, and that the rest of the world can just bend their behavior to suit mine.

I thank Pejathaya for his patience and for his kindness in giving a fundamental lesson without preaching. If I had not asked him about his religion he might have never said a word to me.

DIFFICULT TIMES FOR INDIA

On July 20, 1969, America landed the first man on the moon. I can never forget my experience of that first morning after Neil Armstrong and Buzz Aldrin walked on the moon. As I approached the tea *'ungadi'* where I often drained my morning coffee and ate my first deep-fried chili of the day I was greeted by cheering well wishers.

The men in the tea shop were listening to a radio broadcast, and were talking excitedly. They were better informed than I was about the space mission. When they saw me approach they shouted out congratulations. It seemed as though I was the one who had engineered the mission and walked on the moon. They asked if I knew Mr. Neil Armstrong, and they asked me to convey their congratulations to him.

Not all the Sindhanur villagers were so sure that stepping on the moon was a great thing. A few of them speculated that it may be a bit sacrilegious to interfere with this distant planet. After all, you never walk into someone's house with your shoes on. So, why would we be so thoughtless as to step on this distant sphere that belonged to everyone. A few townspeople thought we had soiled a gift from God.

Most people I met in Sindhanur, however, were excited about the lunar achievement, and wanted to talk about how it was done and what this meant for future space exploration. Over the next several weeks many people came to my house to look at the pictures in Monroe's most recent issues of *Time Magazine*. You would have thought that the U.S. had just won the World Cup. I repeatedly explained to visitors that Peace Corps India had nothing to do with the success of the mission. I think they expected us to convey their best wishes to the

American people.

It wasn't long before the cheery receptions at the tea shops disintegrated into suspicion and consternation. The year 1969 saw India going through a struggle at the higher levels of government. Indira Gandhi's Deputy Prime Minister, Morarji Desai, attempted to steer her away from her attempts to nationalize India's banks and a general shift toward socialist policies. Eventually, the Indian National Congress split into two parties, with Mr. Desai as the leader of one faction.

In 1970, Indira Gandhi continued to govern with a slim majority, and in 1971 many of her socialist economic and industrial policies were enacted, including nationalization of India's banks. In 1970, India was drawn into a civil war taking place in East Pakistan (now known as Bangladesh) called the Bangladesh Liberation War. This became a spark for confrontation in 1971. During 1971, India fought its third war with Pakistan. India also signed a 20-year treaty of friendship with the Soviet Union. Relations with the United States became strained. During the India-Pakistani War, in December of 1971, an estimated two to three million East Pakistan citizens were killed and up to four hundred thousand women were reportedly raped by Pakistani forces. In addition, reports estimated that eight to ten million people fled the fighting to take refuge in India. Eleven Indian air bases were attacked by Pakistan.

The Soviet Union sided with India during this confrontation, and supported the Indian Army. The U.S., on the other hand, leant political and material support to Pakistan. When the U.S. sent the USS Enterprise aircraft carrier and its battle group into the Bay of Bengal, my Indian counterparts in Sindhanur began to ask me some difficult questions.

It was the second time my face became a representation of America. Whether for good news or bad, if you come from that country you are responsible for your people's actions. The young students I met on the streets of Sindhanur no longer asked me for the time, or tried to engage me in trivial conversation. They now bore serious looks of anger and flung hard questions at me in English, *Kannada* and *Urdu*.

Some acquaintances avoided me, or could not make eye contact. Those who engaged in conversation questioned the motives of my country. There was little I could say. If I supported my country's action I would suffer heated exchanges with people who wanted to vent their anger at the U.S.'s actions. Should I condemn the threatening presence of the USS Enterprise in the Bay of Bengal I would be undermining all that my presence in India stood for.

Many of my Indian co-workers and friends, however, were understanding, and hopeful that the war would soon end. It did. By the end of December it was over.

While trouble was brewing in Delhi and India's foreign relations were heating up, small town Sindhanur was less seriously affected. The India-60 volunteers were intent on keeping their political views subdued. The year 1970 passed swiftly as the India-60 PCVs plowed ahead with hearts and minds on productive work. Most of the volunteers managed several projects and most of them were asked daily by their better farmers to come to their fields to advise on plant selection and best practices.

In late 1970, most of the India-60 volunteers ended their two year contracts with the Peace Corps. They underwent medical examinations, prepared final paperwork, selected their preferred method of travel back to their homes in the U.S., packed up their belongings and left India. By January 1971 only a few of the remaining volunteers who had extended their contracts were left in Raichur District. I had asked for three additional months to complete two projects that needed closure.

LIFE AFTER SINDHANUR

Pejathaya studied coffee cultivation diligently. Within a year he came to know the best practices for coffee production, harvesting and curing. He learned how to encourage certain trees to shade the sensitive coffee flowers, and how to use water sprinklers to enhance flowering at the right time of the season. He used the space between the rows of coffee plants to plant pepper and other spices, and he expanded the growing of areca nut palms.

The nut from the areca palm, or betel nut, is eaten by many Indians as a local custom for refreshing one's mouth after a meal and improving digestion. The areca nut is not a true nut, and is deemed by the International Agency for Research on Cancer (IARC) to be carcinogenic to humans. Used for chewing, it is wrapped in a betel leaf along with clove, cardamom, lime and other spices to produce a fresh, peppery taste. It is a mild stimulant. Sales of areca nut buoyed up the loss of income when coffee prices were sub par.

These expanded uses of the estate proved successful in helping the Sulimane Estate survive from its languishing recent past. In spite of depressed coffee prices in many of the 1980s and early1990s, the estate prospered, and with improved prices in the late 90s, Pejathaya was able to not only enjoy the fruits of his hard work but was able to spend more time writing.

At first he wrote articles for publication in local periodicals. His primary focus was on agriculture, but often covered stories of pets and other animals. Some of his short stories were later combined into a children's book. Most of his writings were in his native *Kannada*, however, he wrote his memoirs in an English language book titled, *The Voyage of a Paper Boat*. The opening chapter of that book is reprinted in the fifth chapter of this book.

A highly successful coffee harvest and sustained good prices allowed Pejathaya to bring his wife and two daughters to the United States in 1999.

CAMP DHADESUGUR

It was difficult to leave India. Sindhanur had become my home, and I now had more friends and more work experience in India than I had in the U.S. More important personally, India was the place where I met and married the love of my life. In the little Catholic church in the village of Jawalgera, not far from Pejathaya's Syndicate Bank farm, Father Archie blessed our marriage on the evening of All Saints Day. Dale Magers, the Peace Corps Associate Director, and India-60's Tony Ganey, dressed in a white dhoti, grey vest and long red turban, were present to witness the marriage.

Dee had served as a Peace Corps volunteer in the *Kannada* speaking District of Dharwad. Her program taught vegetable gardening and nutrition to the women in that area. She became interested in the use of soybean as a healthy protein rich food at the same time that I experimented with soybean as a possible commercial crop. We discovered our joint interest in researching soybeans while attending a *Kannada* refresher class.

Not far from the Jawalgera church, on the dirt path crossing over sub-canal No. 54, several of my fellow India-60 Peace Corps Volunteers, two newly arriving Peace Corps instructors, Paul Weinstein and Douglas Davis, their wives (both named Susan), a few Indian friends, four new Peace Corps trainees and Dale Magers, helped us celebrate the taking of our wedding vows. In joy and good feeling after a long day on the road from Hyderabad, we passed around a bottle of Johnny Walker Red and ate a birthday cake.

Dee bought the Johnny Walker Scotch from the duty-free shop at Heathrow Airport on her journey to New Delhi. The two Susan's somehow found a birthday cake in a bakery in

Hyderabad (They said, "They were all out of wedding cakes"). With no cups, or plates or utensils it was a bit of a messy ordeal, but the Tungabhadra irrigation system supplied ample water to wash our sticky fingers.

The moon was bright on that glorious evening. The air was clear and cool. The sound of water falling over the drop on the distributary canal appropriately reminded us of our purpose in this place. We didn't mind drinking from the same Scotch bottle because we knew (hoped) that the strong spirits in the red-labeled bottle would overpower any contagious creatures from an unhealthy participant.

Soon, we had to break up the party, as this was also the night of the beginning of the second of the two Peace Corps Training Programs (India-132). We still had to drive fifteen miles to the Dhadesugur Training Center to meet the rest of the new trainees and instructors.

As we arrived at the main hall of the training center the training staff welcomed us with an archway of celebratory palm fronds and flower petals at the doorstep. We were congratulated by the Indian and American staff and served a matrimonial vegetarian meal on banana leaves in the main hall. After the meal we were given the keys to the Government Inspection Bungalow on the main road. There, we spent our first night.

Early the next day we moved out of the comfort of the bungalow into a grass shack. The Peace Corps had contracted local villagers to construct a bamboo and *apoo* grass house (very much like Pejathaya's Tungabhadra Farm office) for us near the Tungabhadra River. It measured about eight feet by ten feet. They also ran a thin, blue-coated electric wire from the main dormitory to a tall bamboo pole to provide us with one light bulb of illumination. This was our first home.

Who could ask for a better situation? Nights were peaceful and quiet. The setting was very picturesque, as we could sit on the rocks outside our grass shack and watch the sun set over the wide Tungabhadra River. My worksite was just 100 steps uphill from our house. The only problem was being awakened some mornings by a gigantic bullock rubbing its back against our house.

Home Sweet Home, on the banks of the Tungabhadra River

At the same time that Dee flew to India from the States, two dozen new Peace Corps trainees flew to India and traveled by way of New Delhi, Hyderabad and Raichur to Sindhanur *Taluka*. We housed them in a stone dormitory at the Dhadesugur Agriculture Training Centre, also within earshot of the Tungabhadra River. Our goal was to pack a year's worth of language skills, agriculture knowledge and cultural sensitivity into their heads in a span of just ten weeks.

During the two weeks before the second training program, staff met every day, working hard to plan for the ten-week program. The actual training went fine, however, only ten trainees survived to be placed in the field. Training operated six days a week, from early morning until late evening. Trainees begged for more free time, but soon learned that there was nowhere to go and nothing else to do.

So we trained hard, took field trips, and ate local food. Between classes we played volleyball and swam in the Tungabhadra River. Occasionally, we hooked up with local youth to join in an exciting game of Cubbity, a local game somewhat similar to our game of "Capture the Flag."

Joe's and Ken's River Boat in its working days

Joe Emerson, the training Project Director, coaxed me into splitting the cost of a cowhide river ferry. Our boat was about 12 feet in diameter, framed in bamboo and river reed with a hull skin of buffalo hide. It was designed to ferry people and animals across the river. It's round shape made it easy to paddle against the swift current. It could accommodate up to twelve people plus small livestock. The leather had to be kept wet or it would shrink and crack. Once that happened the boat would be useless. Joe and I shared the boating fun with the trainees during our breaks. One fateful day the boat was accidentally left in the sun where it met its doom. It now rests at the bottom of the Tungabhadra.

Of course, we also subjected the trainees to their first village visits. We listened to their anxious complaints before and after their first experience of being deposited in remote villages for a day of cultural immersion. None of them encountered a scorpion during their village visits!

There were those trainees who decided early that they were not meant to spend two years eating *rotis* and drinking *chai*. They quietly said goodbye and were escorted to Bangalore for their homebound tickets. There were those who were deselected for one reason or another, and ten of them graduated and went stoically to meet their host farmers.

My wife and I were on a time-line to leave the country shortly after training. Her excursion air ticket was only good for 120 days. Our plan was to leave the training camp as soon as training ended and the volunteers were placed in their respective villages. We still had to travel to Bangalore for final meetings with staff and to complete the project report before we could set off to see Pejathaya.

As I left the tea *ungadi* in the village on that last day in Dhadesugur a bus pulled to a dusty stop across the roadway. I closed my mouth and eyes to avoid the dust and fumes as I walked past the quickly unloading bus. A frantic shout caught my attention. "Mr. Ken! Mr. Ken!"

I turned to see a familiar form rushing toward me. It was my dear friend Achyuta Ramaiah, the embattled President of the Sindhanur Milk Cooperative. In *Telugu* and broken *Kannada* and bits of English he told me that he traveled to Dhadesugur because he heard that I was soon to leave India and he couldn't let me go without saying goodbye.

"How will our cooperative survive after you leave us. Please stay in India. You have a home here, and you are loved by many." He said, "You can find a nice Sindhanur girl to marry and you will be happy here. Please don't go."

"But Achyuta Ramaiah, I am already married. My wife is here in Dhadesugur," I replied. "My mission with Peace Corps is completed and now I must return to the States."

Achyuta Ramaiah shook my hand and gave me a big bear hug. Never, in the two plus years living in India, had I experienced such a warm show of friendship. His eyes watered slightly as he wished me good luck and asked that I return some time to see his progress.

I had been saying farewells to my Indian friends for the past several months, but none of those previous goodbyes gave me such a strong feeling of kinship and sorrow for departing from this country. My eyes water to remember that roadside parting of the ways.

In Bangalore, each training coordinator summarized the effectiveness of his training, describing what aspects were successful in preparing trainees for the field and identifying which methods were not effective. As Technical Coordinator, I had been assigned two Agriculture Department officials, Mr. Patil and Mr. Hiremath, both of whom were expert in agricultural technology, and were good communicators. My report was easy to write. My only regret was that less than half of the original trainees survived the training to be placed in host villages.

As soon as the compiled report was assembled and edited we were free to go. Dee and I caught the next bus to the Chikkamagluru District to visit Pejathaya.

GETTING AROUND

The high hills of Chikkamagluru District of Karnataka are known as the 'coffee land' of Karnataka, and are fairly remote. Coffee plants require good, well-drained soil, ample rainfall (for *Indian monsooned coffee*) at the right time, and an altitude of at least 2000 feet above sea level.

Pejathaya's coffee estate was located in a remote area where roads were subject to flooding during the monsoon season. Travel to and from the coffee estate was difficult during the rainy season, but a little less arduous in the dry season. Pejathaya tells the story of a bus driver named Gopal, who became a friendly connection to the more active civilization in the distant towns.

DRIVER GOPAL
BY S.M. PEJATHAYA

Driver Gopal was the most popular man in our Bhadra River valley during the sixties and early seventies. He was driving his Tata Mercedes Benz bus from the city of Shimoga to Kalasa, up and down everyday. Shimoga City is the district headquarters of Shimoga district. It is our neighboring district and nearest agriculture-based commercial market. It is a renowned market for 'areca' nuts.

Next to coffee, 'areca' nut is our major agricultural crop. The agricultural community of Bhadra Valley even today sells 'areca' nuts at Shimoga Mandies (Commission Agents) and Areca Nut Growers' Co-operative Society. We get our spray materials from Shimoga. We get advance finance on expected quantity of our crop by these 'areca' nut trading firms before the harvest season. After taking an advance, as a custom we send our harvested 'areca' nuts, after duly processing the harvested crop to these trading firms for trading in open auction.

Processing the half-ripe 'areca' nuts that we harvest from the tall palms is a laborious process. First, we peel kernel part from the green nut and discard the husk. We cut the nuts into halves and then boil them in a concoction of various herbs and natural pigmenting materials. Later we sun dry them carefully on bamboo mats. This process gives our 'areca' the distinct color and taste. If the rates are low during the harvest season, we warehouse the produce until the rates pick up. We accept an advance from these traders depending on the quantity of the crop that we have warehoused with them.

We depended on this city of Shimoga for our many more needs. Shimoga has shops where all sorts of agricultural commodities and implements are available. There we can find good textile shops, electrical shops, hardware stores and fabricating workshops. We depended on this city for all our needs of agricultural implements, vehicles, their spares, cement, fertilizer and pesticides. Shimoga City has many good restaurants, hotels with comfortable lodges, a good number of hospitals and nursing homes. We depend on Shimoga for our healthcare.

Furthermore, Shimoga City boasts of having a good number of cinema halls. There used to be many drama camps and circuses performing during the summer months at Shimoga decades ago. After the advent of television and video cassettes, the drama and circus companies have become things of the past, as people remain glued to their television sets.

Driver Gopal was working for M/s Shanker Transport Company. He was a most reliable senior bus driver with them. Gopal was in his forties. He was a man of average height and medium build. He was a pleasant character with a pleasing smile on his face and always ready to help others. He maintained his bus very well. His bus would start from Shimoga city at 7.30 a.m. and reach Kalasa by 12.15 p.m. On the return journey, it would leave Kalasa at 2 pm to reach Shimoga City by 7.15 p.m. The distance between the two destinations is about seventy-five miles and three-fourth of the route is in our Bhadra River valley.

Nearly half of this winding road was not asphalted and the asphalted stretch had innumerable potholes. The journey used to be very tiresome, bouncy and dusty.

Gopal was a careful driver and each passenger felt very safe when he drove that Tata Mercedes Benz bus. The bus had a very distinctive Alpine horn, the sound of which carried for miles. Gopal was very punctual and village people reckoned their time by the arrival and departure of his bus at their villages.

He was very popular throughout the Bhadra River valley as his was the only bus coming from and returning to Shimoga the same day. The daily newspapers and periodicals would arrive from Shimoga in his bus, as did the postbag to our Balehole post office. Gopal was a very helpful person and would run errands for almost everyone in our neighborhood. Many Children traveled to Shimoga unescorted as their school commenced the new terms and they would return home for their vacations the same way in Gopal's bus. Parents were always sure that Gopal would take care of them on their journey.

Most of the farmers warehoused their 'areca' nut crop soon after the harvest at Shimoga Areca nut 'mandies' and sold them sometime during the year when rates picked up. Apart from coffee, 'areca' nut is still one of the main crops in the Bhadra Valley. More than half of the passengers in his bus were 'areca' nut farmers going to Shimoga or coming home from there. Most of our children studied at Shimoga as it was the nearest educational center with a good number of high schools and colleges having hostel facility. Small shopkeepers in the valley depended on Gopal for fancy items, sweets, biscuits, chocolates, and things like 'bidis', cigarettes and chewing tobacco.

Gopal would bring the medicines if we handed our local doctor's prescriptions. He would bring baby cereal foods and some cosmetic items, which were not available in our villages. He would bring us cricket, badminton sets and volleyballs. Thus, he saved our many trips to Shimoga for the purchase of sundry things. He was very correct with our money and would return the change with the bills issued by the shops.

Driver Gopal would not accept money for his kind of service. With great difficulty we would force him to accept a bunch of plantains, a little of homegrown cardamom or a packet of our areca nut from time to time. He would say that he had not taken any special trouble to do our errand, and it is not fair on his part to accept money for all these courtesies. Driver Gopal knew each of us in the Bhadra Valley and he was part our daily lives. He was friendly with all and had no enemy in this world.

In course of time during the eighties, he retired and along with his retirement, "The great link of humanity" that connected us with the city of Shimoga, just vanished. No one would fill that gap in the years that followed. The transport facility too had improved considerably after Gopal's retirement. The other bus drivers were just 'drivers' and we became just the other 'dumb passengers.'

The age-old human touch disappeared, and, traveling to Shimoga became just a mechanical routine. Now, there is a bus every half an hour, between Shimoga and Kalasa. The roads are metalled and tarred all through. People just consider this trip, just as a 'hop to the city and be back *home' on the same day evening.*

Memory of Gopal and his Mercedes bus always lingers with the old timers. We still cherish those times when a selfless driver Gopal helped us to live a comfortable life in our villages. We all owe him a lot and probably will never pay him back for his good-natured help.

Today, I tell my daughters about Driver Gopal and how he would bring their requirement of medicines, baby foods, biscuits, chocolates and toys as they grew up in our remote estate. I thankfully remember the number of trips he had saved for my neighbors and me. Otherwise, we had to go all the way in person and waste many good man-hours of work as well as money. I am sure we spent all those hours in our farms usefully, to grow something or the other for the betterment of our country. I gratefully appreciate the services that Driver Gopal rendered selflessly to our rural community. Anything that we wanted from the city would arrive by his bus the very next day, positively! How amicable and friendly he was!

Will we come across the likes of Driver Gopal in our life again? How can we repay his good gesture? Probably, we can do that, perhaps, by helping someone as selflessly as he did!

The question is how many of us have a motivation to help others as unconditionally as our dear Driver Gopal? If ever we do likewise, this world will be a better place to live in.

*　　　　*　　　　*

Immediately after completing the project report for the last PCV training program Dee and I visited Sulimane Coffee Estate to spend several days with Pejathaya before leaving India. During his earlier visit to our grass house in Dhadesugur, Pejathaya invited us to visit the coffee estate. I knew that I could not leave India without a final meeting with my good friend, so I happily agreed. Pejathaya gave us detailed instructions about bus numbers and schedules, when to leave Bangalore, where to stay and what to do when we arrived at the last stop.

We made the journey from Bangalore in January 1972. The roads were in good condition and Pejathaya's instructions were precise. I had not learned about Gopal the driver until later, so I am not sure if he was the driver of our bus. All I know is that whoever was driving our bus did a good job, and the journey was a fascinating experience.

Pejathaya met us in his four-wheel drive vehicle and drove us the last few miles to the estate. We had to cross Bhadra River, which was not bridged. During the monsoon the river was swollen with waters gushing from the higher mountains. His estate would become an island and he had to cross in a dugout double-ender boat. January was the end of winter and the river was flowing low. Luckily, his Jeep forded the low flowing Bhadra River with relative ease.

He seemed to be very happy and content in his life on the coffee estate. He loved his new situation. He was the owner-operator of a reasonably large coffee plantation, and he also managed the coffee lands of Saroja's three sisters. He was not the slave, as he had feared, but the master of the situation. His knowledge about intercropping, fertilizer application, chemical sprays and sprinkler irrigation had improved Saroja's coffee and areca nut crop. Within a span of eight months, Pejathaya's crop protection measures and judicious use of fertilizers had already caused the farm to show a profit.

In addition, Pejathaya had planned ahead at least three decades by planting trees, such as coconut, that would become productive many years later. His new Robusta Coffee plants would give a steady yield in about twelve years. The pepper, cardamom and areca plants were already showing profits.

The estate bungalow was located at the end of a long driveway and hidden behind a growth of protective trees and coffee plants. It sat in the lowest level of the Sulimane Valley. Water flowed by gravity to the house, tapped from a perennial pond at a higher level. The roof was covered with red clay tiles to protect the house from the heavy rains, and to cool the house in the hot summers.

The house Pejathaya called home was a large two-story brick and wood structure with ample fenestration. It has an inner courtyard with a fragrant Tulasi (a sacred Hindu plant) in the center. The ceilings and attics were supported by rafters of high quality wood. We saw concrete floors of red oxide-mixed cement that had been polished smooth and shiny.

The kitchen stoves are heated by firewood, which is available in plenty on the property. The spicy hot South Indian Vegetarian curry was served on plantain leaf in a large dining room. The kitchen floors were all smooth concrete slabs painted in light shades of grey. The inner rooms were large and airy, and modestly adorned with family photographs and memorabilia.

Several buildings were situated near the compound. These contained the tools and machinery used in growing, cultivating and harvesting the coffee and other crops grown on the estate. Some of the buildings were housing for workers, others were for storing produce.

Pejathaya proudly walked us through the estate, showing us his sprinkler irrigation equipment and other innovations. He began inter-planting the coffee plants with other crops such as cardamom and black pepper. He planted timber as shade for the coffee, and had begun planting silver oak saplings which would become good shade trees and standards for the pepper vines in about ten years.

As we walked, he told us about "monkey beans." Local monkeys and flying squirrels would often ingest the raw coffee beans but were unable to digest them. Reclaimed coffee beans had become a marketable, even a sought after commodity. In the market it was called "Jackal Coffee," and was a specialty coffee in London in the 1920s.

Sulimane Bungalow; Pejathaya's home in the Bhadra River Valley

Saroja's father had built a very large coffee and areca nut drying yard in front of the house. During our visit, workers harvested areca nuts. As we watched, they boiled them with herbs to instill a red color, and began drying them in the sun. We watched, fascinated, as Pejathaya demonstrated how areca was harvested, cured and prepared for selling in the market.

The nut of the areca palm grows on a tall, slender tree. Pejathaya's nut trees were around thirty feet high. The fearless workers, wearing only shorts, a leather belt and no shirt, shinnied up a tree hand over hand, using their feet to brace against the rough bark of the areca palm. In one hand they held a eight foot long pole. On the end of the pole was a sharp ten inch metal sickle blade.

The belt around their waists held one end of long hemp rope. A worker at the base of the tree maneuvered the rope to keep it from tangling, or snagging and causing the climber to lose his balance. Up, up the worker climbed until he was within reach of a batch of areca nuts by reaching out his pole.

The nut clusters would slide down the pole to the man's hand. He placed the cluster on the rope tied to his waist and allowed it to slide down the rope to the waiting hands below.

Then came the more treacherous act of moving to the next palm tree. The worker, still high up in the palm, would jump to the next tree. By shifting his weight back and forth the palm's thin trunk would sway and bend. When the swaying motion brought him close enough to the neighboring areca palm he would reach out and grab that palm. Being careful to not entangle the rope hanging from his waist, and without dropping the pole in his hand, he would disengage from the first palm and slide over to the second one. Everyone watched, breathlessly, as the worker catapulted into the second tree.

Pejathaya said that only the most audacious workers attempted this. Those who did it successfully considered their expertise as a exploit of courage and distinction. They were the highest paid workers on the estate. Several areca harvesters on other farms had, in the past, paid a high price for their daring. Pejathaya insured these workers with work hazard insurance, and is proud to note that in one hundred years history of the estate no one had ever fallen from the areca nut trees.

ELEPHANTS CAN'T READ

With his small caliber rifle in hand Pejathaya narrated many local stories in an excited, boyish manner as he walked Dee and me through the coffee estate. The rifle was not to kill but to warn monkeys to stay clear of his crops. We enjoyed his stories about his neighboring farmers, his estate workers and the animals that he saw while tending his coffee.

Dee and I loved the solitude of the farm and the feel of the fertile soil under our sandals. The cool, moist vegetation and the wildlife so far from heavy population was like being on a tropical island. We didn't want to leave. Yet, our future awaited us. Somewhere, back across that ocean, our families and our destiny awaited and urged our instincts to keep moving.

We parted company after two days with Pejathaya and his wife Saroja. We couldn't help but sense how happy and content they both were. They had been excellent hosts. As we said our goodbyes we promised to communicate. Our promise to visit them again was sincere, but had an improbable chance of transpiring. They, in turn, exclaimed that they would love to someday visit us in the U.S.

After Pejathaya took up coffee growing in the hills of Karnataka, he began jotting down some of his experiences from his childhood. He went further by developing short stories about the people, places and animals that he met while developing the coconut farm on the coast, irrigating a farm in Raichur District, growing coffee in the hills of Chikkamagluru District and later, as a gentleman "e-farmer" in Bangalore. The term e-farmer is Pejathaya's own, as he manages the coffee estate remotely, using electronic communication with the resident manager.

During the rainy seasons he wrote about his many adventures and experiences. He put together some of his writings in what he calls his memoirs. Some of these stories appeared in *Kannada* language periodicals and, eventually, in *Kannada* language books. Several years after we said goodbye in India, Pejathaya began forwarding some of his short stories. I loved reading them because they are written from the heart, and they represent his personal experiences.

One story Pejathaya related reflects something I've always known about elephants but have never experienced. It is said that elephants have good memories. A popular magazine once claimed that an elephant remembered a hunter several years after the hunter had shot and wounded another elephant from its herd. When that hunter returned for another hunt several years later the elephant charged the unfortunate hunter.

Although most of his writings were in the local *Kannada* script, Pejathaya wrote some stories in English. One of my favorites is this true story about his experience with elephants in a situation that could have cost him or his family serious harm. The elephant remembered the car but did not take notice of the license plate number. Here is Pejathaya's story."

ELEPHANTS CANNOT READ!
BY S.M. PEJATHAYA

We had a memorable time with a tusker (elephant with well developed tusks) during the year 1987. We were traveling across the Bandipur Reserve Forest. We were not going to stay at the Jungle Lodge there. We hail from a coffee jungle and there would be nothing much different in a jungle lodge. We were on a trip to Ooty and Kottagiri for a short holiday.

We traveled in our open Maruti Gipsy jeep. We started early from Bangalore and were at Bandipur National Park by about eight in the morning. We saw herds of deer and stag grazing happily without fearing man. We saw some monkeys. We saw a tusker, a cow and two calves feeding peacefully on the tall grass, a little off the road. They were about 20 yards away. I wanted to photograph them. I kept the engine running and pulled the parking brake. As I lifted my camera to photograph, the tusker trumpeted in rage and charged at my jeep.

I let the camera drop on the sling and stepped on the throttle after throwing off the parking brake. We could feel the whoosh of the giant tusker's breath through the enormous trunk with which it was trying to reach us! The jeep shot forward in no time. It was a great relief to escape from the mountain of muscle and rage. The guy chased us for nearly two kilometers, though we were pushing off at around 25 miles/hour. Finally, the guy stopped near the Tamil Nadu border gate, manned by the forest guards.

After about a month, during my morning walks in Bangalore, I met a neighbor who happened to be one of the partners in one of the Jungle Lodges of Bandipur. During casual talk, he revealed to me that he had hit an elephant hard on the hind legs accidentally in the darkness of the night at Bandipur forest.

He told me that a huge tusker was standing in the middle of the road after a deep bend. The color of the elephant merges with the darkness and it is always very difficult to see the elephant during the darkness in the jungle. He had hit the big tusker's hind legs. The elephant lost its balance and landed on its haunches in the middle of the road. It gave out great cries in pain. He said, fortunately for him, this Jungle Lodge partner guy had hit the elephant from the rear side. Had he hit the elephant from the front or its sides, he wouldn't have returned to tell the story. However, at this juncture, the guy could find enough space to reverse his jeep. His was a green Maruti Gypsy 4WD vehicle just like mine! The elephant had been sitting on its haunches in great pain for nearly twenty minutes. Before the tusker stood up and tried to chase the offending jeep, the guy being a clever jerk, had conveniently reversed his jeep and was watching it from a safe distance. He got away from the elephant before it neared him. He had escaped! He was boasting of his adventure!

But, I was the victim to the anger of the elephant, the very next day! The reason: the elephants cannot read registration numbers! The tusker had mistaken my jeep for the truant one! Yes! Now, I am sure that the elephants cannot read!

After this incident my wife Saroja is damn afraid of the elephants. She would not like to travel through Bandipur forest again.

A LOT OF BULL

The story about elephants not being able to distinguish one license plate from another is typical of Pejathaya's writings, and I always looked forward to his next installment. His new life in the hills of Shimoga District brought on a completely new cast of subjects and inspired many stories. At first Pejathaya was an outsider in his new community, but his accommodating nature, positive attitude and love of people soon won him the respect and love of everyone he met.

Pejathaya lived on the coffee estate for several years. His two daughters were born there, and they had a very happy home. When the two girls reached school age, Pejathaya and Saroja wanted the best possible education for them. This meant that they had to move to where the schools existed. That was the beginning of Pejathaya's career as a commuting farmer.

They moved to the larger town of Shimoga, where the young girls entered school. Pejathaya opened a soft drink bottling business to keep busy, and commuted to the coffee estate on a regular basis. When the daughters needed to enter higher level schools and college, Pejathaya and Saroja moved again, and took up residence in Bangalore. Still, he maintained constant contact with the workers on the estate, and travelled there several times each month. He lived there during the harvest and other busy times.

It became difficult for Pejathaya to travel the long, dusty, rutted roads from Bangalore to his coffee estate. Not only did it take up travel time, but the jolting ride strained his body. As the number of trips decreased to only those necessary during the critical harvesting and planting seasons Pejathaya turned to what he calls e-farming. Through the use of telephone and internet he was able to see and hear much of the action on the coffee estate.

It was during this time that he began to communicate in writing with other agriculturists. He wrote articles for newspapers and farming periodicals. All of his writing at this stage was in the local script, *Kannada*. Some of Pejathaya's best short stories introduce the interesting people he came to know while working at or traveling to the Sulimane Estate. Pejathaya wrote the following story about a neighboring farmer, Mr. Shetty, and his massive bull, Bheema.

SHETTY'S BULL
BY S.M. PEJATHAYA

Mr. Shetty was my neighbor. I say 'was', because he is no more now. He was a planter of good repute and a comprehensive farmer. Apart from coffee, 'areca' nut, cardamom and pepper, he grew horticultural crops like papaya and pineapples.

He had a nice dairy farm and allocated a few acres of his land to grow green fodder that he needed for his cows and buffaloes. During 1970s, our area was considered to be very remote where the power supply and telephones were not reliable. The roads were not asphalted. The situation in our nearest small town, Kalasa, was no different.

Mr. Shetty was a progressive farmer and had many Jersey and Holstein Friesian (HF) Cows. He had difficulty in breeding them. For, due to frequent power failures the freezer at the Veterinary Hospital and Artificial Insemination Center of Kalasa would not function properly, and most of the trials in artificial insemination failed.

To address the issue, Mr. Shetty went to Bangalore and met the bigwigs of the Animal Husbandry Department. He finally succeeded in purchasing a two-month-old HF bull calf from the State's Dairy Research Center. He brought it to the farm in his open jeep and named him Bheema as he was very well built for his age. Bheema acquired his special place in the drawing room of the bungalow itself, near the hearth of Mr. Shetty in the beginning months.

Bheema was petted by everyone in Shetty's household. He was treated like a child separated from his mother. He would be given the best of feeds and tonics, and massaged twice a day by none other than Mr. Shetty himself! When Bheema grew up to become a larger calf, he could not be housed inside the bungalow. In a few months, the drawing room became too small for Bheema!

Mr. Shetty built a small hall for him, next to his bungalow. The place was too elegant to be called as a cowshed.

Mr. Shetty spent more and more of his time petting Bheema as he grew up to become a small bull. He was a pet and a darling of everybody in the estate. Mr. Shetty never wanted Bheema's nose to be pierced, as it would inflict pain to his pet calf. He would not put a halter to Bheema's neck to tie him up. Putting a muzzle tether was also out of question.

Bheema was always free within his shed. Every morning he would go to the field with Mr. Shetty and follow obediently like a domesticated dog when Mr. Shetty went around the estate. He never harmed anyone. He was never tethered even when inside his spacious quarters. Bheema was quite a disciplined fellow. He would never touch any crop or even a blade of grass on his own. He would eat only things offered to him.

Mr. Shetty always wore a wide brimmed hat whenever he went out of the bungalow. On all such occasions, this gentle giant Bheema, who was about three years old, would join and follow him! Whenever Mr. Shetty went out, Bheema would be in the shed.

Despite the great size and weight of about a ton, Bheema was like a gentle child. The very size of Bheema frightened me whenever I went to Mr. Shetty's place. While he was still a calf I began carrying some toffees to feed Bheema, which pleased both Bheema as well as Mr. Shetty. He was very glad that I liked Bheema. I was proud to call Bheema as my friend.

Bheema would demand toffee with a small grunt and for each grunt he would receive one toffee from me. He would sniff at my face in gratitude after consuming a toffee and seek one more with a grunt, till such time I went out of stock! This happened every time. After he had attained his full size, I was really afraid to go near him. Whenever I went to Shetty's estate Bheema would come searching for me and demand his usual toffees.

I knew even a small nudge from him would send me toppling over, but Bheema in turn behaved as if he were a small calf. He was very gentle. I thought Bheema was not at all aware of his great size!

He would always come galloping to me with his demanding short grunts! I always proffered toffees to him as soon as he neared me. When the stock of toffees was over, I tried coolly to move away from him at the earliest.

One day Mr. Shetty had left for Mangalore with his family early in the morning. He had carefully corralled Bheema in his shed after feeding and massaging him. By about ten in the morning the sweeper of the shed carelessly kept the door of the shed open before he started cleaning the shed.

In the meanwhile, our 'little' Bheema thought of taking a stroll in the morning sun and wandered out. The sweeper could not get the 'Gentle Giant' into the shed again by pleading and begging. He tried to raise his voice and shout at Bheema. Bheema was amused at the shouting of this puny person and grunted back at the man to shoo him away!

The nervous worker, in his confusion, picked a small stick to chide Bheema into the shed since he thought that it was not an 'unpardonable mistake' to use a small cane and swish it in the air to turn the young bull back into his shed.

Bheema misunderstood the action and ran away from the shed in panic and disgust. Soon most of the staff and labor were chasing Bheema, who galloped widely all over the estate as he was chased by a contingent of workers. Somebody suggested roping him. At the sight of the rope he became violent. In his rage, he tried to knock down the people who came near him with the rope. Finally, the workers and the staff had to give up. Bheema chose to remain outside his shed and roamed within the estate lands.

Bheema was obviously offended that day and refused to cool down. He continued to grunt and chase anyone who came near him. Every one in Shetty's estate was frightened and worried.

What would their boss say when he returned from Mangalore the next day? He would certainly reprimand each one of them for their carelessness. Mr. Shetty's foreman, Rasheed Saheb, came in search of me to our estate and asked if I could help him. He told me that every one was scared of Bheema and no one would go near him. Rasheed Saheb had no courage to face an angered Mr. Shetty who would take him to task when he returned from Mangalore, the next day. If anything went out of control in an estate, the foreman of the estate would be held responsible.

Rasheed Saheb pleaded with me to come to their estate and suggested I bring a few toffees! He said, I too resembled Mr. Shetty in build and I too wore Khaki pants and wide brimmed hat. He was sure that a pocketful of toffees would do the trick. No doubt, I was scared to face an angered

Bheema. However, my ego would not permit me to admit my fear.

I clambered into my jeep to go to Mr. Shetty's estate. As soon as we opened the main gate and entered the fenced area, Rasheed Saheb coolly got off the jeep to close the gate. He whispered that Bheema was likely to check on the person who had come by a jeep. He told me that Bheema may get angry at the sight of Rasheed and he did not want to be seen at the spot! He had worried Bheema by chasing him all that morning with a band of shouting laborers. He disappeared from the site!

As I slowly drove towards the bungalow, Bheema came bounding in great strides. As he neared, I could hear the hiss of his breathing! I switched off the engine and sat quietly in the comparative safety of a canvas-topped jeep.

For half a minute, Bheema was staring at me with mixed feelings. Then, he came near the jeep and slowly put his muzzle into the jeep and gave a short grunt demanding his toffee! I called "Bheema, Bheema" twice, trying to hide my nervousness. I fed him a toffee. He sniffed my face as if to thank me, I scratched him in the head around his de-horned area. I reached and scratched the area between his jawbones and at the same time got out of the jeep.

I took out another toffee from my pocket and held it out after peeling its paper cover, which he accepted with his usual grunt. I thought the job was half done. I looked away from him and walked a few steps down towards his shed and proffered another toffee. He came after me to accept it with his usual acknowledgement and sniffed my shirt collar. I walked on again and offered three more toffees before we walked into his shed. His manger was piled high with lush-green fodder grass, and his trough was brimming full with fresh spring water.

He took a swill of water and asked for one more toffee, which I gladly gave him. He continued his demand for more toffees and I kept on feeding him. He was grunting for his tenth toffee now, I quietly slipped the last one I had into his mouth. As he was in the process of relishing the sweet, I got out of the main door and closed it securely from outside.

Next day, Mr. Shetty came over to thank me for corralling Bheema. He said, apart from him, I was the only man in the world who could understand the sentiments of his pet Bheema.

In the years to come, Bheema won many prizes at various cattle shows.

He became the most famous breeding bull in our district. He was known to be the only Holstein Friesian (HF) stud bull without a nose ring. He obeyed his master like a puppy in the various cattle shows. Bheema sired hundreds of fine calves.

Bheema is no more, now. I see his progeny continue in our area as I see many HF breed cattle that graze today in the hilly pastures of Kalasa.

*   *   *

This story reminds Tony Ganey of our training in Dhadesugur in 1968, where our Indian instructors taught us to drive the large bullocks (neutered bull, or steer) while they pulled a heavy harrow. Two teams of these giant animals were hitched in tandem. One person was the rear driver and walked behind the teams. A second person was instructed to sit on the yoke of the front team and balance himself (without touching the "ferocious" bullocks) to drive the lead team. This latter activity prescribed huge amounts of courage.

HOLY PILGRIMAGE

Religious and cultural tradition is a very important inherent obligation of the people of India. A strong bond compels children to follow the beliefs of the parent, and the parent of the grandparent, ad infinitum. Even the most sophisticated Indian-born people living in the modern West feel at least a minuscule responsibility to honor their elders and respond to the wishes of the parents, even after the parents have departed this world.

Of all the cultural traditions explained to me by Pejathaya over the years of our acquaintance, I never quite understood the depth of the feeling of duty that a child has for following the wishes of the parent. Many Indians, living in Europe or the United States for several generations, still expect to arrange their children's marriages in the traditional manner. A parent's wishes are carried on the shoulders of the child until the wish becomes a fact and the child is relieved of one more duty.

Of the many stories Pejathaya wrote, his visit to the holy Ganges River was to me the most insightful. The Ganges is considered a sacred river. It is believed that bathing in the river stimulates the remission of sins and facilitates liberation from the cycle of life and death. Pejathaya's story depicts the feelings of the modern Indian man contrasting his struggle to maintain the old ways by being true to the wishes of his parents. Intensify that conflict by adding the need to be true to the feelings and wishes of his modern day spouse.

Tradition and honor for our parents and ancestors is probably not as deeply felt in the American way of life as it is in the lives of many religious Hindus. If the average American saw the Ganges today they would not be willing to put even their little finger in its murky water. If the occasion required us to honor our deceased parents we would likely find an alternative to the Hindu rituals.

The revulsion experienced by Pejathaya and Saroja can be sensed when you read his story. To his everlasting credit, Pejathaya insisted on overcoming his abhorrence of the putrid waters of the Ganges, and he persevered in his mission to follow the wishes of his late, beloved mother.

VARANASI
BY S. M. PEJATHAYA

Varanasi is known as Kashi or Benares. It is one of the most holy places for Hindus. A Hindu must visit Kashi to pay homage to his departed ancestors, and to purify his body and soul by cleansing himself in the Holy Ganges. He shall pray at the temple of Kashi Vishwanath to pardon his sins, which he committed knowingly or unknowingly. The visit to Kashi Vishwanath temple and the temple of Goddess Vishalakshi is a must during the pilgrimage of 'Kashi.' The women buy the exquisite Benares brocade saris to commemorate their visit. Whereas the men folk would buy Benares shawls and the famous 'Spatika beads'[26] to form a 'Japamala.'[27]

A Visit to Kashi is compared to the Haj pilgrimage of the Muslims. It is every Hindu's dream to go on a pilgrimage of 'Kashi' to cleanse himself of his sins and to pray for his departed ancestors. After this great pilgrimage, one is supposed to live a calm and quiet life, almost dejected from worldly affairs and devoting more time to prayer. In memory of this great

---

[26] Naturally occurring crystal beads

[27] Rosary

pilgrimage, as a prevailing custom, many people give up consuming one or two of their favorite vegetables or favorite dishes.

In olden times, Kashi was a very far off place and people took months for the pilgrimage. Many of the pilgrims never returned as they succumbed to death. The death during the pilgrimage was supposed to be very auspicious. The belief prevailed that pilgrims attained 'moksha'[28] if they passed away during the pilgrimage of 'Kashi.' It was supposedly certain that if a person died at Kashi and his last rites were performed there by the side Holy Ganga, he would attain 'moksha.' There would not be further birth for him in this world. Because of this belief, many aged people in olden times opted to spend their last days in Kashi.

The mode of travel was by foot, palanquin, and horseback or by cart. Then the railway transportation was introduced. The travel became easier as the airplanes joined the mode of transport. Now, the man needs only the will and the much needed money to make this trip of pilgrimage.

Despite all these conveniences of travel, we can still see many aged people living their last days in Kashi awaiting death. They live a dejected life there and keep praying the Lord for their moksha.

I heard about 'Kashi' when I was a child, from my grandmother. She could never visit 'Kashi' in her lifetime. I still feel disappointed about this fact. As I grew up, I developed a feeling that I should take my mother to 'Kashi' on pilgrimage. Somehow, I failed to accomplish this. When my mother passed away, our family 'Purohit'[29] told me that a portion of her ashes could be kept aside, later to be immersed in the holy Ganga. That is, if any one of the sons wanted to perform the particular ceremony at 'Kashi.' He told us that there was no time limit to perform the ceremony; but we had to do it during our lifetime. I volunteered to do the same, and I received a small copper urn of her ashes from our Purohit after taking the oath. The ashes could not be taken into the house as per the prevailing custom. It had to be buried under a coconut tree. Therefore, I buried the urn under the coconut palm at my elder brother Balakrishna's place, as I had no house of my own at Bangalore at that time. I was living in a rented apartment.

---

[28] Eternal peace

[29] Priest

The years passed and the coconut tree at my brother's place grew taller and taller to remind me of my oath. Eleven years passed. Finally, I contacted our family Purohit at Bangalore and told him that I had made up my mind to visit Kashi and asked him to introduce me to a Kashi Purohit who would conduct the ritual of immersion of my mother's ashes in the Ganges.

We planned our visit to Kashi during the Dasara holidays in October. We flew to Calcutta and stayed there for three days. From Calcutta we took a plane to Patna and from there, we drove by taxi to Kashi as there was no flight scheduled for that particular day. The road was very bad and it took nearly ten hours to reach Kashi. We stayed at the Best Western Hotel.

It was the 'Durga Pooja' season and every road in Kashi had a 'pooja pendal,'[30] and our taxi could not penetrate deeper into the heart of the city. Our young taxi driver, who called himself Mr. Jha, volunteered to guide us to the Harishchandra Ghat. He parked his car in a safe place. We covered about a kilometer by climbing onto a rickety cycle rickshaw to reach the bank of River Ganga on the northern outskirts of the city.

The wide river flowed very slowly and the water was thick and polluted. We could see the other bank far away very vaguely. The taxi driver hired a wide bottomed boat to ferry us to Harishchandra Ghat which lay down the flow of the great river. We sailed down the numerous bathing Ghats of the great city. People were taking bath in each Ghat. There were a number of purohits performing the rites for their clients. As we sailed down we found a bathing Ghat almost deserted. I questioned the driver as to why a particular Ghat was not crowded at all. He told us that this particular Ghat is known as Narada Maharshi Ghat. In our 'Puranas' Narada Maharshi is a great trouble monger. He always instigated the couples to quarrel. It seems he did not spare even Gods and Goddesses.

The thick blackish green water of the river Ganga carried all sorts of floating impurities. All the sewers in the world seemed to empty into the holy river. A good number of human bodies were cremated along its banks because the local people, as well as the people from far away places, brought their dead for cremation at Holy Varanasi. It is believed that if one's body

---

[30] Kiosk with religious items

is cremated on the banks of the Holy Ganga, the soul would attain the eternal bliss in heaven.

In accordance with this profound belief, bodies are cremated day in and day out all along the banks of Ganga in Kashi. Every Ghat has a long queue. I heard that sometimes a greedy undertaker pushed a partially cremated body into the Holy River to save on the fuel of firewood. Yes! The floating of these half burnt bodies formed a ghastly sight.

I always thought this was an exaggeration, however, we saw a floating arm of a dead body; the crows were perching on it. They pecked on it constantly as no one bothered them. To my bad luck, Saroja saw this scene first. She was taken aback by the sight. My effort to pacify her by saying that it is only a banana tree stem floating on water and the crows were hitching a jolly ride on it went futile. This angered her and she told that banana stems do not have a wrist and fingers at one end! I had to keep quiet, staring at Saroja who was showing signs of great discomfort and indignation. Finally, after passing many Ghats, our driver Mr. Jha told that we had arrived at the great Harishchandra Ghat. We could see a dead body being cremated in front of a small sanctum of Veera Baahu.

The bank of the Great River Ganga was strewn with ashes of the cremated bodies as no one cared to wash ashes away. I descended from the boat and stepped on the ash-colored bank. Saroja just could not think of setting her foot on human ashes and she was hesitating.

Our stalwart taxi driver told Saroja, "Maajee, do not worry! I shall carry you up the steps. You are like a mother to me!"

He just took hold of Saroja as if she were a child and lifted her bodily, and carried her a few steps up and set her on the granite stone pavement of staircase. The stairs led us up to the riverbank road. After a few steps down the road, we reached our Purohit's residence.

Sri Baahu Acharya welcomed us in our mother tongue, Kannada. We paid Mr. Jha and thanked him for his kind services. Mr. Jha told us that it was his pleasure to help a couple who were as old as his parents, and it was his opportunity to be in the Harishchandra Ghat early that morning. He told us that he had brought his bath towel from his taxi and he would take his bath in the holy Harishchandra Ghat and would walk his way to his taxi by a shortcut. Saroja winced at the thought of him taking bath with great pleasure in the polluted waters. He left after receiving an *additional tip from Saroja.*

Sri Baahu Acharya is a great Sanskrit scholar. Now, he is the authorized Kshetra Purohit[31] appointed by our holy Pejavar Mutt of Udupi. He is the only person at Kashi duly authorized to perform all the religious rites for us. His house is by the side of the Mutt. We were welcomed again by his wife. She called us in for breakfast. We told her that we have already had our breakfast. She served us nice cups of tea. The Purohit started his work. I was asked to lay the casket which contained the ashes of my mother in a new earthen pot. He told me that he would send one of his men to follow me to the Harishchadra Ghat where I had to take the holy immersion bath in Ganges before we began the rituals. He seemed to understand Saroja's plight without telling; and he asked her to take bath in his own premises where the City Corporation's purified Ganga water flowed in the taps. She was asked to wear a silk sari after bath. The bathroom was tiled and it was very clean. So, the biggest problem of holy bath for Saroja was solved.

As commanded by him, I had to take three baths in the Ganga that day. I took bath in the polluted waters of Holy Ganga with a positive conviction. I thought that it was my duty to take bath and perform the rites for my mother, father and ancestors. There were thousands of people doing the Karma (ritual) like me at Kashi that day. I went with the assistant Purohit to take bath in the river. I braced myself as I descended the steps and got into waist deep water and took the first dip. I tried to forget the environment, and focus on the purpose of my mission. I self-hypnotized myself forcefully and assumed that the water is not polluted.

The morning was warm as the sun shone. The breeze was gentle. The holy river flowed majestically. I tried to "assume and imagine" that it was crystal clear! The assistant Purohit kept on warning me not to wade further into the great river. After the customary three dips I came out of the polluted water. In fact, it was just like taking a dip in the worst sort of city sewerage water.

I had no way! I had resolved to do it all!

I performed my Japa (daily prayer) on the banks of Ganga and gave 'Arghya' to Gods filling my cupped hands with water of the holy river.

---

[31] Resident Purohit of Kashi

317

Then I hurried back to the Uttaradi Mutt in the wet clothes. The Purohit asked me to carry the pot containing my mother's ashes to the same spot by the riverside again. This time the chief Purohit accompanied me. By the riverside, I was asked to open the cloth covering the casket of my mother's ashes and then, the casket itself.

I saw the ashes and the bone fragments of my dear mother. I could think of only her, and nothing else! I was given a small quantity fresh milk to be poured over the ashes. Then, I was given the Holy water (Thirtha) and some flowers that adorned the Kashi Vishwanath's deity, to be put on the ashes. Then, there were many mantras which I had to repeat as the Purohit dictated me. All of them were meant to grant eternal peace to the departed soul of our dear mother.

Finally, I was asked to wade into the holy river shoulder deep keeping the earthen urn on my left shoulder. I was told to recite the final prayer to my mother's 'moksha'. I was ordered to toss the urn over my left shoulder to my back after making a small hole in the earthen pot to facilitate it to sink into the waters of Ganga very slowly. Purohit asked me not to look back. He was observing the sinking pot as it floated away in the current of Ganga. Finally, he asked me to take three dips in the river after the pot had sunken completely. I followed him to the 'Mutt' (temple) with my clothes dripping. I was asked to squeeze the water out of my clothes and wear them again. I had to make 'Sankalpa' (express my determination or my resolve in Sanskrit prayer form) to offer the holy rituals and prayers for my ancestors.

The next ritual was called "The Pithru Shrarddha and Pithru Tarpana". The first part was "Pinda Pradana" in which I had to lay the small balls of cooked rice on the floor adorned with specific 'Rangoli" designs. Then, I had to give "Tarpana" with Ganga water. The ritual signifies giving food and water to the departed ancestors.

First, I had to offer food and water to the departed soul of our mother, grandmother and great grandmother. Next offering was for my departed father, grandfather and great grandfather. Then, to my late father-in-law, mother-in-law and their parents and grandparents. Then, to all the uncles, aunts and the relatives, who have departed. Finally, to all the ancestors of my side as well as Saroja's side.

Next in line were the 'Gurus.' Then to the teachers who gave us

318

education and knowledge. Later were the friends who have departed; and all the well wishers, who have passed away. After them came the turn of the servants who served the household of Saroja as well as mine.

Finally, came the turn of all the animals like cows, bulls, buffaloes, dogs and other pets which were reared by our household. I prayed for the pet dogs, cats, doves, stags, fawns, civet cats, squirrels, mynah birds, parrots, ducks, a turtle, and a frog that I had raised and befriended in my lifetime. This fond remembrance of gratitude made me immensely happy!

The whole ritual took about two hours and I had to recite all the Sanskrit mantras as dictated by my 'Purohit.' He asked me to put some rice on to a leaf and lay it to the crows outside the building. Finally my wife Saroja was asked to clean up all the rice balls and put them in a large platter. I had to carry the platter down to the river and immerse the big plate in water after getting shoulder deep into the holy waters of Ganga. The fish in the water attacked the food and finished the rice balls within a minute with great fervor.

After dipping myself in Ganga finally for three times, I had to give 'Tarpana' to the Gods and angels, to the holy trees and to the Gods of eight directions and to Yamadharma, the God who dispenses death. Yama Dharma is "The Supreme Justice" to all mortals.

Finally there was a pooja performed by the Purohit to mark the end of the ceremony during which he prayed for all the ancestors, 'gurus,' teachers, well wishers, servants and all those pets and domestic animals that served our household and our lineage. Finally, there was the 'dakshina'[32] to be paid to the 'Purohit' for his services. Sri Acharya told us that it was really an appreciable gesture on our part to come to Kashi from far off Karnataka state to perform the rites for our ancestors. As a Kshetra Purohit, he was very much pleased by our good deed. He was very glad that we had performed the rituals, which are compulsory for every Hindu, as prescribed in our scriptures. So, he commanded us to give only one rupee as dakshina! We were moved by his humble words and were almost in tears, as we realized that we had fulfilled one of our religious obligations in life.

---

[32] Fee paid in gratitude for his services

We had heard that the Purohits of Kashi were worse than bandits, and they took away all that we had as their fee. We were amazed to see this Kshetra Purohit asking for just one rupee as his fee!

Finally Saroja and I took out a reasonable sum and handed it over to him with a Namaskara. He blessed us profusely. He asked us to stay over and have lunch at his place. We told him that our daughters would be waiting for us at our hotel. He told us that it was natural for our daughters to have preferred to stay in the hotel, as most of the youngsters do not want to come to the banks of the Ganga. For they think that Ganga is very much polluted at Kashi, and they are disgusted with the local purohits, as the latter always tried to swindle as much money as they could from the pilgrims on the pretext of performing rituals. Moreover, Sri Acharya told us that their young minds had not matured enough to understand the significance of these rites. One imbibes the Hindu culture with age and the experiences in life, and one day, they too will visit the banks of Ganga with the families of their own. We understood how true his statement was!

Thirty years ago, we could never think that we would one day visit Kashi to perform the rites of our ancestors or I could never imagine myself to take a dip in the highly polluted waters of the Ganga.

Here I did it without any hesitation, with a sense of duty and not once, but three times! The values of the Hindu culture that I had imbibed during the course of my hitherto life had inspired me to do it.

I did it selflessly to appease my ancestors and to follow the command of our scriptures. All the while, I very well knew inwardly that I shall not be repeating the performance in my life again!

The River Ganga was pure and holy many, many years back. Now, she is the most polluted river, yet holy for every Hindu!

Our late prime minister, Sri Rajiv Gandhi had started a project to prevent the pollution of Ganga, but nothing much has happened after his death in this direction.

I still dream of a time when Ganga would flow as an unpolluted river. If at all she once again flowed clean and sparkling, what a pleasure it would be for every Hindu to come to Kashi on his mandatory pilgrimage!

I wish our next generation shall have the opportunity and pleasure of seeing an unpolluted Holy Ganga.

PEJATHAYA SETTLES DOWN

'Settling down' to many of us means having a family, a house that you call home, and a dog. After living and working in several areas of Karnataka, and after traveling around the world as a tourist, observer and writer, Pejathaya finally made Bangalore his home. He did not give up agriculture, as he still manages Sulimane Estate, albeit, using the telephone and the Internet.

He still travels to the coffee estate when necessary, and watches over its progress like a mother hen. He continues to write articles about agriculture in the local periodicals. Nevertheless, Pejathaya has accepted the domestic life and is a happy man today. Along with Saroja, he raised his two daughters in the city, and enjoyed a gentleman's leisure. He prides himself on his succession of automobiles, and devoted much time to man's best friend, his non-vegetarian Great Dane.

THE DAY WE TOOK RAKSHA
TO THE DOG SHOW
BY S. M. PEJATHAYA

Raksha was our pet dog. He weighed about fifty kilos and stood to my waist level. When he kept his paws on my shoulders his head stood well over mine. He was a massive Great Dane. We picked him up as a pup of forty days from a kennel. At the kennel, Raksha showed the liking for my wife and he wanted to accompany her. He sat on Saroja's lap and refused to get down! Of course, he was the best pup of the litter. He was a brindle pup with a black mask and had a special air about him. He had tiger-like black stripes over a smooth fawn-colored body and an expressive face.

As a little boy, I always wanted to have a big dog. I could not afford one. My two daughters Radhika and Rachana wanted a big dog and I had no heart to refuse them. Saroja too wanted a big dog for our house. Thus, we went to a vet and asked him to find a pedigree Great Dane pup for us. Soon the call came from the vet, and we went to the kennel to pick our puppy. My daughters went to the book store to buy two best books on dog care. Then we purchased all odds and ends required to bring up a pup. We named the pup Raksha.[33]

---

[33] "Security" or "protection" in Sanskrit

Raksha had a small bed, a bowl, few toys and a few toilet items like brushes, shampoo and powder. Since he was very tiny, at first, he roamed freely inside our house. He drank only milk then. He was a happy puppy and loved to play. He started to make puddles of urine all over the flooring and occasionally passed motion inside the house.

Our intelligent daughters put a proposition on to us the very next day. They said that they love Raksha very much and that they would share fifty percent of the puppy's work with mummy and dad. We gladly agreed. Then, they told us that they had selected the front end of the puppy, and we had to look after the rear end! We got the point!

Saroja and I had to clean all the litter and puddles while they would feed the dog! Soon, we started him on cereal food. His appetite became enormous in a few days. Saroja had to restrict Raksha to the front reception room of our house. We declared the rest of the house as out of bounds for him. We moved all the furniture from the front room. We kept his bed, eating plate and water bowl in that room. We spread sheets of news paper on the floor to absorb his soiling. He wetted the newspaper intermittently. He would play with the newspaper sheets and tear them to pieces. He would cry every now and then to draw Saroja's attention. He would whimper in low tones to be taken out into the garden for a more serious job. When taken out, he would play in the sun and with the flowers in the garden. He would chase butterflies, and forget the main purpose of coming out. When once brought inside the house, he would do the things that he was supposed to do outside! Saroja accepted all his pranks patiently. She would scrub the floor with disinfectant many times a day to keep that room clean. As Raksha grew up, we stopped the cereal food and put him on bread, milk and eggs.

He finished liters of milk, eggs and quantities of bread at his fourth month. During the school holidays, Raksha would travel with us to the estate in our Fiat car. He would whimper, when he wanted to get down and ease himself. He was certainly a pleasant and a well-behaved puppy.

As soon as we came back from the estate, we hired Mr. Brian as his trainer. Mr. Brian was an ex-Navy man and one of the best dog trainers in Bangalore. Raksha learned basic lessons of obedience and discipline in his fifth month. That November he won the Best of Breed and Best Puppy Prize in the Dog Show in Bangalore. We were very proud of his progress.

However, during the school hours of our daughters, we had to feed the little glutton. He took five or six meals a day. The little guy had two meals of bread and milk, a meal of idli or dosa, a meal of rice, eggs and vegetable and a small meal of a kilo fruits and biscuits. We wanted to bring up Raksha without giving him meat. As he grew up, we increased the eggs to six numbers a day and his milk intake remained at three liters. At one year, he was still growing in size and he established a claim on our breakfast every day in addition to his own breakfast! He would eat ten dosas or ten idlis within seconds in the morning. By eleven in the morning he would eat a kilo of apples or a dozen bananas with equal ease! This gluttony suddenly came to an end at his fifteenth month.

We were to go to our coffee estate all together, but Raksha had attained almost his full size and the rear seat of our small Fiat car was not sufficient to accommodate him and our two daughters. Our vet, Dr. Delvi, ran a boarding kennel for dogs. Raksha was raised as an 'eggetarian.' We requested him to keep Raksha for two weeks and insisted that no meat be given to Raksha. Dr. Delvi agreed.

We missed Raksha very much but we were sure that he was in safe hands. The servant at the kennel had trouble feeding Raksha. As the other dogs in the kennel were given meat, Raksha it seems, went on a hunger strike. He could smell the diet of meat given to the other dogs and craved for it by instinct. Finally, the doctor allowed the servant to feed him meat. Raksha wanted more and more of meat and nothing else. When we returned from the estate, we found that Raksha was cutting down a kilo of meat and two loaves of bread in the evenings. He would accept half liter of milk and a few slices of bread in the morning. He had stopped his mid-day meals. He wanted one big evening meal with meat every day. After coming home, he never resumed his perpetual eating style, much to the disappointment of Saroja, who loved to feed him. He would sniff at his cereal, dosa and idly. But, he would eat none of these! He would not even sniff at banana and apples! We tried to feed Raksha according to his old food chart. He went on fast! He refused even the eggs. Next day also he did the same.

Finally we had to yield. I told Saroja that Raksha belonged to the hound family and the main food of his ancestors was meat and we had no right to deprive him of meat. The problem was, we were vegetarians, and

Saroja would not allow meat into the house. We asked our gardener-cum-watchman to cook and serve Raksha. We purchased a stove and a pressure cooker to cook the meat for Raksha. From that day onwards, Raksha was happy with his own kind of food.

Right from his puppy days, Raksha loved our car. He would behave himself well in the car. When he was small, he would sit like a doll behind us next to the rear glass. In a few weeks he grew up and he could not station himself there. He would sit with the kids in the back seat. He loved to go to a petrol pump, probably because he thought that was the feeding place for the car. He was very friendly with the boys there. He would shake hands with them, and he would coax them to fill our car by making squealing sounds. He was happy when the car was being filled. Once they started to remove the nozzle, he would growl at them. Probably, he was asking them to feed the car more and more, continuously without stopping. This was a permanent joke for him as well as the petrol pump boys!

I bought a new Maruti Suzuki Gypsy Jeep in 1986 and parked it in front of our house by evening. I had planned to get extra washable seat covers for the jeep during the next day and I did not take Raksha for a ride in the new jeep. Raksha was about seven months old then and he was as big as a calf. He shed so much hair and I thought that he would scratch the fragile original seat covers if I made him to sit in my new jeep. He went round the jeep, stood on his hind legs, and peeped inside. He begged me to take him out for a ride. I told him that I shall take him for a ride the next day and went into the house. That evening, Raksha would not eat. He was looking at the new jeep and asking me to take him for a ride. Finally, I had to heed to his suggestion and all of us set out in the new jeep for a ride. I spread a rug on the new seat to protect it, and I asked Raksha to sit on it. Raksha was elated and was very happy! He would bark at any vehicle going in front of us and urge me to overtake. As we came near our house, he whimpered for another round in the new jeep. I obliged him. Finally, we came home after half an hour. As soon as I opened the door, he jumped out and gobbled his dinner happily!

His trainer, Mr. Brian, was a dog lover and a gentleman. They had a mutual liking for each other, and every alternate day he would provide classes for Raksha. If I ever went near them to watch his training, Raksha would behave like an insolent child. He would never pay any attention to *his training in my presence. He would rush to play with me like a kindergarten child. Observing this, Mr. Brian requested me to keep out of sight when he trained Raksha.*

At ten months Raksha was a fully trained dog. Mr. Brian took him to the Dog Show of our City. Saroja and children saw him behaving majestically in the ring as he participated in the junior class. I did not accompany them because Raksha behaved like a spoilt child if he ever saw me. They returned with a shield and a certificate proclaiming Raksha as the Best Junior Dog. The mandatory lessons for Raksha were over after the training period of six months. Mr. Brian oriented Raksha to me, to obey my commands and asked me to exercise Raksha at least for ninety minutes everyday. Next morning, I put a lead on to Raksha's choker chain and took him out at 5:45 in the morning. It was dark, and as we neared a bus stop down the road we could see two street dogs. Raksha growled at them instinctively. The two dogs started barking at us. I was very much annoyed and I coolly picked a stone from the road side and hurled it in the direction of the dogs intending not to hit them, but only to scare them away. This action was interpreted by Raksha as an order to attack! Suddenly the big dog jerked me as he jumped towards the dogs and he was barking wildly! Fortunately, I had slipped the leather hoop of the lead chain to my right wrist. Before I realized anything, I was being dragged by big dog across the tar road. I shouted "No, No!" to Raksha. He did not respond, and I tried in vain to get up as he continued to drag me. I was still being dragged away with greater speed as the two stray dogs turned tail! I was being dragged on my sides, as I did not give up my grip of the lead chain. Suddenly, I remembered the command! I shouted "Stop, Raksha, Stop!" within a fraction of a second my trained dog stopped and stood still! I stood up on my feet and took stock of the damage on my body! My clothes were a mess, all torn due to abrasion. I could feel the burning pain in several places. I abruptly cancelled my program of exercising the dog. We returned home. I requested Saroja to dress the torn patches of skin on my body. And, I told her what had happened. I admitted to the fact that I did not speak the right word of command like a fool. As a result I got this reward.

Next day, Saroja sent for Mr. Brian and requested him to take out Raksha for walks and look after him as long as Raksha lived with us, and his training fee shall continue. At this arrangement, I was very happy! So, was Raksha!

One more year passed, and Raksha participated in the Kennel Club of India (KCI) Dog Show. This time I wanted to watch him. Though Raksha was a grown up dog, he continued to behave like a spoilt brat when I was around. I could not sit with my family when Raksha came to the ring to participate in the events. An American was invited by the KCI to be the chief judge of the dog show. I told Mr. Brian and my family that I shall be watching Raksha from behind the screens of our stall. I would hide behind the partitions of the stall so that Raksha would not be aware of my presence at the show. I did not accompany the team for the registration that morning, as Saroja was the registered owner of Raksha.

Well after the events began, I sneaked into the grounds. I stood behind the screen of our stall to see Raksha perform majestically in the dog show. Saroja and the kids were sitting in the chairs near the ring, whereas I watched the event from my hideout. The events were proceeding as per schedule. The end of the show was nearing. I was peeping at the show attentively when a hand fell on my shoulders. It was our vet. I explained to him the reason for hiding and watching the show. He told me not to worry as all the events were coming to an end and it was the final round. The final round was announced to be over and only the selection of the Champion Dog was due. My vet asked me to accompany him to vet's stall very next to the ring. I entered the vet's stall as the guest of my vet. Raksha happened to be a few feet away standing free without leads and posing for the final stance. The American Judge was examining the excellent stand of Raksha.

At the same moment Raksha noticed me! Everything went haywire for me and Mr. Brian. Raksha at once abandoned his stance to come bounding towards me and he pounced over me. I was knocked down!

Raksha was fed up with the strange people and strange dogs that gathered at the show. It was a relief for him to see me! He started licking my face. I was petting Raksha.

Then, I heard the accented voice of the American Judge. He said, "You sure have an affectionate little dog!" I replied, "Sure, I have one!" He patted Raksha on the head and moved on. The Dog show was over. Raksha received many prizes. He had won the Best of Breed! We were hoping that the Champion Dog prize would come our way.

Finally, after a minute silence the Champion Dog was announced. But, to the disappointment of Mr. Brian and all of us, the championship was given to another dog. It was my mistake altogether, for which I shall never excuse myself! I had sort of hurried near the ring before the champion was adjudged. I had to seek solace to myself with that American's comment.

The American Judge had remarked, "You sure have an affectionate little dog!"

Yes! I really had one!

*   *   *

This story about Raksha is captured in Pejathaya's Kannada language book for children and is in its second printing.

THE STORYTELLER LIVES ON

Pejathaya has written many short stories, and continues to write them. Some of the stories have been printed in *Kannada* books. One story became part of required collegiate reading material at Mangalore University. He has written one book in English, called *The Voyage of a Paper Boat*, which he hopes to publish in the U.S. in the future. As I type this, Pejathaya is still creating stories based on his true life adventures. He often writes weekly articles for a Bangalore publication.

Twice Pejathaya travelled to the foothills of the Himalayas to meet the English writer Ruskin Bond. Mr. Bond wrote his first novel (*The Room On The Roof*) at the age of 17, and was an inspiration to Pejathaya. The two of them spent several days sitting by the fireside in Mr. Bond's Mussoorie bungalow talking about the joys of communicating through writing.

Over the twelve thousand or so miles that separate us, I communicate with Pejathaya on a regular basis. At 5:00 a.m. U.S. Pacific Coast Time I can experience almost a direct conversation with him through the internet before he goes to bed in Bangalore. At 5:00 p.m. my time he is just getting up, and we again can "talk." We sometimes use Skype and FaceTime to chat.

He brought his family to the U.S. in 1999, and spent several weeks with some of his Peace Corps friends and their families. That was the first time I met his two daughters. It seemed as though Pejathaya had turned back the hands of time, as his daughters were as Western as he was on the day I met him. They wore black leather jackets and spoke like American teenagers, with, of course, a distinguishable South Indian accent.

Their interests were in seeing the sights of San Francisco, searching for cowboy hats and visiting a Harley Davidson Motorcycle shop.

We stood on a hill in Marin County and looked down at the Golden Gate Bridge. I couldn't help but be impressed at how small the world had become. We stood in a spot that Pejathaya and I had talked half a lifetime ago. I was deluged with the emotions of seeing him and his family here in the U.S. After so many letters and emails since we last met in the Sulimane coffee estate I could scarcely believe that here he was, the storyteller himself.

Saroja chuckled sympathetically as John Kelly, my wife Dee and I struggled with our mostly forgotten *Kannada*. She didn't know that, with the exception of Dee who was quite fluent in *Kannada*, John and I were never really that good at it when we were in India.

Pejathaya's India had changed dramatically since 1971. The country's major cities were much more sophisticated. He carried the same Nokia cell phone that I carried, and freely called relatives and friends in the U.S. His daughters were highly skilled in computer operation, and borrowed our home computer to regularly check their email and to correspond with their friends in Bangalore.

The entire family was very flexible with some of those cultural preferences that we had been so concerned about. John had bought a complete set of cookware so they wouldn't have to use "impure" pots and utensils for food preparation. Pejathaya was appreciative, but he said it was not necessary, as the entire family was able to adjust to the habits and customs of others.

Pejathaya and Saroja's daughters, Radhika and Rachana, went with my daughter and me on a sightseeing trip to San Francisco. We visited sites of the city, including Coit Tower, the Golden Gate Bridge and the Crookedest Street in the World. We rode on a street car, and at Pier 39, we caught a ferry to the former federal prison on Alcatraz Island where I snapped a picture of the three of them behind the prison bars.

Meanwhile, Pejathaya and Saroja shopped the Indian markets in Berkeley for familiar ingredients and prepared a special vegetarian meal for us. It was a scrumptious meal, and there were more wonderful meals to come from Saroja's creations. Saroja, an excellent cook, could find her way around any kitchen with no problem.

After they toured the Grand Canyon, Disneyland and much of the West Coast, the Pejathaya family said goodbye and continued their journey to the East Coast, where they visited other friends and relatives. We were sad to see them leave, but we look forward to future visits.

We still communicate regularly. Pejathaya has been a catalyst in reuniting Peace Corps India-60 volunteers. His letters and emails create a whirlwind of communication among the volunteers and staff of our group. He recently completed an eight part series of articles in a *Kannada* publication in which he depicted many of the volunteers and their activities.

The Storyteller's paper boat is sailing beyond the compound walls, riding on the current of his experiences and conversations with numerous acquaintances. May his stories sail far into the future.

THE SUM OF IT ALL

The man I met on the flight to Los Angeles in 1968 for Peace Corps training had been partially correct. He had also been partially wrong. That day, he asked me who I thought I would help or change by spending two years as a Peace Corps volunteer. He criticized my answers, implying that I was naive to think that I could accomplish anything other than waste a lot of our country's resources. He said that the only people who would benefit were the volunteers themselves, who would get a two-year, expense-paid vacation in some exotic part of the world.

I was crushed at the time, thinking that his words were angry and resentful. The lecture made me question my motives. Is this really all the Peace Corps is about? Did I misunderstand what I was about to do? His comments, however, forced me to consider what I genuinely expected from this mission. Was it the spirit of helping others or was I only thinking about free travel to explore another culture? What did I expect to accomplish?

In 1968 I was cruising on a wave of emotion that had been stirred up by young President John F. Kennedy. After all, this was the same man who also convinced us that our country could put a man on the moon. I was touched by Kennedy's words in early 1961 when he said the Peace Corps was created, "..to promote world peace and friendship..."

To many of the young adults in the early 1960s, the spirit of being empowered to represent the United States was invigorating, even intoxicating. We immediately thought that 24 months with the Peace Corps was more rewarding than two years working for a Masters degree. For one thing, there was no tuition and no travel costs, and second, the stimulation of living in an alien culture was more alluring than sitting in a boring classroom.

I went anyway. I spent my two years. And, yes, I did benefit a great deal personally by being able to learn a new language and travel to a far-away land. That is something I never could have done on my own meager resources. In retrospect, I did learn a lot, and I did meet many new friends. But was it a two year vacation? Did I leave any lasting improvement in my host country. Was even one Indian person better off that my government-spent thousands of dollars to train and feed me and fly me around the world? These questions had to be answered.

In late 2012, Pejathaya was asked to write an eight-part series for a weekly Bangalore publication. His subject was his experiences with the American Peace Corps during the period between 1968 and 1971, and his contact with the volunteers through 2012. He asked some of the India 60 volunteers to send photographs to enliven the stories. He then sent the link of the resulting articles by email to his friends here in the States. He wrote his articles in the *Kannada* script, which most of us still cannot read. We could, however, follow the gist by looking at the inserted photographs and reading Pejathaya's summaries in his forwarding emails. Thanks to "Google Translation" I was able to read not only most of his stories but also some of the comments from his *Kannada*-speaking readers.

Most of Pejathaya's readers who wrote comments to his articles were very excited about his tales of working alongside the PCVs. Many readers remarked that it was a brave thing these young Americans did, to leave their homes and live in the remote villages. They applauded Pejathaya for his stories, which portrayed the longstanding relationship with the volunteers, and how some of the volunteers had later visited him at his coffee estate, and dined with him many years later in Bangalore.

Negative comments were fewer, but pointed. Several comments referred to the Vietnam War and suggested that the volunteers preferred working in India to fighting in the war. They stopped short of using the phrase "draft dodgers," but their point was clear. Others complained that the American volunteers were insensitive to Indian customs and rituals. Others suggested that the volunteers took jobs away from their Indian citizens. One of the writers must have experienced a lazy volunteer who spent most of his Peace Corps service in his house reading books.

Fair is fair, and I am glad I got to see the wide-ranging perspectives on Peace Corps service. The proud Indian intellectual, skilled professional or fervent patriot may see the Peace Corps as an intrusion into their county's affairs. That perspective is understandable, as Americans would undoubtedly feel the same if a foreigner came to the States with the attitude that they had a better way of teaching our kids, or growing corn, or making cars. What I long to know is, in the villages where we worked, did we accomplish anything worthwhile?

There is no imposing edifice anywhere in Raichur District to speak to the successes of India-60. There are no words or names prominently displayed on a structure or document that shines on to say, "Yes! These guys did great things!"

There are no new inventions or farming processes that speak to the wonders of the Peace Corps volunteers' skills or intelligence. And the records of the Department of Agriculture do not attribute any new crop varieties to the assistance of the Peace Corps.

Then, what good became of our country's investment in our training and two years of support while living in India? Was the traveller in the airplane ride to Los Angeles entirely correct?

We had fun, saw India, and left. That's it?

The Raichur District villagers were surviving before my fellow volunteers and I interrupted their lives. They would have survived without the presence of Peace Corps volunteers. Further, Mrs. Indira Gandhi's wish for the Green Revolution to succeed would have come true without intervention from India-60. So then, where was the value of this experiment?

I surfed the internet looking for a trace of the Sindhanur Cooperative Milk Society. Finding none, I let out a cry of dismay. What happened to those dedicated farmers who got up at 4 a.m., seven days a week, to bring their two liters of buffalo milk to the roadside collection point. What became of Bill's Gerber testing equipment? Was this project just a fleeting experiment, fueled by the active imaginations of bored volunteers, and buoyed up by sympathetic villagers? Did the idea evaporate the day the last volunteer left?

More surprising is that I cannot find a trace of the Sindhanur Tractor Society and its 30 tractors. I learned, however, that one in every six farmers in Sindhanur owns their own tractor. This probably explains the disappearance of the Tractor Society, which was once the largest employer in Sindhanur. Maybe the Society worked itself out of existence.

As demoralizing as this may seem to the volunteers, I gain positive perspective by reading of the successes of Raichur District, and, specifically, Sindhanur *Taluka*. According to my internet search results, Sindhanur is the number one *Sona Masuri* rice growing *taluka* in the state. (*Sona Masuri* is a lightweight and aromatic variety of rice that is exported to the USA, Canada, Europe and elsewhere). Sindhanur also has the highest use of fertilizers and pesticides in the state and is number one for revenue production. The following is a 2013 quote from *Wikipedia, The Free Encyclopedia.*

"Sindhanur is one of the largest revenue making towns in Karnataka. It has almost all the tractor showrooms available in India and it is the second largest tractor selling place in India (first comes Oshiapur in Punjab). One in every six farmers in Sindhanur has his own tractor."

Unfortunately, we will never know whether the successes of Mudiya Gowda and Chandrappa were in any way inspired by 'Mukkunda George.' Except for the encouraging words of Tom's host farmer, we will never know if the Jalihal marketing cooperative would have succeeded without Tom's hard work.

Further, I am confident that the homemakers of Sindhanur don't say, "Thank you, India-60," every time they buy a liter of milk.

Returned volunteers have glorious visions of their influence on their host country. There was, of course, an impact, but it might be much more subtle than they imagine. After all, the mission of Peace Corps, according to its design, was not the building of soaring edifices, or the invention of earthshaking ideas, or scientific discoveries. Rather, the mission statement was much simpler. The Peace Corps mission was designed with three goals in mind.

- Providing technical assistance
- Helping people outside the United States to understand American culture, and
- Helping Americans to understand the cultures of other countries

In short, the Peace Corps purpose was to promote world peace and friendship. In addition, President Kennedy envisioned this program as a means of countering the stereotype of the "Ugly American." He wanted young Americans doing the same work and eating the same food as their hosts.

I would like to quote a man from Karnataka who worked in the farm irrigation industry in Raichur and Bellary Districts. Mr. Abhay Golikeri made this comment after reading a draft of this book in September 2013 and offering his suggestions:

As you have mentioned in one place, if we think about who benefited and to what extent, I personally feel that humanity benefited. People from two different culture(s) were made to live together for a little over 2 years, which saw the simple and poor Raichur farmers learn so much about Agriculture from the Peace Corps volunteers. Not just that. They also had a glimpse of a totally different culture and divergent views, and they did this without moving out from their home. In India, we revere people like Dr. Norman

Borlaug and JFK. We are also grateful to volunteers like you from the American Peace Corps.

Dr. Norman Ernest Borlaug was the American agronomist who is credited with the title of "the father of the Green Revolution." He developed a high-yielding, disease resistant variety of wheat that was introduced into Indian agriculture in the early 1960s, along with improved cultivation methods.

Mr. Golikeri's comment makes me feel that maybe my two years in India was worthwhile after all.

Oh, yes! Contrary to what I stated above about transparency, there is one trace of physical evidence that still exists, to reflect the fact that India-60 volunteers once worked in Raichur District.

Sirens blaring, an emergency vehicle runs the roads of Raichur District to help provide medical treatment for rural villagers. An ambulance service, largely supported by donations from former Peace Corps staff and volunteers, has been operating in the District for the past several years. The SanJeeVini Ambulance Service was dedicated to two India-60 volunteers who passed away. These two volunteers, Mike Quaid and Willie James, were loved by their Indian counterparts for their tireless efforts to improve life in their respective villages.

Ambulance service in Raichar District

For the things we could not accomplish during our short, two year volunteer stint with Peace Corps, we have very little to show, except, maybe this small token of our love for the people of India. However, we know we have made lasting friendships with many Indian people. Some, like Pejathaya, stay in touch regularly. Pejathaya demonstrates his strong belief in the power of communication, by keeping the channels open. Thanks to his writings he keeps the feeling warm.

Several former India-60 PCVs travelled to India in 2010. A group of them, including Tom Holmes, Chuck Lenth, Richard Wines and Billy Danielson visited Pejathaya and enjoyed a day and a meal with him in Bangalore. I was told that these men and their spouses were treated like returning royalty when Pejathaya hosted them.

Richard and his wife again travelled to India in July 2013 and presented Pejathaya with an inscribed plaque that held a photograph of India-60 volunteers that was taken in Bangalore, India in 1969.

*S.M. Pejathaya with commemorative plaque
from India-60 PCVs and friends*

The inscription is in both English and *Kannada* script and it thanks Pejathaya for his work with the Peace Corps volunteers and the inspiration he gave to India-60 by keeping the communication channels open.

Like the paper boats of his childhood, Pejathaya's exciting journey survived all the obstacles along life's fast moving stream and sailed beyond the courtyard barrier into the great world beyond. His successful journey continues its voyage, as he continues to record his insights about the life and humanity that line the shores of his boat's progress. With a smile on his face and a stiff upper lip, he looks for new ports, and dreams to venture forever onward.

The India-60 volunteers have likewise followed their dreams, and each has scored success in his choice of profession and life style. The two or three years they spent as volunteers in India gave each of them a special perspective, and each has tailored his next phase in life with the lessons on understanding another culture. Each India-60 volunteer learned to be sensitive to the ideas of others regardless of their country of origin. That, by itself, helps make this a better world.

ACKNOWLEGEMENTS

The hand sketched images adorning each of Pejathaya's stories were prepared by Shri Yathish Siddakatte of Bantwal Taluk, Karnataka, India. Mr. S. M. Pejathaya commissioned Mr. Siddakatte to prepare the sketches for his memoirs, and subsequently contributed the sketches to this joint effort.

Mr. Pejathaya's stories incorporated in this book are included with his permission, and were extracted from his first English language book, called *The Voyage of a Paper Boat*. This book, *Paper Boat*, is a collaborative effort between S. M. Pejathaya and Ken Kerkhoff.

The names of characters in this book are the actual names of the Peace Corps Volunteers, Peace Corps Officials and trainers as well as the Indian government officials and other persons as presented herein. I apologize for any unintended misspellings of persons' names.

The names of some India places, names and words, when translated into English, can be spelled in several ways. No disrespect is intended if the reader disagrees with the spelling or usage of those words.

Finally, I would like to acknowledge the many wonderful Indian people who shared their lives with my India-60 associates and me and had the patience to forgive our lack of understanding of their language and culture.

GLOSSARY

Acharya	Guide or instructor in religious and educational matters. Family surname common in India, but especially in West Bengal
Andhra	As in the state of Andhra Pradesh where Telugu is the spoken language.
Anna	A former Indian monetary unit equal to a fraction of an Indian Rupee:
Apoo	Wild, tall grass that grows by the waterways; can be used for making mats and thatching roofs
Areca Nuts	The seed of the areca palm
Ayurvedic	(Practitioner) traditional Hindu healer who used the Ayurveda system of medicine, including balance in bodily systems, diet, herbs and yogic breathing.
Bahamans	Devotional songs
Bajra	Pearl millet; grows well in areas of drought, low soil fertility and high temperatures
Bajra roti	Flat bread made from millet (bajra)
Baksheesh	A tip, or a gift
Banyan	Shirt
Beedie	Thin, Indian cigarette filled with a tobacco flake and tied with a string Beedis (also, bidis) like small, local made cigars
Betal leaves	Leaves of the betel plant, used to make Paan, an after meal stimulant

345

Bharatnatyam	Classical Indian dance
Bhuja	A spicy snack mixture made with a blend of grain noodles, peas, peanuts and sultanas (dried grapes)
Bili Jola	White sorghum
Brahmin	The Hindu priestly caste into which one is born
Brinjals	Eggplant vegetable
Bunt	Small Indian community of north and South *Kannada* Districts. A farmer clan
Canara	British slang for *Kannada* (See also Kanara)
Chai	Reference to tea in numerous languages
Chamara	A type of fan used in Hindu pooja made from Yak hair mounted on a wood handle
Champak	A very fragrant flower found in a tree; Magnolia Champaca
Chapatis	Unleavened flatbread made from wheat and toasted on a flat iron
Chikka Dhani	Younger boss, or boss' younger brother
Choultry	Free lodging for pilgrims near holy temples
Chulah	Coal or wood fired cooking stove
Chutney	South Asian condiments
Copra	Dried coconut kernel
Cuddapah (stone)	Slate stone from a place called Cuddapah in Andhra Pradesh
Curds	Plain Indian yogurt
Dakshina	Payment for the services of a priest
Dhanya Lakshmi puja	Dhanya means grains; Hindus give thanks to the Goddess Lakshmi for the bountiful grain harvest.
Dhoti	Traditional Indian men's garment; rectangular unstitched cloth wrapped around legs and waist and knotted at the waist

Diwali	Ancient Hindu festival called the festival of lights, also called Deepavali
Doodh peda	A dessert made by boiling milk until it becomes a solid and adding some sugar and Cardamom
Dukaan Wallah	Shopkeeper. Examples: *Paan Walla*; *Tambool* seller
Durga pooja	Annual Hindu festival celebrating the Hindu goddess *Durga*; in October or November, also called *Dussera*
Dussehra	(Also *Dasara or Dussera*) An important Hindu festival; marks end of Durga Pooja
Gaur	North Indian bison
Ghat	A series of steps leading down to a body of water
Ghee	Clarified butter used in Indian cooking
Gingili	Oil from sesame seeds
Godown	From Portuguese, a shed, barn, or warehouse
Gotra	Lineage of ancestors from the ancient Rishi Clan
Gothra	Pronounced with father's name and surname to denote line of ancestry
Govindaraja Patna	Most famous temple in Tirupati, Andhra Pradesh, India. The Temple Town of Tirupathi or Govindaraja is below the temple of Thirumala
Gram Panchayat	Smallest Village administration unit with elected members
Gram Sevak	Gram means village; sevak refers to worker
Guru	A Sanskrit term meaning a spiritual teacher or master. Anyone who has followers
Gurukula	A traditional Sanskrit residential school run by a Guru and his family

Haaka Shikars	A hunt organized by a group of people
Haakadars	Beaters who scare the animals out of the forest for the hunters
Hakim	Title often used for learned philosophers doctors of Persian medicine in Indian villages
Hanuman	The Hindu God who took the image of a monkey
Harijan	Means "Children of God" but refers to *untouchable* people of India
Haulage	Business of being a hauler
Henna	Temporary colorful design made on hands and legs using dye from the henna tree.
Hole' yemme'	River buffalo
Holi festival	A spring celebration known as the festival of colors
Holige'	A sweet flatbread made from a split yellow grain (lentil)
Howdah	A covered litter for riding on the back of an elephant
Hutchellu	*Guizojia Abyssinia,* an herb that produces oil, like sesame and used for dry chutney
Idlis	Steamed rice cakes, often eaten as a breakfast food
Jaali tree	See Naganagowda Jaali tree
Jaggery	A course brown sugar made in India from the sap of palm trees or sugar cane juice
Jahagirdar	A person who owns vast lands
Jambul tree	A tropical evergreen tree that bears a blackberry like fruit
Japa mala	A string of 108 beads (rosary) used by Hindus and Buddhists in prayer or meditation
Jathraas	Local temple fairs
Jola (bili jola)	White sorghum
Jowar	Sorghum

K.D.	Known delinquent. Colonial British identified criminals with this title, and branded them K. D.
Kaasina Sara	Heavy chain decorated with gold sovereigns
Kai maddu	A *Kannada* term for the act of slow poisoning of a person's food
Kambli	Rough hewn woolen blanket
Kanara	Also Canara, The *Kannada* speaking region in Southern India's Karnataka coastal area (a British term)
Kannada	Language spoken in the Indian State of Karnataka
Kapok	A large, robust tree that produces a cotton like fiber locally known as silk cotton
Kappal roti	Expedition food. A dry rice roti; (kappal means boat). Keeps for 20 days.
Kardi	The Hindi equivalent for Safflower
Karmar	A very good firewood tree with heavy oil content. It can be cut and used directly after cutting
Karnataka	Originally know as Mysore State, is located in South West India
Kashi	The City of Banners; the Holy City for Hindus
Kattambali	A maize cereal dish prepared with Yogurt
Kaurava army	In the Mahabharata epic Kaurava formed an army of his rival's enemies
Khatas	Land holding rights
Khichdi	Rice and lentils boiled with sautéed vegetables
Kodapaanas	Long necked water pitchers
Konkan	Pertaining to the far western coast of India. Also, a language spoken in Goa and parts of Maharashtra

Koorigi	Kannada expression for an area of four acres. Also, a Koorige is a bullock-pulled seed drill which covers about four acres per day
Koppe	Rain shield that covers head and upper body
K-tea	From the Urdu word Khadak, for strong. Khadak Tea is strong, boiled with milk and sugar
Kumkum	Vermillion powder used for social and religious markings. Married Indian women wear a dot of vermillion on their foreheads
Kurukshetra	The battlefield of Mahabharatha epic. Where the famous 18 day war took place and Pandava brothers won
Lantana	A tropical evergreen shrub
Lungi	A length of cotton fabric worn like a sarong
Machan	A raised platform used by Indian farmers to watch over and protect their crops
Mahout	A person who trains, handles and cares for the temple elephant
Mamoo	*Kannada*, Tulu or Urdu word for maternal uncle
Mandies	Crop warehouses
Mecca	Eternal bliss attained after death
Moksha	Eternal peace
Munshi	An accountant, a Persian word originally the name of a contractor, writer or secretary, later used in the Mughal Empire and British India for a teacher as well as an accountant or clerk.
Mutt	A hermitage where a Swami lives with his deity
Naanu	*Kannada* term for "me" or "I"

Naganagowda Jaali	A tree; *Prosopis juliflora,* also called Bellary Jaali, grows in arid regions of Karnataka, and is good for forage, erosion control, cooking fuel, making implements and small structures.
Namaskara	Also, *'Namaste:* An Indian greeting with joined palms. A mark of giving high respect
Nandi	The bull of Lord Shiva
Nale	Also, *'Naale':* Kannada word for "tomorrow"
Nizam	of Hyderabad: Former monarch or potentiate ruler of pre-independence Hyderabad State
Nullah	Also *'nallah':* North Karnataka word for stream or watercourse
Paan	Indian betel leaves from a betel vine. Can be considered a stimulant
Paddy	Rice before threshing or in the husk
Panchayat	System of local government. Village council.
Parvati	Mother Goddess; consort of Shiva
Patel	Village headman known as *Sarpanch* in Hindi
Pathan	A Muslim from Afghanistan. They came like mercenaries to India
Payasa	A sweet porridge prepared from cereal and coconut milk or Milk
Pendal	Improvised shelter with a temporary roof. A mongrel with no pedigree
Peon	Servant; office helper
Pie dog	A feral dog common in Indian villages
Pilichaundi	Spirit of tiger worshipped by villagers of South & North Kanara Districts (*Kannada* Districts of the Coastal Karnataka)

Pooja pendal	A temporary shelter with temporary roof prepared for a Pooja or Puja
Poonac	Extracted cake of oily substances. Eg. coconut cake, groundnut cake, gingili cake; usually used as animal fodder
Puja, 'pooja,'	Prayer or adoration
Pundi palle soppu	A leafy vegetable, also Gonkura, or Hibiscus sabdariffa
Pundit	A scholar or a Learned Person. Originates from Sanskrit Panditha.
Punjabi	A language spoken by inhabitants of the Punjabi region
Purohit	A priest who performs Pooja or Havan (worship through Fire)
Raja	King. A term for a monarch or princely ruler in India
Ramayana	A great epic story of India's culture and religion
Rasam	Extract. A soup like dish. An extract of Tamarind, salt & Chili usually eaten with rice
Razakar	The Razakars were a private militia organized by Qasim Razvi to support the rule of Nizam Osman Ali Khan, of Hyderabad
Rotis	Flat unleavened bread
Rupee	Official Indian currency
Saab or *sahib*	A common Hindi, Urdu and Punjabi term for master, teacher or a learned person
Saar	A small Karnataka coastal stream; a perennial source of water
Sahib	See saab
Salaam	Salutation, Salutes. Means 'peace be with you'
Sambar	A spicy vegetable curry

Sanskrit	Ancient Indian language
Sarpanch	Another word for village headman
Savaari Gaadi	Covered bullock cart
Sevak	As in Gram Sevak: Government paid village worker
Shandy	A weekly farmers' market
Shikar	Organized hunting as a sport. From Persian.
Shiva	God of destruction of Evil
Spatika beads	Crystal beads used in an Indian rosary
Sultana	A pale yellow seedless grape made into a raisin
Supari	Scented areca nut powder or a piece of processed areca nut
Swamiji	A Guru or A Hermit or a Religious Head
Tabla	Twin drum percussion instrument. Thumped with palms only.
Taluka (Taluk)	An administrative division similar to a U.S. county
Tamarind	A sour fruit used in Indian cooking. *Tamarindus Indica*
Tamboola	*Betel* leaves, *Areca* nut, slaked Lime chewed as a stimulant. Some people add chewing tobacco with Tamboola. Sanskrit,
Tarpana	From Sanskrit, refers to an offering made to a devine entity with water let down from cupped hands
Thokku	A chutney made from tamarind, salt, etc.
Thread ceremony	An Indian initiation ritual involving presentation of a sacred thread worn across the torso. It is compulsory for a Brahmin boy to wear a thread. This is called Upanayana or Brahmopadesha
Til (oil lamp)	Sesame oil lamp lit during pooja

Tilak	A mark worn on the forehead or other parts of the body daily, or for special religious occasions
Tumbige'	A small brass, copper or aluminum water pot used in rural India for personal hygiene. In Raichur District they call this *thembigi*. It is called *chombu* in Tulu language
Ungadi	A small shop; a tea shop`
Upadhyaya	A teacher *(Acharya)*
Upma	South Indian breakfast dish like a thick porridge
Urdu	A language spoken by the Muslims of the region of Hindustan
Vijayanagara Empire	Southern India empire established in 1336 but declined after a major military defeat in 1565
Walaikum assalaam	*Wa 'alaykum al-salaam* is an Arabic greeting often used by Muslims around the world translating nearly to "And unto you peace"
Wallah	Someone who does or sells something. A soda wallah sells soda pop

ABOUT THE AUTHOR

With a passion for travel and adventure developed at an early age Ken Kerkhoff traveled much of Asia, Europe and Africa. In India he employed his agriculture skills to assist the Government of India win its Green Revolution.

Ken holds a BA and an MBA. He won his first short story contest at the age of ten. His correspondence from India was printed in his hometown newspaper. He writes both creative non fiction and fiction.

ABOUT THE CO-AUTHOR

Born in a remote village on the west coast of India, S.M. Pejathaya had the ambition of sailing the high seas as an Indian naval officer. After earning a physics degree in college his plan was interrupted when he agreed to develop a coconut farm for his family. He wrote about the wild tigers, buffalo and boar that roamed his land. Pejathaya became proficient in agriculture and was soon hired by a major Indian bank to manage an inland dry land farm. He married and became a coffee farmer in the highlands of South India. He wrote short stories during the prolonged monsoon rains, and eventually published four books in his native language. Pejathaya writes from the heart. His stories about animals and people tug at the heart, like Murali, the elephant that played cricket, and Diwaker, the blind boy who was gifted an eye by the love of his life.

Pejathaya and Kerkhoff crossed paths in their 20s and struck up an immediate friendship. The common denominators were working in agriculture and story telling. After 45 years these two close friends communicate long distance on a regular basis.

Made in the USA
San Bernardino, CA
26 December 2015